Tomi

Tomi Reichental's Holocaust Story

'a powerful tale … deserves to be shared in Irish classrooms and in classrooms around the world'
InTouch Magazine

'accessible and honest'
Belfast Telegraph

First published 2018 by The O'Brien Press Ltd
12 Terenure Road East, Rathgar, Dublin 6, Ireland
Tel: +353 1 4923333
Fax: +353 1 4922777
books@obrien.ie
www.obrien.ie
Reprinted 2019.

The O'Brien Press is a member of Publishing Ireland.

ISBN: 978-1-84717-975-3

Based on *I Was a Boy in Belsen* by Tomi Reichental with Nicola Pierce

10 9 8 7 6 5 4 3 2
23 22 21 20 19

Printing and bound by Scandbook AB, Sweden.

The paper in this book is produced using pulp from managed forests.

Front and back cover photographs courtesy of the Reichental family.
Front cover: Tomi Reichental.
Back cover (back row from left): Laco Mayer (Tomi's cousin, who survived Buchenwald), Bandy Scheimowitz (a cousin), Miki (Tomi's brother), Dury Scheimowitz (cousin), Kati (cousin, murdered in Auschwitz); front row: Eva Mayer (Chava, cousin), Tomi, Tikva (cousin).

Published in:

Tomi

Tomi Reichental's Holocaust Story

retold by

Eithne Massey

Illustrations by Emma Byrne

THE O'BRIEN PRESS
DUBLIN

Contents

Foreword by Tomi Reichental page 7

Part I

THE FARM

1 **Summer** 11

2 **Winter** 17

3 **Leaving the Village** 26

Part II

THE HUNT

4 **Hated** 34

5 **Sent Away** 43

6 **Hunted** 48

7 **Hiding** 55

8 **Trapped** 65

9 **The Journey** 72

10 **Tomi's Father** 83

Part III

THE CAMP

11 In the Forest 92

12 The Showers 99

13 Living in Belsen 105

14 Halt! 112

15 *Mazel Tov!* 118

16 Omama Rosalia 125

Part IV

THE RETURN

17 Liberation! 132

18 The Human Laundry 142

19 Father 149

Epilogue: Remembering 161

Afterword by Gerry Gregg 170

Foreword

This story is based on what happened to me, Tomi Reichental, and my family and millions of other people like me in the years 1939–45.

Once upon a time, I lived in a little paradise. It was called Merašice. It was the place I grew up in. My father, Arnold, was a farmer. My grandparents had the village shop. We were at the heart of everything that happened in our little corner of Slovakia.

My older brother Miki and I had the run of the place. I recall endless days of fun and games, winter and summer. My mother, Judith, smothered us with affection and spoiled us with treats. My favourite was her delicious home-made ice cream.

Life was good. We were lucky boys who wanted for nothing, surrounded by the love of a big family.

Then one day it all changed.

After living in Merašice for hundreds of years, we were told, 'You people are strangers in this land. Jews are no longer welcome here.' Then our nightmare began.

Life would never be the same again. The paradise that was Merašice was lost for ever. At the age of six, I began to fear for the future. One day, we said goodbye to our cousins, aunts and uncles. We never saw them again.

By the age of nine, I was on the run for my life and later ended up in Bergen-Belsen concentration camp. By the time I was ten, I had seen all there was to see.

Tomi Reichental

PART I

The Farm

1

Summer

'Tomi!' The voices were full of laughter. It was Chava and Miki, coming nearer and nearer to his perch high in the tree. Tomi had gone higher than he ever had before, hoping the green leaves would hide him.

'Tomi! We are coming! We can see you!'

That was Laco's voice, deeper than the others. So he was there too. Laco was the oldest cousin, the leader of the group of eight who met every summer at Tomi's house. He was sure they could not possibly see him, up so high with the green branches below. Not one of them had looked up.

Then Miki called out, 'Come out, come out, wherever you are! You can't hide from us!' His older brother's voice was mocking.

But if I stay very still, thought Tomi, *if I don't even allow myself to breathe, maybe they will go by and I will not be caught.* The breeze swayed the branches gently, bringing with it the scent of hay. Through the branches he could see the wheat fields, just turning gold, and the black and white cows in the distance, their tails flicking lazily to keep off the flies. All part of his father's farm.

Earlier that summer, Omama, his grandmother, had told him a story about a hidden treasure, buried deep in the earth. Afterwards, he had spent hours hunting for treasure in the fields. His father had come upon him digging beside the stream and asked him what he was up to. He smiled when Tomi told him. 'Look around you, my son. The land is all the treasure we need. The harvest fields are our gold. And there are diamonds in the wet grass when the sun lights it up in the morning!'

Tomi laughed and said, 'I see what you mean, Apuko! And the cows eat up the diamonds, and they come out in the milk!'

'I'm not sure our milk has diamonds in it, especially when you see the price we get for it. But we have enough to live on. And that's all we need.' His father held out his hand for Tomi to take. They had walked home through the wheat fields with the dogs racing beside them.

Soon the wheat and barley would be harvested and milled. Later again, the tiny green apples all around him would turn red and be picked, stored over the winter in the apple-loft. Tomi loved that time of year.

He loved every time of the year, because each time brought new, good things, but his favourite time was springtime, when the trees in the orchard were covered in blossom. He would lie in the new grass under the trees during the first long evenings and watch the white petals drift down like snow. Sometimes he could see the storks flying home across the sky to their nest in the old church tower.

'We know where you are, Tomi, and we're coming to get you!' Chava had joined in with her older cousins, her voice high-pitched and excited. Chava got excited very easily. She lived in the city and was sometimes frightened by the animals on the farm. It made Tomi feel big and brave to explain to her that the cows were just curious when they came running across the fields to see her.

Tomi stayed as still as he could, hoping no one would look up. Now he could see Laco's, Miki's and Chava's heads beneath his perch – Laco's dark, the tallest of the group, Chava's and Miki's lighter, like Tomi's own blond hair.

Chava's long hair was braided up every morning by Aunt Margo, but today, after a morning spent climbing trees and crawling through haystacks, the braids had come down and were unravelling around her shoulders.

Now there was another voice calling – it was Tomi's mother, his *anuka*.

'Children! Come to the summer house! Ice cream!'

'Ice cream!' Tomi dropped from his branch, landing right in front of Laco and Miki and Chava, making them jump. They shrieked with laughter and raced towards the tiny wooden hut, where they crowded in around the table. Mariška was there, dishing out home-made ice cream into their bowls, along with raspberries and strawberries and the first plums.

She had put a jar filled with wildflowers in the middle of the table. There were cornflowers and poppies, the bright blues and reds of her brightly coloured skirt and headscarf. Mariška helped his mother in the house, and she was one of the kindest people Tomi knew.

Then Tomi's mother appeared with the small sweet cakes that he loved so much. Anuka was taller than Mariška, and her clothes were more quietly coloured and somehow different. But then his mother *was* a little different from the local women. Like Chava, she had been brought up in town and had only begun to live in the country after she married Tomi's father, who had taken over the farm when his parents decided to set up a shop in the village.

Both Tomi's parents were different in small ways from most of the villagers. They read more and were more interested in what went on in the world outside the village.

They had a radio and listened to the news and to music almost every evening. Most people in the village did not have a radio, and no one else had a motorcycle. His father's pride and joy, the cousins loved to have a go on it when they came to visit.

There were six of his cousins gathered around the table now: the boys, Laco, Bandy and Juraj, and the girls, Kati, Chava and Tikva. They came from the cities to visit. Every summer, the cousins came and ran wild on the farm, fishing in the little rivers, getting in the way of the harvesters when they decided to help and getting their feet so dirty that Mariška would scold Tomi and Miki as she scrubbed them clean before bedtime. 'What children you are! I have never seen such dirt! You cannot be putting those feet in the clean sheets!' Mariška did all the washing and was very proud of the whiteness of her sheets, sheets that had to be scrubbed as hard as their feet.

'Any more ice cream, Teta Judith?' asked Laco. Tomi's mother smiled and scooped some more out. 'You are all getting so tall! I don't know if it's a good idea to feed you any more. You won't be able to fit on that bench the next time you come here.' They all knew that Tomi's mother was teasing; there was always plenty of good things in the farmhouse.

'The next time we come it will be the winter holidays,' replied Laco. 'We won't need ice cream – we will have snow!'

Scraping the last of the fruit and the melting ice cream from the bottom of his bowl, Tomi looked around at the smiling faces and hoped nothing would ever change. And, for some time, nothing did.

2

Winter

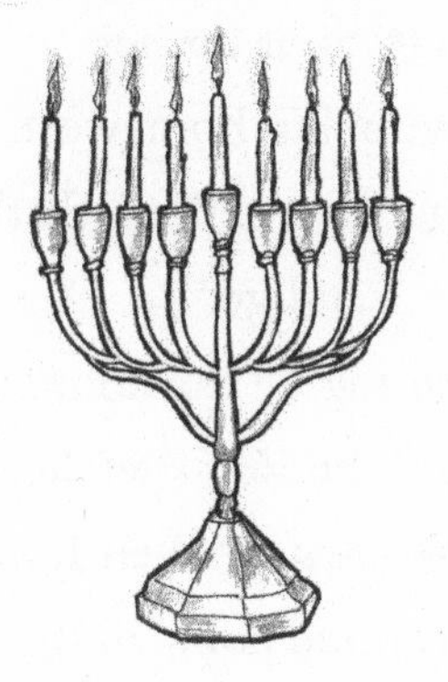

'Tomi, I want you to pop around to the shop and get some sugar from Omama.'

'Right now?' Tomi asked. It was so warm and cosy in the house, and he knew that outside would be freezing.

'Yes, right now. Father Harangozo is coming over later, and I want to make some cakes for him.'

Tomi groaned. 'Can't Miki go?'

Miki glared at his brother. Tomi glared back. He didn't know why he was always the one who was asked to do errands. His mother said it was because Miki was four years older and had more schoolwork. But Tomi thought it was because Miki would always put up an argument about why he couldn't do the chore just then. It sometimes took so long for him to do as he was asked that his mother would complain that she could have got it done herself in the time it took to get Miki to do it for her.

'Miki is busy with his homework.' She held out the canister for the sugar. 'Now, Tomi, that's enough. Just do as you have been asked, and go.'

Tomi had been sitting on the floor by the stove, the dog's head against his lap. The dog stretched his long legs lazily towards the fire and yawned when Tomi pulled himself up.

Tomi didn't really mind going to the shop, which was just around the corner. Having to pull on a heavy coat and hat and gloves and boots when the shop was so close, however, seemed ridiculous to him, but his mother always insisted that he did. It was bitterly cold outside, and she thought Tomi was delicate. She was always trying to force him to eat the vegetables that he hated, telling him that they would make him grow big and strong.

He muttered a little as he pulled on his boots and took his hat and scarf from the brightly painted dresser. His mother smiled at him. She knew that he quite liked going around to his grandparents' shop. Omama would sometimes give him one of her wonderful cakes, Opapa a sweet or two. Just to get rid of him and Miki, he always said, but although his face was stern when he said that, his eyes would twinkle.

Outside, Tomi was glad of his boots, for the snow had been falling for some time and was piled high on the ground. It was dusk already, the sun a red ball in the west. In the east the first stars were showing.

Tomi loved the snow. He loved the way it changed the village into somewhere strange and magical. All the familiar things in the yard were now mysterious humps and bumps, and everything seemed so clean and pure. It made Merašice feel like a little world of its own.

Soon the Christmas holidays would be here, and he and Miki would be able to take their special toboggan – the best in the village – and ride for hours, up and down the hill by the church. Then, like every year, some of the cousins would arrive for a winter visit, and they would join in the fun. And then it would be Christmas, and even though the family did not celebrate the Christian feast, Tomi and Miki, like every other child in the village, would put their shoes on the windowsill on Christmas Eve for them to be filled with goodies.

Tomi loved their own Jewish festival of Hanukkah, the festival of lights, celebrating the Holy Temple of Jerusalem. Over the eight days of Hanukkah, a candle would be lit each evening until all the branches of the special candlestick, the Menorah, were alight. Their Jewish friends from the neighbouring villages would come around to their house to celebrate. They would eat the treats that had been carefully prepared and drink Anuka's wonderful home-made fruit liquors, served in the crystal glasses she was so proud of.

Tomi and Miki would not be allowed to use these glasses until after their Bar Mitzvah, when they became adults. Like the silver cutlery and the good sheets and pillowcases, the pretty china and the ornaments, they were looked after carefully. Anuka explained to Tomi that all these things had been wedding gifts. They were to be used only on special occasions, and they were to last a lifetime, maybe even beyond, to be handed on to Tomi and his brother when they were grown up and had left the house to get married.

The lights of the little shop, and the Hanukkah candles lighting up the window, glowed warmly against the snow. The shop was the only one in the village, and what his grandparents did not have in stock they made sure to get for their customers.

Tomi pushed open the door, shaking snow from his boots. Inside, the space was stacked with everything and anything. It always astonished him that in a place so full of so many things, Omama and Opapa could put their hand on whatever was asked for straight away.

'And how is my little one today?' Omama asked, smiling. 'Have you come for a story or a cake?'

Tomi shook his head and held up the canister. 'Anuka sent me for some sugar. Father Harangozo is coming tonight to play cards, so she is making cakes.'

Omama smiled. 'He is a good man, the priest. He knows all the secrets of the village and says nothing! I will give you some cheesecakes to take back with you.'

Tomi thought his grandmother was a little bit like the priest. She would sit in her own special chair behind the counter, smiling, knitting away, always ready to chat to whoever came in. People loved to talk to her, and they told her things they told nobody else. Omama didn't give penance or punishment, like the priest did, she just smiled and nodded. And listened. She was a good listener. Small and plump, she always wore a crisp white apron over her skirts, and her hands were always busy, with cooking, with knitting, with sewing, with mending. They were only still when she would pull Tomi onto her knee and tell him stories, like Little Red Riding Hood and Hansel and Gretel.

Opapa was different: he didn't waste time chatting. He was very serious about keeping up Jewish traditions, more so than Apuko and Anuka. He arranged to have all their meat killed in the kosher way and recited the blessing over the challah, the special bread they ate on Saturdays, the Sabbath. This was their special day, just like Sunday was the Sabbath day for Christians. On that day, Mariška arrived early to the Reichental house because they were not allowed to do any work. It was the only day in the week when Tomi felt different from his neighbours.

There was the sound of a cart pulling up outside the shop, and a stranger came barging in, slamming the door behind him, shaking snow from his coat all over the floor. Tomi could not help staring. They rarely got strangers in Merašice, just the travelling workers who came around to do jobs like putting glass in windows or mending pots and pans.

This man was tall and rough-looking and spoke with an odd accent. He looked around swiftly and scowled at Tomi. Then he said to Opapa, 'So you must be those Jews then. I am looking for Ludo Nedelka.'

Omama came out from the back with some cheese-cakes for Tomi as his grandfather explained how to find the Nedelka house. The stranger grunted. He poked one of the cakes, which Omama had put on the counter, and Tomi thought how rude he was. He would have had his hand slapped if he had done that.

'Is this some kind of Jewish cake?' the stranger asked, staring at Omama. She said calmly, 'It's a local recipe. These cakes are the very best in Slovakia.'

The stranger growled something, picked up the cake and took a large bite out of it. Tomi was furious. He was about to tell the stranger just what he thought when he saw his grandfather shake his head at him very slightly.

The stranger stuffed the rest of the cake into his mouth, threw a small coin on the counter and left, slamming the door behind him. They could hear him shouting at his horse and the clatter of hooves as he left.

'What was wrong with that man?' Tomi asked. 'Why was he so rude?'

His grandmother shrugged. 'No need to worry about that,' she said. 'He's just a rude man. Luckily not very many people are like him. Most people respect us.'

'And those who don't are just jealous of us,' said Opapa, his voice angry. 'Just because we have a little – a very little – more than they have. As if that wasn't all down to hard work and effort. That's our strength, that and keeping the family together.'

Opapa looked very stern as he said this, and Omama looked at him anxiously. She said quietly, 'Hush, now, Tomi doesn't need to hear this. As I said, most people respect us – why even the priest is a good friend of your parents, Tomi. You had better get back with that sugar or there will be no cake for him tonight. Just hold on one minute and I will get you another cheesecake.'

All evening, Tomi puzzled over what had happened. Why had the man spoken to his grandparents like that? Was there something wrong with being Jewish? Was that why the man did not like them? Tomi didn't feel any different to anyone else in the village. It was true, as Opapa said, their family did have a little more than some others – a little more land, a house built of bricks instead of mud. They didn't go to the church, but why was that so important?

Father Harangozo, who was playing cards and enjoying the cakes and the fine plum brandy, said jokingly, 'You are much quieter than usual tonight, Tomas!'

Father Harangozo was small and stout and smiled a lot. He was Hungarian, and often he and Tomi's parents chatted in that language.

'He's been like that since he went over to the shop,' said Anuka. 'I hope he didn't get a chill. Are you warm enough, Tominko?'

Tomi nodded.

'Is something bothering you?' asked his father.

Tomi shrugged. He didn't like being the focus of all this attention, and he didn't know whether he wanted to tell all these adults what was worrying him. Perhaps he was being silly and they would laugh at him.

They were looking at him expectantly, and the card-playing had stopped. Even Miki was looking up from his book.

Tomi started hesitantly. 'It was this man.' He stopped.

'What man?' asked his mother.

'He came into the shop, and he was so rude, and talked about us being Jews. Opapa seemed angry. Did that man not like us because we are Jewish?'

Tomi's parents were silent. Miki looked on intently and said nothing. The priest sighed and said, 'If that is the case, he is a very stupid and un-Christian man. He should know that we are all God's children, Tomas, and that your family is a very fine one. Why, I do not know how I would survive without your parents' good company.'

'Or Judith's plum brandy,' said Apuko, and everyone laughed.

That night in bed, Tomi thought about the stranger for a long time. He was glad that there was no one like that living in Merašice. It always seemed safe from the outside world, and especially safe at times like this when the snow came.

With the shutters closed, he could not see the snow falling, but he knew it was there. *The snow will keep us safe*, he thought sleepily. *We are quite safe, really, in spite of men like that one who came here today.*

Safe and sound, safe and sound, he thought drowsily, repeating the words in his head until he went to sleep. And, for a little while, they were.

3

Leaving the Village

The snow had arrived early that year and stayed without melting. Hannukah ended, and then Christmas came. On Christmas Eve, the boys put their shoes on the windowsill, and, as always, overnight they were magically filled with toys and sweets.

The snow went on and on, to the point where even Tomi had grown a little tired of playing on the toboggan and feeling the cold bite his cheeks every time he left the house. At last it started to melt, and the icicles began to drip away to nothing from the eaves of the houses where they had hung all winter. The whiteness turned to slush and then became little streams in the village street, and Tomi was allowed to leave the house with first one and then two fewer layers of warm clothes and scarves.

Finally, the village square was clear enough to play football. But something had changed. Though the boys were still happy to have Miki, who was a brilliant player, and Tomi, who played goal, on their teams, they did not call them by their names anymore. When it was time to pass the ball, instead of shouting, 'Come on, Miki!' or, 'Come on, over here, Tomi!', it was 'Hey, the Jew scored!' and 'Pass the ball to the Jew!' The fact that they were Jewish had become more important than their names.

Though the boys did not know it, the real changes started before that, in September 1941, when Jews were forbidden to visit places like parks and cinemas, when they could no longer ride a bicycle and no longer had the right to travel freely. Tomi's father's motorcycle was now kept in the shed: it had suddenly become illegal for him to have one.

Tomi's parents started to have whispered conversations, and exchanged glances whenever an envelope with an official crest on it arrived. Miki and Tomi would take turns to ask, 'What is the letter about?', but they never got an answer. Other letters arrived, more than ever before because now the strict travel restrictions for Jews meant that the rest of the family could not visit as often as they used to.

By May, things had got much worse. Opapa was forced to close up the shop that had been part of village life for so long. The neighbours muttered and shook their heads. They said it was a shame to lose such a good shop and complained that they would have to travel miles to get the things that used to be on their doorstep.

Tomi felt that some of the villagers and even some of his companions at school didn't look at him in quite the same way as before. He was Jewish. He was different. And in some people's minds, being different meant there was something wrong with them.

Then came the summer holidays and the news that he and his brother could not go back to the local school when the holidays were over. When he heard this, Tomi secretly hoped that it meant he would not have to go to school at all. He could go off to the fields every day and play with Miki.

Hidden behind the table one evening, he listened while his parents discussed what might be the best thing to do. Anuka was sewing, her face set in a frown, while Apuko, in from the fields, was pulling off his boots.

'We can't leave them without an education,' his mother said. 'What are we going to do?'

Maybe you can, thought Tomi. *I'm fine with that!*

His father sighed. 'I don't know what we *can* do. We will have to send them somewhere where there is a Jewish school. That's the only kind they will be allowed attend now.'

There was a silence, and then his father said thoughtfully, 'What about sending them to stay with my sister Renka? In Nitra? There's a Jewish school there.'

Anuka sighed. 'It's so far away if anything happens to them …'

'I can't see what other choice we have. You know that Renka will look after them well.'

'I suppose you are right. But it will be so strange not to have them at home. And Tomi is so small – only six.'

I'm not all that small! thought Tomi, but he knew better than to say anything. There was something exciting about the idea of going to live in a town – although it was a little scary at the same time. And Aunt Renka and her family, especially his cousin, Martuska, were always kind when they visited.

His father said, 'And he will have Mikinko to keep an eye out for him.'

'He will need it. The world is changing so fast – and sometimes I am afraid—'

At this moment, the sneeze that Tomi had been holding in came out in an explosion.

'What are you doing there, Tomas?' said Anuka angrily. Tomi was scolded, and nothing more was said about his mother's fears.

By the time the summer holidays were over, everything had been arranged. Anuka was to bring the two boys to Nitra.

They were sad leaving Mariška and Apuko and the farm, but Mr Duraj, who always drove them to the station in his horse and cart, cheered them up by cracking jokes.

They had been to Nitra before. It was a big town, with a castle on the hill above the town, and a river, where Miki and Tomi sometimes went fishing with their cousins. Tomi had wanted to bring their fishing rods, but Miki had shaken his head. 'There's no point. Don't you remember? Jews aren't allowed fish any more.'

The train was as much fun as ever, and then it was just a short walk through the narrow cobbled streets of the town to Aunt Renka's house. The school was only down the street from where she lived, and Anuka pointed it out to them. 'You'll love it there, you will see!' she said cheerfully.

Anuka shared the dinner Aunt Renka had prepared for them but could not stay the night as the house was quite full now with Aunt Renka, her family and the two boys. Before she left she hugged her sons hard and told them to do as they were told and to be good for Aunt Renka. Then she told Miki that he was to mind his little brother.

'I don't need minding!' said Tomi. He made sure to let Anuka see how grown up he was by not crying when she left, even though he really wanted to.

Aunt Renka spent that evening sewing yellow stars on both of their new coats, to be ready for the next day.

'What is that for, Aunt Renka? Is it a kind of school uniform?' Tomi asked.

Aunt Renka didn't exactly smile. She said quietly, 'You are a big boy now, Tominko. That means you have to wear this any time you leave the house. From now on, all Jewish boys and girls over five have to wear a yellow star when they go out.'

Aunt Renka brought Tomi to the school the next morning. Anuka had been right: school was fun. The day started off with games so the children could get to know one another, and everyone was friendly.

At twelve o'clock, when the bell rang, he remembered that Aunt Renka had said she would not be able to collect him. Because Miki was not going to finish school until later, Tomi would have to make the trip back to the house on his own.

He was feeling quite proud of himself as he made his way down the street. Then something whizzed past his head, missing his cheek by a hair's breath. It landed just beyond him: a sharp-edged stone.

PART II

The Hunt

4
Hated

Tomi looked over towards the path. There were three boys about his own age, standing outside a corner shop. Something about the way they were staring at him made him nervous, and one of them seemed to have something in his hand.

'Jew! Jew!' They hissed the words out at him.

For a moment, he stood, frozen. Then he ran and ran until he reached Aunt Renka's house. When he got there, he wondered if the boys had really thrown a stone at him. He could hardly believe that people could be so mean to him when he had done nothing to them.

And it got worse.

'Dirty Jew! Smelly Jew! Pig!'

Tomi began to hate the trip to and from school. Going

there was not so bad, because most people were just thinking about getting to school or work themselves, but going home was horrible. There were always boys, most of them older than Tomi, hanging around the street corners, bored, just waiting for a Jewish person to pass so they could call them horrible names and, more and more often, fire stones as well as insults at them.

One winter's evening, as he came around the bend outside the butcher's, Tomi stopped in his tracks. He could see a group of boys sitting on the windowsill outside the shop, laughing and pushing each other. *Maybe I should turn back before they see me*, he thought. But where could he go? In any case, one of the boys had already spotted him. 'Look at the little Jewboy!' he mocked. 'All wrapped up in his nice winter coat!'

One of the other boys narrowed his eyes. 'That coat is far too good for a filthy Jew!' he said.

'Maybe we should take it off him?' another suggested.

Tomi started to run. The boys dived, but they did not catch him. As he ran by them, something landed on the yellow star. It was a huge glob of spit. Tomi could hear the boys congratulating the one who had done it. 'Good shot!' they shouted, their laughter loud and high in the cold winter air.

Tomi had always thought that laughter was something good. Now he realised that it could be cruel.

When he reached Aunt Renka's home, he was in tears. He burst into the kitchen and ran to the sink, trying to get the spit off the yellow star as quickly as possible. Miki was already home, and Cousin Martuska was preparing lunch, stirring a pot of stew at the stove.

Tomi was especially fond of Martuska, who as far back as he could remember had always been cheerful and smiling. She had finished school and had been planning to go to university, but that was no longer permitted for Jews. She could not work either, so now she spent a lot of time at home. It didn't make her grumpy, though; she was still as smiling and hopeful as ever. If there was a thunderstorm going on, Martuska would just say that all the rain would make the grass grow better for the cows.

'What's the matter, Tominko?' she asked, going over to hug him.

'Don't touch me!' Tomi scrubbed furiously at the yellow star with the washcloth.

Martuska took out her handkerchief and wiped his face, then held it up to his nose. 'Blow hard and you will feel better.' He did, and he did feel a little better for a moment. Then he could feel the sobs rising again. Martuska hugged him harder. 'Now, take off your coat and come and have some good hot stew and tell me what happened,' she said.

'The boys – the boys at the butcher's – they spat at me.'

Tomi was starting to feel better, knowing that he was safe at home now. 'Why do they do things like that to us? Why do they call us such horrible names? What's wrong with being a Jew? I don't want to be Jewish!'

Martuska sighed. 'Never say that. You should be proud of being Jewish. Aren't you proud of the family?'

Tomi didn't know what to say. He was so confused. Of course he was proud of his parents, of his aunts and uncles, of his grandparents. But he hated when people treated him in such a horrible way. And they treated him in a horrible way because of his Jewish family.

Martuska ladled some stew into a bowl. She said, 'Now, come and sit at the table. You too, Mikinko. We are Jews, and, just at the moment, people are being told again and again that the Jews are responsible for all the bad things that happen – for there being very little work, for people being poor. They are being told that because we are different we are guilty of doing bad things. But it is not we who are guilty, but them. Try not to think about what those boys did. They are the dirty ones, to treat people like that. You just do your best to keep out of their way, and don't draw any attention to yourself. All this will pass over, wait and see – there will be better times ahead!'

The teachers at the Jewish school said the same. 'Try to keep out of the way of trouble. Don't draw attention to yourself. Don't laugh or chatter in the streets. Be quiet and do your best not to be seen.' The teachers were going through the same thing themselves: the name-calling, stone-throwing, harassment – and not just from boys at the street corner. Sometimes they couldn't make it to class because they had been stopped by the police. Because they wore the yellow star too, everyone knew they were Jewish.

So the time in Nitra was not a good one for Tomi, despite the company of his cousins. He counted down the days until Christmas when he could go home. He couldn't wait to be back with Opapa and Omama, Anuka and Apuko. Back in the village. Back with people who would be kind.

When it finally came, Christmas was wonderful, as always, though very quiet. Opapa never left the house any more. The loss of the shop had really upset him, and he spent a lot of time just sitting in his chair, sometimes reading but mostly half asleep. Omama spent a lot more time in her chair too, but she kept knitting and sewing, and she still captured Tomi on her lap to tell him stories of magical forests and wolves and witches and gingerbread houses.

Going tobogganing wasn't as much fun as it used to be. There was a new kind of guard in the village, who stared at the children as if they had no right to be out having fun in the street. These Hlinka guards spent their time striding around in black uniforms and matching shiny boots – looking as if they owned the place, as more than one villager grumbled. Mariška told Tomi's mother that she had heard from her husband that when these guards got drunk in the local pub they would shout songs about how wonderful Slovakia was at the top of their voices and then come out with crazy ideas about getting rid of all the Jews.

Anuka would hush her.

Tomi tried to talk to Miki about what was happening. Miki had visited Aunt Margo in Bratislava, and Tomi had heard him telling their mother that the Hlinka guards were everywhere there, cracking their whips and bullying anyone they saw wearing a yellow star.

'They have meetings where they wear swastika armbands and cheer the president, who talks all the time about lazy, greedy Jews. He says we are taking the wealth of the country away from everyone else. In some other places, everything is being taken away from the Jews. They are being rounded up and sent off—'

Anuka interrupted him, with a warning glance towards Tomi. 'That's enough! I don't want you talking about this kind of thing in front of the little ones!'

'Shouldn't Tominko know what's going on? Shouldn't we be trying to do something about it?'

'There is nothing we can do, Miki,' Anuka said. 'We will just try to keep going here and hope for the best.'

'Are you sure there is nothing, nothing at all we can do to make things better?'

Anuka shook her head. 'Try not to think too much about it, Mikinko. And, as I said, say nothing about this to anyone but myself and your father.'

She turned to Tomi. 'I don't want you thinking about this, Tominko. Just remember always that Miki is your big brother and that he will look out for you.'

When the holidays ended, Tomi felt a weight settle like a stone on his stomach. He tried to hide his tears as Mr Duraj collected them to bring them to the train station. Back to Nitra. Back to the stone-throwing and the insults. Back to the fear of walking to school. Term time stretched out in front of him.

The end of Tomi's misery came sooner than he expected. Just a few weeks later, when he arrived for school one morning, he found the gates locked. Jews were no longer allowed to go to school. Miki looked at the gates and said, 'This is another thing they are taking away from us because we are Jews. Now we are not even allowed to learn to read and write.'

Tomi didn't care what the reason was. He was going home. Within a few days, Mr Duraj was driving them back to Merašice. There were hugs and kisses all round when they reached the house.

Tomi could hardly contain his excitement. *So that's the end of that,* he thought happily. *No more school!* However, Apuko was determined that both his sons would get an education.

He found a local man, living a few miles away, deep in the countryside, who said he would teach the two children.

Tomi and Miki had a very different walk to school now. Instead of city streets and mocking voices, they made their way to their lessons through the woods and fields. With the approach of spring, the track that led through an arch of overhanging trees to the tutor's house became a magical green tunnel. The birds sang in the surrounding forest. The two boys talked about everything and exchanged secrets. They became very close to each other. They had to. They had no other friends in the village.

The summer made the tunnel of trees even greener, and wild flowers grew underneath. The peaches and the plums ripened in the garden and the orchard of the farmhouse, but no cousins came to visit. Tomi's parents laughed less, and in the background there was always worry. They said less and less to the children about what was going on. Even so, Tomi and Miki began to realise that people had started to disappear.

A letter came to say that Uncle Desider, who had worked as a surgeon in Moravia, and who had been arrested some time before, had been sent to a prison in Germany. The family had been very worried about him but could do nothing to help him. Desider sent letters from the prison, but after a while there were no more letters and no way of knowing what might have happened to him.

Then there was the visit of their cousin Martuska. She was one of the thousands of young Jewish people who were told they were being sent away to work in camps in other countries. Martuska was, as always, laughing and smiling when she visited Merašice, just before she left, and she was really excited about the trip. 'They won't let us work here. They won't let us study here. I'm happy to go somewhere they might let us do both! And there are so many of my friends and other cousins going … it will be fun!'

'Promise you will write to me!' said Tomi. 'Promise you will let us know what's happening.'

'I promise! And when I come back to visit you, I will bring you the biggest box of sweets I can find.'

But after Martuska left there were no letters – not from her, not from any of the cousins. Tomi never saw the box of sweets she promised. And he never saw his cousin again.

Now Tomi realised that conversations stopped as soon as he or Miki walked into a room. There were stories not told and things hidden. And Miki told him nothing either, just closed his lips firmly and looked stubborn, no matter how many times Tomi asked him to talk to him about what was going on.

5

Sent Away

It was strange to see so little of the cousins that summer. Tomi and Miki drew further and further away from the village boys who had been their friends. They didn't play football anymore, except to kick the ball to each other, which wasn't much fun. Tomi could see Miki getting impatient with him sometimes – he really was no competition for his older brother.

It wasn't that all of the other children refused to play with them – some of them would have been happy to have Tomi and Miki on their team. But Tomi and Miki knew that the boys and their families would be in trouble with the Hlinka guards if they were seen playing football with Jews. Because everything had changed. There were new words being used, words like 'fraternisation' and 'collaboration'. Tomi didn't really know exactly what they meant, apart from trouble for his family.

His father had been writing letter after letter to the local council. Tomi knew that it had something to do with his family getting permission to stay on the farm. Every time a reply came from the authorities, he watched his father and mother open the envelope together, and breathe huge sighs of relief when it told them they could stay in their own home, in their own village, for another couple of months. More and more family members were being sent off, away from Slovakia – some to the east, some to the north – with no news about what happened to them after they were taken away.

It was August, a long, bright, summer evening, with the blackberries blooming and the apples already russet red. Tomi was outside, playing with the sheepdog, when he saw a big black car approaching their house. Two men, dressed completely in black, both tall and unsmiling, got out and knocked on the door of what had once been the shop. Tomi looked on as the door opened, and Opapa came out, followed closely by Omama, drying her hands on a towel. His mother and father came running from their own house. One of the men was dressed as a policeman, and the other was a local Hlinka guard.

It's Ludo, thought Tomi. Ludvik, one of the Nedelka family. *Ludo knows us. He won't do anything horrible to our family.*

Ludo's face was set in a hard expression, and his voice was harsh as he read from a paper that he pulled out from the pocket of his black uniform. 'By the orders of the Ministry of the Interior, Jew Jecheskel Reichental and his wife Katarina are to go immediately with the defence officer. You are permitted to bring only what is absolutely essential.' Then he added, 'Be quick, we are not here to waste time.'

For a moment, there was a stunned silence, and then Apuko said, 'Ludo, this is crazy. My family and I – we are farmers, we are needed here. We have a permit to stay.'

'Well, show it to me then,' said Ludo.

'It's on the way. We have been waiting for ages for it. You can check with the office in Bratislava. We should get it any day now.'

Nedelka said nothing for a moment. Then, in a voice like a machine, he said, 'I have my orders. If you don't have a permit, your parents must come with me.'

'But Ludo … We grew up together. You have known my family all our lives. We went to school together. You used to come on errands to my father's shop.'

Tomi stood, watching, stunned at what was happening. His grandparents, like so many others, were being taken away. Horror mixed with disbelief. Surely their old neighbour would not take his beloved Opapa and Omama away? Surely?

Then, Tomi saw Ludvik Nedelka's face twitch slightly and realised something horrible. Ludo didn't care that what he was doing was destroying Tomi's family. In fact, somewhere inside it was making him feel good. He was enjoying looking big in front of the policeman, and he was really enjoying having power over people that he had perhaps always been a little jealous of.

Tears were flowing down Tomi's mother's face when she came over to her son and pulled him tight to her. Part of Tomi wanted to hide his face in her apron, but another part needed to know what was going on.

'Hurry up,' said Ludo Nedelka again. 'Don't keep us waiting.'

Omama sighed. 'We have to go,' she said to Opapa. 'Come, let's get our things.' She untied her apron and went into the house, where she gathered together some food and some clothes. She stood for a moment looking around her kitchen, as if saying her goodbyes to all the things that had been part of her life for so many years. The table where the whole family had gathered to celebrate the start of the Sabbath. The big black oven, where she had cooked so many wonderful cakes. The herbs hanging to dry, the blue bowl filled with purple plums. She had just made one of her nicest cakes, and it was cooling on the windowsill, filling the kitchen with the scent of vanilla.

Tomi saw Ludo, who had followed them into the house as if he suspected they would somehow escape through the window or the chimney, give it a greedy glance. *If he takes a piece*, thought Tomi fiercely, *I'll go and bite his hand. I will.*

Opapa was putting on his coat, his hands shaking. Omama went over to help him.

'Don't worry, Apuko,' said Tomi's father. 'I will come and get you as soon as the permit comes through. You will be back home with us in a couple of days, I promise you.'

His father said nothing, just embraced him – a short embrace, for Nedelka was harassing them to move along. The old couple walked side by side to the waiting car, their heads bowed.

The permit arrived two days later, dated for two weeks before Tomi's Omama and Opapa were arrested. Even by the cruel new laws of Slovakia, there was no reason why they should have been taken away.

6

Hunted

'They are coming!' Mariška burst through the door from the farmyard. She continued breathlessly, 'Mr Duraj sent little Stefan to tell us that the Hlinka are on the prowl. They are only a few minutes away!'

There was not a moment to be lost.

'Tominko, you take the blankets, and Mikinko, get the food bag.' Even as Anuka spoke she too was gathering up what they would need. 'Which one will we go to, Arnold? The hayfield or the haystack in the yard?'

'If they are that close, it had better be the haystack.' Apuko grabbed the bucket they would use for a toilet. This had all been planned carefully.

Tomi and Miki were first to reach the big haystack in the farmyard and burrow quickly into it. Their parents arrived moments later. There they sat, silent and still, and waited. Soon they heard the shriek of a motor stopping. Loud voices. The noise of heavy boots on the gravel. Then silence.

Looking around him, at the little bits of hay in his mother's hair and in his father's moustache, Tomi felt a giggle rise. Diving into the haystacks had always been strictly forbidden to the children. It felt so odd to be doing this with his parents, almost like playing hide and seek.

Apuko gestured at Tomi to keep quiet. He tried his best, but it was hard with the hay tickling his nose. It was also hard to stay still when he thought the Hlinka guards might be coming nearer and nearer the haystack. Perhaps they would poke it with sticks, to see if there was anyone hidden within. That thought made Tomi stop wanting to giggle straight away.

The family waited for what seemed like hours. There was an occasional small rustle, but it was only a rat or some small animal moving through the hay. It was very hard to keep quiet and still for so long. The day grew darker.

Rapid footsteps came towards them. Someone pushed back the hay, and all of them tensed. A familiar voice said,

'It's only me, Mariška.' She was speaking in a whisper so the family knew the guards must still be nearby. 'I've brought you food,' she said, her face red and comically framed in the hay. 'They are still looking for you, so I think you had better stay in there tonight.'

It was a long, cold and uncomfortable night. In the morning, Mariška came to tell them that the guards had left. This was the first of many times the family hid from the guards. Soon hiding became as normal to Tomi as playing football or following his father around the farm. Tomi wondered if there would ever again come a time when there would be parties in the summer house, games of hide and seek in the orchard. It seemed unlikely.

A new 'Operation' had been started by the Hlinka guards. Operation Chytácka was basically an all-out hunt for Jewish families. The guards would go from village to village, looking for Jews to arrest. It didn't matter if they had a permit to stay, they would still be forced from their homes and sent away.

The Hlinka guards were not liked by the country people – they treated them very badly – so a great many Jewish families were warned by their neighbours if the Hlinka were out on a hunt. The Reichentals were well prepared. Tomi's father had organised a number of hiding places for the family: the shack belonging to their old friend, Mr Duraj; spots in the cornfield, where the tall stems would hide them from sight; and, of course, the giant haystack in the farmyard.

It was coming into the end of autumn now, an autumn full of fear. For weeks after Opapa and Omama were taken away, Tomi's father wrote letter after letter to the authorities, explaining that there had been a mistake and asking that his parents be released and sent home.

At first, Tomi was sure that his father would be able to do what he said. Opapa and Omama would come back to the farm, and everything would be like it had been before. Every day, he would ask hopefully if there was any news about his grandparents. Their house was so quiet with no one in it, and he missed Omama's cakes and stories and hugs. After a few weeks, he stopped asking. He could see that his questions hurt his father. Eventually, a letter came saying that his grandparents had been sent far away. There was nothing more that anyone could do to try to get them back.

The weeks went by; the season turned, just like always. The crops were harvested. The apples and pears ripened and were picked. Mariška continued to come to clean the house. Apuko worked the farm, and Anuka cooked the children's favourite food for their Friday meal. But nothing was the same. The world, which Tomi felt had become somehow smaller, somehow tighter, over the passing months, but which had still been a safe one, turned into a colder, darker place. He would wake at night imagining the tall black shape of Ludvik Nedelka coming from the shadows, taking his grandparents away. And now there was the fear that he would come and do the same to Tomi's parents. To Mikinko. To Tomi himself.

And then a January night came when no warning was received, and there was a sharp crack on the door. The family pulled themselves out of bed and gathered together. Apuko said, 'Boys, sit on the couch, back from the door.'

Miki half moved forward, as if he felt that he should be at his father's and mother's side, but he did what he was told. There in the doorway stood Ludvik Nedelka, together with another rough-looking Hlinka guard. He shoved past Tomi's father so that he was standing in the middle of the little sitting room. 'You have thirty minutes to pack one small suitcase each. Bring only essentials. Then you must hand over the keys of the residence and come with us.'

Apuko opened his mouth to speak, but before he could say anything, Miki was on his feet, shouting. 'How dare you? This is our home! How dare you torment us all the time? Why us, when your own children sleep safe at home? What have we done to you that you treat us like this? It isn't right! We have done nothing wrong! We are good people! My little brother is only seven!'

There was a shocked silence. Even Nedelka didn't seem to know what to say.

Tomi's father pulled the two officers into the kitchen. Mother said nothing, just gently pushed Miki back onto the couch. He sat there, not looking at anyone, his face still red with fury. He was trembling, but Tomi could not tell whether it was from anger or from fear at what he had done. It seemed that he had shocked even himself with his outburst. Anuka put her arm about him to hold him close, but still he would not look at her.

The three men came back into the room, Nedelka stuffing something into his pocket. 'We will be back in an hour. Be ready to go then.' His voice was not so loud now, and he did not look at Miki.

Father sighed when they left. 'It's the haystack again tonight. I think Nedelka's visit might have been his own idea. He just wanted me to give him money. That's why we didn't hear about it from our usual contacts. But it means that we really are not safe.'

These days, Miki and Tomi had very little to do. Their tutor could no longer teach them. It was too dangerous for him to have anything to do with Jews, and, in any case, Anuka worried about the long journey there and back through the forest.

Quite apart from what was happening to the Jews, the whole country was now in the middle of a war. They spent a lot of time watching the bombers – giant, shiny bees – pass over their house on the way to the capital, Bratislava.

Little cousin Chava was sent from the city to stay with them because she was so frightened of the bombings.

Listening to the news on the radio in the evening, Tomi realised that there was no safe place anywhere. Other news came to them too: of deportations, of deaths, and then of Uncle Dieter's execution.

In the middle of all this, in the middle of all the talk about 'filthy Jews' and how they should be thrown out of their towns and villages, there were still people who were loyal friends to the Reichental family. Mariška and Mr Duraj still worked for them, and some visitors continued to come to the house. Father Harangozo, who still came to play cards, lamented the way the world had gone. 'It's like everything has gone crazy!' he said. 'How can people act like this to their neighbours?'

Miki and Tomi were playing with their toy planes by the fire. Their father exchanged a glance with his wife, put down his cards and said, 'Father Harangozo, we need your help.'

7

Hiding

Father Harangozo nodded. 'If you want me to convert you to become Christians, that will not be a problem.'

Anuka shook her head. 'No, we don't want to convert. I know other people have done that, to avoid being deported. But look at the Lowys. They converted and were still taken away. We are not safe here anymore, and we need to leave Merašice – at least I and the two boys do.'

Both Tomi and Miki had stopped their game and were staring at their mother.

Lately, there had been more conversations cut short than usual. Almost every time they came into a room, Apuko and Anuka stopped talking to each other. The boys had realised that something was up. But neither of them had suspected this.

Miki said anxiously, 'What about Apuko? We can't leave without him!'

His father tried to smile. 'They need me here to till the land and harvest the crops. I will be safe enough. In any case, I am not going to leave the farm and let it go to rack and ruin. I have to look after the land. I have friends here, and I have known the village and the countryside around it all my life. I promise you that I will be safer here on my own than I would be with the rest of you here. Now listen, and I will tell you the plan. You are to go to live with Omama Rosalia. She will come to Bratislava …'

Miki tried to say something, but his father shook his head sternly. He looked very like Opapa. 'No, Mikinko, be still and listen. And Tominko, don't look so upset. I am sure it won't be long before we are all back here together.'

Tomi could almost see the words form in Miki's mouth – 'That's what you said to Omama and Opapa' – but thankfully the priest cut in. 'So what do you need me to do? Do you want me to sort out Christian identity papers for you and the boys?'

Anuka nodded eagerly. 'Yes, and we need you to teach them how to look like Christians. We are lucky they both have fair hair and blue eyes. Father, is it too much to ask? We don't want to put you in any danger.'

The priest shook his head. 'You are my good friends, and you are good people. It's my duty to help you. It is what

God wants. No human being should be treated the way your people are being treated.' He paused, looked at the anxious faces around him, and smiled. 'And I want you all to come back here when all this horror is over, so I can have a glass of your plum brandy and people in the village I can talk Hungarian to and play a decent game of cards with!'

So Tomi and Miki Reichental became Tomi and Miki Vyda. Father Harangozo organised papers for them, and Anuka told them again and again to forget they had ever been called Reichental. 'When anybody asks you your name, you are Vyda, not Reichental. Never, ever forget this!' She hugged Tomi and said, 'Soon we will move to a small village, far from here, where no one knows the Reichentals. You two are going to have to learn Catholic ways as quickly as you can – it will be the most important lesson you will ever learn.'

Tomi and Miki went every day to the priest's house and learned how to bless themselves, how to behave in the church and how to say prayers like the Rosary and the Lord's Prayer. The priest told them lots of stories about saints, which Tomi quite liked, though they were not as good as the stories Omama used to tell, and he wondered how his strict grandfather would feel about him listening to them.

The need to leave became even more urgent towards the end of the summer, when German police, called the

Gestapo, marched into Slovakia to help the Hlinka in their hunt for Jewish families. Word started to come through about huge camps and gas chambers, about hideous things being done to the Jewish people who had been rounded up. Some things were reported in the newspapers, but mostly the news came through letters from cousins and by word of mouth from the villagers and the few remaining Jewish people in the area.

All the news was bad. All over Europe, hundreds – thousands – of men, women and children were being sent on long journeys to unknown places. Nobody ever came back.

By September, Tomi's parents had decided that it was time for Tomi, Miki and their mother to leave. Tomi had never seen his father cry, but when it was time to say goodbye there were tears and more tears. Mariška was there, and she cried too, hugging the boys she had known since the day they were born. Even Mr Duraj seemed a little red-eyed as he set his horse in a fast trot towards the railway station.

There was very little traffic on the road. They passed the deserted synagogue, and then the road led them past the forest. The sun was going down and slanted through the trees, making it seem like an enchanted wood in one of Omama's stories. They reached the top of the hill and looked down into the valley where the town of Hlohovec lay; beyond it was Leopoldov, and the station.

By the time they got to the bottom of the hill, it was dark. At the entrance to Leopoldov, there was a sudden kerfuffle: a group of soldiers, shouting at them to stop. Mr Duraj pulled up reluctantly and said crossly, 'I can't delay. I need to make the train to Bratislava and I am late already!'

The soldier who had stopped them nodded and seemed about to let them go on. One of the soldiers was staring hard at Tomi and Miki's mother. 'These are Jews! These are Jews!' he shouted excitedly.

Tomi knew a moment of paralysing fear. Mr Duraj whipped up the horse and took off, leaving the soldiers shouting and cursing behind them. Every minute, Tomi expected to feel a bullet whizz past his ear or even lodge itself into his neck, but for some reason the soldiers didn't open fire.

Mr Duraj, shaking a little, dropped them and their baggage just outside the station, and Tomi's mother thanked him with tears in her eyes. 'You saved our lives. Those soldiers could have shot you. We will never forget this.'

Tomi felt like crying too. Mr Duraj had always been so kind to them all. He helped them hide, letting them sleep in his little hut for many of the nights the Hlinka guards were on the prowl. Although sleep was maybe the wrong word, because none of the family ever got much sleep there. Mr Duraj snored very loudly, and the hut was filled with dozens of fleas that were only too happy to feast on them.

But, fleas or no fleas, Mr Duraj had been one of the people, like Mariška, and like Father Harangozo, who had not only never looked at them differently, when Jews started to be treated like the enemy, but who had helped them in every way they could.

They had to fight their way through the station, which was packed with crowds boarding the train to Bratislava. The station was full of Hlinka guards and Gestapo officers, obvious by the black swastika on a red armband they wore on their coats.

To start their life as the Vyda family, the family was headed first to Bratislava, where Margo and her family were living in hiding. Their grandmother, Omama Rosalia, was to join them there.

All three Reichentals held their breath while the guard examined the false papers Father Harangozo had given them. The guard frowned as he examined their papers and looked at them very closely. Tomi tried not to look at his mother or brother in case he somehow made it obvious that they were really Jews. Then the guard gave an abrupt nod and gestured them onwards.

When they took their seats on the train, Tomi's mother let out a sigh of relief. Tomi whispered, 'That guard looked so cross I was worried.' His mother shook her head at him very slightly, and Miki said, in a high, loud voice, 'What have we to be worried about? Our papers are in order, and we have the right to go anywhere we choose!' He was glaring at Tomi as he said this, and Tomi realised that he should not have said anything. Who knew who might be listening, among the crowds of women with baskets and men lighting cigarettes? So many people would be proud to let the Gestapo know they had spotted a Jew.

It took two hours to reach the capital, and it was a silent and nerve-wracking journey. Towards the end, Tomi did manage to sleep a bit. He was woken up by his mother shaking him gently. 'We are here, Tominko. We have to go to the Reduta cinema.'

For a moment, Tomi thought they were somehow going to live in the cinema. Did that mean that he could watch movies every day? In fact, their new home was a tiny flat in the backyard of the house next door to the cinema. They would stay there for a couple of weeks before meeting up with Omama Rosalia and moving to a village in the country. The nicest part of what had been a long and horrible day was that Aunt Margo was there to welcome them and help settle them in. She and Chava, along with Uncle Dula and Cousin Laco, were living in hiding in a villa in Bratislava.

The next morning, they had a visit from their Uncle Geza and Hella, his Swiss girlfriend. Hella seemed impossibly glamorous to the boys. She warned them about the air raids. 'There's one nearly every day now,' she said, 'but you can't go to the shelter. It's too risky. The best place to go is probably the coal bunker.' Tomi's mother made a face at this, and Hella laughed. 'I know, the boys will look like nothing on earth when they come out of it, but at least it's safe and solid!'

Geza and Hella came to their rescue just a few days later when there was a knock on the door. Two men from the Slovak secret services stood there. 'You are Jews. Come with us,' one of them said.

Anuka shook her head, trying to appear as calm as possible. 'I can show you our papers ... We are not Jews.'

The man hardly looked at the cards. He shrugged. 'We know that you are Jews.'

There was another knock on the door, and one of the officers went to open it. Uncle Geza and Hella stood there.

'Your IDs.'

Geza said, 'I am afraid I have left mine at home.'

Hella looked as cool as could be. 'I have mine,' she said, 'and I am a Swiss citizen. Let's go into the other room for a moment.'

They heard a mumbled conversation through the door, and Tomi's mother exchanged glances with Geza. They all knew that Hella was giving the men money, probably lots of money. Once again, greed ruled.

They were so grateful to Hella. Tomi's mother tried to thank her, but before she could do it properly, Hella shook her head and said, 'They will be back. They know you are Jews. You are going to have to move, straight away. It's not safe here anymore.' She sat down wearily and looked at each of the family in turn. 'And we came here with some bad news, I'm afraid.'

'What is it?' asked Tomi's mother. 'Please don't tell me something has happened to Arnold.'

Geza put his arms around her and pushed her gently onto a chair. 'I'm sorry, Judith, but we have got word that Arnold has been arrested.'

There was a sob from Tomi's mother, and Hella pulled the two boys into a hug, as if hoping she could pass some strength to them.

Anuka pulled herself together, and, clutching the handkerchief she had used to wipe away her tears, said in a broken voice, 'What has happened? Where is he?'

'We don't know any details. We are not even sure it was him who was arrested yesterday in Merašice. But it doesn't seem likely that it could be anyone else.'

'He should have come with us! He should have stayed with his family. Why did he have to stay on that stupid farm? He always loved it too much.'

Hella said soothingly, 'I'm sure he will be all right.'

Tomi's mother gulped back her tears and looked over at her two boys. 'Yes, of course he will be all right. We are all going to get through this. We will all get home to Merašice and we will be together.'

Yes, Tomi thought. *He has to be all right. I won't even think about it, and we will see him soon, or at least get news.* But a voice in his head whispered, *All right? Like Uncle Desider? All right like Omama and Opapa, who have been sent who knows where? Father is being sent to those places, to the camps, where terrible things are being done to Jews. How can he be all right?*

8

Trapped

The very next morning, Anuka found the family a new home. It was an apartment in a large house in the country. She explained to Tomi and Miki, 'There are other people in the house, so we have to make sure that they believe we are Christians. You two will have to leave every morning, as if you were going to school, and go into the forest. You will have to hide there for the time you would normally be at school. You need to be quiet as mice, so no one hears you.'

'What if it's raining?' asked Miki. 'Is there nowhere else we can go?'

Their mother shook her head. 'Nowhere as safe as the woods. I know it will be hard – especially the bit about staying still and quiet for you, Tomi – but it's really, really important.'

Tomi started to grumble. A whole day stuck in the forest! And not just once, but day after day.

Anuka said abruptly, 'That's enough, Tominko. These are bad times for everyone. The place Margo has found is even worse than ours. They are in what is supposed to be an empty house, so they have to spend every day with the shutters closed, and they can't use any light at night either. Poor Chava has to spend all day and all night in the dark and in silence. And she is such a chatterer – it is so hard for her. At least our life is a bit closer to normal.'

'And at least we don't have to hide in the coal bunker,' Miki whispered to Tomi when they arrived at the big country house.

The days were getting colder, and it was hard having to leave the warmth of the house every morning and make their way into the forest, knowing they could not come back for hours. While they were there, they were not able to talk or play games in case anyone heard them. It was a strange life, and very uncomfortable on the days it rained. They would arrive home soaked to the skin, muddy and miserable. Tomi spent a lot of time wondering whether things would ever change. Was he going to spend his life being hunted, hiding, trying to become invisible? And where was his father? Was he all right? Had he been brought to one of the camps where terrible things happened?

But there were also days when the sky was blue and the birds sang. The boys were so quiet that sometimes the forest creatures came close to them because they did not realise the boys were there. They saw lots of squirrels, some foxes and badgers, and sometimes even deer. Miki pretended to be a hunter and shot them with a twig, but because he didn't make the BANG noise that would have frightened them they stayed peacefully grazing for a long time.

Tomi thought of the tunnel of green he and Miki used to take to the schoolmaster's house and wondered if he would ever be so free again. It had not felt free at the time, and he had complained about the way the path got muddy and how the lessons were sometimes hard and sometimes boring. But his family had been together, and he had felt safe. There was very little safety now. Like the forest creatures, they were hunted.

At least the forest creatures had their home in this wood – their dens and their nests. He and Miki and their mother had no real home at all now. With their father gone, he was sure that the Merašice farm would be left to become overgrown, the house empty with no more coats or hats on the old dresser. No one to mend the barn when the wind took a tile off. No one to weed the courtyard.

He tried to explain his feelings to Miki. 'We have nowhere now. We have no home, no farm. Not even a name. Everything is gone.'

Miki tried to console him. He whispered, 'At least we have our mother and each other. Once we stick together things cannot get really bad. And did you hear that Omama Rosalia and Aunt Margo and Cousin Chava are coming to join us very soon?' Miki stopped abruptly when a nearby noise startled them, but it was only a jay taking off from the branches of an old oak tree. 'Let's see how long we can sit still and stare at each other without smiling!' he said. So they did. Tomi was the one who cracked first, falling in a fit of helpless, silent laughter as Miki crossed his eyes comically at him.

They waited impatiently for the arrival of Omama Rosalia. Everything would be so much better when they could go with their cousins and Aunt Margo and their grandmother and live together in peace in a small village. Tomi was especially looking forward to seeing Chava. Even though she was a girl, and sometimes had funny ideas, they had always got on well and played well together – they were very close to being the same age.

The morning when Uncle Geza was to bring Omama to meet them finally arrived, and they made the journey into the city. Anuka put their suitcases in a locker at the station. 'Geza told me to meet Omama in a shop beside the cinema,' she said, bringing the boys to a photographic shop nearby. 'I want you two to wait here until I come back. I should only be a few minutes. When I come back,

I will have Omama Rosalia with me!' She was pink with excitement at the thought of seeing her mother again.

Inside the shop, the boys waited. And waited. And waited. Tomi stared at the shop display until he felt he knew every camera and every piece of equipment in it by heart. They could not tell for how long they had waited. Then they heard the church bell tolling twelve. Tomi was getting restless, and Miki was getting cross with him for the way he kept fidgeting.

And then, finally, the door opened. Tomi jumped up to run to Omama and hug her. It had been such a long time since he had seen her.

But he stopped in his tracks. It was not his grandmother and his mother at the door. It was two men, tall and blond, wearing long black leather coats. Each had a swastika on his red armband. Tomi shrank back.

One of the men stepped forward and grabbed Miki by the shoulder. 'You are a Jew?'

Miki shook his head. 'No,' he said, his voice firm in a way that astonished Tomi. 'I am not a Jew. My name is Miki Vyda.'

'You are a dirty little Jew.'

Tomi's heart sank. The Vyda name had been the talisman they had held onto, believing that it would save them.

Miki shook his head again.

'You are Jewish,' said the man. Then he slapped Miki across the face, leaving an angry weal. 'Tell me the truth. We have your mother.'

Miki said again, 'My name is Miki Vyda. This is my brother, Tomi Vyda. We are not Jewish.'

Tomi knew that Miki would keep saying that no matter how many times they hit him.

Now they turned on Tomi. 'You are Jewish, aren't you?' the taller man said.

Tomi shook his head. 'My name is Tomi Vyda,' he said, his voice shaking only a little. 'I am not Jew—'

Before he could finish the word 'Jewish', the man hit him in his face, so hard that he was nearly knocked off his feet. He could hardly hear with the pain. Miki jumped forward and grasped the man's arm to stop him hitting Tomi again. 'No! Stop! He's only little. Don't hit him. Yes, we are Jewish.'

The man laughed. 'You could have saved yourselves a beating if you had just admitted that in the beginning. But when can you expect the truth from Jews?'

The men bundled the two boys across the road to the shop beside the cinema. Their mother was there, and Tomi and Miki ran to her. Their grandmother and Uncle Geza were there too and some other people whom Tomi did not know. Omama Rosalia hugged them tightly and said, with tears in her eyes, 'Ah, my little boys, this is not the meeting we were meant to have. Someone has betrayed us!'

Omama's face was covered in bruises where she had been punched, time after time. She had been caught as soon as she entered the shop where the meeting had been arranged to take place. And when Anuka came to the shop, she had been identified as a Jew by the fact that her maiden name was the same as her mother's. Because it wasn't an obviously Jewish name Father Harangozo had thought that there was no need to change it. The boys had been found because the suitcases in the station were full of their clothes. When the Gestapo found two small boys left alone, waiting for their mother, they knew exactly who they were.

'You know, this pair doesn't look Jewish,' remarked the Gestapo man, looking at Miki and Tomi.

'Can't you let them go then?' said Anuka, a note of desperate hope in her voice. But the Gestapo man just laughed.

Chava and Margo, Laco, Uncle Dula and Geza had all been caught. One of the family who owned the villa they were staying in had cracked under interrogation by the Gestapo. Now thirteen members of Tomi's family were on their way to the Gestapo headquarters in Bratislava.

9

The Journey

The Gestapo headquarters was full of people, but everyone there was silent. Nobody wanted to draw attention to themselves by speaking. There were quiet hugs of welcome for the cousins and aunts and uncles, but, as Omama Rosalia had said, this was not the reunion anyone had hoped for. Tomi and Miki didn't say a word either; they were used to keeping quiet, and all Tomi wanted to do was hold on to Anuka. That was his great fear: that his mother and brother – the only safety in this frightening world – would be taken away from him.

As the long day went on, more and more people were brought into the dimly lit basement corridor where they were being held. Each one kept their head bowed, carefully avoiding each other's eyes. They knew that letting the guards see that they knew each other could bring all of them further into danger.

Some were wearing coats and had small cases, as if they had been on their way to the station. Some were still in their indoor clothes. When evening came, one or two very small children were brought in still in their pyjamas, hurriedly wrapped in blankets to keep out the October cold. The building they were held in, Aunt Margo whispered, had once been the home of a rabbi. Now a Nazi flag hung over the door, and the walls were covered in Nazi slogans and the hated swastika.

Some people at the wall slid down to sit on their hunkers or on the floor. Tomi's mother stood upright, holding her boys close to her. Tomi shifted from one foot to the other, wondering how long they would have to stay like this. What would he do if he needed to use the toilet? That was the thought that scared and shamed him most – he could not bear the thought of having to ask to leave his mother.

Then he noticed that Anuka had taken the ID cards out of her bag. She glanced around quickly and then slid them under the carpet on the floor. Tomi opened his mouth to ask why. Anuka put her finger to her lips. Later, she told him that she was hiding the IDs so that Father Harangozo would not get into trouble.

All around them, children cried quietly or hid their faces against their parents. Cousin Chava did not even meet Tomi's eye; she spent the time with her head buried in her father's arm. Everyone realised that the hunt was over. They were trapped.

By the next day, there was hardly room for people to sit on the floor. All through the night a child had been crying and asking when they could go home. Tomi knew that home was the last place they would be taken. During the long morning, the only news they were given was that they would be moved somewhere else, though no one said where. Finally they heard the noise of trucks arriving, and everyone was herded outside. Tomi and his family – his mother had made sure they were close to the rest of the family in the queue – were loaded onto them.

They were taken to Sered', where there was a labour camp for Jewish people. The camp had started off as a place where Jews worked as slaves, making everything from uniforms for the army to tiny, delicate toys. But all that had changed. By the time Tomi was sent there, the place had fallen apart. There had been an unsuccessful uprising against the Nazis in Slovakia, and now most Jews were no longer held at Sered' but were sent to camps in other countries. The camp had become nothing more than a stop on the way to other, much darker places.

Ordered into a little hut, Tomi sniffed. He could smell the scent of new wood. It reminded him of the carpenter's shop in Merašice, where their toboggan had been made. How far away the village seemed now. How strange to think that other families were still living a normal life, still warm and safe in their homes.

Everyone had to stay in the hut, which was packed full of people. During the night, Tomi was woken by a keening noise. It was an old woman he had seen in the truck, crying. She was calling out for her children to come and save her from this terrible place. But her children were nowhere near, and, thought Tomi, even if they had been there, there was nothing they could have done.

The days went by slowly, broken up only by the call to *Achtung*, which meant that everyone had to gather together as quickly as they could. Each time this happened, a thousand people or so were selected to be moved on to another place, another camp, in Germany or Poland. Anuka would stand still and tight-lipped while the list of chosen names was called out. When it finished, Tomi saw her shoulders slump, and she relaxed in front of his eyes. They were safe for another day.

Tomi puzzled over the way the camp commander divided the people who were called. Women over sixty and mothers with small children were put on the left and everyone else was put on the right. Much later, he found out that the ones on the left were considered less useful for work and so were more likely to be sent to the gas chambers.

Then, one morning, their names were called out. 'Judith Reichental! Miklos Reichental! Tomas Reichental!'

The time had finally come. All of Tomi's family, his uncles, his aunts, his cousins, were to be moved on from Sered'.

Everyone was brought outside and lined up in the sunlight in front of a long table of Hlinka guards and German soldiers. 'Jews, you are to place anything of value here on the table. I know your kind: you will try to hide anything you can from us. Be warned – you won't get away with this. You will be shot if we find you are hiding any valuables!'

Why, Tomi wondered, *did every word or order that came out of the guards' mouths have to be shouted or snarled?*

The man doing most of the shouting, the one in charge, looked ordinary: heavy eyebrows, dark-haired, with wide, thin lips. He didn't look like a monster out of a nightmare. Yet there he was, roaring at them, telling them he would shoot them if they hid so much as an earring or a coin from him.

People all around Tomi began to take off their watches, their rings, their lockets. His family had nothing of value so they looked on as the guards searched the people passing the table, making sure they were not hiding anything in their clothes. It was embarrassing to see the women being frisked by the guards, and Tomi hoped they wouldn't do anything like that to his mother or his aunt. He felt his legs shake as they walked past the long table. Now they were on the other side.

'Halt!'

He looked back in horror. Aunt Margo had been stopped. She had a green jacket over her arm. The man with the heavy eyebrows had pulled it roughly from her and held it up to his companions. 'A smuggler!' he shouted triumphantly, and began to shake out the jacket. Aunt Margo stood as still as a rock as he went through each of her pockets. He pulled out an old tram ticket and waved it in triumph. Wrapped inside was a couple of cents. Margo must have bought the ticket and wrapped it around the change.

She stood, white and still, and the rest of the family looked on in horror. Then the man laughed and threw the jacket back at her. 'Move along, Jews,' he shouted. He kept laughing as if what he had done was the biggest joke in the world.

They moved along.

It was madness. Everyone was being hustled onto the waiting trains. Tomi watched as his uncles and older cousins, Ludo and Gerej, Dula and Osy, were sent to the right. There was no time to say goodbye to them. Childless women between the ages of thirteen and sixty were made board one particular train. Some of them were dragged screaming from their parents and husbands.

Everything happened in so much of a rush that it was only later that Anuka told them about the terrible choice she had been forced to make. Miki was only twelve, but he was tall and so could have passed for thirteen. He might have been sent off with his uncles and older cousins, but, as Anuka whispered to Tomi, 'If your father was with us I would have sent Miki with him, but as he is not I have to keep you both close by. I can only hope that I made the right decision.'

The train was made up of cattle trucks, wooden boxes on wheels, and the group was herded roughly into one of them, the guards shouting '*Schnell! Schnell!* Faster! Faster!' But the people being herded onto the train moved with silent dignity. Even the babies were quiet.

There were over fifty people crushed into the truck that Tomi, Miki, their mother and grandmother, Aunt Margo and Chava were piled into. They were the very last ones to get on. There were no steps, so Margo and Anuka had to help Omama Rosalia on board.

'Anuka, it stinks,' said Tomi.

It did stink. The smell was of animals and of human waste. There was nothing in the truck apart from a couple of buckets which were to be used for toilets. It was so crowded they could hardly move. Then the door slammed shut and they were in darkness.

Day after day and night after night went by, and during each one the stench in the carriage became worse and the state of those travelling more terrible. There was no way of knowing when the horror of darkness and noise would end, or if it would ever end. Within a couple of days, one of two elderly sisters travelling in the truck became very ill. Her sister held her and pleaded with her to get better, but it was soon quite clear that unless she got some kind of medical help she would not live for long.

Tomi spent hours with his hands over his ears, trying not to hear the woman's sobs. When her sister died, she became hysterical. They shared the rest of the journey with the dead woman and her sister, who could not stop weeping and moaning.

Very few people spoke. The noise of the engine was so loud that it was hard to hear what anyone was saying. In any case, there was very little to talk about: nothing changed as day after day the train went further and further away from home.

'I don't care where we are going,' sobbed Chava one morning, when the smell in the train seemed especially bad, 'as long as we can get out of here!' Tomi nodded – he felt the same.

'Shh, don't say that!' said Aunt Margo, exchanging glances with Tomi's mother. They both knew that at the end of this journey there might well be one of the gas chambers they had heard about, that this journey in the dark might well be leading into the darkness of death. Although the children had heard of gas chambers, their parents had tried to keep the details about the mass killings from them. They were certainly not going to tell them now.

Then, after what felt like a lifetime in the stinking darkness, the train shrieked to a halt. The doors clanged open, and guards, muttering curses about dirty Jews, took the buckets out to empty them and handed in bread. It was the first food given to them since the journey started.

Tomi peered out through the gaps in the slats of the carriage wall. He had often seen cattle crowded into railway cattle trucks and had felt sorry for them, knowing that they were probably on their way to their deaths. Now he was the one looking out.

As far as he could see they were no longer in Slovakia. The station signs were in German and people on the platform were also all speaking in German. Margo crouched beside him. She whispered to Tomi's mother, 'Do you think we are in Germany? Does this mean we won't be sent to Auschwitz?'

'Hush,' whispered Tomi's mother. But she nodded.

On the seventh day, it rained all day. The water came in through the gaps in the boards in the truck. Trying to cheer everyone up, Margo whispered, 'If Martuska was here, she would say that the rain was a good thing! It's cleaning us up!' They all tried to smile. But the fact was that the rain made the filth on the floor of the truck slippery and greasy, which made it even harder to stay upright and out of the dirt.

That evening, the train came to a sudden halt, making half the people in it slip and slide onto the floor. There was noise and confusion everywhere – barking dogs and

German soldiers shouting, '*Schnell! Schnell!*' Bright light flooded into the carriage, almost blinding them after so many days in darkness. 'Move faster, Jewish bitches!'

Tomi clutched his mother's hand for dear life. Miki's shoulder was grabbed by one of the soldiers, and he was dragged back into the carriage. He had to help carry the old lady's body out, and for a few minutes of pure panic they thought that they had lost him. But then he was back, his face pale, nodding to his mother – who gave him a fierce hug. They were still all together.

The soldiers were screaming at them to hurry up as they herded them like cattle, cracking their whips. It didn't take much to make them use the whips on a woman or child.

They stumbled along to the sound of those shouts, barking dogs, whip cracks and curses, through the cold autumn rain. They walked until they came to a forest, the rain still pelting down, the mud sucking at their shoes as if it wished to stop them going further.

By now, it was almost completely dark. They could just about see a muddy path leading through the forest into deeper darkness. Now the dogs were silent, apart from the occasional howl that reached them through the noise of the wind and rain. *It's like the forest in the story of Hansel and Gretel that Omama used to tell*, thought Tomi. *But if there was a trail of breadcrumbs here, I'd eat them, not follow them.*

At the end of the journey, after hours of struggling along the path, the sharp rain cutting into their faces like tiny needles, there was no gingerbread house waiting for them. Instead, through the black night, they could just about make out high walls with barbed wire stretched across the top and smoke belching out from a tall chimney.

10

Tomi's Father

The Reichentals had hoped that Tomi and Miki's father, a farmer and well known and liked in the community, would be safe from capture. But within a few days of his family leaving Merašice, the worst happened. Arnold had been out walking with his dogs, enjoying a small break from the work he had been putting into the farm and from the worry of the past few weeks. He missed Judith and his boys, but at least, he thought, they would be safe and away from the threat of being captured.

Just at the edge of the village, the dogs started to chase a cheeky crow. Arnold was so busy laughing at the antics of the pair that he did not notice an ominous black van pull up beside him. Inside was Ludo Nedelka, his old classmate. Ludo was grinning. Arnold knew that there was no point appealing to Ludo's better nature. By now he knew that Ludo did not have one.

'That's the Jew!' came the call, and Arnold was pulled roughly into the van. The dogs growled and looked confused as he was hustled away from them. One of them tried to climb in too but was kicked roughly away by the guard. 'Go home, boys,' Arnold shouted. Hopefully someone would look after them and the other animals. Then he realised that his own situation was far worse than that of the animals he cared for.

He was brought to the nearest detention centre, without even being given a chance to collect any belongings from the house. He soon realised that he was going to be sent to one of the camps – whether to be gassed or to be worked as a slave and starved to death he could not tell.

After a couple of days at the detention centre, Arnold was loaded into an overcrowded cattle truck. He sat quietly as the train pulled away, bringing him further and further from Merašice and the land he loved. There was hardly any talk among the men in the truck. Everyone there knew that their luck had run out. All except one. Arnold was so lost in his own worries that he did not pay much attention when he saw one of his companions pulling out a blade and sawing away at the heavy chain that kept the door of the cattle truck locked. But suddenly the chain dropped to the floor, and the man pulled open the door, letting in the cold night air and the rain on the wind as the train raced through the darkness. The man shouted, 'I am going to make a break for it. Jump, jump now if you want to save yourselves!' Then he disappeared into the blackness.

Arnold gazed after him for just a moment. There was no time to think. He was right beside the door. Almost without realising it, he too had jumped. There was a terrible blast of pain as his shoulder hit a telegraph pole and his body hit the train track. Then he realised something wonderful: he was in agony, but he was alive!

It was very dark, but on one side of the track the countryside was open, and Arnold thought he could make out the lights of a road. On the other side, there was the dark bulk of a forest. He tried to pull himself up, but the pain in his shoulder was so bad he could hardly move. When he tried to lift it from the ground, he fell back, moaning quietly.

Then he heard a shout. 'Don't worry, I'm a friend.'

From his position lying flat on the train tracks he could see mud-covered boots, and he blinked as the beam of a torch lit his face. 'I'm Martin. Can you walk? If you can, we need to move quickly. We need to get across the track. The forest will hide us.'

Martin helped Arnold to get up off the ground. As soon as he was up, Arnold found that he could walk. It hurt a lot, but he realised that if he did not get into the shelter of the woods he would be picked up by the Nazis.

As they made their slow and halting journey towards the trees, Martin explained that he was one of the other people who had jumped from the train. He even knew the man who had sawed the chain in two. 'He's a Hungarian, and he has escaped many times before! Before all this mess started he was a safecracker so he knows all about keeping his nerve.'

The two men reached the outskirts of the forest. Arnold was still in terrible pain but now at least he had hope. Martin said that if they were lucky they might meet up with some partisans in the woods. The partisans were people who lived in hiding, who were supporting the Allied armies so that they could fight against the horror of Nazism that had overtaken their country.

The two men walked until they were well inside the cover of the forest. Martin said, 'We can rest a little now. We are away from the patrols here.'

Arnold nodded thankfully. 'Yes, that would be good.' He had begun to feel like he could not take another step.

They made themselves as comfortable as they could on the floor of the forest and slept until the first light crept through the branches of the trees.

When Arnold woke up, the pain was still there, so he decided not to move for a bit. He lay with his eyes open, looking at the light on the red and gold leaves. He remembered telling his son that their gold was the corn in the fields. *Well*, he thought, *I still have gold. I still have my freedom and the hope that my family has managed to avoid capture*. Carefully, so as not to hurt his arm, he took a photo from his pocket.

Martin stirred and pulled himself up. 'What have you got there?' he asked.

'My family.'

'What has happened to your family?' Martin asked.

'I am – I was – a farmer in a small village near Nitra called Merašice. My wife and my two boys went to Bratislava to be with relatives, for safety. They were given false papers so I hope that they will be all right. If they had been captured with me I am sure they would not have had a chance, so I must be thankful for that.'

Martin said, 'There are families that will hide Jewish people, you know, some for money, some out of the goodness of their hearts. But the patrols are getting more and more frequent. It seems like they want to wipe out every last one of us. What did we ever do to the Germans or the Poles or the Slovakians that has made so many of them side with that monster Hitler?'

Arnold sighed. 'I don't know. I know that in my own case, Ludo Nedelka, the local Hlinka guard, was always a bit jealous of my family being a little richer than some of the other people in the village. It was not much more, and we worked very hard for it. I think the times are hard these days. And when times are hard it's easy to choose one group of people and decide that they are the reason for all the bad things that are happening.'

Martin nodded. 'That's true. To be any way different now is to be guilty. They are sending Roma and homosexual people to the camps too, and people with disabilities ... but mostly us Jews. At least your wife and children should be safe. You must keep yourself strong for when you all meet up again.'

'I wonder when that will be. Will we see the end of this war? Whatever happens, the world will never be the same again. We can never go back to the way we were before. We can never forget that these terrible things have happened.'

'You would be surprised how quickly people forget, pretend such things did not happen.'

'Martin, do you think that this could be the end of our people? Do you think that the Nazis will win?'

Martin shook his head. 'No. I believe that there are good people out there who will fight against this evil. There are rumours that the Germans are weakening.'

'I hope you are right.'

There was silence. Then Martin said, 'Can I see the picture?'

'It was taken a couple of years ago. The boys have grown but have not changed much otherwise.'

'Look how blond the little one is! It should be easy to pass him off as a Gentile – the same with the older boy, though his hair looks darker. What age is he?'

'He's twelve.'

'He looks tall for his age. And your wife – she is very pretty, and elegant, in her striped jacket. She has such a kind face. You must be so proud of them all!'

'I am. Look how happy they all are in the photo – that is before things got bad. But my Judith would smile and keep her spirits up even in the midst of the darkest days. She will take care of the boys. And they are good boys; Tomi is full of mischief, and Miki is more serious. They are both such clever boys – they take after their mother!'

Martin stretched and pulled himself up. It was time to move on.

The forest was hard going, especially for Arnold with his injuries from the fall. They kept each other going with stories about their families and their past. Martin had never been out of Slovakia, and he was fascinated by Arnold's tales of Venice, where he and Judith had gone on their honeymoon. 'A city floating on water! I would give a lot to see that.'

'Ah, it seems very long ago now … But then so does the farm – it feels so far away. I hope there is someone looking after the animals.'

'Don't you worry about that. I have seen it happen in other places: they move someone in straight away to take the place of the Jews who have been deported. It is like they are trying to wipe away the fact we ever existed, were ever part of the community.'

'Well, whoever it is, I hope they are good to the pony. And to the dogs. They are all hard workers and faithful, good beasts.'

PART III

The Camp

11

In the Forest

Even the dogs, held on long leashes by the Nazi officers, were dripping and exhausted when the sad convoy finally reached the clearing in the forest. It was hard to take in what they were seeing. The skyline was dominated by the tall chimney that seemed to belch out black smoke, letting clouds of ash fall all around it. Beyond it were trees and more trees, the continuation of the seemingly endless forest that they had been travelling through.

It was certainly some kind of camp, and, even in the darkness, it was obvious that it was huge, with row after row of huts, and with watchtowers and barbed-wire fences and high walls on all sides. Later they would learn that the name of the camp was Bergen-Belsen, but that night they were told nothing.

They were brought to a large hut full of bunks, with a single stove burning at one end of it. Then the guards left. Too exhausted even to change out of their wet clothes, everyone fell onto the hard bunks. Tomi lay for a few seconds, just glad to be out of the wind and rain. Then he began thinking of the story of Hansel and Gretel. The chimney reminded him of the oven belonging to the witch. He dreamed about the witch when he fell, almost immediately, into sleep.

The witch was just about to push Hansel into the oven when Tomi woke up with a start. It felt as if he had only been asleep for a couple of minutes. There were shouts and screams coming from all around him. 'Roll-call! Hurry up! Faster! Get up! Get out into the yard, you lazy Jews!'

Anuka helped Tomi with his shoes, tattered now from the long walk. His feet were still wet and cold, and they hurt when she pulled his shoes on.

It was a bright morning, and the air was sharp as the exhausted travellers walked outside into a large courtyard. Most were still half in a daze. Nobody had any idea what would happen next, and some were so tired that they didn't really care.

Waiting for them was a camp guard, a man in tall boots, surrounded by women guards. Each one of the women was perfectly turned out, with bright red lipstick on and curled hair. Some were quite fat, but some were slim and pretty, with blonde hair and blue eyes. They were like dolls just out of their boxes, or golden-haired princesses in a fairy tale, thought Tomi.

Some even had the same bland smiles as dolls. But they were dressed as guards, and many held leather straps. The man held a whip behind his back. When Tomi looked up, he could see other guards, watching from the towers that surrounded the camp. Those guards had guns.

The guards were shouting orders in German, but most people could not understand what they were saying. For a few minutes, there was confusion. Then suddenly Tomi heard his Aunt Margo's voice. Apuko had sometimes complained that Aunt Margo could be a little bossy. Tomi knew he could not get away with anything with her – she had once locked him in his bedroom until he had done his homework. Now she was taking control. She whispered fiercely to her companions, 'Get into lines! Look as if you know what you are doing. If we show them order they won't get angry and start taking potshots at us!'

And people did. People generally did as Aunt Margo asked, because she always sounded as if she knew the right thing to do. Also, for their own self-respect, they wanted to show that they were still human beings, not animals to be prodded into line.

As this was going on, the SS officer pointed at Margo and said, '*Sprechen sie Deutsch?* Do you speak German?'

Margo stood straighter and said calmly. '*Ja*. Yes.'

The officer spoke again. 'You are in charge of this block. You will be the one the Jews go to with any questions and problems. You will organise the roll-call twice a day – and if anyone is missing, you will be responsible. In fact, if anyone is missing, you will be shot. You must make sure the block is clean at all times. You and four others will be in charge of giving out the food. Pick four women now to get breakfast from the kitchen.'

Almost everyone perked up at the thought of breakfast. Tomi's stomach rumbled when he thought of food. Never in his life had he had so little to eat in so long a time. He wondered if they would just get some nice white bread or if there might be salami or cheeses as well, maybe even jam or an apple.

Back in the hut, the Reichentals changed into dry clothes from their suitcases and then sat on their beds waiting eagerly. But when Aunt Margo and her companions returned, looking grim, they had no white bread and no cheese or jam or salami.

'What's the matter, Tominko? Why are you crying?'

Tomi shook his head, unable to speak. It was such a disappointment to see the sour, watery coffee and the black, hard bread. He choked out, 'I can't eat that, I can't.'

Anuka said, 'Now don't make a fuss, Tomi. It's all we have, and you have to eat something.'

Margo added, 'And drink the coffee. We can't drink the water from the taps here because it is infected. They told me so in the kitchen. Tomi, come on now, eat up. Look at Chava, she is trying her best.' It was true that Chava was nibbling at the corner of the crust, her face screwed up in disgust.

Tomi took a tiny bite from the bread, but the taste was so horrible he choked on it and coughed it up.

'Children, come over here,' Omama Rosalia whispered. She had her suitcase open and was rummaging in it. 'Quiet now: this is just for you three!' Like a magician pulling a rabbit from his hat, she pulled a huge salami out of her suitcase.

Tomi thought he had never seen anything so lovely.

'This will help get the bread down,' Omama said comfortingly. 'But we can only have a small slice each, because we do not know how long this will have to last us.'

As soon as the meal was finished, Aunt Margo and Anuka decided that the children needed a good wash. All of them were filthy after their journey in the cattle truck and through the forest. This was nearly as unpleasant as the breakfast. The washroom had no walls, and the three children froze as Margo and Anuka sluiced them down with icy water.

But the worst was yet to come.

'Yeeugh!' Chava was gagging, and everyone else had their hands held over their noses and mouths. The smell in the train had been terrible, but this was ten times worse. They were looking in horror at the latrines. There were no proper toilets, just a long trench dug in the ground, with a wooden bench with holes in it where people sat. There was no privacy. Tomi was so small that his feet didn't reach the ground, and he was terrified that he would fall into the stinking mess below.

Margo exchanged a look with Tomi's mother, who was thinking sadly of her spotless kitchen and the outhouses in Merašice, scoured every day by herself or Mariška. 'It's going to be hard to keep the children free from germs and disease here,' she said quietly, and Margo nodded. On her trip to the kitchen she had heard that more and more people were being sent into the camp, thousands of them, from all over Europe, and there was not the food or space or facilities for them to live properly.

She also wondered about the crematorium. In other camps, such as Auschwitz, thousands of people were being killed in gas chambers every day. The young and the old and anyone who was not useful as a worker were most at risk. In their family's case, that included Omama Rosalia and the three children.

The rest of the morning was spent standing in line for what felt like hours to Tomi. He amused himself by making faces at a boy of around his own age who was standing in the line next to him and who had a remarkable ability to make his eyes cross. Even with the cold and misery around him, Tomi couldn't help but laugh.

The boy was very thin and dark. His mother, who was also thin and dark, seemed even more anxious than most of the people in the lines. She kept pulling on the boy's arm to try to get him to stop messing about, and Tomi heard her whisper, 'Stop it, stop it right away, you will get us into trouble.' But the boy just grinned and continued with his antics. When his mother reached the top of the queue and called out her son's name to the officer, Tomi learned that it was Samuel and that he was from Bratislava.

All the details about the new arrivals were taken down: name, date of birth and country of origin. They were each given a number on a piece of cloth which had to be sewn on their coat. Tomi hated his number even more than he had hated the yellow star. It made him feel as if he wasn't a human any more, just one of the countless numbers in the camp.

Then it was time for lunch, which was boiled beets and potatoes and which smelt so bad that once again Tomi could not eat. He felt really tired after the train journey and the long walk through the forest, but even if he had been full of energy, there was nothing to do in the camp. What was more, his mother did not want to let him or Miki out of her sight. After a supper of black bread and watery coffee, which again Tomi could not get down, everyone – adults and children alike – curled up on their bunks and went to sleep.

12

The Showers

Life in the camp settled down to a kind of routine. Every day was the same. A freezing start: roll-call. A freezing, miserable end: roll-call. Sometimes they were left standing for hours in the rain and sleet as the guards slowly called out the list of numbers.

One morning, an especially nasty day with an icy wind coming from the east, the guard came to the second-last number then stopped. She was dressed in a heavy waterproof coat with shining high boots and wore very bright red lipstick. 'Wait, I think I made a mistake. I don't have the full list here; we will have to start all over again.'

There was a sharp intake of breath from nearly everyone there. They had been thinking that they would soon be able to get inside. One old woman groaned, and the guard gave her a sharp look. 'You'll be lucky if I don't have to do it a third time, with all that noise!' They stood in silence as each number was called one more time.

As the days went by, Chava, Miki and Tomi explored the camp. It was divided up into sections, according to nationality and whether those in the section could be put to work or not. Every day, work parties went out of the camp, but Tomi's section was in the mothers and children part, so they were just ignored for most of the time between roll-calls.

The children discovered the crematorium at the edge of the forest, with its huge chimney that belched out smoke day and night. They discovered the mortuary, where the bodies of those who had died were brought before going to the furnace for cremation. And they discovered the kitchens, a totally forbidden zone.

When Margo found out that the children had been spotted near the kitchens, she met them at the door of the hut looking like a thundercloud. 'If I ever, *ever*, hear that you have been near the kitchens again, I am telling you none of you will be able to sit down for a week. The guards have beaten people to a pulp just for coming too near. Do you all understand? You could get yourselves killed just by sticking your silly little noses in the door. Do you understand, Chava and Tomi? And you, Miki, I would have expected a bit more sense from you!'

They never went close to the kitchens again.

Another week passed, and then three more days. At roll-call, they stood waiting for an hour in the rain for the SS guard to appear. When she finally came marching into the courtyard she was not alone. With her was a group of armed soldiers. Tomi whispered to Anuka, 'Why are all the guards there?'

She whispered back: 'Hush, don't draw attention to yourself.'

The roll was called, as usual.

Then the SS guard shouted, 'Return to your huts and fetch your blankets and towels. You are going to be taken to the showers.'

At those words, Tomi felt a shiver pass through the group. Tomi did not know why. He had not heard the details of what was happening in Auschwitz. In the Polish camp, people were told that they were being sent for a shower. But when they went into the shower rooms, it was not water that came from the showerheads but poison gas. Thousands of men, women and little children had been killed that way.

Tomi didn't know about this, so he was quite happy at the thought of a shower. He said, as they made their way back to the huts to fetch their blankets and towels, 'Maybe we will have hot water! Wouldn't Mariška be amazed to see me so happy to get washed!'

His mother said nothing, and when one of the older women whispered to her, 'Do you believe them? What do you think?' she said nothing. She just shrugged and nodded towards the children.

Tomi saw that there were tears in her eyes. He quietened down. Something was not right. He tried to ask what was going on. 'What is it, Anuka? Why are you upset? Don't you want us to be cleaned up?' But she was bustling away with her Don't Interrupt Me expression, and at the doorway Margo was calling, 'Hurry up! They are getting impatient!'

As they were led in single file along the edge of the fence, there was almost complete silence. Tomi saw one woman throw away her wedding ring, muttering something about not letting the German swine take her gold. It seemed to Tomi that not one of the adults would meet his eye, and when he looked at Miki he wouldn't either. Only Chava looked back at him, as puzzled as he was.

They finally reached a large concrete building with a chimney. Some of the women gasped, and others cried out. Tomi and Chava exchanged glances. What was going on?

'Faster! Faster!' shouted the guards.

Inside the building there was a long hall, filled with a chemical smell that made Tomi's eyes water and stung his throat. He started to cough, as did many others. Some of the women were openly sobbing now. He could not understand why people looked so frightened. What was so scary about taking a shower?

The guards shouted something in German, and Margo translated: 'We have to take off all our clothes and leave everything on the trolleys.'

Tomi tried not to look around as all the women undressed. Even in the overcrowded huts, he had never seen a woman with no clothes on, and he was embarrassed. It didn't help that the guards were standing around laughing and slyly mocking them. He could not understand what they were saying, but he could understand the tone easily enough.

One of the soldiers came up to Chava and picked up a lock of her long blond hair. '*Dieses Kind ist nicht Jüdisch! Sie muss Arierin sein!* This child is not Jewish! She has to be Aryan,' he said.

'*Sie ist mein Kind! Gehen sie! Gehen Sie!* She is my child! Go away!' shouted Margo, and the soldier, when he saw one of the SS women looking at him, walked away.

As each person undressed, they were given a bar of soap and pushed through a metal door. Inside was a huge room with a concrete floor and shower heads all over the ceiling. When the very last person entered, the door was slammed shut.

Some of the women cried quietly. Some whispered comforting words to their children. Some said nothing, just held their children tight. Anuka grabbed Miki and Tomi and held them close to her. They could feel her heart racing. They could feel the way she was pulling air into her body in long, harsh gasps. Across from them, Margo held Chava with her face buried into her shoulder, stroking her hair. Margo's face was very white.

Tomi had never seen, even during the worst of times, such fear in their eyes. Like every other woman in the room, they looked up towards the shower heads, waiting to see what would come from them.

They waited and waited. Then there was a gurgling noise and a sudden rush of warm water. Chava wriggled out of her mother's grasp and held up her hands to the water. Tomi and Miki, released by their mother, who was hugging Margo and sobbing, began to fool around and splash each other. All the women were smiling and half crying, some hugging each other, kissing their children, laughing as the children ran from one showerhead to another.

Then they were led out again, to where their clothes and towels had been left in piles for them to collect. They smelt clean, and they were warm and dry. Later, Margo was told that the showers were to disinfect them and to stop the spread of disease in the camp.

Perhaps it won't be so bad here, thought Tomi. *Though the food is horrible and there is nothing to do all day*. What he did not know was that this was the last warm water he would see for many, many months. In fact, it was the last shower any of the inmates of Tomi's block would have before the spring.

13

Living in Belsen

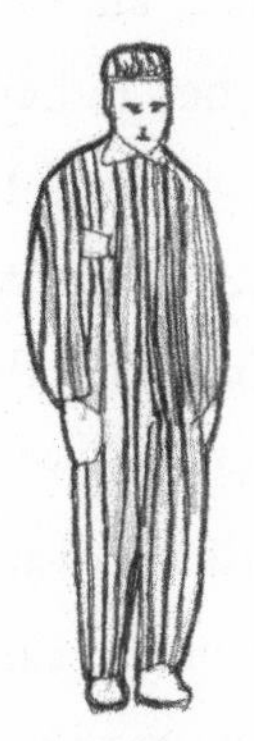

The camp at Belsen had been built for German building workers, before the war started. Then it had become a prisoner-of-war camp, and now it was a concentration camp where Jews and other people whom the Nazis considered not part of the master race were held.

There were many different sections to the camp, and the people held there were from all over Europe. At about the same time as Tomi and his family reached Belsen, a young Dutch girl, Anne Frank, was brought there with her sister, Margot. Tomi never met the Frank sisters, and he did not hear the story of Anne's famous diary until long after the war was finished. The people in the Dutch section of the camp were treated slightly better than most, as many were exchanged for German prisoners of war. But everyone in

Belsen risked starvation and disease, and Anne and Margot did not survive.

Tomi and Miki and Chava began to play with the other children in the blockhouse, although their mothers preferred them to play together rather than with the others. They were afraid that they would hear stories about what was happening in the other camps, where death came with showers. They were also afraid that the children would catch some disease – the camp was full of very sick people.

Some of the inmates didn't want to have anything to do with the other people in the camp. There was one girl, Miri, who never talked to anyone. But there were others who became Tomi's friends: Palo and his mother, Lydia, and Naomi and her older sister, Judith, who was always ready to make up games to entertain the smaller children.

Tomi also made friends with Sam, the boy who had been making faces on his very first morning in Belsen. They explored places they were not supposed to go near, like the crematorium. Tomi told Sam about life on the farm, and Sam told him a little bit about his past. 'I am double trouble, because my mother is Jewish and my father was Roma. I don't even know my grandma because the family didn't want to have anything to do with my mother after she married my father. You are lucky to have your brother and your grandma and your cousin with you. We have nobody but each other.'

'What about your father?'

'He died last year, before we were captured. Mutti said that maybe he was lucky not to be alive to see all this. He would have hated so much to be locked up. Where is your father?'

Tomi shook his head. 'We don't know.' Talking to Sam made Tomi wonder if he would ever see his father again.

One morning, after the long and pointless wait for roll-call, they were sent back for their bedding and clothes and had to follow one of the guards to a new part of the camp. On the way, Tomi realised how very big the camp was and how many people were crowded into it. They passed long high walls with barbed wire on top that separated each part of the camp and cut it off from the outside world. It seemed that every last inch of land was used to erect another hut and stuff it full of prisoners. They saw hundreds of them, wearing grubby loose jackets and trousers, striped like pyjamas. There were even stripes on the caps the men wore.

Every other place Tomi had lived, even in the cities, there had been flowers and vegetables growing. Here, nothing was planted and so nothing grew. All the food was brought in from outside. 'It's so quiet, even the birds in the forest don't sing. And nothing grows here,' said Anuka sadly.

'I am growing!' said Tomi proudly. In spite of the lack of food, he was stretching, and it was a real problem because the only clothes he had were the ones they had brought with them. His shoes were too small, and his shirt hardly buttoned across his chest. Later, as times got even harder in Belsen, it would hang loose on him.

'Not as much as I would like! Not as much as you would if you were given proper food!' said Anuka. 'But you are both getting big. And Miki will be turning thirteen in December. Time for his Bar Mitzvah!'

'Well, I know I won't be having one here,' said Miki gloomily, kicking a stone out of his way. Margo hushed them – the SS guard was saying something.

They reached a hut: number 207. 'Home sweet home,' Margo said, grinning a little twisted grin. 'This is ours,' she added. 'And I have a surprise for you.' When they entered the hut, she pointed to a partition which made a separate room. 'That's our room,' she said. 'We have a little bit of extra space and some privacy from the others.'

Tomi looked around. 'How many people are in this hut?'

'Three hundred and thirty. And we are the only ones with a private room.'

Anuka was looking around her in delight. 'This will make such a difference!' she said. 'Look, there's even an electric light bulb!'

The room was very bare. There were six narrow beds and no room to walk around. The suitcases had to go under the beds. There was one little window, and the view was of the latrine, a few scrubby trees and, beyond them, a barbed-wire fence. But the family felt as happy as if they had been given rooms in a luxury hotel. Here they would not have to listen to the groans and the fights of the other inmates. Here they could feel secure that no one was going to try to steal their shoes or their clothes. One poor old woman had even had her false teeth stolen from under her pillow as she slept.

Sam was still in the old camp, so Tomi rarely saw him now, but one day he managed to make his way back and met Sam at the wall of the crematorium. They arranged to meet every Wednesday at the same place.

When Tomi came back from his exploring, he was whistling cheerfully because for once he had not seen anything horrible. In fact, he thought he had glimpsed a squirrel in one of the big trees at the fence – and he had seen his friend.

His mother caught his arm as he came in. 'Be quiet, Tomi. Something very sad has happened. Miri is dead.'

Miri. She was the girl who had kept apart from everyone else. From the beginning, she wouldn't talk to Tomi or Chava or Miki. She rarely talked to anyone but her mother. She was thirteen, and her family was a wealthy one. She couldn't believe that this had happened to them, that they too had been captured and were now in a camp.

During the past few weeks Miri had stopped talking completely and refused to eat the food her mother tried to coax into her mouth. Every morning it took all her mother's pleas to get her up for roll-call; sometimes Margo had to help. Now Miri had given up on life completely. 'I think she preferred death to this life she was living,' said her mother.

She held her daughter in her arms and wept over her until Margo came and said gently, 'We need to let the guards know, but before that perhaps you would like to prepare little Miri?'

'Prepare her for what? For the crematorium?' The mother's voice was bitter, and she looked at the other mothers as if it was somehow their fault that her child had died while theirs were still alive. It made it worse that Miri's body was to be burnt. Jewish people always buried their dead.

The mothers combed Miri's hair and laid her out as best they could outside the hut. They watched over her as her body was piled onto a handcart already half full of dead bodies and brought to where the great chimney rose up into the grey sky.

That evening, there was little said in the blockhouse. Even the littlest children were shocked into silence by Miri's death. Then Lydia, Palo's mother, called all the children over to her. Somehow she had managed to bring a children's book with her into the camp, the story of a bird called Cimcara. Lydia didn't just read the story – she made the children part of it. 'Come on, children,' she said. 'Tell me what you think Cimcara's world is like.'

'It's a farm!' cried Tomi.

'Yes, so it's a farm.'

'On the edge of a forest, but a nice forest, not like this one with its dark pine trees!' cried Chava.

'It has got meadows and a little river!' This was Palo.

'And there's a dog there called Jacko!' shouted another child excitedly. 'Jacko is the best dog ever. He barks when there are strangers, and he even barked when my little brother went too close to the stream on our land.'

'And there is a lovely house,' one of the girls chimed in dreamily, 'with lovely furniture and linens ...'

'And it has a red roof!'

'Inside, there is white bread and crab-apple jelly!'

'And lovely meatballs and sauce!'

'And a chest full of blankets!'

'And no one is ever hungry or cold – it's summer all the time!'

And so it went on, with each child talking a little about the best parts of their past.

That night, before he went to sleep, Tomi pictured Cimcara's world in his mind. It was just like Merašice. When he woke up to the cold of the morning, he lay with his eyes closed and tried to imagine it again: the woods full of birdsong, the sky full of sunlight.

When he opened his eyes, the sky was still as grey as iron. He was still in Belsen.

14

Halt!

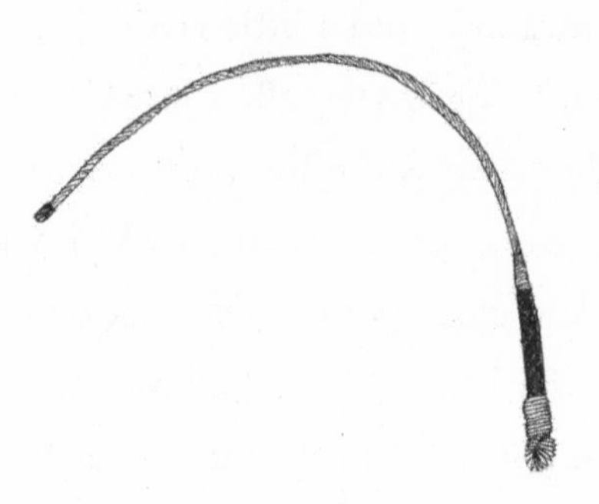

Tomi thought the guards used their whips just because they liked to hear the noise of the lash against their victim. They seemed to like the cries and moans too. One day, when he was out wandering the camp with Sam, Tomi saw blood flowing from an old lady's arm where a guard had caught her with a lash of a whip. The blood was as bright and as red as the lipstick the women guards wore. When some of the women ran to help her – she had fallen to the ground with the shock – the guard lashed the whip again to keep them away.

Sam, standing frozen with fear beside Tomi, whispered to him to not move an inch and to be sure not to catch the eye of the guard. When they finally were able to creep away, Tomi was nearly in tears because of what he had seen.

‘We should have tried to do something!’ he said.

Sam snorted. ‘There is nothing we could have done. And I have seen worse than that – I have seen a guard stamp on the chest of a woman who had fallen down on her back. Someone told me they once saw one of the dogs rip apart an old man.’

‘These guards are monsters. How can they be human?’

Sam looked grim. ‘Oh, they are human. My mother says that people can do the most horrible things when they know they have the power. Here there is nothing to stop them treating the people in the camp as badly as they want.’ It was true. Anything the guards considered theft or disobedience could be punished by death – by beating or by shooting.

The roll-calls were the part of the day that everyone dreaded. At roll-call they did not even have the comfort of being able to huddle together for warmth. They had to stand in straight lines, arms by their sides, in the pitch dark and the cold.

Very few people had any clothes other than what they had been wearing when they were captured. Some still wore the summer clothes they had on when the Nazis had dragged them from their homes. They stood as still as they could as they listened for their names to be called, the harsh voices echoing across the bleak courtyard.

The coldest day yet arrived, with snow and hard frost, and everyone breathed a sigh of relief when at last the roll-call was over, the final number called. Now they could get back inside and try to get some warmth from the stove, the thin blankets and the human heat of the people huddled together in the wooden shed.

After the morning roll-call, there was always the same chore for the Reichental children. Anuka insisted that they wash themselves every morning, to keep down the number of lice that crawled over their bodies and through their hair. It was the lice that spread the terrible diseases like typhus. Tomi and Miki spent hours hunting lice on their bodies and cracking them dead. They would sometimes have competitions to see how many they had killed in a day.

When they came back and were huddled in their blankets in the blockhouse, Miki whispered to Tomi, 'I heard you crying last night. You know, you must try to be as quiet as possible when you are upset. It just makes things worse for Anuka when she hears you.'

Tomi felt the tears well up again and tried to choke them down. It was all bad enough without Miki giving out to him. 'I know. I try to be as quiet as I can. But I'm so miserable. I want to go back to the farm and see the fields and the animals and get away from this stinky mud and having to wash in freezing water. There's nothing to do here. We are just being kept like animals in a pen until—'

Miki put his hand over Tomi's mouth. 'Don't say anything. Don't even think anything. Just keep hoping that we will all be together again. With Apuko and the uncles and the cousins.

We will all be together in the orchard, playing hide and seek.' Suddenly, Miki grinned. 'Let's go out. I have a plan.'

'Where are you going?' asked their mother as they pulled on their coats, by now very ragged and torn.

'Just outside,' said Miki. 'Chava, do you want to go too?'

Chava shook her head. She was playing with Omama's long hair. Every evening, Omama made a ceremony of taking down her hair, unplaiting it and combing it slowly. Then in the morning she plaited it again, coiling it at the back of her head. Chava was helping her, though when she did it the style was more a bird's nest than a neat bun. But she loved to do it, and Omama Rosalia, with a few deft touches, would usually get her hair in order and thank Chava for her help.

As soon as Tomi went outside, he was sorry he had said he would join Miki in his expedition. As the weather got colder and snow and ice covered the camp, they had been going outside less and less. But today Miki had something more adventurous planned. They were always building new huts in Belsen, a sign that yet more prisoners were being sent to the already overcrowded camp. 'Did you notice the bits of wood sticking out of the snow where they are building the new huts?'

Tomi shook his head. He had been too busy shaking with the cold and feeling hunger gnaw inside his stomach to notice anything.

'We can take some of that wood and burn it in the stove. No one will notice!' The two boys went over to where the wood was sticking up out of the snow. They pulled up some of the smaller pieces as quickly as they could, then began to run back towards the hut.

'*Halt! Halt!*' They had been seen! They didn't stop or look back, just ran as fast as they could to the safety of the hut, throwing the wood under the bed nearest the door and covering the edge with one of the blankets. Their mother and Margo looked at them in horror, and Margo whispered furiously, 'What have you done?'

'*Blockalteste!* Come out!' came a voice at the door, and Margo, pale as a ghost, went outside. The boys exchanged looks, and Tomi was astonished to see that Miki was shaking. He had not seen him look so afraid since the day they were captured in the photography shop.

They could hear voices outside the door. Miki could just make out what was being said and translated for Tomi. 'Two people were seen running with stolen property … this block will be searched to find the guilty ones.'

Tomi was so frightened he could not breathe properly. If the guard found the wood, he and Miki would be beaten, possibly executed. The door opened, and one of the guards looked in. Each member of the family stood up beside their bed, staring straight ahead, careful not to meet the guard's eye.

The woman yanked the covers off Tomi's bed and looked underneath to check if the wood was there. Then the second bed, the third, the fourth and then the fifth. One bed left to check: the one near the door where the wood was. The guard started to bend down towards the sixth bed, then changed her mind. 'Nothing here!' she shouted, then went into the main room where she screamed abuse at the other mothers and grandmothers and children for at least twenty minutes as she checked each bed, finding nothing but the pitiful belongings in the suitcases brought so far from so many homes.

When she left and Margo returned to the room, Tomi and Miki had already tearfully promised their mother that they would never do anything like that again.

'You must remember,' said Margo sternly, 'that I have seen people beaten to death for doing things like that. And you must remember that it is not just your lives you put at risk when you do stupid things like that, but the lives of all of us. Yes, I know you just wanted to help, but there is nothing any of us can do here without being seen. We have no freedom. We are watched all the time.'

15

Mazel Tov!

In spite of the fear, cold and hunger that were part of daily life in Belsen, Tomi and his friends continued to play together, and the older girls and women in their hut tried their best to create some fun for the little ones in the middle of all the misery. Judith, who was fifteen and the older sister of Tomi's friend, Naomi, was one of the people who made life in the camp bearable. She spent hours playing with the small children, organising games, teaching them Hebrew songs and making little figures from wool, then hiding them for the children to find. She was the one who made sure that Miki's birthday on 18 December was celebrated.

It was a very special birthday. In Jewish tradition, as soon as a boy turns thirteen, he is considered an adult.

If the family had been at home in Merašice, there would have been a huge celebration with the whole family and all their Jewish friends. They would have had a ceremony in the synagogue where Miki would have read from the Torah, and then a party at home in their house with lovely food and music. Everyone would have dressed up in their best clothes, and there would have been singing and dancing and games and stories.

It was not quite like that in Belsen. In fact, Miki had expected nothing at all for his birthday. But Judith had other plans. When the family came in from the freezing roll-call, there was a smell of roasting potatoes and something that looked like a tiny cake.

'It's a day of celebration!' Judith said. She had managed to get hold of a few little potatoes, which were roasting on the stove. The cake was three slices of bread piled on top of each other, covered in margarine and sprinkled with sugar. There was even a single candle on top. When the cake and potatoes had been divided up into tiny morsels so that everyone got a share, everyone wished Miki *Mazel tov!* Then the whole hut joined in the singing.

At the end of the day, Anuka gathered the boys to her, kissed them goodnight and said, as she always said, 'Don't worry, we will all be all right.' And somehow, after a day when they had managed to celebrate in spite of the horrors of the camp, they believed her.

For Christmas, Judith collected a few branches from a fir tree and stuck them together so they looked a little like a Christmas tree. This she decorated with strips of coloured paper. When the guard came around, she and the children sang 'Silent Night'. Judith even had a little gift for the guard, and on that day, for once, there was very little shouting and no beatings. Things were about as good as they got in Belsen on that Christmas day, despite the fact that the weather was now freezing and there was snow and ice on the ground when the roll-calls were made.

Soon after Christmas, Aunt Margo came back from the kitchens with some bad news. There was to be a new commander in the camp. His name was Josef Kramer. 'He's meant to be worse than the one before,' she whispered. 'He is coming from Auschwitz. There, he allowed all the guards to have whips – in fact, he encouraged them to use them. And in Auschwitz ...' Her voice trailed off.

By now, Chava and Tomi knew all about the gas chambers in Auschwitz. Many Jews had been sent from there to Belsen, because the Russian Army was advancing from the east, and news of the scale of the mass murders had spread around the camp. The people who came from Auschwitz were in an even worse state than those who had been living in Belsen.

As usual, the rumours and gossip had got it right. When Josef Kramer took over, the long hours standing in the snow became longer; there were more beatings and shootings; and the food rations grew smaller and smaller.

December had been freezing. January was worse. However, towards the end of the month, news started to creep through the camp that the German army was in full retreat and that there might even come a day when the Russians would arrive and liberate the camp.

Although Tomi wanted more than anything to get away from the camp, he was finding it hard to imagine that there really was a world outside this dreadful place. He was cold and hungry all the time. The hut itself seemed the only secure place in the world, so there were days when he had to be pushed to go outside. His grandmother was the one who insisted that he take a least a little walk every day. 'Tominko,' she would say, 'you have to bring your old *omama* out for her walk. If I don't have you, I might slip on the ice and break all my bones! And I have to keep walking or my old bones will stop working altogether!'

There were other days when he couldn't stand being stuck inside, looking at the same grey faces, listening to the same voices, to his mother and Margo arguing over the best way to cook goulash, when they had not eaten goulash for what felt like years. On these days he would run outside, hoping to meet Sam or indeed anyone his own age so they could play wild games and pretend they were ordinary children for a while.

But Sam had changed. Often Tomi went to their meeting place and waited for what felt like hours. More and more often Sam did not make it. Tomi still went, hoping that perhaps the next time Sam would turn up. When he did, Sam would just say that he had been 'a bit sick'. He didn't have the energy now to play any games. Every time Tomi saw him he looked thinner and paler.

There was a bright patch in the darkness. For a few nights in a row that winter, the youngest children from Tomi's block were led in secret to the hut where the Hungarian girls who worked in the kitchens lived. The hut was packed but warm with people and movement and within minutes each of the children had been assigned to one of the girls and given food they had only dreamed of during the previous months: bread with margarine and jam, soup and good black coffee, even a little milk.

The friendly girls had become experts at sneaking food from the kitchens and had decided to share some of it with the starving children. The girls were very kind and petted and played with them, making them feel like real children again. But these secret evening journeys only lasted for a short while. One evening, their guide did not appear.

Tomi never learned what had happened and could only guess that someone had betrayed the girls to a guard. He tried very hard to not think of what might have been their punishment if they had been found out. He hoped they had stopped because it had become too dangerous, not because they had been caught.

Around this time, a new guard was sent to Belsen: Irma Grese. They waited an hour in the freezing sleet for her to turn up for her first roll-call. When she finally arrived, she carried a vicious-looking whip which she flicked impatiently as the numbers were called out. Tomi glared at her blond hair piled in plaits around her head, her bright red lipstick, her shiny nails, her heavy coat and high black boots. She wore heavy perfume, as if trying to keep the awful smells of Belsen away from her.

Irma Grese came to Belsen with the reputation of being one of the most dangerous of the Nazi guards. Tomi had learned how vicious the doll-like women could be, shouting abuse non-stop at the inmates and kicking, slapping or punching them just as often as they felt like it. But even among them Irma Grese was considered cruel. It was said that she liked to set half-starved dogs on people she caught doing anything out of order, even taking a piece of mouldy bread from the kitchen.

She looked only a few years older than Miki, yet here she was, in command of the coughing grandmothers, the mothers, the teenagers, the small children who were too afraid to cry in case they drew attention to themselves. And yes, this morning she decided that the numbers were out.

'Halt! We need a recount!' By now, everyone knew the best thing to do was to stay silent and try not to show any expression at all.

'Oh, such grumpy faces!' she mocked. 'I suppose you are going to go back to your blockhouse and complain about this! You Jews are all the same, always moaning!'

Tomi's mother used to say that you could get used to anything, but Tomi never got used to the misery of those morning roll-calls, to the hunger pains in his stomach, to the dreadful feeling of never, ever having enough to eat. It was even harder to get used to the cries and sometimes screams of the dozens of sick people – some of them with no family or friends to look after them – or to the cartloads of bodies taken every day to the crematorium.

Things had always been bad in Belsen. The noise and the smells. The constant fear. The rats who plagued them, skittering around the huts in search of food. The greyness of everything. The beatings. The cold. The hunger. But as the winter grew more bitterly dark and cold, and snowy January turned into February where the paths were covered in freezing slush, and every day the icy rain fell, things got even worse.

Omama Rosalia became ill.

16

Omama Rosalia

Tomi was sitting by his grandmother's bed. She had become very quiet, not talking to her daughters. She smiled gently at the children but did not say anything to them either. Up until now, she had been the one trying to get Tomi to swallow the black bread and stinking soup. But now she just sat, staring in front of her, wrapped in her own world of weakness and pain. Now she really did need Chava to help her braid her hair – she could no longer do it on her own. For a while, she still struggled outside for the daily wash, but for the rest of the day she just sat on her bed, staring at nothing.

On this dark wintry afternoon, Tomi was holding Omama Rosalia's hand and thinking about food. The gnawing in his stomach never stopped. It felt as if a rat had got in and was eating him from the inside. There were days when he could think of nothing else.

It was the same with everyone. His mother and aunt would spend hours discussing recipes. They had long arguments about the best way to cook certain dishes. Today it was cheesecakes. They had very different views on how to bake them. Margo said, 'When we get out of here, we will cook both kinds and see which is the winner.'

The boys exchanged glances. Was that ever going to happen? Or would they just be left here until the food ran out? Every day, more and more people arrived so there was less and less food to go around.

Many of their friends, both adults and children, had become what they called *Muselmänner*. This was a slang word for people who were starving to death and who had given up hope for the future. Everywhere you went in the camp there were people sitting on the ground, leaning listlessly against each other, waiting to die. Their bones stuck out from their ragged, filthy clothes, and their eyes, when they were open, were dull – they did not respond to anything around them. The *Muselmänner* were so thin they reminded Tomi of skeletons, and, like skeletons, they did not speak or move.

Now no one called out greetings to the boys as they went past, like they used to do when they first arrived in Belsen. No one had the energy. The crematorium could no longer cope with the number of the dead, so the corpses were left out where they died. There were fields of bodies, mounds of bodies over a metre high.

Some people who had lost their loved ones and who felt there was no reason to live ran towards the barbed-wire fences, knowing that by the time they reached them they would be shot dead by the guards in the watchtowers. They were left there too – hanging like tattered washing on the lines of steel.

While some of the people in the camp had given up hope, others had become desperate and were willing to do anything to survive. To get food, they stole from each other. Margo now had to bring a stick with her when she went with her assistants to bring the food from the kitchen to the hut. During nearly every trip she was attacked by starving women trying to get hold of something to eat.

As Tomi sat with his grandmother, trying to keep his mind off what was going on around him by thinking of Mariška's roast chicken, Margo came in, almost in tears. 'I can't bear that I have to beat them away like dogs. Although I don't think I have ever seen even a dog so hungry or so desperate. One of them tried to bite me today.'

Her sister sighed. 'But Margo, we need to eat, even the little they give us. If you let them take the food, what would happen then? We would starve and so would everyone in this block.'

One morning, Margo came back from the kitchen with her face even grimmer than usual. 'They have stopped the roll-calls. It's because the guards are afraid of catching typhus. It's an epidemic now – the whole camp has fallen apart. They are keeping as far away from us as possible. They are even putting Hungarian prisoners of war – old men – up on the towers to guard us.'

'That's why you need to keep washing, boys,' said Tomi's mother. 'The typhus is spread by the lice, and washing keeps them a little under control.'

'But we are still covered in lice!' objected Tomi. 'It feels like there is an army of them walking over me sometimes.' He spent half his time picking lice out of his and Miki's hair and clothes.

'A horrible German army!'

'Let's kill them all!' said Miki.

Chava was crying. 'I hate them! I hate the lice.'

'Never mind, Chava, come out and play.'

Chava shook her head. 'I don't like the war games you play with the other boys. And I don't like seeing all the bodies. They stare at me.'

Tomi went out. It was true that there were bodies everywhere now. He and his friends had become so used to the terrible sight of corpses heaped on top of each other that they even used the piles to hide behind when they played their favourite games of battles between evil Germans and good Jews, battles which the Jews always won.

Tomi jumped as a boy leapt out from behind a pile of bodies and pointed at him, his finger a gun. 'You are dead, you dirty German!' he shrieked, and Tomi, as the rules of the game decreed, dropped to the ground, hardly even aware that there was a corpse looking him in the eye only inches away.

He still met Sam sometimes. One day, when they were out wandering around the camp, they saw an old man waving at them from the top of one of the watchtowers. He was one of the Hungarian prisoners who were now used as guards. The old man was smiling, and he seemed to have something in his hand.

'He's eating something!' said Sam, 'Maybe he will throw something down!'

Sure enough, as soon as the guard finished eating, he threw down his crusts to the two boys waiting underneath. They could not believe their luck!

They came back the next day, and the next, and each time the guard threw them bread. But the news spread quickly, and soon there were hordes of other children fighting for the food. The bigger boys always got the food so in the end Tomi gave up the battle. He was too small, and he didn't have enough energy to fight.

Omama Rosalia grew weaker and weaker. Then one night Tomi woke to a strange sound. It was his mother weeping. He had never heard his mother sob like that before.

No matter how bad things had seemed, Anuka had always smiled and said, 'Things will get better, don't you worry.'

Now there were tears streaming down her face. Aunt Margo was crying too. They were holding each other tight, standing at Omama Rosalia's bedside.

'What's wrong, Anuka?'

Although he asked, Tomi already knew the answer. His mother said, 'Omama is leaving us now.' The only sound in the room was the rasping noise of Omama trying to pull air into her lungs. She managed to whisper, 'Please, open the window.'

The family looked at each other, and then Miki went and opened the window, letting out the precious heat.

There was a deep sigh.

And then she was gone, and the room was very quiet.

The family waited for Omama's body to be taken away. None of them was crying now. This grief had gone beyond tears. The men with the handcart came, and her body was brought away, and piled up with so many, many others.

Tomi crept out later to see if he could find her body, but he never did, and perhaps it was just as well.

PART IV

The Return

17

Liberation!

The camp had become one terrible, stinking toilet. Except for the noise of the children, who still called out to each other as they played hide and seek behind the piles of corpses, there was almost complete silence.

The dogs had disappeared – taken away, or, some people whispered, killed and eaten by the few remaining guards. The numbers of rats increased, and people could do no more than look away when they saw them at the bodies that lay everywhere.

Even though the people in the camp were silent, the noise level overhead got louder every day. The city of Hanover, not far away, was being bombed. Most of the children spent their time watching the sky. They watched the fighter planes dip and dive. Every time a German plane was brought down, they cheered with all their might, their joy giving them the strength to dance around a little. The more German planes falling through the air, blazing, the more chance that the hell they were living in would end.

Tomi and his friends no longer had to be afraid of being punished by the guards – they hardly saw the guards anymore, even though more and more prisoners arrived from Auschwitz. The Russian Army was moving further and further west. *Perhaps*, thought Tomi, *perhaps after all we will get out of here.*

There had been other small signs of change. The first signs of spring. The first day without frost. Even in Belsen, the little green grasses and weeds struggled through the cracks in the stone and concrete. The ferns from the forest wound their tendrils around the barbed-wire fences. Tomi kept his eyes on the sky, a sky which was no longer an unrelenting grey – there were some days when it was blue. The days began to stay brighter for longer.

It was a strange time. People were waiting for something, but they were not quite sure what. Many were waiting for the day when death came to take them, or to take their fathers, or mothers, or sisters, or brothers, or friends.

And then, one morning, Miki came running into the hut, almost speechless with excitement. He had been out early to watch for planes. 'Anuka, there are no more guards on the watchtowers! They have all gone!'

Anuka looked at Margo. 'Do you think it is a trick? Do they want us to think we can leave, and then as soon as we reach the barbed wire they will shoot us?'

Margo shook her head. 'I have no idea what's going on. We hear nothing now.'

So everyone stayed in the camp.

Exhaustion and sickness had hit almost every family. Those who had the energy to leave the camp and walk away into the forest would not leave the old and the sick who had no strength left to go anywhere. In any case, who knew what might be waiting for them outside? The whispers continued, saying that the Russians were advancing every day, that they would come with food and medicine and that all the horror would finally be over.

They soon realised that almost all the SS guards had disappeared too. But this meant that there was no more food being brought into the camp. Then the pipes stopped bringing water. So none of the thousands of people in the camp had any food or water. They waited day after day, with Margo going to the kitchens every morning in case, by some miracle, food arrived. It did not.

Tomi spent a long time looking for Sam, but, when he eventually found him, Sam would not talk to him. His mother was holding him in her arms, her face wretched. She tried to smile at Tomi. 'Sam is really weak now,' she said.

'He will hardly even talk to me. Just give him a little hug to let him know you are here.'

Tomi hugged his friend, but Sam would not even look at him. Tomi knew what was happening. Sam's body was weak, it was true, but the big problem was with his spirit. Like Miri, he had lost hope.

Tomi went back to the hut and sat hunched on his bed in the corner of the room, his knees drawn up to his chest. He placed his hands over his ears and tried not to hear. He put them over his nose and mouth so he would not smell the smell, worse than human waste. He could feel something crawling slowly over his skin. He could feel the cold seeping through the thin wood of the hut. He closed his eyes tightly.

He was still in Belsen.

There was a low rumbling noise, and everyone jumped up. What was going on? Then the shouts and the cries started. 'They have come! We are free! We are free!' Everyone who could walk staggered as fast as they could from their huts. Some even found the energy to run towards the fences. A whole convoy of tanks was approaching the gates of Belsen, and they were not German tanks. They were coming to free the camp.

People were hugging each other, helping each other to make the journey towards the gates and the line of tanks. Some were laughing, almost hysterically. Some were standing bemused, unable to believe that the liberators had finally come.

A German soldier, one of the few guards left, was watching what was going on. He was drunk and half dressed, and he began to wave his gun in the air, shouting at the people who were running. He couldn't bear to see what was happening. Allied soldiers were coming to liberate the camp. The Jews he had been taught to hate would walk free. The master race had been defeated. Hitler's plan that the Germans would rule the world had collapsed.

The soldier was shouting in German, but no one paid any attention to him. That seemed to drive him crazy, for he took up his gun and fired at one of the women running towards the fence. She fell to the ground, killed just as she had been set free. But, unlike so many others, she died knowing that the Germans had been defeated.

The tanks made their way through the camp, soldiers in the turrets announcing through loudspeakers, 'You are liberated. This is the British Army.'

'Wasn't it the Russians who were supposed to come?' said Tomi to Miki.

'I don't care who it is. We are free, Tomi. We can find Apuko and go back to Merašice!'

Father. What had happened to him? That was the big question now.

Chava said, 'And I will see my daddy and Laco again too!' Then she asked, doubtfully, 'And everything will be the same as it was?'

Miki shrugged. 'I am not sure about that.' Seeing Chava's face drop, he added, 'Most likely it will be. The main thing is, we are free.'

Tomi looked around him. There were thousands of people still running towards the fence. Some of the women were struggling to pull pine branches from the trees to throw in the path of the army. They knew it was a tradition to throw flowers in the path of victorious soldiers, but no flowers bloomed in Belsen so the dark pine branches were the next best thing.

Tomi spotted Sam and his mother. She was half dragging him as they made their way towards the tanks, but their faces were transfigured by joy.

As well as those who ran to greet the tanks, there were thousands more too sick or weak to move – and thousands more lying dead on the ground in piles. Many people were sharing their beds with their dead loved ones, unable to find the strength or the will to get up.

The soldiers looked horrified as they moved through the camp. They held their hands over their mouths and noses to keep out the smell of death. Some carried handkerchiefs soaked in petrol over their noses. Some of them threw up, some of them prayed, and some of them cursed as they saw the state of the living and the dead. All of them looked deadly pale, as if they were seeing ghosts.

In the middle of the chaos, they heard one tough-looking soldier whisper to another, in a shocked voice. Aunt Margo, who knew a little English, translated for Tomi. 'Half of them are like skeletons, walking around. Just skin and bone. How is it that they are even still alive?'

His companion nodded, equally shocked. 'And how did they survive in this filth? They must be crawling with lice and fleas and who knows what else. Look at those poor kids' – the man was pointing at Tomi and Chava – 'they look like they haven't had a square meal, or a wash, in months. Here, kid, take some of this ...'

Tomi was about to take the chocolate the soldier was holding out to him, but Anuka came running up and said, 'Tomi must eat slowly. If he eats too fast he will make himself sick.'

The soldier had no idea what Tomi's mother was saying, but he nodded and smiled. Tomi wanted to stuff himself with all the good things that were coming out of the tins the soldiers handed out to everyone. Anuka made him eat a little at a time. But as soon as his stomach got used to having food in it, he made up for lost time: sausages, bacon, Irish stew, steak and kidney pie, rice puddings, cheese and jam, apple juice, orange juice. He found an oddly shaped square tin and opened it carefully. Inside was a delicious mixture of meat and herbs, a solid wedge. He looked at it, puzzled. One of the soldiers passing by laughed and patted him on the shoulder. He made gestures to show Tomi how good it was, rubbing his stomach and smiling. 'Try it! It's good! It's called corned beef!' Tomi tried it and liked it best of all the food they were given.

The soldiers were kind to the children and allowed them to spend time with them. As the days went on, Tomi and his friends got to know them better. Even though it was hard to understand what they were saying, their smiles and gestures managed to communicate a lot.

The soldiers had rounded up the SS guards and forced them to deal with the corpses that lay all over the camp. It was their turn to do the hard and horrible work of burying the bodies of all the people they had helped to kill by starving them and making them live in inhuman conditions. That was quite a turnaround.

As Tomi looked on, he shouted, 'Hey, *schnell* there, go faster!' and soon all the children were shouting at their former tormentors, telling them to go faster, faster. The women guards, who had always been so beautifully turned out, their boots gleaming as they kicked the inmates of the camp, were now exhausted, filthy creatures, terrified of catching disease from the corpses they had to load onto handcarts. The carts brought the bodies to the mass graves that had been dug by the male guards. Now they all had to look into the face of the evil things they had done. Their bland smiles totally disappeared.

'What will happen to them?' Tomi asked one of the soldiers, a smiling man who spoke a little Slovak and who always had a stick of chewing gum to give to the army of small boys who followed their heroes around. The soldier shrugged. 'They will be put on trial, and most of them – especially the big guns – will probably be hanged.' One of the journalists who had come to write about the camp was passing by. He said, grimly, 'Hanging is too good for them.'

Tomi had already run off. He had discovered the joy of being able to move around without fear. Free to explore the camp, they found the SS uniform stores and dressed up in gold tassels and braided hats. They discovered the repair shop for the tanks and cars of the German army. He, Sam and Miki spent hours in the turrets of the tanks, turning them in all directions as they fought and won battles against the Nazis.

There was more drama when the British soldiers rounded up people from the neighbouring towns and villages and brought them to the camp to see what had been going on under their noses. The people were mostly quiet, although one or two kept saying loudly that they had known nothing at all about what had been going on there.

Watching them being led through the rotting corpses and filthy yards, Aunt Margo said grimly that she reckoned they had not wanted to know. 'It's easy to ignore bad things going on if it is more comfortable to pretend that they are not happening.'

18

The Human Laundry

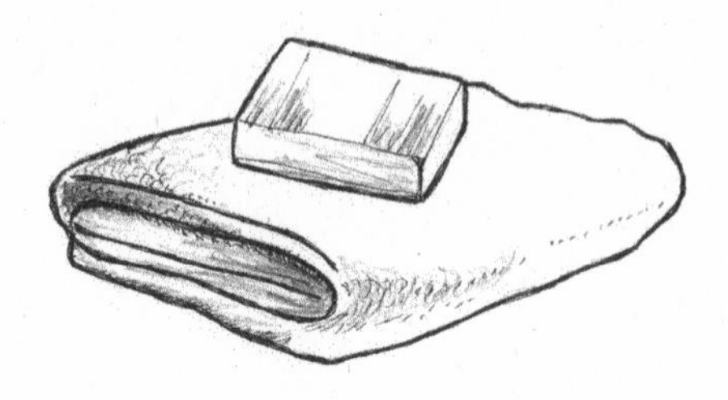

The relief and joy the family had felt at the liberation faded when Aunt Margo became ill with typhus. Too weak to move from her bed, she refused to eat. Tomi's mother looked after her for a few days but then realised that they needed to get her into hospital for the medicines and the specialist care they would give her there.

There were so many sick people in the camp that the tank store had been cleared and turned into a hospital. Thousands of people were suffering from typhus and typhoid, and others had been so damaged by starvation that they would not survive without hospital care.

Tomi's mother didn't want Margo to go to the hospital on her own. 'There are so few nurses and doctors, and Margo needs someone to look out for her. She is not able to do it herself, she is too weak.' She looked at her youngest son. 'Tominko,' she said, 'how would you feel about going to the hospital with Margo? You need hospital care too – you are so thin and weak. I am worried that you have not got any stronger, and in hospital you will get the medicine you need. If you go with Aunt Margo, you could make sure that she eats and drinks enough and that the doctors don't forget about her. Is it too much to ask you? Would you be afraid?'

Chava started to cry. 'I want to go with my mama!'

Tomi's mother said, 'Your mother will just fret about you if you are with her. Tominko is the one who really needs to go. We need someone to go who is not afraid to speak out and ask for things. Tomi is less shy than you – in fact, this is one time when his cheekiness is a good thing! What do you think, Tominko?'

Margo was muttering something feverishly. She looked really bad.

Tomi thought for a minute. On the one hand, he could hardly imagine being away from his mother and Miki. What if anything happened to them while he was away? It was still hard to believe that they were safe now. On the other hand, it would mean that he would get away from the horrors that still surrounded them.

The weather had got much better, but that meant that the bodies in the camp had started to smell much worse.

Sometimes it was hard not to throw up when the wind brought the smell of dead people in their direction. It seemed to be taking for ever to bury all the thousands of people who had died. And it was hard to watch the bodies carted away day after day. The novelty of shouting at the guards had worn off, and now it all just seemed very sad and terrible.

One thing was sure: Aunt Margo did need his help. It was awful to see someone so energetic and cheerful, as she had been even during the worst of times, look so desperately weak and ill. He couldn't bear the thought of losing her now, now that they had a chance of freedom and new life. He nodded. 'I'll go with her,' he said.

As soon as they arrived in what the camp members called 'the human laundry', Tomi wondered if agreeing to go with Aunt Margo had been such a good idea. They had to be thoroughly deloused, and the chemical smell made them both sneeze and cough and their eyes water up. Tomi was scrubbed more thoroughly than he had ever been by Mariška, even on her most energetic days. He was given a pair of pyjamas, but they were so big that the top reached right to the ground, like a nightshirt.

'Everything is so clean!' he whispered to Margo.

One of the nurses heard him. 'Yes, this is how the world should be for sick people. It keeps the germs away. Now, there's a little bed made up for you beside your aunt, so hop into it. Try to sleep.'

The bed had clean white sheets, and the blankets were warm. Tomi lay there, breathing in the smell of sheets washed in soap and dried in sunshine. When he woke up, a kind nurse was bringing breakfast. 'What's your name, young man?' she asked. 'You had better eat up all that bread and jam – you look as if you need it!' No more horrible, gritty black coffee and rotten bread. Everyone drank out of white cups, and everything tasted wonderful.

Tomi soon realised that his mother had been right when she said that Margo would need someone with her. The hospital was packed. There were people running about all day and sometimes during the night too. The nurses complained that it was overcrowded and that they did not have enough staff. But they were very kind. They not only made a pet of Tomi but also fed him goodies between the square meals he was now being given. He just wanted to eat all the time these days, as if making up for the months and months with hardly any food.

Aunt Margo, on the other hand, although she was over the worst of the disease, was refusing to eat anything. She had even stopped drinking. The nurses told Tomi that she would die very quickly if she did not eat and drink. He tried to coax her: 'Just a little mouthful, Teta, for Chava!' But his aunt's mouth remained firmly shut against the spoon he was holding up.

At other times, she would cry out for her husband. Sometimes she was sure he and Laco had come to fetch her home. It frightened Tomi. He knew that if his aunt lost touch with what was really going on it would be very hard to pull her back. He racked his brains to think of what might make her want to keep on living. Of course, the very best thing would be to have Uncle Dula and Cousin Laco come to see her, but who knew where they were, or even if they were still alive.

Apart from her husband and child, the only other thing she begged for was cigarettes. 'A cigarette! All I want is a cigarette,' she would moan. Tomi had no cigarettes, but by this stage he had made friends with many of the nurses. They were shocked when he came to them asking for cigarettes, but when he told them his plan they agreed to help.

So, one day, just at dinnertime, Tomi went up to Margo's bed, cigarette and matches in hand. 'Look what I have got for you!' For once Aunt Margo didn't shout out or call to her husband. Instead, she breathed a great sigh. 'Oh, Tominko, you wonderful child. Give one to me, quickly now. You will have to help me light it.'

'Not so fast,' said Tomi. 'Let's make a deal. I will give you half the cigarette if you eat your dinner and drink some water. Look, they are coming with it now.'

'Don't be ridiculous! Give it to me now!' Margo grabbed at the packet, but Tomi was too quick for her. He laughed. This was like the days in Merašice when his mother bribed him to eat his dinner with the promise of one of Omama's wonderful cakes. Margo had done the same with Chava when the meal was something with too much cabbage in it.

'Tomi! Do what you are told! I need a cigarette!'

'You will get one when you eat some dinner.'

Margo sighed. She looked longingly at the packet, and Tomi wondered how long he could keep refusing her the only thing in life she seemed to want.

'Very well then.'

He helped Margo sit up in the bed. Then he helped her to eat the stew, sometimes feeding her, sometimes helping her shakily bring the food to her mouth. When it was all finished, he broke the cigarette in two and put one half of it between her lips. He lit it, and Margo pulled on it with a deep sigh.

One of the nurses came up and ruffled his hair. 'I see your plan is working, young Tomi. I am sure the nurses will be happy to supply you with cigarettes as long as Margo has to be bribed to eat. Just make sure you don't start smoking them yourself!'

It took a few weeks before Margo was well enough to leave the hospital. As she grew stronger, she no longer demanded the cigarettes as a bribe. She became impatient to be with Chava again, and Tomi missed his mother and his brother and cousin. They were delighted when they joined the rest of the family at the temporary camp that had been set up outside Belsen, in the Wehrmacht barracks. It was clean and warm and disease-free – a heaven after Belsen.

While Margo was in hospital, Chava had been ill too, but Tomi's mother had refused to let her go to hospital on her own and had nursed her through her illness. She was still weak but was on the road to recovery. She was in bed when her mother, equally pale and shaky, came into her room, but she stretched out her arms and squealed with joy, 'Anuka! You are back! You are back!'

Margo went over and hugged her tightly. 'Yes, my dear one, and I will not go away again. But Chava, you will have to say a special thank-you to your cousin Tomi. He has been a real hero. I am sure that he has saved my life!'

19

Father

Tomi loved the new camp. There was a shiny canteen full of food. It was warm and dry and safe. It even had a cinema. The cinema was meant to be just for the British soldiers, but sometimes they allowed the children to go in too. The movies were all in English, so Tomi didn't understand a word that was being said, but he really enjoyed feeling as if he was doing something ordinary, something he would have done before the months of hiding and the horrors of the camp.

He also loved watching the jeep races and football matches that were organised for the soldiers and for the people in the camp. He felt that he was a real boy again, a real human being. The people around him treated him well, talked to him, laughed at him and encouraged him to play and to be as cheeky as he liked.

One question hung over the whole family. What had happened to Apuko and Laco and Uncle Dula? Similar questions were being asked by every family. Most of them had been separated from their wives or husbands, their parents or their children. Their names were sent to Prague to be put on the lists of survivors, and they waited, day after day, for a response from any of their relatives.

One day, Sam came running up to Tomi. He had put a little flesh on his bones now, and his eyes were shining with excitement. 'My grandmother got in touch to see if we were still alive! We are going to her house in Budapest.'

'I thought your grandmother didn't want anything to do with you and your mother.'

Sam shrugged and then grinned. 'Mutti says that Grandmother has probably realised after all this that we need to stick together, that life is too short to cut off the people you love. But I don't care why! Whatever the reason, we will have a real home now. Mutti has told me about the house and the trees and the river … it sounds wonderful! You will have to come to visit.'

'And you will have to come to Merašice, to see the orchard and the farm and the summerhouse. And to eat loads of ice cream!'

Tomi knew that he would miss Sam, but he was really happy that he was going to his mother's home and to his family.

Many of the people in the camp were leaving and beginning the long journey back to their countries, back to their homes. Stories came back to the camp of happy reunions with family and friends. But not everyone went home to a happy ending. Some of the Jews who made the long journey home were met by neighbours who did not want them back. They discovered that their houses had been raided and that their furniture, clothes and even bedclothes had been taken. No one would say who had done it. In some cases, even their homes were gone, taken over by neighbours they had once thought of as friends. Many of these families had no choice but to make the journey back to the Belsen refugee camp, people with no homeland, and no homes.

The first time Tomi met one of these families, grey-faced with exhaustion and disappointment, he felt a shiver of fear. What if they never found Apuko? What if the farm was gone? What would happen to them then? Where would they go? Anuka and Aunt Margo whispered to each other, hoping the children would not hear. But the children knew very well what they were whispering about.

Every day they made the trip to the noticeboard, every day hoping for a message from Arnold Reichental. Every day there was no message. Until, one day … 'There he is!' Tomi's mother was laughing and crying at the same time, clutching in her hand the card addressed to Judith Reichental.

It was in Arnold's handwriting, and on the back it said, 'I am alive. I am waiting for you in the village.'

'He's alive!' Anuka hugged her sons and then pulled Aunt Margo and Chava into a tight embrace. 'I am sure you will get a card like that soon! Oh, I can't believe it! All of us have survived. Boys, you will see your father very, very soon!'

It was July before the arrangements were made for the family to leave Germany for Slovakia. Margo and Chava had still heard no news about Uncle Dula and Laco. Margo had sworn she would not set foot in Bratislava until she found her son and her husband, but in the end they all boarded the bus for the long journey back. Before they left the camp, Tomi made sure to say goodbye to the soldiers and the nurses who had been so kind.

This was a very different journey from the nightmare journey to Bergen-Belsen. They were given water and biscuits to take with them. Though the bus was old and slow, now they had seats, and they could see the landscape outside the windows, the dark pine forests and the pretty German villages they were passing through. Tomi did not like to look out at the towns so much. Many of them had been bombed and were nothing more than big piles of rubble.

It took days for them to reach Prague. On the first night, they stopped in a small German town where the returning refugees were to be given lodging by Germans. Tomi's family was led to a tall white house, bright and clean, with red geraniums and green shutters. The woman who opened the door smiled a little nervously at them, and looked very relieved when she realised that Margo spoke good German. Then she began talking nineteen to the dozen. 'Your beds are made up upstairs. And I have food for you on the table – our own good eggs and boiled potatoes – and some of my honey that I managed to save from before the war. Or would you prefer to wash first? But of course you must do what you wish! You are my guests.'

Tomi looked at the table where there was a feast laid out. He just wanted to dive straight into it. Anuka saw his face and shook her head. 'First bring your bags upstairs and wash yourselves,' she said, 'then we will eat.' Tomi and Miki raced upstairs and washed as quickly as they could.

When they were seated around the table and Aunt Margo began to pile food onto Chava's plate, she shook her head. 'No. I won't eat that. They might want to poison us.'

Tomi's mouth was already so full of food that he could not answer, but Miki laughed. 'Don't be crazy, Chava. There is no way the Germans can do anything to us now.'

'Miki is right,' said Aunt Margo, more gently. This is all good food. Eat up, Chava. The milk is lovely.'

'I can't! I can't put that food in my mouth. Look at all the people that were killed in the camp. The Germans hate us!' Chava was crying now, sobbing that she wouldn't, she couldn't eat the food.

Anuka and Aunt Margo exchanged a glance, and the kind German woman looked on, puzzled. 'Is there something with the food she doesn't like? I can get her something else if she wishes.' *Wow*, thought Tomi, a German worried about what we want to eat.

Aunt Margo translated what the woman had said to Chava. Chava just shook her head and kept her mouth firmly closed. In the end, Aunt Margo let her be.

For the entire time the bus travelled through Germany they stayed in the houses of the German people. These people had been required to take the refugees in, but they were kind and generous. Many made a point of saying that they had known nothing of what had been happening in the camps.

Chava could not get used to the idea that Germans were not her enemies, that they did not want to kill her. She refused all the food offered, and all the way to Prague she lived on the biscuits she had brought from the army canteen.

When they reached Prague, they stayed in a refugee centre, very glad that the journey was over. 'Prague is our new national capital city,' explained Anuka. 'The Czech Republic and Slovakia are one country now.'

'What will happen to Bratislava?' asked Tomi.

'It will still be there. It just won't be where the government is any more.'

'Will the castle go too?' asked Tomi. It was his big memory of the city – that and the photography shop where they had been captured. His mother and Margo laughed and assured him that the castle would still be there.

'Well, I won't be going back to Bratislava until I get news of my family,' said Margo firmly. 'I never want to see the place again if my boy and my husband are dead.'

'In that case, Margo, I will stay with you.'

'No, Judith, you must go back to your own home.'

Tomi's mother shook her head. 'We would never have survived Belsen without you. I am not leaving you now.'

Margo, usually so composed, was almost crying. She hugged her sister. 'And I would never have survived the hospital without your Tomi. But let us hope there is word soon.'

And there was.

Margo was on one of her many daily trips to check the boards of survivors when she bumped into a woman who grasped her arm and exclaimed, 'Margo! What on earth are you doing here?' It was an old friend from Bratislava. 'Don't you know that Laco is waiting for you at home?'

'Laco has survived! And Dula?' asked Margo. 'Is there any news of him?'

The friend shook her head. 'I have no news. But no news can be good news. You had better go back and see your son in any case, Margo!'

The family boarded the train to Bratislava on a beautiful day at the beginning of August, the height of summer, with everything ripening for the harvest. It was a slow journey in an ancient train that seemed to stop every ten minutes for security checks. After many long hours, the four towers of Bratislava Castle came into sight. Tomi's mother sighed. 'There were times when I thought I would never see that again!' she said.

Tomi said, 'But you always told us everything would be all right and that we would all be back together someday!'

His mother smiled. 'It was bad enough that Margo and I were worried out of our minds. I wasn't going to let you children get upset too.'

'So you didn't know for sure that everything would be all right?'

Anuka just kept smiling and said, 'Well, it was in the end, wasn't it? We will soon see your father.'

At the station, Uncle Artur and Laco were standing waiting for them, waving frantically as the train drew into the station. Margo peered closely, then she bent her head and held Chava tight. They realised what this meant. Uncle Dula had not survived the camps.

On the platform, Margo and Chava hugged Laco as if they would never let him go. He was as thin as a rake but had got much taller. *He looks almost grown up*, thought Tomi. Laco smiled and smiled and smiled when he looked at his sister and mother.

Uncle Artur told them that two of Tomi's mother's brothers had died in Buchenwald, and her sister Adela in Auschwitz. Then they had to give him the news that his mother had died in Belsen. Yet, despite the sadness, there were joyful tears. They had survived. They were alive.

Laco had prepared food for them at home. They had only just begun to eat when there was a knock on the door, and all food was forgotten. Apuko was there, almost as thin as they were. The family held each other in a close embrace. Apuko still had the same warm hug that had always made Tomi feel so safe. He seemed exactly the same as when they had left him in Merašice all those months ago, but he was amazed at how tall his sons had grown. He was delighted to tell them how he had survived the war. He told them about his escape from the train and how he had stayed in hiding with a group of people who were fighting in secret against the Nazis. Then he said, 'You know what? We are going to head back to Merašice this very afternoon. I can't wait to show you! The farm and house were well looked after while we were away – nothing has changed.'

There were tears when the time came to part from Margo and Chava and Laco, and Anuka made them promise to come and visit Merašice very soon. As she gave a last hug to Chava, she whispered, 'You will have to come and eat lots of fruit and other good things so you can put some weight on your bones. Living all that time on biscuits can't have been good for you!'

The journey to Leopoldov station took two hours, and, as they came closer to home, everything from the fields to the houses became more and more familiar. Most familiar of all was Mr Duraj, waiting at the station with his horse and cart, delighted to see them all and anxious to fill them in with all the details of what had been happening in the village since they left.

'Only ten months,' said Anuka, 'but it feels like a lifetime.'

Mr Duraj smiled. 'Well, not so much has changed around here. Pavel Polacek was the man assigned the farm by the Nazis. But he never regarded it as his own.'

'I know Pavel, he's a good farmer,' said Tomi's mother.

'Yes,' said Apuko. 'He has kept everything as it was. He didn't even change the pictures on the walls of the house. And he has looked after the farm well. All the animals, even the dogs, are well and happy.'

Mr Duraj laughed. 'I heard him say that while you were away, every time they passed the place on the road where you were picked up by the Hlinka, the dogs would run around and sniff and whine, as if wondering where you were.'

The forest had never looked so green and alive as when they made their way down the winding road towards the village. The sky had never looked so blue. And everywhere there were birds singing.

Tomi could hardly keep still with the excitement of coming home, and when they reached the driveway to the house he leapt out of the cart and ran towards the door, where he was enfolded in the arms of Mariška, who was crying and laughing at the same time. The dogs were jumping around and barking joyfully, begging to be petted.

There was a feast of good things and much joy that evening. They were home, they were a family together, and they could rejoice. Stories were told, and told again: his father's escape from the train, Tomi's bribery of Aunt Margo when she was ill. No one talked of the horrors they had seen in the camp. Instead, they talked about all the good people who had helped them survive Belsen: the kind Hungarian kitchen girls, the watchtower guard who had thrown the children bread, the nurses who had looked after Tomi in the hospital, the soldiers who had fought and risked their lives.

Before he fell asleep that night, safe in his old bed with the window open to the stars, Tomi thought of all the ones who had not survived, who had not been helped. All the lost ones, the ones who would never go home. So many dead, killed because people had decided that they were somehow less than human, that their lives had no value.

The stars were very bright in the sky, and there were even a few shooting stars lighting up the short August night. He thought about his friend Sam, perhaps in Budapest by now, and wondered if sometime in the future he would travel to see him. *It would be nice to travel*, he thought, *but not just yet.* Now there were the last ripening days of summer to enjoy, leading into apple time and then the turning of the year. The snow would fall over Merašice and cover everything in its soft white blanket of quiet. Then the festive season would arrive, with parties and wonderful food and huge log fires and stories to tell again – not of all that had been lost but of a magical world where creatures like Cimcara lived and the birds sang in the trees all summer long.

Tomi closed his eyes.

EPILOGUE

Remembering

Tomi opened his eyes.

The light through the leaves had dazzled him for a moment. He was standing at the edge of the wood close to Merašice, the wood they had driven past so many times in Mr Duraj's cart, the wood they had passed coming home after the horrors of Belsen. He had been telling his family about those trips. They were gathered a little way away, discussing whether they would need more petrol for the car journey back to Bratislava.

It had been a long, long time since Tomi had been in Merašice.

Very soon after the family returned to the farm, politics once again changed the world of the village. When Slovakia came under the rule of Communist Russia, Jews were not made welcome, and there did not seem to be a place any more for farmers like Tomi's father, who worked his own land.

A new Jewish homeland was being built, and so the family had moved from the farm and the village to Israel, very excited about being part of the new nation, the first Jewish nation for thousands of years.

Miki and Chava still lived there. Tomi visited them often. He had loved it in Israel, but he had been given the opportunity to go to Germany to study engineering, and, despite the astonishment of some of his friends, he had taken it up. He had worked in Germany and London and Italy, and had finally ended up living in Ireland, where he had married and raised his family.

But through the years when the Communist state had made it difficult to get back to Slovakia, he had seen the orchard in his dreams.

He tried not to think about Belsen. He never, ever spoke about his time there, even to people who were very close to him. Ireland had not been part of the great war against Nazism, so it was easy enough to pretend that he had forgotten what had happened.

But he never had.

Then, one day, he had been visiting his son at his home in Dublin. Everyone had been sitting out in the garden: his son, his grandson and his daughter-in-law. She had said, 'Go on then, Josh, ask Granda.'

Tomi looked at his grandson, who for once seemed a little shy. He was about Tomi's age when he had been taken to the camp.

'I was wondering, Granda, if you would come with me into school one day. We are doing World War Two in History, and the teachers know that you were living in Slovakia while all that terrible stuff was happening. Would you mind very much telling my class about what it was like?'

The boy looked at him hopefully, and Tomi sighed. He sat back in his seat under the apple tree and looked upwards into the green branches, covered with the little red apples. For years, he had been telling himself that it was best to forget, best to move on and live his life, to make sure that his future was not damaged by the nightmare of the past. But now he had made his future, and his life had been a good one.

As he looked up into the branches of the apple tree, he realised that it was time to talk about what had happened to him so long ago. There were fewer and fewer people around to tell their stories of what had been done to them, of what they had survived. He wondered if people were even beginning to forget what had happened. To many people, his life was history, a story told with no connection to a real, living person. There were even some people who denied that what he had gone through had happened. *We were there*, thought Tomi. *It happened. I have to start telling the story*. So he said yes.

Tomi was very upset after that first class visit. He thought it had been a disaster, as some of the children were in tears when he left. But in fact he discovered that all the children had been very moved by his story. He discovered that he had a gift for telling the story of what had happened to him.

As well as telling the story over and over again to classes of young people, Tomi wrote a book about his past, especially about the time when his family were in hiding and when they were in Belsen. Then, one day, he decided it was time to visit Belsen itself. The camp had been burnt to the ground after the liberation, to make sure all traces of the terrible diseases that had rampaged there would be cleared, but it was kept as a memorial to the thousands of people who had died there and as a reminder of what the Nazis had done.

It had been very strange to go back there and see the place empty and silent, except for the visitors who walked quietly through the flat fields. Some of them had tears in their eyes as they read the inscriptions and the lists of names.

The forest still surrounded the camp. Tomi listened. Still no birds singing. But it was very peaceful. *How strange*, he thought, *this place of misery has become almost beautiful. One would never be able to guess what awful things happened here, if not for the notices and memorials. The earth has covered up the horror.*

The visitors looked as if many of their parents, perhaps even their grandparents, had not been born when the horrors of Belsen had taken place. *The further back in time it goes,* thought Tomi, *the harder it will be to explain.*

Even finding where Hut 207 had been was not easy. In the end, he did find it. The huts had been burnt down, but each was marked by an outline. He stood there a long time with Chava and Miki, who had made the trip with him. Chava had brought a bronze plaque with her so that their grandmother could finally have a memorial in her honour.

'Omama, why would people have done things like that?' a small boy asked a woman, who looked to Tomi more like a daughter than a granny. They were speaking Slovakian. He waited for a moment to hear what the grandmother had to say. 'I don't know, Tomas,' she said. 'I do not understand how or why people do such terrible things. Perhaps we can never understand.'

'It couldn't happen now, could it? That was so long ago, years and years and years.'

'It seems long ago to you, but my parents' friends and family ... many of them died here. My papa was one of the lucky ones.'

'Not so very lucky though.'

'No, not so very lucky. Tomas, perhaps there will always be people who will do such awful things. And there will be people who stand to one side and let it happen. And then there will be the ones who do something about it when they see people being treated badly by others – the ones who will stop the gang calling a little girl names because her skin is dark instead of pale, or because she wears a headscarf, or because she doesn't believe in the same god as they do. Luckily for us all there will still be the other kind of people – the ones who will stand up to the bullies who torment those who are just a little bit different. Do you understand?'

'Yes, I think so,' said the small boy. 'Look, here comes Dada and Peter.'

The pair was joined by a man with dark hair and a smaller boy, walking hand in hand. The little boy ran to his brother and started tugging his hand. 'Tomi, I want to play a game. Can we play hide and seek?'

The two adults exchanged a look. The father shook his head. 'No, Peter, not here. When we go back to the hotel, you can go to the playground. But not here.'

Tomi thought of that family now, of what the grandmother had said, as he watched the light filter through the branches. It was true. The evil that had created the camps had not been burnt away when the huts in Belsen were set on fire. It was still there in the human heart, waiting for a chance to grow again.

But the goodness was there too. Tomi thought of the goodness he had known in the past. He thought of gentle Omama

Rosalia and wished her rest and peace. He thought of the many, many members of his family who had been killed. He thought of his laughing cousin, Martuska, who never had the chance to live a rich, full life, like the one he had enjoyed. He thought of his grandparents – his father's parents. They had finally learned that they had died in Auschwitz.

He thought of his father, of the long letters they had exchanged before he died. Of his mother, who had lived until she was ninety-six and who, just before she passed away, had been able to recognise him and call him her Tominko. *We are still a family*, thought Tomi. *We went through all that, and we brought each other through.*

He was on his way back from a visit to the house in Merašice. The village was the same in some ways, different in others. The road was much bigger and better, but the village dogs still lay in the spring sun, looking very like the ones they had kept on the farm. The fields still stretched out beyond the village, green with new growth. And Mariška was still alive, a very old lady now.

She had been the first person he had gone to see. When he had made his way up the path to the entrance of her house, he had seen an elderly woman sitting in the sun. He knew it was his old friend straight away. 'Mariška, do you remember me at all?'

She looked confused, so Tomi said, 'It's me, Mariška, Tomi Reichental!'

'Jesus Maria, Tominko!' Mariška had tears in her eyes as she hugged him, calling excitedly to her daughter to come and meet little Tominko, who was not so little any more.

Tomi and his family had gone around the village, with Tomi introducing them to the people he had known. Finally, they came to Tomi's old house. It had been neglected, and the fruit trees had been cut down. He went inside and saw that the old dresser he remembered from his childhood was still there in the house. He decided that he would rescue this little piece of his past and bring it to Ireland. The dresser was worn and its paint was faded and scratched, but it could be made new.

Tomi's last pilgrimage to the past was to this forest, the forest he had passed so many times, which he had seen on so many trips out of the village and on so many journeys home. Some of the journeys had been happy, some filled with grief and fear, some bittersweet.

He peered in through the trees, at the light slanting through the darkness. Sun and shadow flickered before him. Darkness and light, good and evil. Even now, he had no easy answers to his questions about the good and the evil that lived in the human heart.

The trees on the edge of the wood were crab-apples, their blossoms tiny and delicate, shining in the late April sun. Something fell on his face, very gently. He brushed it off. There was something on his hand: white and clean and new. It could have been a flake of snow, or pale ash from some great chimney.

It was apple blossom.

Afterword

This book is based on the boyhood experiences of Tomi Reichental. It is a story you, the reader, will never forget. It is a story we must all learn from. It is only when we put ourselves into the shoes of a nine-year-old boy who survived the cruelty of the Holocaust that we can begin to imagine what Tomi went through. Even then, it will only seem like a bad dream. For Tomi, there were years of fear, months of hunger and many long freezing nights to endure before he woke up and walked free in April 1945 from the horrific nightmare of Bergen-Belsen.

Sadly, most of Tomi's family did not come home. Cousins were gassed at Auschwitz. Uncles were worked to death in Buchenwald. His grandmother, Rosalia, starved to death beside him in Bergen-Belsen. All told, thirty-five of Tomi's relatives perished in what Jews call 'The Shoah'.

For over seventy years, Tomi asked himself, 'Why?' It is a small word, but a big question.

Tomi's not the only survivor to ponder on the reasons for this merciless slaughter of a whole race of people. Primo Levi was a young Italian chemist who ended up in Auschwitz because he too was a Jew. One day, Levi, exhausted from endless days of hard, punishing labour and little nourishment, was ordered to do another pointless chore. He turned to the SS guard overseeing the prisoners and asked, 'Why?'

'Why? Here there is no why.'

But there is a why. There is an explanation for what happened to Tomi, and his family, and millions like them.

In Germany in the 1930s, the people put their trust in Adolf Hitler and his Nazi Party. Hitler swore to make Germany great again. He promised to make Germany so strong it would one day dominate all of Europe and beyond for a thousand years. To do that, he said, the Nazi Party would have to get rid of the people preventing Germans from taking what should be theirs.

The group of people that Hitler blamed for all that was bad in the world was the Jews. This was an evil fantasy. But the Führer's message of hate held Germans spellbound. Those who resisted the Nazis were jailed. Many were executed. Soon Adolf Hitler had everything his own way in Germany. Then he went to war to conquer Europe and murder every Jewish man, woman and child his death squads could get their hands on. The Nazis called this sinister plan 'the Final Solution'. From September 1939 until the last day of the war, in May 1945, Hitler's stormtroopers and their accomplices killed Jews wherever they could find them.

Tomi's story is a warning. The freedoms that we sometimes take for granted are precious. It is the duty of all of us to defend them from those who believe that only some people should enjoy the rights we were born with.

Tomi's terrifying experience began with a yellow star. It ended among thousands of corpses in a forest in the middle of a war-ravaged Europe.

That's what hate did. That's 'why'.

Gerry Gregg

APPETIZERS

APPETIZERS

150 DELICIOUS RECIPES SHOWN IN 220 STUNNING PHOTOGRAPHS

CHRISTINE INGRAM

greene&golden

This edition is published by greene&golden,
an imprint of Anness Publishing Ltd, Blaby Road,
Wigston, Leicestershire LE18 4SE; info@anness.com

www.annesspublishing.com

If you like the images in this book and would like to investigate using them for publishing, promotions or advertising, please visit www.practicalpictures.com for more information.

A CIP catalogue record for this book is available from the British Library.

Publisher: Joanna Lorenz
Senior Managing Editor: Conor Kilgallon
Recipes: Catherine Atkinson, Alex Barker, Angela Boggiano, Carla Capalbo, Kit Chan, Jacqueline Clarke, Maxine Clarke, Andi Cleveley, Roz Denny, Joanna Farrow, Rafi Fernandez, Silvano Franco, Christine France, Sarah Gates, Shirley Gill, Nicola Graimes, Rosamund Grant, Carole Handslip, Deh-Ta Hsiung, Peter Jordan, Elisabeth Lambert Ortiz, Ruby Le Bois, Clare Lewis, Sara Lewis, Sally Mansfield, Sue Maggs, Sallie Morris, Jenny Stacey, Hilaire Walden, Laura Washburn, Steven Wheeler, Kate Whiteman, Elizabeth Wolf-Cohen and Jenni Wright
Photography: Karl Adamson, Edward Allwright, Steve Baxter, James Duncan, John Freeman, Ian Garlick, Michelle Garrett, Peter Henley, John Heseltine, Janine Hosegood, Amanda Heywood, David Jordan, Maria Kelly, Dave King, Don Last, William Lingwood, Patrick McLeavey, Michael Michaels, Thomas Odulate and Sam Stowell
Designed and Edited for Anness Publishing Ltd by the Bridgewater Book Company Ltd
Production Controller: Wendy Lawson

NOTES

Bracketed terms are intended for American readers.
For all recipes, quantities are given in both metric and imperial measures and, where appropriate, in standard cups and spoons. Follow one set of measures, but not a mixture, because they are not interchangeable.
Standard spoon and cup measures are level. 1 tsp = 5ml, 1 tbsp = 15ml, 1 cup = 250ml/8fl oz.
Australian standard tablespoons are 20ml. Australian readers should use 3 tsp in place of 1 tbsp for measuring small quantities.
American pints are 16fl oz/2 cups. American readers should use 20fl oz/2.5 cups in place of 1 pint when measuring liquids.
Electric oven temperatures in this book are for conventional ovens. When using a fan oven, the temperature will probably need to be reduced by about 10–20°C/20–40°F. Since ovens vary, you should check with your manufacturer's instruction book for guidance.
The nutritional analysis given for each recipe is calculated per portion (i.e. serving or item), unless otherwise stated.
If the recipe gives a range, such as Serves 4–6, then the nutritional analysis will be for the smaller portion size, i.e. 6 servings. The analysis does not include optional ingredients, such as salt added to taste.
Medium (US large) eggs are used unless otherwise stated.
Front cover shows Parmesan fish goujons – for recipe, see page 27.

PUBLISHER'S NOTE

Contents

Introduction 6

DIPS AND NIBBLES **8**

SOUPS, PÂTÉS AND TERRINES **50**

VEGETARIAN DISHES **98**

FISH AND SHELLFISH **134**

POULTRY AND MEAT **172**

SALADS **194**

Guide to techniques 216

Index 222

Introduction

Appetizers can be the best part of a meal and many people prefer them to larger courses. Indeed, they are so popular that sometimes whole dinner parties consist entirely of a variety of appetizers. You can see the attraction – "starters" by definition indicate small portions, which means there can be a huge and delicious selection of different and interesting dishes. Of course, for the cook, having to provide such a medley of diverse foods can be quite a challenge (although one you may well feel equal to), but for the guests it will be nothing less than a complete delight!

In some countries, appetizers or "starters" have become an institution. Tapas, in Spain, are a meal in their own right, and the Italians' antipasto is so varied and delicious that you'd be forgiven for wishing to stop right there with the artichokes and superb dried hams, and forget entirely about the pasta and meat that follow.

If you're planning a sophisticated dinner party, it is possible to start with a simple but tasty appetizer such as Pork and Peanut Wontons with Plum Sauce or Leek and Onion Tartlets, which can be served easily beforehand with drinks. Your choice of appetizer should take its cue from the food you intend to serve as a main course. Choose this with care, as the appetizer will set the tone for the rest of the meal. Select something fairly light, such as grilled king prawns (jumbo shrimp) or a simple salad if you

BELOW *Serve Potted Prawns with crunchy brown toast or crackers.*

ABOVE: *A very tasty starter can be easily made from a few simple ingredients.*

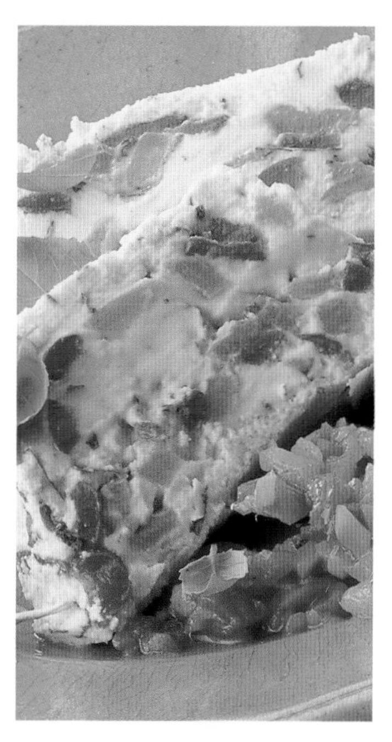

ABOVE: *A terrine makes a colourful addition to any menu.*

ABOVE: *Salads make great starters, as they are quick and simple to prepare.*

plan to serve a roast meat or hearty stew. If, on the other hand, you are barbecuing fish or grilling chicken, you could decide on something much more elaborate such as Wild Mushroom and Fontina Tarts, or fish or vegetable terrines, which look pretty and taste wonderful. Or, for an Oriental meal, you could serve Chicken Satay with Peanut Sauce.

However, you shouldn't feel too constrained by the ethnicity of your meal. Today, the trend is to serve foods that complement each other. A Mediterranean-style starter such as Charred Artichokes with Lemon Oil Dip could happily come before an Indonesian green curry. Similarly, Malayan Prawn Laksa would be fine before a French or Italian-style meal.

Those rules that do exist are related to texture and taste. For example, if you're making a soufflé or roulade as a main course, choose something crunchy as a starter.

The recipes in this book are extremely versatile and can be used for a range of occasions such as a buffet party, a light lunch, as finger food for an informal dinner party or as pre-dinner nibbles. And the beauty of many of the dishes is that they are incredibly simple and quick to make and can look stunning with very little effort – they will get any meal off to the best possible start.

USING THIS BOOK

This book is ideal for first-time cooks with a passion for appetizers, who will benefit from the detailed Guide to Techniques section at the end of the book as well as the more straightforward Dips and Nibbles section at the front. It will also appeal to the more experienced cook, who will find elaborate dishes in the Soups, Pâtés and Terrines section, as well as more difficult recipes to tackle in the Fish and Shellfish and Poultry and Meat sections.

Dips and nibbles

The recipes in this section are perfect for many occasions. Treats such as Parmesan Thins and Duck Wontons with Spicy Mango Sauce can be served as part of a buffet or as finger food at a drinks party. Dips lend piquancy and interest to finger food. Potato Skins with Cajun Dip make an unusual and exciting starter or try hot crispy Celeriac Fritters with cold Mustard Dip for an exciting flavour combination.

Hummus bi tahina

Blending chickpeas with garlic and oil creates a surprisingly creamy purée that is delicious as part of a Turkish-style mezze, or as a dip with vegetables. Leftovers make a good sandwich filler.

SERVES 4–6

150g/5oz/3/4 cup dried chickpeas
juice of 2 lemons
2 garlic cloves, sliced
30ml/2 tbsp olive oil
pinch of cayenne pepper
150ml/1/4 pint/2/3 cup tahini paste
salt and ground black pepper
extra olive oil and cayenne pepper, for sprinkling
flat leaf parsley sprigs, to garnish

1 Put the chickpeas in a bowl with plenty of cold water and leave them to soak overnight.

2 Drain the chickpeas, place in a pan and cover with fresh water. Bring to the boil and boil rapidly for 10 minutes. Reduce the heat and simmer gently for about 1 hour until soft. Drain in a colander.

3 Process the chickpeas in a food processor to a smooth purée. Add the lemon juice, garlic, olive oil, cayenne pepper and tahini paste and blend until creamy, scraping the mixture down from the sides of the bowl.

4 Season the purée with plenty of salt and ground black pepper and transfer to a serving dish. Sprinkle with a little olive oil and cayenne pepper, and serve garnished with a few parsley sprigs.

COOK'S TIP

For convenience, canned chickpeas can be used instead. Allow two 400g/14oz cans and drain them thoroughly. Tahini paste can now be purchased from most good supermarkets or health food shops.

Nutritional information per portion: Energy 265kcal/1101kJ; Protein 10g; Carbohydrate 12.6g, of which sugars 0.8g; Fat 19.7g, of which saturates 2.8g; Cholesterol 0mg; Calcium 210mg; Fibre 4.7g; Sodium 15mg.

Potato skins with Cajun dip

Divinely crisp and naughty, these potato skins are really simple to make. They are great on their own or served with this piquant dip as a garnish or on the side.

SERVES 4

2 large baking potatoes
vegetable oil, for deep-frying

FOR THE DIP
120ml/4fl oz/½ cup natural (plain) yogurt
1 garlic clove, crushed
5ml/1 tsp tomato purée (paste) or 2.5ml/½ tsp green chilli purée or ½ small green chilli, chopped
1.5ml/¼ tsp celery salt
salt and ground black pepper

1 Preheat the oven to 180°C/350°F/Gas 4. Bake the potatoes for 45–50 minutes until they are tender.

2 Cut the potatoes in half and then scoop out the flesh, leaving a thin layer on the skins. Keep the flesh for another meal. Cut the potatoes in half once more.

3 To make the dip, mix together all the ingredients and chill.

4 Heat a 1cm/½in layer of oil in a pan or deep-fryer. Fry the potatoes until they are crisp and golden. Drain on kitchen paper, then sprinkle with salt and black pepper. Serve the potato skins with a bowl of dip or a dollop of dip in each skin.

Nutritional information per portion: Energy 210kcal/871kJ; Protein 2.7g; Carbohydrate 12.5g, of which sugars 3.3g; Fat 17g, of which saturates 2.2g; Cholesterol 0mg; Calcium 61mg; Fibre 0.7g; Sodium 35mg.

Celeriac fritters with mustard dip

Celeriac is an unusual vegetable with a deliciously subtle flavour. Here it is used to make hot, crispy fritters which taste fabulous combined with a cold mustard dip.

SERVES 4

1 egg
115g/4oz/1 1/2 cups ground almonds
45ml/3 tbsp freshly grated Parmesan cheese
45ml/3 tbsp chopped fresh parsley
1 celeriac, about 450g/1lb
lemon juice
oil, for deep-frying
salt and ground black pepper
sea salt flakes, to garnish

FOR THE DIP
150ml/1/4 pint/2/3 cup sour cream
15–30ml/1–2 tbsp wholegrain mustard

1 Beat the egg well and pour into a shallow dish. Mix together the almonds, Parmesan and parsley in a separate dish. Season well.

2 Peel and cut the celeriac into batons about 1cm/1/2in wide and 5cm/2in long. Drop them into a bowl of water with a little lemon juice added to prevent discoloration.

3 Heat the oil to 180°C/350°F. Drain and then pat dry half the celeriac batons. Dip them into the beaten egg, then into the ground almond mixture, coating the pieces completely and evenly.

4 Deep-fry the fritters, in batches, for 2–3 minutes until golden. Drain on kitchen paper. Keep warm while you cook the remaining fritters.

5 Mix the dip ingredients together with salt to taste. Spoon into a bowl. Sprinkle the fritters with sea salt flakes.

Nutritional information per portion: Energy 514kcal/2123kJ; Protein 14.3g; Carbohydrate 4.7g, of which sugars 4g; Fat 48.8g, of which saturates 11g; Cholesterol 81mg; Calcium 301mg; Fibre 3.7g; Sodium 349mg.

Basil and lemon dip

This lovely dip is based on fresh mayonnaise flavoured with lemon juice and two types of basil, green and opal. Serve with crispy potato wedges for a delicious starter.

SERVES 4

2 large egg yolks
15ml/1 tbsp lemon juice
150ml/¼ pint/⅔ cup olive oil
150ml/¼ pint/⅔ cup sunflower oil
4 garlic cloves
handful of fresh green basil
handful of fresh opal basil
salt and ground black pepper

1 Place the egg yolks and lemon juice into a blender or food processor and process them briefly until they are lightly blended.

2 In a jug (pitcher), stir together the oils. With the machine running, pour in the oil very slowly, a little at a time. Once half of the oil has been added, the remaining oil can be incorporated more quickly. Continue processing to form a thick, creamy mayonnaise.

3 Peel and crush the garlic cloves. Alternatively, place them on a chopping board and sprinkle with salt, then flatten them with the heel of a heavy-bladed knife and chop the flesh. Flatten the garlic again to make a coarse purée.

4 Tear both types of basil into small pieces and then stir into the mayonnaise along with the crushed garlic.

5 Add salt and pepper to taste, then transfer the dip to a serving dish. Cover and chill until ready to serve.

COOK'S TIP

Make sure all the ingredients are at room temperature before you start to help prevent the mixture from curdling.

Nutritional information per portion: Energy 210kcal/871kJ; Protein 2.7g; Carbohydrate 12.5g, of which sugars 3.3g; Fat 17g, of which saturates 2.2g; Cholesterol 0mg; Calcium 61mg; Fibre 0.7g; Sodium 35mg.

Guacamole

Avocados discolour quickly, so make this sauce just before serving. If you do need to keep it for any length of time, cover the surface of the sauce with clear film and chill in the fridge.

SERVES 6

2 large ripe avocados
2 red chillies, seeded
1 garlic clove
1 shallot
20ml/2 tbsp olive oil, plus extra to serve
juice of 1 lemon
salt and ground black pepper
flat leaf parsley leaves, to garnish

1 Halve the avocados, remove the stones and scoop out the flesh into a large bowl.

2 Using a fork or potato masher, mash the avocado until smooth.

3 Finely chop the chillies, garlic and shallot, then stir into the mashed avocado with the olive oil and lemon juice. Season to taste with salt and ground black pepper.

4 Spoon the mixture into a small serving bowl. Drizzle over a little olive oil and scatter with a few flat leaf parsley leaves. Serve straight away.

Nutritional information per portion: Energy 108kcal/445kJ; Protein 1.6g; Carbohydrate 3.1g, of which sugars 2.3g; Fat 9.9g, of which saturates 2.1g; Cholesterol 0mg; Calcium 13mg; Fibre 2.3g; Sodium 8mg.

Thai tempeh cakes with **dipping sauce**

Made from soya beans, tempeh is similar to tofu but has a nuttier taste. Here, it is combined with a fragrant blend of lemon grass, coriander and ginger, and formed into small patties.

MAKES 8 CAKES

1 lemon grass stalk, finely chopped
2 each garlic cloves, spring onions (scallions) and shallots, finely chopped
2 chillies, seeded and finely chopped
2.5cm/1 in piece fresh root ginger, chopped
60ml/4 tbsp chopped fresh coriander (cilantro), plus extra to garnish
250g/9oz/2¼ cups tempeh, sliced
15ml/1 tbsp lime juice
5ml/1 tsp caster (superfine) sugar
45ml/3 tbsp plain (all-purpose) flour
1 large egg, lightly beaten
vegetable oil, for frying
salt and freshly ground black pepper

FOR THE DIPPING SAUCE

45ml/3 tbsp each mirin (sweet rice wine) and wine vinegar
2 spring onions (scallions), finely sliced
15ml/1 tbsp sugar
2 chillies, finely chopped
30ml/2 tbsp chopped fresh coriander (cilantro)

1 To make the dipping sauce, mix together the mirin, vinegar, spring onions, sugar, chillies and coriander in a small bowl and set aside.

2 Place the lemon grass, garlic, spring onions, shallots, chillies, ginger and coriander in a food processor or blender. Process to a coarse paste. Add the tempeh, lime juice and sugar, then blend until combined. Add the flour and egg, and season. Process again until the mixture forms a coarse, sticky paste.

3 Take a heaped serving-spoonful of the paste mixture at a time and form into rounds with your hands. The mixture at this stage will be quite sticky.

4 Heat enough oil to cover the base of a large frying pan. Fry the tempeh cakes for 5–6 minutes, turning once, until they are golden on both sides. Drain on kitchen paper and serve warm with the dipping sauce, garnished with the extra chopped fresh coriander.

Nutritional information per portion: Energy 79kcal/332kJ; Protein 4.5g; Carbohydrate 9.1g, of which sugars 4.3g; Fat 2.3g, of which saturates 0.4g; Cholesterol 26mg; Calcium 192mg; Fibre 0.8g; Sodium 15mg.

Lemon and coconut dhal

A warm spicy dish with tangy lemon and coconut flavours, this can be served either as a dip with warmed pitta bread or as an accompaniment to cold meats.

SERVES 8

5cm/2in piece fresh root ginger
1 onion
2 garlic cloves
2 small red chillies, seeded
30ml/2 tbsp sunflower oil
5ml/1 tsp cumin seeds, plus extra to garnish
150g/5oz/2/3 cup red lentils
250ml/8fl oz/1 cup water
15ml/1 tbsp hot curry paste
200ml/7fl oz/scant 1 cup coconut cream
juice of 1 lemon
25g/1oz/1/4 cup flaked (sliced) almonds
salt and ground black pepper

1 Use a vegetable peeler to peel the ginger and finely chop it with the onion, garlic and chillies.

2 Heat the sunflower oil in a large, shallow pan. Add the ginger, onion, garlic, chillies and cumin. Cook for about 5 minutes, until the onion is softened but not coloured.

3 Stir the lentils, water and curry paste into the pan. Bring to the boil, cover and cook gently over a low heat for about 15–20 minutes, stirring occasionally, until the lentils are just tender and not yet broken up.

4 Stir in all but 30ml/2 tbsp of the coconut cream. Bring to the boil and cook, uncovered, for a further 15–20 minutes, until the mixture is thick and pulpy. Off the heat, stir in the lemon juice. Season to taste.

5 Heat a large frying pan and cook the flaked almonds for one or two minutes on each side until golden brown. Stir about three-quarters of the toasted almonds into the dhal.

6 Transfer the dhal to a serving bowl; swirl in the remaining coconut cream. Scatter the reserved almonds on top with the cumin seeds and serve warm.

Nutritional information per portion: Energy 190kcal/791kJ; Protein 6g; Carbohydrate 12.2g, of which sugars 1.9g; Fat 13.4g, of which saturates 7.9g; Cholesterol 0mg; Calcium 22mg; Fibre 1.3g; Sodium 11mg.

Baba ganoush with **Lebanese flatbread**

Baba ganoush is a delectable aubergine dip which comes from the Middle East. Tahini – a sesame seed paste with cumin – gives the dish a hint of spice.

SERVES 6

2 small aubergines (eggplants)
1 garlic clove, crushed
60ml/4 tbsp tahini
25g/1oz/¼ cup ground almonds
juice of ½ lemon
2.5ml/½ tsp ground cumin
30ml/2 tbsp fresh mint leaves
30ml/2 tbsp olive oil
salt and ground black pepper

FOR THE FLATBREAD
4 pitta breads
45ml/3 tbsp sesame seeds
45ml/3 tbsp fresh thyme leaves
45ml/3 tbsp poppy seeds
150ml/¼ pint/⅔ cup olive oil

1 First make the Lebanese flatbread. Split the pitta breads through the middle and open them out. Mix the sesame seeds, chopped thyme and poppy seeds in a mortar. Crush them with a pestle to release the flavour.

2 Stir in the olive oil. Spread the mixture over the cut sides of the pitta bread. Grill (broil) until golden. When cool, break into pieces and set aside.

3 Grill (broil) the aubergines, turning them frequently, until the skin is blackened and blistered. Remove the skin, then chop the flesh roughly and leave to drain in a colander.

4 Squeeze out as much liquid from the aubergine as possible. Place the flesh in a blender or food processor, then add the garlic, tahini, ground almonds, lemon juice and cumin, with salt to taste. Process to a smooth paste, then roughly chop half the mint and stir into the dip.

5 Spoon the paste into a bowl, scatter the remaining mint leaves on top and drizzle with the olive oil. Serve with the Lebanese flatbread.

Nutritional information per portion: Energy 451kcal/1878kJ; Protein 9.3g; Carbohydrate 29.5g, of which sugars 3.1g; Fat 33.8g, of which saturates 4.7g; Cholesterol 0mg; Calcium 204mg; Fibre 4.2g; Sodium 225mg.

Quail's eggs with **herbs** and **dips**

For al fresco eating or informal entertaining, this colourful platter of contrasting tastes and textures is delicious. Choose the best seasonal vegetables available.

SERVES 6

1 large Italian focaccia or 2–3 Indian parathas or other flatbread
olive oil
1 large garlic clove, finely chopped
small handful of chopped fresh mixed herbs, such as coriander (cilantro), mint, parsley and oregano
18–24 quail's eggs
salt and ground black pepper

FOR THE DIPS

30ml/2 tbsp home-made mayonnaise
30ml/2 tbsp thick sour cream
5ml/1 tsp chopped capers
5ml/1 tsp finely chopped shallot
salt and ground black pepper

TO SERVE

225g/8oz fresh beetroot (beet), cooked in water or cider, peeled and sliced
1/2 bunch spring onions (scallions), trimmed and roughly chopped
60ml/4 tbsp red onion or tamarind and date chutney
high quality olive oil
coarse sea salt and mixed ground peppercorns

1 Preheat the oven to 190°C/375°F/Gas 5. Brush the focaccia or flatbread liberally with oil, sprinkle with garlic, the herbs and seasoning and bake for 10–15 minutes, or until golden. Keep warm.

2 Put the quail's eggs into a saucepan of cold water, bring to the boil and boil for 5 minutes. Arrange in a serving dish. Peel the eggs if you wish or leave guests to do their own.

3 To make the dip, combine the mayonnaise, soured cream, capers, shallot and seasoning.

4 To serve, cut the bread into wedges and serve with dishes of the quail's eggs, mayonnaise dip, sliced beetroot, chopped spring onion and chutney. Serve with tiny bowls of coarse salt and ground peppercorns, together with olive oil for dipping.

Nutritional information per portion: Energy 344kcal/1446kJ; Protein 15.7g; Carbohydrate 43.6g, of which sugars 8.3g; Fat 13.2g, of which saturates 3.4g; Cholesterol 260mg; Calcium 151mg; Fibre 2.7g; Sodium 478mg.

Chilli bean dip

This deliciously spicy and creamy bean dip is best served warm, either with triangles of lightly grilled pitta bread or a large bowl of crunchy tortilla chips.

SERVES 4

2 garlic cloves
1 onion
2 green chillies
30ml/2 tbsp vegetable oil
5–10ml/1–2 tsp hot chilli powder
400g/14oz can kidney beans
75g/3oz mature (sharp) Cheddar cheese, grated
1 red chilli, seeded
salt and ground black pepper

1 Finely chop the garlic and onion. Seed and finely chop the green chillies.

2 Heat the vegetable oil in a heavy pan or deep frying pan and add the garlic, onion, green chillies and chilli powder. Cook gently for about 5 minutes, stirring regularly, until the onions are softened and transparent, but not browned.

3 Drain the kidney beans, reserving the liquid. Blend all but 30ml/2 tbsp of the beans to a purée in a food processor.

4 Add the puréed beans to the pan with 30–45ml/2–3 tbsp of the reserved liquor. Heat gently, stirring to mix well.

5 Stir in the whole beans and the Cheddar cheese. Cook gently for about 2–3 minutes, stirring until the cheese melts. Add salt and pepper to taste.

6 Cut the red chilli into thin strips. Spoon the dip into four individual serving bowls and scatter the chilli strips over the top. Serve warm.

COOK'S TIP

For a dip with a coarser texture, do not purée the beans; instead mash them with a potato masher.

Nutritional information per portion: Energy 244kcal/1018kJ; Protein 12.7g; Carbohydrate 20.2g, of which sugars 4.6g; Fat 12.6g, of which saturates 4.8g; Cholesterol 18mg; Calcium 234mg; Fibre 7.1g; Sodium 538mg.

King prawns in crispy batter

Serve these delightfully crispy prawns with an Oriental-style dipping sauce or, for something a little different, offer a simple tomato sauce or lemon wedges for squeezing.

SERVES 4

120ml/4fl oz/1/2 cup water
1 egg
115g/4oz/1 cup plain (all-purpose) flour
5ml/1 tsp cayenne pepper
12 raw king prawns (jumbo shrimp), unpeeled
vegetable oil, for deep-frying
flat leaf parsley, to garnish
lemon wedges, to serve

FOR THE DIPPING SAUCE
30ml/2 tbsp soy sauce
30ml/2 tbsp dry sherry
10ml/2 tsp clear honey

1 In a bowl, whisk the water with the egg. Add the flour and cayenne, and whisk to make a smooth batter.

2 Carefully peel the prawns, leaving just the tail sections intact. Make a shallow cut down the back of each prawn, then pull out and discard the dark intestinal tract.

3 To make the dipping sauce, mix the soy sauce, dry sherry and honey in a small bowl until well combined.

4 Heat the oil in a large pan or deep-fryer, until a cube of stale bread browns in 1 minute.

5 Holding the prawns by their tails, dip them into the batter, one at a time, shaking off any excess. Drop the prawns carefully into the oil and fry for 2–3 minutes until crisp and golden brown. Drain on kitchen paper and serve with the dipping sauce and lemon wedges, garnished with parsley.

Nutritional information per portion: Energy 278kcal/1162kJ; Protein 8.9g; Carbohydrate 25g, of which sugars 3g; Fat 15.7g, of which saturates 2.1g; Cholesterol 96mg; Calcium 69mg; Fibre 0.9g; Sodium 601mg.

Parmesan fish goujons

Use this batter, with or without the cheese, whenever you feel brave enough to fry fish. This is light and crisp, just like authentic fish-and-chip shop batter.

SERVES 4

375g/13oz plaice or sole fillets, or thicker fish such as cod or haddock
a little plain (all-purpose) flour
oil, for deep-frying
salt and ground black pepper
dill sprigs, to garnish

FOR THE CREAM SAUCE
60ml/4 tbsp sour cream
60ml/4 tbsp mayonnaise
2.5ml/½ tsp grated lemon rind
30ml/2 tbsp chopped gherkins or capers
15ml/1 tbsp chopped mixed fresh herbs, or 5ml/1 tsp dried

FOR THE BATTER
75g/3oz/¾ cup plain (all purpose) flour
25g/1oz/¼ cup grated Parmesan cheese
5ml/1 tsp bicarbonate of soda (baking soda)
1 egg, separated
150ml/¼ pint/⅔ cup milk

1 To make the sauce, mix the cream, mayonnaise, lemon rind, gherkins or capers, herbs and seasoning together, then chill in the fridge.

2 To make the batter, sift the flour into a bowl. Mix in the other dry ingredients and some salt, and then whisk in the egg yolk and milk to give a thick yet smooth batter. Then gradually whisk in 90ml/6 tbsp water. Season and chill in the fridge.

3 Skin the fish and cut into thin strips of similar length. Dip the fish lightly in seasoned flour.

4 Heat at least 5cm/2in oil in a large, heavy pan with a lid. Whisk the egg white until stiff and gently fold into the batter until just blended.

5 Dip the floured fish into the batter, drain off any excess and then drop gently into the hot fat.

6 Cook the fish in batches, so that the goujons don't stick to one another, for only 3–4 minutes, turning once. When the batter is golden and crisp, remove the fish with a slotted spoon. Place the goujons on kitchen paper on a plate and keep warm while cooking the rest. Serve hot, garnished with sprigs of dill and accompanied by the cream sauce.

Nutritional information per portion: Energy 358kcal/1497kJ; Protein 24.2g; Carbohydrate 21.4g, of which sugars 3.2g; Fat 20.2g, of which saturates 5.9g; Cholesterol 116mg; Calcium 243mg; Fibre 1.4g; Sodium 293mg.

King prawns with **spicy dip**

The spicy dip served with this dish is equally good made from peanuts instead of cashew nuts. Vegetarians can enjoy this, too, if you make it with vegetables or tofu cubes.

SERVES 4–6

24 raw king prawns (jumbo shrimp), unpeeled
juice of 1/2 lemon
5ml/1 tsp paprika
1 bay leaf
1 thyme sprig
vegetable oil, for brushing
salt and ground black pepper

FOR THE SPICY DIP

1 onion, chopped
4 canned plum tomatoes, plus 60ml/4 tbsp of the juice
1/2 green (bell) pepper, seeded and chopped
1 garlic clove, crushed
15ml/1 tbsp cashew nuts
15ml/1 tbsp soy sauce
15ml/1 tbsp desiccated (dry unsweetened shredded) coconut

1 Peel the prawns, leaving the tails on. Place in a shallow dish and sprinkle with the lemon juice, paprika and seasoning. Cover and chill in the fridge.

2 Put the prawn shells in a pan with the bay leaf and thyme, cover with water, and bring to the boil. Simmer for 30 minutes; strain the stock into a measuring jug. Top up with water, if necessary, to 300ml/1/2 pint/1 1/4 cups.

3 For the dip, place the ingredients in a blender or food processor and process until smooth. Pour into a pan with the stock and simmer over a moderate heat for 30 minutes, until the sauce is fairly thick.

4 Preheat the grill (broiler). Thread the prawns on to small skewers, then brush the prawns on both sides with a little oil and grill (broil) under a low heat until cooked, turning once. Serve with the dip.

Nutritional information per portion: Energy 80kcal/334kJ; Protein 9.9g; Carbohydrate 3g, of which sugars 2.3g; Fat 3.2g, of which saturates 1.7g; Cholesterol 98mg; Calcium 46mg; Fibre 0.9g; Sodium 283mg.

Beef satay with a **hot mango dip**

Strips of tender beef are flavoured with a warmly spiced marinade before being cooked on skewers, then served with a tangy fruit dip.

MAKES 12 SKEWERS

450g/1lb sirloin steak, 2cm/¾ in thick
15ml/1 tbsp coriander seeds
5ml/1 tsp cumin seeds
50g/2oz/⅓ cup raw cashew nuts
15ml/1 tbsp vegetable oil
2 shallots or 1 small onion, finely chopped
1cm/½in piece fresh root ginger
1 garlic clove, crushed
30ml/2 tbsp each tamarind and soy sauce
10ml/2 tsp sugar
5ml/1 tsp rice or white wine vinegar

FOR THE MANGO DIP
1 ripe mango
1–2 small red chillies, seeded and chopped
15ml/1 tbsp fish sauce
juice of 1 lime
10ml/2 tsp sugar
1.5ml/¼ tsp salt
30ml/2 tbsp fresh coriander (cilantro)

1 Soak 12 bamboo skewers for 30 minutes. Slice the beef into long narrow strips and thread, zigzag-style, on to the skewers. Lay on a flat plate and set aside.

2 For the marinade, dry-fry the seeds and nuts in a large wok until evenly brown. Transfer to a mortar with a rough surface and crush finely with the pestle. Peel and chop the ginger. Add the oil, shallots or onion, ginger, garlic, tamarind and soy sauces, sugar and vinegar.

3 Spread this marinade over the beef and leave to marinate for up to 8 hours. Cook the beef under a moderate grill (broiler) or over a barbecue for 6–8 minutes, turning to ensure an even colour. Meanwhile, make the mango dip.

4 Cut away the skin and remove the stone (pit) from the mango. Process the mango flesh with the chillies, fish sauce, lime juice, sugar and salt until smooth, then add the coriander and serve with the beef.

Nutritional information per portion: Energy 62kcal/263kJ; Protein 9g; Carbohydrate 2.9g, of which sugars 2.8g; Fat 1.7g, of which saturates 0.8g; Cholesterol 19mg; Calcium 5mg; Fibre 0.3g; Sodium 205mg.

Pork balls with a minted peanut sauce

This makes an unusual and exotic starter for a dinner party or as part of a buffet. The recipe is equally delicious made with chicken breasts.

SERVES 4–6

275g/10oz leg of pork, trimmed and diced
1cm/1/2in piece fresh root ginger, grated
1 garlic clove, crushed
10ml/2 tsp sesame oil
15ml/1 tbsp each sherry and soy sauce
5ml/1 tsp sugar
1 egg white
salt and white pepper, to taste
350g/12oz/scant 1 3/4 cups long grain rice, cooked for 15 minutes
50g/2oz ham, diced
1 iceberg lettuce, to serve

FOR THE PEANUT SAUCE
15ml/1 tbsp coconut cream
75ml/2 1/2fl oz/1/3 cup boiling water
30ml/2 tbsp smooth peanut butter
juice of 1 lime
1 red chilli, seeded and finely chopped
1 garlic clove, crushed
15ml/1 tbsp chopped fresh mint
15ml/1 tbsp chopped fresh coriander (cilantro)

1 Place the diced pork, ginger and garlic in a food processor, and then process for 2–3 minutes until smooth. Add the sesame oil, sherry, soy sauce and sugar and blend with the pork mixture. Finally, add the egg white, salt and white pepper.

2 Spread the cooked rice and ham in a shallow dish. Using wet hands, shape the pork mixture into thumb-size balls. Roll in the rice to coat and pierce each ball with a bamboo skewer.

3 To make the peanut sauce, put the coconut cream in a measuring jug and cover with the boiling water. Place the peanut butter in another bowl with the lime juice, chilli, garlic, mint and coriander. Combine evenly then add the coconut.

4 Place the pork balls in a bamboo steamer and steam over a saucepan of boiling water for 8–10 minutes. Arrange the pork balls on lettuce leaves on a plate, with the sauce to one side.

Nutritional information per portion: Energy 337kcal/1409kJ; Protein 17.5g; Carbohydrate 47.9g, of which sugars 1g; Fat 7.8g, of which saturates 3g; Cholesterol 33mg; Calcium 35mg; Fibre 0.7g; Sodium 322mg.

Pork and **peanut wontons** with **plum sauce**

These crispy filled wontons are delicious served with a sweet plum sauce. The wontons can be filled and set aside for up to eight hours before they are cooked.

MAKES 40–50 WONTONS

175g/6oz/1½ cups minced (ground) pork or 175g/6oz pork sausages, skinned
2 spring onions (scallions), finely chopped
30ml/2 tbsp peanut butter
10ml/2 tsp oyster sauce (optional)
40–50 wonton skins
30ml/2 tbsp flour paste
vegetable oil, for deep-frying
salt and ground black pepper
lettuce and radishes, to garnish

FOR THE PLUM SAUCE

225g/8oz/generous ¾ cup dark plum jam
15ml/1 tbsp rice or white wine vinegar
15ml/1 tbsp dark soy sauce
2.5ml/½ tsp chilli sauce

1 Combine the minced pork or skinned sausages, spring onions, peanut butter, oyster sauce, if using, and seasoning, and then set aside.

2 For the sauce, combine the plum jam, vinegar, soy and chilli sauces in a serving bowl and set aside.

3 To fill the wonton skins, place 8 wrappers at a time on a work surface, moisten the edges with the flour paste and place 2.5ml/½ tsp of the filling on each one. Fold in half, corner to corner, and twist.

4 Fill a wok or deep frying pan one-third with vegetable oil and heat to 190°C/375°F. Have ready a wire strainer or frying basket and a tray lined with kitchen paper. Drop the wontons, 8 at a time, into the hot fat and then fry until they are golden all over, for about 1–2 minutes. Lift out on to the paper-lined tray, using a slotted spoon and sprinkle with fine salt.

5 Serve the wontons with the plum sauce, garnished with the lettuce and radishes.

Nutritional information per portion: Energy 56kcal/236kJ; Protein 1.5g; Carbohydrate 7.9g, of which sugars 4.1g; Fat 2.3g, of which saturates 0.4g; Cholesterol 3mg; Calcium 8mg; Fibre 0.2g; Sodium 35mg.

Chicken satay with **peanut sauce**

These skewers of marinated chicken can be prepared in advance and served at room temperature. Beef, pork or even lamb fillet can be used instead of chicken if you prefer.

MAKES ABOUT 24

450g/1lb skinless chicken breast fillets
oil, for brushing
sesame seeds, for sprinkling
red pepper strips, to garnish

FOR THE MARINADE
90ml/6 tbsp vegetable oil
60ml/4 tbsp tamari or light soy sauce
60ml/4 tbsp fresh lime juice
2.5cm/1in piece fresh root ginger, peeled and chopped
3–4 garlic cloves
30ml/2 tbsp light brown sugar
5ml/1 tsp Chinese-style chilli sauce or 1 red chilli, seeded and chopped
30ml/2 tbsp chopped fresh coriander (cilantro)

FOR THE PEANUT SAUCE
30ml/2 tbsp smooth peanut butter
30ml/2 tbsp soy sauce
15ml/1 tbsp sesame or vegetable oil
2 spring onions (scallions), chopped
2 garlic cloves
15–30ml/1–2 tbsp fresh lime or lemon juice
15ml/1 tbsp brown sugar

1 Prepare the marinade. Place all the marinade ingredients in a food processor or blender and process until smooth and well blended, scraping down the sides of the bowl once. Pour into a shallow dish and set aside.

2 Into the same food processor or blender, put all the peanut sauce ingredients and process until well blended. If the sauce is too thick, add a little water and process again. Pour into a bowl and cover until ready to serve.

3 Slice the chicken breast fillets into thin strips, then cut the strips into 2cm/¾in pieces. Add the chicken pieces to the marinade in the dish. Toss well to coat, cover and marinate for about 3–4 hours in a cool place, or overnight in the fridge.

4 Preheat the grill (broiler). Line a baking sheet with foil and brush lightly with oil. Thread 2–3 pieces of marinated chicken on to skewers and sprinkle with the sesame seeds. Grill (broil) for 4–5 minutes until golden, turning once. Serve with the peanut sauce, and a garnish of red pepper strips.

Nutritional information per portion: Energy 48kcal/200kJ; Protein 4.8g; Carbohydrate 2.2g, of which sugars 2.1g; Fat 2.2g, of which saturates 0.4g; Cholesterol 13mg; Calcium 3mg; Fibre 0.1g; Sodium 105mg.

Duck wontons with **spicy mango sauce**

These Chinese-style wontons are easy to make using ready-cooked smoked duck or chicken, or even leftovers from the Sunday roast.

MAKES ABOUT 40

15ml/1 tbsp light soy sauce
5ml/1 tsp sesame oil
2 spring onions (scallions), finely chopped
grated rind of 1/2 orange
5ml/1 tsp brown sugar
275g/10oz/1 1/2 cups chopped smoked duck
about 40 small wonton wrappers
15ml/1 tbsp vegetable oil
whole fresh chives, to garnish (optional)

FOR THE MANGO SAUCE
30ml/2 tbsp vegetable oil
5ml/1 tsp ground cumin
2.5ml/1/2 tsp ground cardamom
1.5ml/1/4 tsp ground cinnamon
250ml/8fl oz/1 cup mango purée (made from 1 large mango)
15ml/1 tbsp clear honey
2.5ml/1/2 tsp Chinese chilli sauce (or to taste)
15ml/1 tbsp cider vinegar
snipped fresh chives, to garnish

1 First prepare the sauce. In a medium pan, heat the oil over a medium-low heat. Add the ground cumin, cardamom and cinnamon and cook for about 3 minutes, stirring constantly.

2 Stir in the mango purée, honey, chilli sauce and vinegar. Remove from the heat and leave to cool. Pour into a bowl and cover until ready to serve.

3 Prepare the wonton filling. In a large bowl, mix together the soy sauce, sesame oil, spring onions, orange rind and brown sugar until well blended. Add the duck and toss to coat well.

4 Place a teaspoonful of the duck mixture in the centre of each wonton wrapper. Brush the edges with water and then draw them up to the centre, twisting to seal and form a pouch shape.

5 Preheat the oven to 190°F/375°C/Gas 5. Line a large baking sheet with foil and brush lightly with oil. Arrange the wontons on the baking sheet and bake for 10–12 minutes until crisp and golden. Serve with the mango sauce garnished with snipped fresh chives. If you wish, tie each wonton with a fresh chive.

Nutritional information per portion: Energy 95kcal/404kJ; Protein 6.8g; Carbohydrate 14.7g, of which sugars 0.4g; Fat 1.9g, of which saturates 0.4g; Cholesterol 28mg; Calcium 35mg; Fibre 0.7g; Sodium 36mg.

Cheese aigrettes

Choux pastry is often associated with sweet pastries, such as profiteroles, but these little savoury buns, flavoured with Gruyère and dusted with grated Parmesan, are just delicious.

MAKES 30

90g/3½ oz/scant 1 cup strong white bread flour
2.5ml/½ tsp paprika
2.5ml/½ tsp salt
75g/3oz/6 tbsp cold butter, diced
200ml/7fl oz/scant 1 cup water
3 eggs, beaten
75g/3oz mature Gruyère cheese, coarsely grated
corn or vegetable oil, for deep-frying
50g/2oz/⅔ cup freshly grated Parmesan cheese
ground black pepper

1 Mix the flour, paprika and salt together by sifting them on to a large sheet of greaseproof paper. Add a generous amount of ground black pepper.

2 Put the diced butter and water into a medium pan and heat gently. As soon as the butter has melted and the liquid starts to boil, quickly tip in all the seasoned flour at once and beat very hard with a wooden spoon until the dough comes away cleanly from the sides of the pan.

3 Remove the pan from the heat and cool the paste for 5 minutes. Gradually beat in enough of the beaten egg to give a stiff dropping consistency that still holds a shape on the spoon. Mix in the Gruyère.

4 Heat the oil for deep-frying to 180°C/350°F. Take a teaspoonful of the choux paste and use a second spoon to slide it into the oil. Make more aigrettes in the same way. Fry for 3–4 minutes then drain on kitchen paper and keep warm while cooking successive batches. To serve, pile the aigrettes on a warmed serving dish and sprinkle with Parmesan.

Nutritional information per portion: Energy 84kcal/348kJ; Protein 2.2g; Carbohydrate 2.4g, of which sugars 0.1g; Fat 7.3g, of which saturates 2.7g; Cholesterol 28mg; Calcium 46mg; Fibre 0.1g; Sodium 58mg.

Parmesan thins

These thin, crisp, savoury biscuits will melt in the mouth, so make plenty for guests. They are a great snack at any time of the day, not just for parties.

MAKES 16–20

50g/2oz/½ cup plain (all-purpose) flour
40g/1½ oz/3 tbsp butter, softened
1 egg yolk
40g/1½ oz/⅔ cup freshly grated Parmesan cheese
pinch of salt
pinch of mustard powder

1 Rub together the flour and the butter in a bowl using your fingertips, then work in the egg yolk, Parmesan cheese, salt and mustard. Mix to bring the dough together into a ball. Shape the mixture into a log, wrap in foil or clear film and chill in the fridge for 10 minutes.

2 Preheat the oven to 200°C/400°F/Gas 6. Cut the Parmesan log into very thin slices, 3–6mm/⅛–¼in maximum, and arrange on a baking sheet. Flatten with a fork to give a pretty ridged pattern. Bake for 10 minutes or until the biscuits are crisp but not changing colour.

Nutritional information per portion: Energy 36kcal/148kJ; Protein 1.2g; Carbohydrate 2g, of which sugars 0.1g; Fat 2.6g, of which saturates 1.5g; Cholesterol 16mg; Calcium 29mg; Fibre 0.1g; Sodium 34mg.

Spicy peanut balls

Tasty rice balls, rolled in chopped peanuts and deep-fried, make a delicious starter. Serve them as they are, or with a chilli sauce for dipping. Make sure there are plenty of napkins to hand.

MAKES 16

1cm/½ in piece fresh root ginger
1 garlic clove, crushed
1.5ml/¼ tsp turmeric
5ml/1 tsp sugar
2.5ml/½ tsp salt
5ml/1 tsp chilli sauce
10ml/2 tsp fish sauce or soy sauce
30ml/2 tbsp chopped fresh coriander (cilantro)
juice of ½ lime
225g/8oz/2 cups cooked white long grain rice
115g/4oz/1 cup peanuts, chopped
vegetable oil, for deep-frying
lime wedges and chilli sauce, to serve

1 Peel and chop the ginger and process with the garlic and turmeric in a food processor or blender until the mixture forms a smooth paste. Add the sugar, salt, chilli sauce and fish sauce or soy sauce, with the chopped fresh coriander and lime juice. Process again briefly to mix the ingredients.

2 Add three-quarters of the cooked rice to the paste and process until smooth and sticky. Scrape into a mixing bowl and stir in the remainder of the rice. Wet your hands and shape the mixture into thumb-size balls.

3 Roll the balls in the chopped peanuts, making sure they are evenly coated.

4 Heat the oil in a deep-fryer or wok. Deep-fry the peanut balls until crisp. Drain on kitchen paper and then pile on to a platter. Serve the peanut balls hot with lime wedges and chilli sauce.

Nutritional information per portion: Energy 123kcal/512kJ; Protein 2.9g; Carbohydrate 12.4g, of which sugars 0.8g; Fat 6.8g, of which saturates 1g; Cholesterol 0mg; Calcium 7mg; Fibre 0.4g; Sodium 45mg.

Pickled quail's eggs

These Chinese eggs are pickled in alcohol and can be stored in a preserving jar in a cool dark place for several months. They make delicious bitesize snacks at a drinks party.

SERVES 12

12 quail's eggs
15ml/1 tbsp salt
750ml/1¼ pints/3 cups distilled or previously boiled water
15ml/1 tsp Sichuan peppercorns
150ml/¼ pint/⅔ cup spirit such as Mou-tal (Chinese brandy), brandy, whisky, rum or vodka
dipping sauce and toasted sesame seeds, to serve

1 Boil the quail's eggs for about 4 minutes until the yolks are soft but not too runny.

2 In a large saucepan, dissolve the salt in the distilled or previously boiled water. Add the peppercorns, then allow the water to cool and add the spirit.

3 Gently tap the eggs all over but do not peel them. Place in a large, airtight, sterilized jar and fill up with the liquid, totally covering the eggs. Seal the jar and then leave the eggs to stand in a cool, dark place for 7–8 days.

4 To serve, remove the eggs from the liquid and peel off the shells carefully. Cut each egg in half or quarters and serve whole with a dipping sauce and a bowl of toasted sesame seeds.

Nutritional information per portion: Energy 20kcal/82kJ; Protein 1.7g; Carbohydrate 0g, of which sugars 0g; Fat 1.5g, of which saturates 0.4g; Cholesterol 51mg; Calcium 8mg; Fibre 0g; Sodium 19mg.

Crispy spring rolls

These small and dainty spring rolls are ideal served as appetizers or as cocktail snacks. If liked, you could replace the mushrooms with chicken or pork, and the carrots with prawns.

MAKES 40 ROLLS

225g/8oz fresh beansprouts
115g/4oz small leeks
115g/4oz carrots
115g/4oz bamboo shoots, sliced
115g/4oz mushrooms
45–60ml/3–4 tbsp vegetable oil
5ml/1 tsp salt
5ml/1 tsp light brown sugar
15ml/1 tbsp light soy sauce
15ml/1 tbsp Chinese rice wine or dry sherry
20 frozen spring roll skins, defrosted
15ml/1 tbsp cornflour (cornstarch) paste
flour, for dusting
oil, for deep-frying

1 Cut all the vegetables into thin shreds, roughly the same size and shape as the beansprouts.

2 Heat the vegetable oil in a wok and stir-fry the vegetables for about 1 minute. Add the salt, sugar, soy sauce and wine or sherry and continue stirring the vegetables for 1½–2 minutes. Remove and drain away the excess liquid, then leave to cool.

3 To make the spring rolls, cut each spring roll skin in half diagonally, then place about a tablespoonful of the vegetable mixture one-third of the way down on the skin, with the triangle pointing away from you.

4 Lift the lower edge over the filling and roll once. Fold in both ends and roll once more, then brush the upper pointed edge with a little cornflour paste, made by mixing together 4 parts cornflour with about 5 parts cold water until smooth, and roll into a neat package. Lightly dust a tray with flour and place the spring rolls on the tray with the flapside underneath.

5 To cook, heat the oil in a wok or deep-fryer until hot, then reduce the heat to low. Deep-fry the spring rolls in batches (about 8–10 at a time) for 2–3 minutes or until golden and crispy, then remove and drain. Serve the spring rolls hot with a dipping sauce, such as soy sauce, or mixed salt and pepper.

Nutritional information per portion: Energy 38kcal/161kJ; Protein 1.1g; Carbohydrate 6.6g, of which sugars 0.6g; Fat 1g, of which saturates 0.1g; Cholesterol 0mg; Calcium 15mg; Fibre 0.5g; Sodium 88mg.

Tapenade and **quail's eggs**

A purée made from capers, olives and anchovies, tapenade is popular in Mediterranean cooking. It complements the taste of eggs perfectly, especially quail's eggs.

SERVES 8

8 quail's eggs
1 small baguette
45ml/3 tbsp tapenade
frisée lettuce
3 small tomatoes, sliced
black olives, pitted
4 canned anchovy fillets, drained and halved lengthways
a little chopped parsley, to garnish

1 Boil the quail's eggs for 3 minutes, then plunge them straight into cold water to cool. Crack the shells and remove them very carefully.

2 Cut the baguette into slices on the diagonal and spread each one with some of the tapenade.

3 Arrange a little frisée lettuce, torn to fit, and the tomato slices on top. Halve the quail's eggs and place them on top of the tomato slices.

4 Quarter the olives, place one quarter on each and finally add the anchovies. Garnish with parsley.

Nutritional information per portion: Energy 157kcal/666kJ; Protein 6.3g; Carbohydrate 28.4g, of which sugars 1.8g; Fat 2.8g, of which saturates 0.6g; Cholesterol 37mg; Calcium 76mg; Fibre 1.5g; Sodium 523mg.

Eggy Thai fish cakes

These tangy little fish cakes, with a kick of Eastern spice, make great party food, dipped in an Oriental-style sauce. If they are made slightly larger, they are a great appetizer, too.

MAKES ABOUT 20

225g/8oz smoked cod or haddock (undyed)
225g/8oz fresh cod or haddock
1 small fresh red chilli
2 garlic cloves, grated
1 lemon grass stalk, very finely chopped
2 large spring onions (scallions), chopped
30ml/2 tbsp Thai fish sauce (or 30ml/ 2 tbsp soy sauce and a few drops anchovy essence)
60ml/4 tbsp thick coconut milk
2 large (US extra large) eggs, lightly beaten
15ml/1 tbsp chopped fresh coriander (cilantro)
15ml/1 tbsp cornflour (cornstarch)
oil, for frying
soy sauce, rice vinegar or Thai fish sauce, for dipping

1 Place the smoked fish in water and leave to soak for 10 minutes. Dry on kitchen paper. Roughly chop the smoked and fresh fish and place in a food processor.

2 Seed and finely chop the chilli, then add with the garlic, lemon grass, spring onions, the sauce and the coconut milk, and process until well blended with the fish. Add the eggs and coriander and process for a few more seconds. Cover with clear film (plastic wrap) and chill in the fridge for 1 hour.

3 To make the fish cakes, flour your hands with cornflour and shape teaspoonfuls of the mixture into neat balls, then coat them with flour.

4 Heat 5–7.5cm/2–3in oil in a medium pan until a crust of bread turns golden in about 1 minute. Fry the fish balls 5–6 at a time, turning them carefully for 2–3 minutes, until they turn golden all over. Remove with a slotted spoon and drain on kitchen paper. Keep the fish cakes warm until all are cooked. Serve with dipping sauces.

Nutritional information per portion: Energy 60kcal/250kJ; Protein 6.2g; Carbohydrate 0.9g, of which sugars 0.2g; Fat 3.5g, of which saturates 0.5g; Cholesterol 29mg; Calcium 15mg; Fibre 0.1g; Sodium 152mg.

Samosas

Throughout the East, these tasty snacks are sold by street vendors and eaten at any time of day. Filo pastry can be used to produce a lighter, flakier texture.

MAKES ABOUT 20

1 packet 25cm/10in spring roll wrappers
30ml/2 tbsp plain (all-purpose) flour, mixed with water
vegetable oil, for deep frying
coriander (cilantro) leaves, to garnish

FOR THE FILLING

25g/1oz/2 tbsp ghee or unsalted butter
1 small onion, finely chopped
1cm/½in piece fresh root ginger, peeled and chopped
1 garlic clove, crushed
2.5ml/½ tsp chilli powder
1 large potato, about 225g/8oz, cooked until just tender and finely diced
50g/2oz/½ cup cauliflower florets, lightly cooked, chopped small
50g/2oz/½ cup frozen peas, thawed
5–10ml/1–2 tsp garam masala
15ml/1 tbsp chopped fresh coriander
squeeze of lemon juice
salt

1 Heat the ghee or butter in a large frying pan and fry the onion, ginger and garlic for 5 minutes until the onion has softened. Add the chilli powder and cook for 1 minute, then stir in the potato, cauliflower and peas. Sprinkle with garam masala and set aside. Stir in the coriander, lemon juice and salt.

2 Cut the spring roll wrappers into three strips (or two for larger samosas). Brush the edges with a little flour paste. Place a small spoonful of filling about 2cm/¾in in from the edge of one strip.

3 Fold one corner over the filling to make a triangle and continue folding until the strip has been used and a triangular pastry has been formed. Seal any open edges with the paste.

4 Heat the oil to 190°C/375°F and deep-fry the samosas, a few at a time, until golden. Drain on kitchen paper.

5 Serve hot, garnished with the coriander.

Nutritional information per portion: Energy 56kcal/235kJ; Protein 1.3g; Carbohydrate 10g, of which sugars 0.8g; Fat 1.4g, of which saturates 0.2g; Cholesterol 0mg; Calcium 16mg; Fibre 0.7g; Sodium 8mg.

Chorizo pastry puffs

These flaky pastry puffs make a really superb accompaniment to a glass of cold sherry or beer. For best results, choose a mild cheese, as the chorizo has plenty of flavour.

SERVES 8

225g/8oz puff pastry, thawed if frozen
115g/4oz cured chorizo sausage, finely chopped
50g/2oz/1/2 cup grated cheese
1 small (US medium) egg, beaten
5ml/1 tsp paprika

1 Roll out the pastry thinly on a floured work surface. Using a 7.5cm/3in cutter, stamp out 16 rounds.

2 Preheat the oven to 230°C/450°F/Gas 8. Put the chopped chorizo sausage and grated cheese in a bowl and toss together lightly.

3 Lay one of the pastry rounds in the palm of your hand and place a little of the chorizo mixture across the centre. Using your other hand, pinch the edges of the pastry together along the top to seal. Repeat the process with the remaining rounds to make 16 puffs in all.

4 Place the pastries on a non-stick baking sheet and brush lightly with the beaten egg. Dust the tops of the pastries lightly with a little paprika.

5 Bake the pastries in the oven for 10–12 minutes, until puffed and golden. Serve the chorizo pastry puffs warm, dusted with the remaining paprika.

Nutritional information per portion: Energy 183kcal/763kJ; Protein 5.4g; Carbohydrate 12.1g, of which sugars 0.6g; Fat 13.1g, of which saturates 3g; Cholesterol 36mg; Calcium 73mg; Fibre 0.1g; Sodium 258mg.

Grilled asparagus with salt-cured ham

This is a very simple but delicious dish. Serve this tapas when asparagus is plentiful and not too expensive. If you can't find Serrano ham, use Italian prosciutto or Portuguese presunto.

SERVES 4

6 slices of Serrano ham
12 asparagus spears
15ml/1 tbsp olive oil
sea salt and coarsely ground black pepper

1 Preheat the grill to high. Halve each slice of the ham lengthways and wrap one half around each of the asparagus spears.

2 Brush the ham and asparagus lightly with the olive oil and sprinkle with the salt and coarsely ground black pepper.

3 Place under the grill (broiler). Grill for 5–6 minutes, turning frequently, until the asparagus is tender but still firm. Serve immediately.

Nutritional information per portion: Energy 73kcal/305kJ; Protein 7.1g; Carbohydrate 2g, of which sugars 1.9g; Fat 4.1g, of which saturates 0.8g; Cholesterol 15mg; Calcium 26mg; Fibre 1.5g; Sodium 301mg.

Prawn toasts

These crunchy sesame-topped toasts are simple to prepare and make an ideal quick appetizer, using a food processor to prepare the topping.

MAKES 64

225g/8oz cooked, peeled prawns (shrimp), well drained and patted dry
1 egg white
2 spring onions (scallions), chopped
5ml/1 tsp chopped fresh root ginger
1 garlic clove, chopped
5ml/1 tsp cornflour (cornstarch)
2.5ml/$^1/_2$ tsp salt
2.5ml/$^1/_2$ tsp sugar
2–3 dashes hot pepper sauce
8 slices firm-textured white bread
60–75ml/4–5 tbsp sesame seeds
vegetable oil, for frying
shredded spring onion, to garnish

1 Put the first nine ingredients in the bowl of a food processor and process until the mixture forms a smooth paste, scraping down the side of the bowl from time to time.

2 Spread the paste over the bread slices, then sprinkle over the sesame seeds, pressing to make them stick. Remove the crusts, then cut each slice diagonally into four triangles, and each in half again. Make 64 triangles in total.

3 Heat 5cm/2in vegetable oil in a heavy pan or wok, until hot but not smoking. Fry the triangles in batches for about 30–60 seconds, turning the toasts once. Drain on paper towels and keep hot in the oven while you cook the rest. Serve hot with the spring onion.

Nutritional information per portion: Energy 194kcal/814kJ; Protein 12.1g; Carbohydrate 28.1g, of which sugars 5.2g; Fat 3.8g, of which saturates 0.6g; Cholesterol 98mg; Calcium 108mg; Fibre 0.9g; Sodium 217mg.

Five-spice rib-sticker

Spicy and sweet sticky ribs are a popular choice in Chinese restaurants. Here, you can create your own, but make sure you choose the meatiest spare ribs you can, to make them a real success.

SERVES 8

1kg/2¼ lb pork spare ribs
10ml/2 tsp Chinese five-spice powder
2 garlic cloves, crushed
15ml/1 tbsp grated fresh root ginger
2.5ml/½ tsp chilli sauce
60ml/ 4 tbsp muscovado (molasses) sugar
15ml/1 tbsp sunflower oil
4 spring onions (scallions)

1 If the spare ribs are still joined together, cut between them to separate them (or ask your butcher to do this). Place the spare ribs in a large bowl.

2 Mix together all the remaining ingredients, except the spring onions, and pour over the ribs. Toss well to coat evenly. Cover the bowl and leave to marinate in the fridge overnight.

3 Cook the spare ribs under a preheated medium-hot grill (broiler), turning frequently, for 30–40 minutes. Brush occasionally with the marinade.

4 While the ribs are cooking, finely slice the spring onions – on the diagonal. To serve, place the ribs on a serving plate then scatter the spring onions over the top.

Nutritional information per portion: Energy 309kcal/1297kJ; Protein 38.3g; Carbohydrate 8g, of which sugars 8g; Fat 14g, of which saturates 4.7g; Cholesterol 123mg; Calcium 46mg; Fibre 0.1g; Sodium 75mg.

Skewered lamb with **red onion salsa**

This summery tapas dish is ideal for outdoor eating, although, if the weather fails, the skewers can be cooked indoors rather than barbecued. The salsa makes a refreshing accompaniment.

SERVES 4

225g/8oz lean lamb, cubed
2.5ml/1/2 tsp ground cumin
5ml/1 tsp paprika
15ml/1 tbsp olive oil
salt and ground black pepper

FOR THE SALSA

1 red onion, very thinly sliced
1 large tomato, seeded and chopped
15ml/1 tbsp red wine vinegar
3–4 fresh basil or mint leaves, coarsely torn
small mint leaves, to garnish

1 Place the lamb in a bowl with the cumin, paprika, olive oil and plenty of salt and pepper. Toss well until the lamb is coated with spices.

2 Cover the bowl with clear film (plastic wrap). Set aside in a cool place for a few hours, or in the fridge overnight, so that the lamb absorbs the flavours.

3 Spear the lamb cubes on four small skewers – if using wooden skewers, soak first in cold water for 30 minutes to prevent them from burning.

4 To make the salsa, put the sliced onion, tomato, red wine vinegar and basil or mint leaves in a small bowl and stir together until thoroughly blended. Season to taste with salt, garnish with mint, then set aside while you cook the lamb skewers.

5 Cook on a barbecue or under a preheated grill (broiler) for 5–10 minutes, turning frequently, until the lamb is well browned but still slightly pink in the centre. Serve hot, with the salsa.

Nutritional information per portion: Energy 135kcal/563kJ; Protein 11.4g; Carbohydrate 2g, of which sugars 1.6g; Fat 9.2g, of which saturates 3.4g; Cholesterol 43mg; Calcium 10mg; Fibre 0.5g; Sodium 51mg.

Soups, pâtés and terrines

There are endless possibilities for making soup and the recipes here range from a light Hot-and-Sour Soup to the hearty Vermicelli Soup. Pâtés and terrines are great for impressing your guests. Try the Grilled Vegetable Terrine, which looks stunning, or the deliciously rich Chicken Liver Pâté.

Gazpacho with avocado salsa

Tomatoes, cucumber and peppers form the basis of this classic, chilled soup. Add a spoonful of chunky, fresh avocado salsa and a scattering of croûtons for a delicious summer starter. This is quite a substantial soup, so follow with a light main course, such as grilled fish or chicken.

SERVES 4–6

2 slices day-old bread
600ml/1 pint/2½ cups chilled water
1kg/2¼ lb tomatoes
1 cucumber
1 red (bell) pepper, seeded and chopped
1 green chilli, seeded and chopped
2 garlic cloves, chopped
30ml/2 tbsp extra virgin olive oil
juice of 1 lime and 1 lemon
few drops of Tabasco sauce
salt and ground black pepper
handful of fresh basil, to garnish
8–12 ice cubes, to serve

FOR THE CROÛTONS

2–3 slices day-old bread, crusts removed
1 garlic clove, halved
15–30ml/1–2 tbsp olive oil

FOR THE AVOCADO SALSA

1 ripe avocado
5ml/1 tsp lemon juice
2.5cm/1in piece cucumber, diced
½ red chilli, finely chopped

1 Make the soup first. In a shallow bowl, soak the day-old bread in 150ml/¼ pint/⅔ cup of the chilled water for 5 minutes.

2 Meanwhile, place the tomatoes in a heatproof bowl; cover with boiling water. Leave for 30 seconds, then peel, seed and chop the flesh.

3 Thinly peel the cucumber, cut in half lengthways and scoop out the seeds with a teaspoon. Discard the seeds and chop the flesh.

4 Place the bread, tomatoes, cucumber, red pepper, chilli, garlic, oil, citrus juices, Tabasco and the remaining chilled water in a food processor or blender. Blend until mixed but still chunky. Season and chill well.

5 To make the croûtons, rub the slices of bread with the cut surface of the garlic clove. Cut the bread into cubes and place in a plastic bag with the olive oil. Seal the bag and shake until the bread cubes are coated with the oil. Heat a large non-stick frying pan and fry the croûtons over a medium heat until crisp and golden.

6 Just before serving make the avocado salsa. Halve the avocado, remove the stone (pit), then peel and dice the flesh. Toss the avocado in the lemon juice to prevent it browning, then mix with the cucumber and chilli.

7 Ladle the soup into bowls, add the ice cubes, and top with a spoonful of avocado salsa. Garnish with the basil and hand round the croûtons separately.

COOK'S TIP

For a superior flavour choose Haas avocados with the rough-textured, almost black skins.

Nutritional information per portion: Energy 164kcal/685kJ; Protein 3.5g; Carbohydrate 16.6g, of which sugars 7.9g; Fat 9.7g, of which saturates 1.7g; Cholesterol 0mg; Calcium 40mg; Fibre 3.1g; Sodium 112mg.

Chilled prawn and cucumber soup

If you've never served a chilled soup before, this is the one to try first. Delicious and light, it's the perfect way to celebrate summer. Try crab meat, or cooked, flaked salmon fillet as an alternative.

SERVES 4

25g/1oz/2 tbsp butter
2 shallots, finely chopped
2 garlic cloves, crushed
1 cucumber, peeled, seeded and diced
300ml/½ pint/1¼ cups milk
225g/8oz cooked peeled prawns (shrimp)
15ml/1 tbsp each finely chopped fresh mint, dill, chives and chervil
300ml/½ pint/1¼ cups whipping cream
salt and ground white pepper

FOR THE GARNISH

30ml/2 tbsp crème fraîche or sour cream (optional)
4 large, cooked prawns (shrimp), peeled with tail intact
fresh chives and dill

1 Melt the butter in a pan and cook the shallots and garlic over a low heat until soft but not coloured. Add the cucumber and cook the vegetables gently, stirring frequently, until tender.

2 Stir in the milk, bring almost to the boil, then lower the heat and simmer for 5 minutes. Tip the soup into a blender or food processor and purée until it is very smooth. Season to taste with salt and ground white pepper.

3 Pour the soup into a bowl and set aside to cool. When cool, stir in the prawns, chopped herbs and the whipping cream. Cover, then transfer the soup to the fridge and chill for at least 2 hours.

4 To serve, ladle the soup into four individual bowls and top each portion with a dollop of crème fraîche or sour cream, if using. Place a prawn over the edge of each dish. Garnish with the fresh chives and dill.

Nutritional information per portion: Energy 439kcal/1817kJ; Protein 18.9g; Carbohydrate 7.5g, of which sugars 7.1g; Fat 37.2g, of which saturates 23.1g; Cholesterol 255mg; Calcium 212mg; Fibre 0.5g; Sodium 245mg.

Hot-and-sour soup

This light and invigorating soup originates from Thailand. It is traditionally served at the beginning of a formal Thai meal to stimulate the appetite.

SERVES 4

2 carrots
900ml/1½ pints/3¾ cups vegetable stock
2 Thai chillies, seeded and finely sliced
2 lemon grass stalks, outer leaves removed and each stalk cut into 3 pieces
4 kaffir lime leaves
2 garlic cloves, finely chopped
4 spring onions (scallions), finely sliced
5ml/1 tsp sugar
juice of 1 lime
45ml/3 tbsp chopped fresh coriander (cilantro)
salt, to taste
130g/4½ oz/1 cup Japanese tofu, sliced

1 To make carrot flowers, cut each carrot in half crossways, then, using a small sharp knife, cut four V-shaped channels lengthways. Slice the carrots into thin rounds and set aside.

2 Pour the vegetable stock into a saucepan. Reserve 2.5ml/½ tsp of the chillies and add the rest to the pan with the lemon grass pieces, the lime leaves, garlic and half the spring onions. Bring the mixture to the boil, then reduce the heat and simmer for 20 minutes. Remove from the heat, strain the stock and discard the flavourings.

3 Return the stock to the pan, add the reserved chillies and spring onions, the sugar, lime juice, coriander and salt to taste.

4 Simmer for 5 minutes, then add the carrot flowers and tofu slices, and cook the soup for a further 2 minutes until the carrot is just tender. Serve hot.

Nutritional information per portion: Energy 43kcal/180kJ; Protein 3.4g; Carbohydrate 3.9g, of which sugars 3.6g; Fat 1.7g, of which saturates 0.2g; Cholesterol 0mg; Calcium 202mg; Fibre 1.4g; Sodium 13mg.

Spanish garlic soup

This is a simple and satisfying soup, which is based on one of the most popular ingredients that is used in the Mediterranean region – garlic!

SERVES 4

30ml/2 tbsp olive oil
4 large garlic cloves, peeled
4 slices French bread, 5mm/¼in thick
15ml/1 tbsp paprika
1 litre/1¾ pints/4 cups beef stock
1.5ml/¼ tsp ground cumin
pinch of saffron threads
4 eggs
salt and ground black pepper
chopped fresh parsley, to garnish

1 Preheat the oven to 230°C/450°F/Gas 8. Heat the oil in a large pan. Add the whole garlic cloves and cook until golden. Remove and set aside. Fry the bread in the oil until golden, then set aside.

2 Add the paprika to the pan, and fry for a few seconds, stirring. Stir in the beef stock, the cumin and saffron, then add the reserved fried garlic, crushing the cloves with the back of a wooden spoon. Season with salt and ground black pepper then cook for about 5 minutes.

3 Ladle the soup into four ovenproof bowls and gently break an egg into each one. Place the slices of fried French bread on top of the eggs and place in the oven for about 3–4 minutes, or until the eggs are set. Sprinkle with chopped fresh parsley and serve immediately.

COOK'S TIP

Use home-made beef stock for the best flavour or buy prepared stock from your supermarket – you'll find it in the chilled counter. Never use stock cubes as they contain too much salt.

Nutritional information per portion: Energy 253kcal/1061kJ; Protein 11.8g; Carbohydrate 26.5g, of which sugars 1.5g; Fat 12g, of which saturates 2.5g; Cholesterol 190mg; Calcium 82mg; Fibre 2g; Sodium 318mg.

Soya beansprout soup

This soup has a hint of spiciness and a refreshing nutty flavour. It is quick and easy to make and is reputed to have a calming effect on the stomach.

SERVES 4

200g/7 oz/generous 2 cups soya beansprouts
1 red or green chilli
15 dried anchovies
1 spring onion (scallion), finely sliced
3 garlic cloves, chopped
salt

1 Wash the soya beansprouts and trim off the tail ends.

2 Halve and seed the chilli and cut it diagonally into thin slices.

3 Add 750ml/1¼ pints/3 cups water to a pan with the dried anchovies. Bring to the boil. After boiling for 15 minutes remove the anchovies and discard them.

4 Add the soya beansprouts and boil for 5 minutes, ensuring the lid is kept tightly on the pan. Add the spring onion, sliced chilli and garlic, and boil for a further 3 minutes. Add salt to taste, and serve.

Nutritional information per portion: Energy 41kcal/173kJ; Protein 4.6g; Carbohydrate 2.7g, of which sugars 1.2g; Fat 1.4g, of which saturates 0.2g; Cholesterol 7mg; Calcium 46mg; Fibre 1g; Sodium 445mg.

Spinach and **tofu soup**

This soup is really delicious as well as being very quick to make. If fresh spinach is not in season, watercress or lettuce can be used as an alternative.

SERVES 4

1 x 200g/7oz block tofu
115g/4oz spinach leaves
750ml/1¼ pints/3 cups vegetable stock
15ml/1 tbsp light soy sauce
salt and ground black pepper

1 Rinse the tofu then cut into 12 small pieces, each about 5mm/¼in thick. Wash the spinach leaves thoroughly and cut them into small pieces.

2 In a wok or large pan, bring the stock to a rolling boil. Add the tofu and soy sauce, bring back to the boil and simmer for about 2 minutes.

3 Add the spinach and simmer for a further minute. Skim the surface, then add salt and ground black pepper to taste, and serve.

Nutritional information per portion: Energy 50kcal/208kJ; Protein 5.5g; Carbohydrate 1.2g, of which sugars 0.9g; Fat 2.6g, of which saturates 0.3g; Cholesterol 0mg; Calcium 337mg; Fibre 0.6g; Sodium 310mg.

Avocado soup

This is a simple but delicious soup. To add a subtle garlic flavour, rub the cut side of a garlic clove around the soup bowls before adding the soup.

SERVES 4

2 large ripe avocados
1 litre/1¾ pints/4 cups chicken stock
250ml/8fl oz/1 cup single (light) cream
salt and ground white pepper
15ml/1 tbsp finely chopped coriander (cilantro), to garnish (optional)

1 Cut the avocados in half, remove the stones and mash the flesh. Put the flesh into a sieve and using a wooden spoon, press the avocado through into a warmed bowl.

2 Heat the chicken stock with the cream in a saucepan. When the mixture is hot, but not boiling, whisk it into the puréed avocado.

3 Season to taste with salt and pepper. Serve immediately, sprinkled with the coriander, if using. The soup may be served chilled, if liked.

COOK'S TIP

Avocados are ripe when they yield slightly if gently pressed at the stalk end.

Nutritional information per portion: Energy 263kcal/1087kJ; Protein 3.5g; Carbohydrate 2.8g, of which sugars 1.8g; Fat 26.4g, of which saturates 10.7g; Cholesterol 34mg; Calcium 64mg; Fibre 2.6g; Sodium 23mg.

Vermicelli soup

This hearty soup brings a taste of the Mediterranean to the table. The inclusion of fresh coriander adds a piquancy to this soup and complements the tomato flavour.

SERVES 4

30ml/2 tbsp olive or corn oil
50g/2oz vermicelli
1 onion, roughly chopped
1 garlic clove, chopped
450g/1lb tomatoes, peeled, seeded and roughly chopped
1 litre/1¾ pints/4 cups chicken stock
1.5ml/¼ tsp sugar
15ml/1 tbsp finely chopped fresh coriander (cilantro)
salt and ground black pepper
chopped fresh coriander (cilantro), to garnish
25g/1oz/¼ cup freshly grated Parmesan cheese, to serve

1 Heat the oil in a frying pan and sauté the vermicelli over a moderate heat until golden brown. Move it about continuously to avoid burning. Remove the vermicelli with a slotted spoon or tongs and drain on kitchen paper.

2 Purée the onion, garlic and tomatoes in a food processor or blender until smooth. Return the frying pan to the heat. When the oil is hot again, add the purée to the pan. Cook, stirring constantly to prevent sticking, for about 5 minutes or until thick.

3 Transfer the purée to a saucepan. Add the vermicelli and pour in the stock. Season with sugar, salt and pepper. Stir in the coriander, bring to the boil, then lower the heat, cover the pan and simmer the soup gently until the vermicelli is tender.

4 Serve in warmed soup bowls, sprinkle with chopped fresh coriander and offer the grated Parmesan cheese separately.

Nutritional information per portion: Energy 141kcal/589kJ; Protein 4.4g; Carbohydrate 13.3g, of which sugars 3.5g; Fat 7.9g, of which saturates 2.2g; Cholesterol 6mg; Calcium 86mg; Fibre 1.1g; Sodium 79mg.

Baby carrot and fennel soup

Sweet tender carrots find their moment of glory in this delicately spiced soup. Fennel provides a subtle aniseed flavour that does not overpower the carrots.

SERVES 4

50g/2oz/4 tbsp butter
1 small bunch spring onions (scallions), chopped
150g/5oz fennel bulb, chopped
1 celery stick, chopped
450g/1lb new carrots, grated
2.5ml/½ tsp ground cumin
150g/5oz new potatoes, peeled and diced
1.2 litres/2 pints/5 cups chicken or vegetable stock
60ml/4 tbsp double (heavy) cream
salt and ground black pepper
60ml/4 tbsp chopped fresh parsley, to garnish

1 Melt the butter in a large pan and add the spring onions, fennel, celery, carrots and cumin. Cover and cook for about 5 minutes, or until soft.

2 Add the diced potatoes and chicken or vegetable stock, and simmer the mixture for a further 10 minutes.

3 Liquidize the soup in the pan with a hand-held blender. Stir in the cream and season to taste. Serve in individual soup bowls and garnish with chopped parsley and fennel leaves.

COOK'S TIP

For convenience, you can freeze the soup before adding the cream, seasoning and parsley.

Nutritional information per portion: Energy 244kcal/1010kJ; Protein 2.5g; Carbohydrate 16.8g, of which sugars 10.6g; Fat 19g, of which saturates 11.7g; Cholesterol 47mg; Calcium 62mg; Fibre 4.4g; Sodium 122mg.

Chilled asparagus soup

This soup provides a delightful way to enjoy a favourite seasonal vegetable. Choose bright, crisp-looking asparagus with firm, slender stalks for the best effect.

SERVES 6

900g/2lb fresh asparagus
60ml/4 tbsp olive oil
175g/6oz/1½ cups sliced leeks or spring onions (scallions)
45ml/3 tbsp flour
1.5 litres/2½ pints/6¼ cups chicken stock or water
120ml/4fl oz/½ cup single (light) cream or natural (plain) yogurt
salt and ground black pepper
15ml/1 tbsp minced fresh tarragon or chervil

1 Cut the top 6cm/2½in off the asparagus spears. Blanch these tips in boiling water for 5-6 minutes until they are just tender. Drain. Cut each tip into 2 or 3 pieces, and set aside. Trim the ends of the stalks, removing any brown or woody parts. Chop the asparagus stalks into 1cm/½in pieces.

2 Heat the olive oil in a heavy pan. Add the leeks or spring onions and cook over a low heat for 5–8 minutes, until softened. Stir in the chopped asparagus stalks, cover and cook for a further 6–8 minutes. Add the flour and stir well. Cook for 3–4 minutes, uncovered, stirring occasionally. Add the stock or water and bring to the boil, stirring frequently, then reduce the heat and simmer for 30 minutes. Season the soup to taste with salt and pepper.

3 Purée the soup in a food processor or blender and strain, if necessary. Stir in the tips, most of the cream or yogurt, and the herbs. Cool then chill well. To serve, stir well, season and garnish with the remaining cream or yogurt.

Nutritional information per portion: Energy 163kcal/676kJ; Protein 6.4g; Carbohydrate 10.2g, of which sugars 4.3g; Fat 11g, of which saturates 6.5g; Cholesterol 27mg; Calcium 82mg; Fibre 3.2g; Sodium 54mg.

Fresh tomato soup

Intensely flavoured sun-ripened tomatoes need little embellishment in this fresh-tasting soup. On a hot day, this Italian soup is also delicious chilled.

SERVES 6

1.3–1.6kg/3–3½ lb ripe tomatoes
400ml/14fl oz/1⅔ cups chicken or vegetable stock
45ml/3 tbsp sun-dried tomato paste
30–45ml/2–3 tbsp balsamic vinegar
10–15ml/2–3 tsp caster (superfine) sugar
small handful of basil leaves, plus extra to garnish
salt and ground black pepper
toasted cheese croûtes and crème fraîche, to serve

1 Plunge the tomatoes into boiling water for 30 seconds, then refresh in cold water. Peel away the skins and quarter the tomatoes. Put them in a large saucepan and pour over the chicken or vegetable stock. Bring just to the boil, reduce the heat, cover and simmer the mixture gently for 10 minutes until the tomatoes are pulpy.

2 Stir in the tomato paste, vinegar, sugar and basil. Season with salt and pepper, then cook gently, stirring, for 2 minutes. Process the soup in a blender or food processor, then return to the pan and reheat gently. Serve in bowls topped with one or two toasted cheese croûtes and a spoonful of crème fraîche, garnished with basil leaves.

Nutritional information per portion: Energy 49kcal/210kJ; Protein 1.9g; Carbohydrate 9.5g, of which sugars 9.5g; Fat 0.7g, of which saturates 0.2g; Cholesterol 0mg; Calcium 19mg; Fibre 2.4g; Sodium 38mg.

Malayan prawn laksa

This spicy prawn and noodle soup tastes just as good when made with fresh crab meat or any flaked, cooked fish. You can also use ready-made laksa paste, available from specialist stores.

SERVES 3–4

115g/4oz rice vermicelli or stir-fry rice noodles
15ml/1 tbsp vegetable or groundnut oil
600ml/1 pint/2½ cups fish stock
400ml/14fl oz/1⅔ cups thin coconut milk
30ml/2 tbsp Thai fish sauce
½ lime
16–24 cooked peeled prawns (shrimp)
salt and cayenne pepper
60ml/4 tbsp fresh coriander (cilantro) sprigs and leaves, chopped, to garnish

FOR THE SPICY PASTE
2 lemon grass stalks, finely chopped
2 fresh red chillies, seeded and chopped
2.5cm/1in piece fresh root ginger, peeled and sliced
2.5ml/½ tsp dried shrimp paste
2 garlic cloves, chopped
2.5ml/½ tsp ground turmeric
30ml/2 tbsp tamarind paste

1 Cook the rice vermicelli in a large pan of boiling salted water according to the instructions on the packet. Tip into a large sieve or colander, then rinse under cold water and drain. Set aside and keep warm.

2 To make the spicy paste, place all the ingredients in a mortar and pound with a pestle. Or, if you prefer, put the ingredients in a food processor or blender and then process until a smooth paste is formed.

3 Heat the oil in a large pan, add the paste and fry, stirring constantly, for a few moments to release the flavours, but be careful not to let it burn. Add the fish stock and coconut milk and bring to the boil. Stir in the fish sauce, then simmer for 5 minutes. Season with salt and cayenne to taste, adding a squeeze of lime. Add the prawns and heat through for a few seconds.

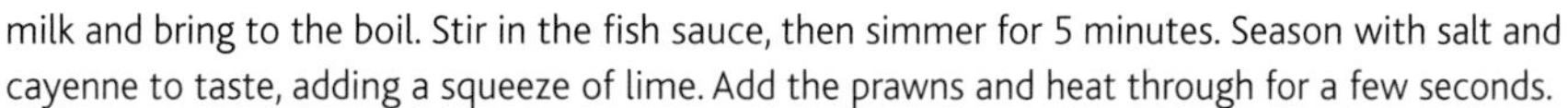

4 Divide the noodles among three or four soup plates. Pour the soup over, making sure that each portion includes an equal number of prawns. Garnish with coriander and serve piping hot.

Nutritional information per portion: Energy 194kcal/814kJ; Protein 12.1g; Carbohydrate 28.1g, of which sugars 5.2g; Fat 3.8g, of which saturates 0.6g; Cholesterol 98mg; Calcium 108mg; Fibre 0.9g; Sodium 217mg.

Tortellini chanterelle broth

The savoury-sweet quality of chanterelle mushrooms combines well in a simple broth with spinach-and-ricotta-filled tortellini. The sherry adds a lovely warming effect.

SERVES 4

350g/12oz fresh spinach and ricotta tortellini, or 175g/6oz dried
1.2 litres/2 pints/5 cups chicken stock
75ml/5 tbsp dry sherry
175g/6oz fresh chanterelle mushrooms, trimmed and sliced, or 15g/½ oz/ ½ cup dried chanterelles
chopped fresh parsley, to garnish

1 Cook the tortellini according to the packet instructions. Bring the chicken stock to the boil, add the dry sherry and fresh or dried mushrooms and then simmer for 10 minutes.

2 Strain the tortellini, add to the stock, then ladle the broth into four warmed bowls, making sure each contains the same proportions of tortellini and mushrooms. Garnish with the chopped parsley and serve.

Nutritional information per portion: Energy 204kcal/859kJ; Protein 7.6g; Carbohydrate 23.4g, of which sugars 1.5g; Fat 4.3g, of which saturates 0.1g; Cholesterol 0mg; Calcium 106mg; Fibre 1.6g; Sodium 185mg.

Curried parsnip soup

The spices, which impart a delicious, mild curry flavour that carries an exotic breath of India, are the perfect way to bring out the sweetness of the parsnips.

SERVES 4

25g/1oz/2 tbsp butter
1 garlic clove, crushed
1 onion, chopped
5ml/1 tsp ground cumin
5ml/1 tsp ground coriander
4 parsnips, peeled and sliced
10ml/2 tsp medium curry paste
450ml/3/4 pint/scant 2 cups chicken stock
450ml/3/4 pint/scant 2 cups milk
60ml/4 tbsp sour cream
squeeze of lemon juice
salt and ground black pepper
fresh chives, to garnish
bread, to serve

1 Heat the butter in a large pan and add the garlic and onion. Fry gently for 4–5 minutes, until lightly golden. Stir in the cumin and coriander and cook for a further 1–2 minutes.

2 Add the parsnips and stir until well coated with the butter, then stir in the curry paste, followed by the stock. Cover the pan and simmer for 15 minutes, until the parsnips are tender.

3 Ladle the soup into a blender or food processor and process until smooth. Return the soup to the pan and stir in the milk. Heat gently for 2–3 minutes, then add half the sour cream and all the lemon juice. Season well. Serve in bowls topped with swirls of the remaining sour cream and the chopped fresh chives, accompanied by the bread.

Nutritional information per portion: Energy 150kcal/623kJ; Protein 4.7g; Carbohydrate 7.8g, of which sugars 6.8g; Fat 11.4g, of which saturates 7g; Cholesterol 32mg; Calcium 170mg; Fibre 0.8g; Sodium 112mg.

Split pea soup

This tasty winter soup is a perfect family starter, and is great for cooking when you have lots of left-over food, such as cold ham and vegetables, from the holidays.

SERVES 4–6

25g/1oz/2 tbsp butter
1 large onion, chopped
1 large celery stick with leaves, chopped
2 carrots, chopped
1 smoked gammon (smoked or cured ham) knuckle, 450g/1lb
2 litres/3½ pints/8½ cups water
350g/12oz/1½ cups split peas
30ml/2 tbsp chopped fresh parsley, plus extra to garnish
2.5ml/½ tsp dried thyme
1 bay leaf
about 30ml/2 tbsp lemon juice
salt and ground black pepper

1 Melt the butter in a large heavy pan. Add the onion, celery and carrots and cook until soft, stirring occasionally.

2 Place all the remaining ingredients in the pan. Bring to the boil, cover and simmer gently for 2 hours.

3 After 2 hours, once the peas are very tender, remove the gammon knuckle. Leave it to cool a bit, then remove the skin and cut the meat away from the bones. Discard the skin and bones, then cut the meat into chunks as evenly sized as possible.

4 Return the chunks of gammon to the soup. Discard the bay leaf. Taste and adjust the seasoning with more lemon juice, salt and pepper. Serve hot, sprinkled with fresh parsley.

Nutritional information per portion: Energy 244kcal/1033kJ; Protein 17.2g; Carbohydrate 35.2g, of which sugars 3.4g; Fat 4.8g, of which saturates 2.5g; Cholesterol 19mg; Calcium 40mg; Fibre 3.5g; Sodium 254mg.

French onion and morel soup

French onion soup is appreciated for its light beefy taste. Few improvements can be made to this classic soup, but some richly scented morel mushrooms will impart an intense, savoury flavour.

SERVES 4

50g/2oz/4 tbsp unsalted butter, plus extra for spreading
15ml/1 tbsp vegetable oil
3 onions, sliced
900ml/1½ pints/3¾ cups beef stock
75ml/5 tbsp Madeira or sherry
8 dried morel mushrooms
4 slices French bread
75g/3oz Gruyère, Beaufort or Fontina cheese, grated
30ml/2 tbsp chopped fresh parsley

1 Melt the butter with the oil in a large frying pan, then add the sliced onions and cook gently for 10–15 minutes until the onions are a rich mahogany brown colour.

2 Transfer the browned onions to a large pan, cover with beef stock, add the Madeira or sherry and the dried morels, then simmer for 20 minutes.

3 Preheat the grill (broiler) to a moderate temperature and toast the French bread on both sides. Spread one side with butter and heap with the grated cheese. Ladle the soup into four flameproof bowls, float the cheesy toasts on top and grill (broil) until they are crisp and brown. Alternatively, grill (broil) the cheese-topped toast, then place one slice in each warmed soup bowl before ladling the hot soup over it. The toast will float to the surface. Scatter over the chopped fresh parsley and serve.

Nutritional information per portion: Energy 304kcal/1263kJ; Protein 8.8g; Carbohydrate 22.6g, of which sugars 8g; Fat 20.1g, of which saturates 10.9g; Cholesterol 45mg; Calcium 225mg; Fibre 2.8g; Sodium 349mg.

Wild mushroom soup

Wild mushrooms are expensive, but dried porcini have a concentrated flavour, so only a small quantity is needed. The beef stock helps to strengthen the earthy taste of the mushrooms.

SERVES 4

25g/1oz/1 cup dried porcini mushrooms
30ml/2 tbsp olive oil
15g/½ oz/1 tbsp butter
2 each leeks and shallots, thinly sliced
1 garlic clove, roughly chopped
225g/8oz/3 cups fresh wild mushrooms
about 1.2 litres/2 pints/5 cups beef stock
2.5ml/½ tsp dried thyme
150ml/¼ pint/⅔ cup double (heavy) cream
salt and ground black pepper
thyme sprigs, to garnish

1 Put the dried porcini in a bowl, add 250ml/8fl oz/1 cup warm water and leave to soak for 20–30 minutes. Lift out of the liquid and squeeze over the bowl to remove as much of the soaking liquid as possible. Strain all the liquid and reserve to use later. Finely chop the porcini.

2 Heat the oil and butter in a large saucepan until foaming. Add the sliced leeks, chopped shallots and garlic and cook gently for about 5 minutes, stirring frequently, until soft.

3 Chop or slice the fresh wild mushrooms and add to the pan. Stir over a medium heat for a few minutes until they begin to soften. Pour in the stock and bring to the boil. Add the porcini, their soaking liquid, the dried thyme and salt and ground black pepper. Lower the heat, half cover the pan and simmer the soup gently for 30 minutes, stirring occasionally.

4 Pour about three-quarters of the soup into a blender or food processor and process until very smooth. Return the purée to the soup remaining in the pan, stir in the cream and heat through. Check the consistency and add a little more stock or water if the soup is too thick. Taste for seasoning. Serve hot garnished with thyme sprigs.

Nutritional information per portion: Energy 287kcal/1183kJ; Protein 2.6g; Carbohydrate 3.5g, of which sugars 2.7g; Fat 29.3g, of which saturates 15.4g; Cholesterol 59mg; Calcium 38mg; Fibre 1.9g; Sodium 35mg.

Spinach and **rice soup**

Use very fresh, young spinach leaves in the preparation of this light and fresh-tasting soup. If you cannot find Pecorino cheese, you can use the slightly milder tasting Parmesan instead.

SERVES 4

675g/1½ lb fresh spinach, washed
45ml/3 tbsp extra virgin olive oil
1 small onion, finely chopped
2 garlic cloves, finely chopped
1 small fresh red chilli, seeded and finely chopped
115g/4oz/generous 1 cup risotto rice
1.2 litres/2 pints/5 cups vegetable stock
salt and ground black pepper
60ml/4 tbsp grated Pecorino cheese

1 Place the spinach in a large pan with just the water that clings to its leaves after washing. Add a large pinch of salt. Heat gently until the spinach has wilted, then remove from the heat and drain, reserving any liquid.

2 Either chop the spinach finely using a large knife or place in a food processor and process to a fairly coarse purée.

3 Heat the oil in a large saucepan and gently cook the onion, garlic and chilli for 4–5 minutes until softened. Stir in the rice until well coated, then pour in the stock and reserved spinach liquid. Bring to the boil, lower the heat and simmer for 10 minutes. Add the spinach, with salt and pepper to taste.

4 Cook for a further 5–7 minutes, until the rice is tender. Check the seasoning and adjust if needed. Serve with the Pecorino cheese.

Nutritional information per portion: Energy 293kcal/1215kJ; Protein 13g; Carbohydrate 26.8g, of which sugars 3.4g; Fat 14.7g, of which saturates 4.4g; Cholesterol 15mg; Calcium 476mg; Fibre 3.8g; Sodium 400mg.

Broccoli soup with garlic toast

This is an Italian recipe, originating from Rome. For the best flavour and colour, use the freshest broccoli you can find and a good-quality Parmesan cheese, such as Parmigiano-Reggiano.

SERVES 6

675g/1½ lb broccoli spears
1.75 litres/3 pints/7½ cups chicken or vegetable stock
salt and ground black pepper
30ml/2 tbsp fresh lemon juice
freshly grated Parmesan cheese (optional), to serve

FOR THE GARLIC TOAST
6 slices white bread
1 large garlic clove, halved

1 Using a small sharp knife, peel the broccoli stems, starting from the base of the stalks and pulling gently up towards the florets. (The peel comes off very easily.) Chop the broccoli into small chunks.

2 Bring the stock to the boil in a large pan. Add the chopped broccoli and simmer for 20 minutes, or until soft.

3 Purée about half of the soup in a blender or food processor and then mix into the rest of the soup. Season with salt, pepper and lemon juice.

4 Just before serving, reheat the soup to just below boiling point. Toast the bread, rub with garlic and cut into quarters. Place 3 or 4 pieces of toast in the base of each soup plate. Ladle on the soup. Serve at once, with grated Parmesan cheese, if using.

Nutritional information per portion: Energy 98kcal/413kJ; Protein 7.2g; Carbohydrate 14.6g, of which sugars 2.4g; Fat 1.5g, of which saturates 0.2g; Cholesterol 0mg; Calcium 91mg; Fibre 3.4g; Sodium 139mg.

Chilled tomato and **sweet pepper soup**

This recipe was inspired by the most well-known chilled soup, Spanish gazpacho. However, the difference is that this soup is cooked first, then chilled.

SERVES 4

2 red (bell) peppers, halved, cored and seeded
45ml/3 tbsp olive oil
1 onion, finely chopped
2 garlic cloves, crushed
675g/1½ lb ripe well-flavoured tomatoes
150ml/¼ pint/⅔ cup red wine
600ml/1 pint/2½ cups chicken stock
salt and ground black pepper
chopped fresh chives, to garnish

FOR THE CROÛTONS

2 slices white bread, crusts removed
60ml/4 tbsp olive oil

1 Cut each red pepper half into quarters. Place skin-side up on a grill (broiler) rack and cook until the skins are charred. Transfer to a bowl and cover with a plate or pop into a plastic bag and seal.

2 Heat the oil in a large pan. Add the onion and garlic and cook gently until soft. Meanwhile, remove the skin from the peppers and roughly chop the flesh. Cut the tomatoes into chunks.

3 Add the peppers and tomatoes to the pan, then cover and cook gently for 10 minutes. Add the wine and cook for a further 5 minutes, then add the stock and salt and pepper and continue to simmer for 20 minutes.

4 To make the croûtons, cut the bread into cubes. Heat the oil in a small frying pan, add the bread and fry until golden. Drain on kitchen paper and store in an airtight box once cool.

5 Process the soup in a blender or food processor until smooth. Pour into a clean glass or ceramic bowl and leave to cool thoroughly before chilling in the fridge for at least 3 hours. When the soup is cold, season to taste.

6 Serve the soup in bowls, topped with the croûtons and garnished with chopped chives.

Nutritional information per portion: Energy 292kcal/1216kJ; Protein 3.4g; Carbohydrate 18.8g, of which sugars 11.8g; Fat 20.4g, of which saturates 3g; Cholesterol 0mg; Calcium 40mg; Fibre 3.5g; Sodium 92mg.

Smoked haddock pâté

Arbroath smokies are small haddock that are beheaded and gutted, but not split, before being salted and hot-smoked, creating a great flavour.

SERVES 6

butter, for greasing
3 large Arbroath smokies, about 225g/8oz each
275g/10oz/1¼ cups soft white (farmer's cheese)
3 eggs, beaten
30–45ml/2–3 tbsp lemon juice
ground black pepper
chervil sprigs, to garnish
lemon wedges and lettuce leaves, to serve

1 Preheat the oven to 160°C/325°F/Gas 3. Carefully butter six ramekin dishes.

2 Lay the smokies in an ovenproof dish and heat through in the oven for 10 minutes. Carefully remove the skin and bones from the smokies, then flake the flesh into a bowl.

3 Mash the fish with a fork and work in the cheese, then the eggs. Add lemon juice and pepper.

4 Divide the fish mixture equally among the ramekins and place in a roasting pan. Pour hot water into the roasting pan to come halfway up the dishes. Bake for 30 minutes, until just set.

5 Allow to cool for 2–3 minutes, then run a knife point around the edge of each dish and invert on to a warmed plate. Garnish with chervil sprigs and serve with the lemon wedges and lettuce.

Nutritional information per portion: Energy 307kcal/1274kJ; Protein 22.2g; Carbohydrate 1.5g, of which sugars 1.5g; Fat 23.7g, of which saturates 7.3g; Cholesterol 166mg; Calcium 59mg; Fibre 0g; Sodium 723mg.

Smoked salmon pâté

This pâté is made in individual ramekins lined with smoked salmon so that it looks really special. Taste the mousse as you are making it, and add more lemon juice and seasoning if necessary.

SERVES 4

350g/12oz thinly sliced smoked salmon (wild if possible)
150ml/¼ pint/⅔ cup double (heavy) cream
finely grated rind and juice of 1 lemon
salt and ground black pepper
melba toast, to serve

1 Line four small ramekin dishes with clear film (plastic wrap). Then line the dishes with 115g/4oz of the smoked salmon cut into strips long enough to flop over the edges.

2 In a food processor fitted with a metal blade, process the rest of the salmon with the double cream, lemon rind and juice, salt and plenty of ground black pepper.

3 Pack the lined ramekins with the smoked salmon pâté and wrap over the loose strips of salmon. Cover the ramekins with clear film and chill for 30 minutes. Invert on to plates; serve with Melba toast.

Nutritional information per portion: Energy 311kcal/1293kJ; Protein 22.9g; Carbohydrate 0.8g, of which sugars 0.8g; Fat 24.1g, of which saturates 13.2g; Cholesterol 82mg; Calcium 36mg; Fibre 0g; Sodium 1654mg.

Herbed liver pâté pie

Serve this highly flavoured pâté with a glass of Pilsner beer for a change from wine, and some spicy dill pickles to complement the strong tastes.

SERVES 10

675g/1½ lb minced pork
350g/12oz pork liver
350g/12oz/2 cups diced cooked ham
1 small onion, finely chopped
30ml/2 tbsp chopped fresh parsley
5ml/1 tsp German mustard
30ml/2 tbsp Kirsch
5ml/1 tsp salt
beaten egg, for sealing and glazing
25g/1oz sachet aspic jelly
250ml/8fl oz/1 cup boiling water
ground black pepper
mustard, bread and dill pickles, to serve

FOR THE PASTRY

450g/1lb/4 cups plain (all-purpose) flour
275g/10oz/1¼ cups butter
2 eggs plus 1 egg yolk
30ml/2 tbsp water

1 Preheat the oven to 200°C/400°F/Gas 6. For the pastry, sift the flour and salt and rub in the butter. Beat the eggs, egg yolk and water, and mix into the flour. Knead the dough until smooth. Roll out two-thirds on a lightly floured surface and use to line a 10 x 25cm/4 x 10in hinged loaf tin. Trim any excess dough.

2 Process half the pork and all of the liver until fairly smooth. Stir in the remaining pork, ham, onion, parsley, mustard, Kirsch, salt and black pepper. Spoon into the tin and level the surface.

3 Roll out the remaining pastry and use it to top the pie. Seal the edges with egg. Decorate with pastry trimmings and glaze with egg. Make 4 holes in the top. Bake for 40 minutes, turn the oven down to 180°C/350°F/Gas 4 and cook for another hour. Cover with foil. Cool in the tin.

4 Make up the aspic jelly with the boiling water. Dissolve, then cool. Make a small hole near the pie edge and pour in the aspic. Chill for 2 hours. Serve in slices with mustard, bread and dill pickles.

Nutritional information per portion: Energy 576kcal/2407kJ; Protein 32.9g; Carbohydrate 36g, of which sugars 1.6g; Fat 33.7g, of which saturates 18.1g; Cholesterol 273mg; Calcium 87mg; Fibre 1.5g; Sodium 888mg.

Chicken liver pâté

This rich-tasting, smooth pâté will keep in the fridge for about 3 days. Serve with thick slices of hot toast or warmed bread – a rustic olive oil bread such as ciabatta would be a good partner.

SERVES 8

115g/4oz chicken livers, thawed if frozen, trimmed
1 small garlic clove, chopped
15ml/1 tbsp sherry
30ml/2 tbsp brandy
50g/2oz/¼ cup butter, melted
2.5ml/¼ tsp salt
fresh herbs and black peppercorns, to garnish
hot toast or warmed bread, to serve

1 Preheat the oven to 150°C/300°F/Gas 2. Place the chicken livers and chopped garlic in a food processor or blender and process until they are smooth.

2 With the motor running, gradually add the sherry, brandy, melted butter and salt.

3 Pour the liver mixture into two 7.5cm/3in ramekins. Cover the tops with foil but do not allow the foil to come down the sides too far.

4 Place the ramekins in a small roasting pan and carefully pour in boiling water so that it comes to about halfway up the sides of the ramekins.

5 Carefully transfer the pan to the oven and bake the pâté for 20 minutes. Leave to cool to room temperature, then remove the ramekins from the pan and chill until needed. Serve the pâté with toast or bread, garnished with herbs and peppercorns.

Nutritional information per portion: Energy 70kcal/290kJ; Protein 2.6g; Carbohydrate 0.1g, of which sugars 0.1g; Fat 5.5g, of which saturates 3.4g; Cholesterol 68mg; Calcium 2mg; Fibre 0g; Sodium 49mg.

Sea trout mousse

This deliciously creamy mousse makes a little sea trout go a long way. It is equally good when made with salmon. Serve with crisp Melba toast or triangles of lightly toasted pitta bread.

SERVES 6

250g/9oz sea trout fillet
120ml/4fl oz/½ cup fish stock
2 gelatine leaves, or 15ml/1 tbsp powdered gelatine
juice of ½ lemon
30ml/2 tbsp dry sherry or dry vermouth
30ml/2 tbsp freshly grated Parmesan
300ml/½ pint/1¼ cups whipping cream
2 egg whites
15ml/1 tbsp sunflower oil, for greasing
salt and ground white pepper

FOR THE GARNISH

5cm/2in piece cucumber, with peel, thinly sliced and halved
fresh dill or chervil, chopped

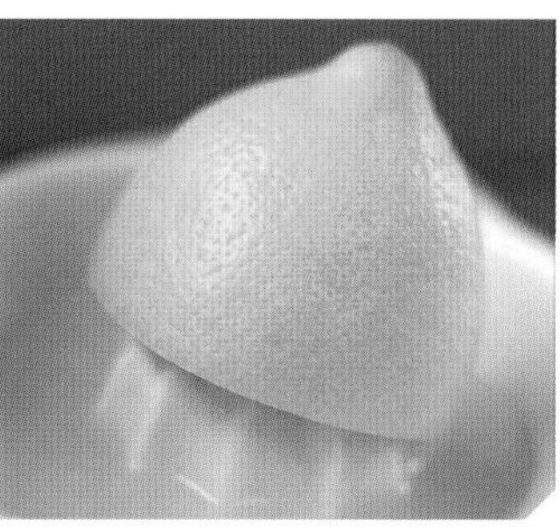

1 Put the sea trout in a shallow pan. Pour in the stock and heat to simmering point. Poach the fish for 3–4 minutes, until it is lightly cooked. Strain the stock into a jug and leave the trout to cool slightly.

2 Add the gelatine to the hot stock and stir until it has dissolved completely. Set aside until required.

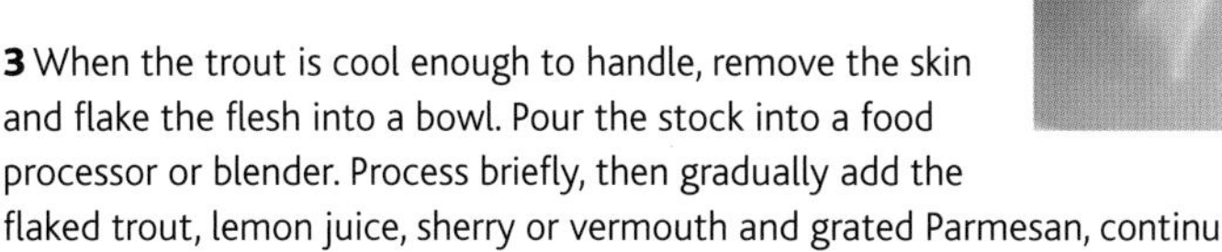
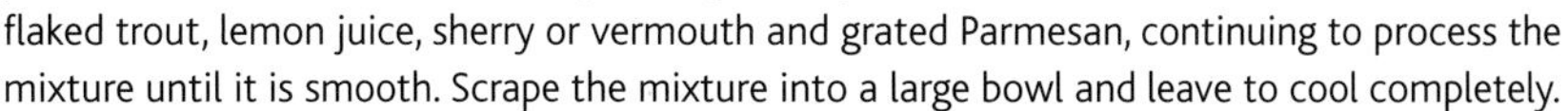

3 When the trout is cool enough to handle, remove the skin and flake the flesh into a bowl. Pour the stock into a food processor or blender. Process briefly, then gradually add the flaked trout, lemon juice, sherry or vermouth and grated Parmesan, continuing to process the mixture until it is smooth. Scrape the mixture into a large bowl and leave to cool completely.

4 Lightly whip the cream in a bowl; fold it into the cold trout mixture. Season to taste, then cover with clear film (plastic wrap) and chill in the fridge until the mousse is just starting to set. In a grease-free bowl, beat the egg whites with a pinch of salt until they are softly peaking. Using a metal spoon, stir about one-third into the fish mixture to slacken it slightly, then fold in the rest.

5 Lightly grease six ramekins or similar individual serving dishes. Divide the mousse among the prepared dishes and level the surface. Place in the fridge for 2–3 hours, until set. Just before serving, arrange a few slices of cucumber and a herb sprig on top and scatter over a little dill or chervil.

Nutritional information per portion: Energy 241kcal/999kJ; Protein 12.3g; Carbohydrate 1.8g, of which sugars 1.8g; Fat 20g, of which saturates 14.5g; Cholesterol 9mg; Calcium 104mg; Fibre 0.1g; Sodium 127mg.

Salmon rillettes

This economical way of serving salmon, with only one little fillet required per head, makes an impressive starter and can be made in advance and stored in the fridge.

SERVES 6

350g/12oz salmon fillets
175g/6oz/3/4 cup butter, softened
1 celery stick, finely chopped
1 leek, white part only, finely chopped
1 bay leaf
150ml/1/4 pint/2/3 cup dry white wine
115g/4oz smoked salmon trimmings
generous pinch of ground mace
60ml/4 tbsp fromage frais (low-fat cream cheese)
salt and ground black pepper
salad leaves, to serve

1 Lightly season the salmon. Melt 25g/1oz/2 tbsp of the butter in a medium heavy pan. Add the celery and leek and cook for about 5 minutes. Add the salmon and bay leaf and pour the white wine over. Cover and cook for about 15 minutes until tender.

2 Strain the cooking liquid into a pan and boil until reduced to 30ml/2 tbsp. Cool. Meanwhile, melt 50g/2oz/4 tbsp of the remaining butter and gently cook the smoked salmon trimmings until they turn pale pink. Leave to cool.

3 Remove the skin and any bones from the salmon fillets. Flake the flesh into a bowl and add the reduced, cooled cooking liquid.

4 Beat in the remaining butter, with the ground mace and the fromage frais. Break up the cooked smoked salmon trimmings and fold into the salmon mixture with all the juices from the pan. Taste and adjust the seasoning if you need to.

5 Spoon the salmon mixture into a dish or terrine and smooth the top level. Cover with clear film (plastic wrap) and chill. The prepared mixture can be left in the fridge for up to 2 days.

6 To serve the salmon rillettes, shape the mixture into oval quenelles using two dessert spoons and arrange on individual plates with the salad leaves. Accompany the rillettes with brown bread or oatcakes, if you like.

Nutritional information per portion: Energy 370kcal/1530kJ; Protein 17.2g; Carbohydrate 0.9g, of which sugars 0.7g; Fat 31.4g, of which saturates 16.5g; Cholesterol 98mg; Calcium 30mg; Fibre 0.4g; Sodium 568mg.

Potted salmon with **lemon and dill**

This sophisticated starter would be ideal for a dinner party. Preparation is done well in advance, so you can concentrate on the main course. If you cannot find fresh dill, use dried dill.

SERVES 6

350g/12oz cooked salmon, skinned
150g/5oz/2/3 cup butter, softened
rind and juice of 1 large lemon
10ml/2 tsp chopped fresh dill
salt and ground white pepper
75g/3oz/3/4 cup flaked (sliced) almonds, roughly chopped

1 Flake the salmon into a bowl and then place in a food processor together with two-thirds of the butter, the lemon rind and juice, half the dill, and plenty of salt and pepper. Blend until the mixture is quite smooth.

2 Mix in the flaked almonds. Check the seasoning and pack the mixture into small ramekins.

3 Scatter the other half of the dill over the top of each ramekin. Clarify the remaining butter, and pour over each ramekin to make a seal. Chill. Serve with crudités.

Nutritional information per portion: Energy 370kcal/1531kJ; Protein 14.8g; Carbohydrate 1.2g, of which sugars 0.9g; Fat 34.1g, of which saturates 14.7g; Cholesterol 82mg; Calcium 64mg; Fibre 1.4g; Sodium 182mg.

Potted prawns

The tiny brown prawns that were traditionally used for potting are very fiddly to peel. Since they are rare nowadays, it is easier to use peeled, cooked prawns instead.

SERVES 4

225g/8oz/2 cups peeled prawns (shrimp)
225g/8oz/1 cup butter
pinch of ground mace
salt, to taste
cayenne pepper
dill sprigs, to garnish
lemon wedges and thin slices of brown bread and butter, to serve

1 Chop a quarter of the prawns. Melt 115g/4oz/½ cup of the butter slowly, carefully skimming off any foam that rises to the surface with a metal spoon.

2 Stir all the prawns, the mace, salt and cayenne into the pan and heat gently without boiling. Pour the prawns and butter mixture into four individual pots and leave to cool.

3 Heat the remaining butter in a clean small pan, then carefully spoon the clear butter over the prawns, leaving behind the sediment.

4 Leave until the butter is almost set, then place a dill sprig in the centre of each pot. Leave to set completely, then cover and chill.

5 Transfer the prawns to room temperature 30 minutes before serving with lemon wedges for squeezing over and thin slices of brown bread and butter.

Nutritional information per portion: Energy 461kcal/1901kJ; Protein 10.3g; Carbohydrate 0.4g, of which sugars 0.4g; Fat 46.6g, of which saturates 29.4g; Cholesterol 230mg; Calcium 55mg; Fibre 0g; Sodium 448mg.

Roast pepper terrine

This terrine is perfect for a dinner party because it tastes better if made ahead. Prepare the salsa on the day of serving. Serve with a warmed Italian bread such as ciabatta or focaccia.

SERVES 8

8 (bell) peppers (red, yellow and orange)
675g/1½ lb/3 cups mascarpone
3 eggs, separated
30ml/2 tbsp each roughly chopped flat leaf parsley and shredded basil
2 large garlic cloves, roughly chopped
2 red, yellow or orange (bell) peppers, seeded and roughly chopped
30ml/2 tbsp extra virgin olive oil
10ml/2 tsp balsamic vinegar
a few basil sprigs
salt and ground black pepper

1 Place the whole peppers under a hot grill (broiler) for 8–10 minutes, turning frequently. Then put into a plastic bag until cold before skinning and seeding them. Chop seven of the peppers lengthways into thin strips.

2 Put the mascarpone in a bowl with the egg yolks, herbs and half the garlic. Add seasoning. Beat well. In a separate bowl, whisk the egg whites to a soft peak, then fold into the cheese mixture until they are evenly incorporated.

3 Preheat the oven to 180°C/350°F/Gas 4. Line the base of a lightly oiled 900g/2lb loaf tin (pan). Put one-third of the cheese mixture in the tin and spread level. Arrange half the pepper strips on top in an even layer. Repeat until all the cheese and peppers are used, ending with a layer of the cheese mixture.

4 Cover the tin with foil and place in a roasting pan. Pour in boiling water to come halfway up the sides of the tin. Bake for 1 hour. Leave to cool in the water bath, then lift out and chill overnight.

5 A few hours before serving, make the salsa. Place the remaining skinned pepper and fresh peppers in a food processor. Add the remaining garlic, oil and vinegar. Set aside a few basil leaves for garnishing and add the rest to the processor. Process until finely chopped. Tip the mixture into a bowl, add salt and ground black pepper to taste and mix well. Cover and chill until ready to serve.

6 Turn out the terrine, peel off the lining paper and slice thickly. Garnish with the reserved basil leaves and serve cold, with the sweet pepper salsa.

Nutritional information per portion: Energy 581kcal/2425kJ; Protein 21.9g; Carbohydrate 78.1g, of which sugars 74.6g; Fat 21.8g, of which saturates 9.8g; Cholesterol 107mg; Calcium 105mg; Fibre 18.9g; Sodium 74mg.

Asparagus and **egg terrine**

For a special dinner this terrine is a delicious choice yet it is very light. Make the hollandaise sauce well in advance and warm through gently when required.

SERVES 8

150ml/1/4 pint/2/3 cup milk
150ml/1/4 pint/2/3 cup double (heavy) cream
40g/11/2oz/3 tbsp butter
40g/11/2oz/3 tbsp flour
75g/3oz herbed or garlic cream cheese
675g/11/2 lb asparagus spears, cooked
a little oil
2 eggs, separated
15ml/1 tbsp chopped fresh chives
30ml/2 tbsp chopped fresh dill
salt and ground black pepper
dill sprigs, to garnish

FOR THE ORANGE HOLLANDAISE SAUCE

15ml/1 tbsp white wine vinegar
15ml/1 tbsp fresh orange juice
4 black peppercorns
1 bay leaf
2 egg yolks
115g/4oz/1/2 cup butter, melted and cooled slightly

1 Put the milk and cream into a small pan and heat to just below boiling point. Melt the butter in a medium pan, stir in the flour and cook to a thick paste. Gradually stir in the milk, whisking as it thickens and beat to a smooth paste. Stir in the cream cheese, season to taste with salt and ground black pepper and leave to cool slightly.

2 Trim the asparagus to fit the width of a 1.2 litre/2 pint/5 cup loaf tin (pan) or terrine. Lightly oil the tin and then place a sheet of baking parchment in the base, cut to fit. Preheat the oven to 180°C/350°F/Gas 4.

3 Beat the yolks into the sauce mixture. Whisk the whites until stiff and fold in with the chives, dill and seasoning. Layer the asparagus and egg mixture in the tin, starting and finishing with asparagus. Cover the top with foil.

4 Place the terrine in a roasting pan; half fill with hot water. Cook for 45–55 minutes until firm.

5 To make the hollandaise sauce, put the vinegar, juice, peppercorns and bay leaf in a small pan and heat until reduced by half.

6 Cool the sauce slightly, then whisk in the egg yolks, then the butter, with a balloon whisk over a very gentle heat. Season to taste and keep whisking until thick. Keep the sauce warm over a pan of hot water.

7 When the terrine is just firm to the touch remove from the oven and allow to cool, then chill. Carefully invert the terrine on to a serving dish, remove the baking parchment and garnish with the dill. Cut into slices and pour over the warmed sauce.

Nutritional information per portion: Energy 359kcal/1483kJ; Protein 6.6g; Carbohydrate 7.1g, of which sugars 3.2g; Fat 34.1g, of which saturates 20.2g; Cholesterol 175mg; Calcium 87mg; Fibre 1.6g; Sodium 179mg.

Grilled vegetable terrine

A colourful, layered terrine, this appetizer uses many of the vegetables that are associated with the Mediterranean and long, balmy summer evenings.

SERVES 6

2 large red (bell) peppers, quartered, cored, seeded
2 large yellow (bell) peppers, quartered, cored, seeded
1 large aubergine (eggplant), sliced lengthways
2 courgettes (zucchini), sliced lengthways
90ml/6 tbsp olive oil
1 large red onion, thinly sliced
75g/3oz/½ cup raisins
15ml/1 tbsp tomato purée (paste)
15ml/1 tbsp red wine vinegar
400ml/14fl oz/1⅔ cups tomato juice
15g/½oz/2 tbsp powdered gelatine
fresh basil leaves, to garnish

FOR THE DRESSING

90ml/6 tbsp extra virgin olive oil
30ml/2 tbsp red wine vinegar
salt and ground black pepper

1 Place the peppers skin-side up under a hot grill (broiler) and cook until the skins are blackened. Transfer to a bowl and cover. Leave to cool. Arrange the aubergine and courgette slices on separate baking sheets. Brush them with oil and cook under the grill, turning occasionally, until they are tender and golden.

2 Heat the remaining olive oil in a frying pan, and add the sliced onion, raisins, tomato purée and red wine vinegar. Cook gently until the mixture is soft and syrupy. Set aside and leave to cool in the frying pan.

3 Lightly oil a 1.75 litre/3 pint/7½ cup terrine then line it with clear film (plastic wrap), leaving a little hanging over the sides. Pour half the tomato juice into a pan, and sprinkle with the gelatine. Dissolve over a low heat, stirring to prevent any lumps from forming.

4 Place a layer of red peppers in the base of the terrine, and pour in enough of the tomato juice with gelatine to cover. Continue layering the vegetables, pouring tomato juice over each layer. Finish with a layer of red peppers. Add the remaining tomato juice to the pan, and pour into the terrine. Give it a sharp tap, to disperse the juice. Cover and chill until set.

5 To make the dressing, whisk together the oil and vinegar, and season. Turn out the terrine and remove the clear film (plastic wrap). Serve in thick slices, drizzled with dressing and garnished with basil leaves.

Nutritional information per portion: Energy 296kcal/1229kJ; Protein 3.5g; Carbohydrate 20.2g, of which sugars 19.7g; Fat 22.9g, of which saturates 3.4g; Cholesterol 0mg; Calcium 42mg; Fibre 3.8g; Sodium 169mg.

Haddock and **smoked salmon terrine**

This is a fairly substantial terrine, so serve modest slices, perhaps with fresh dill mayonnaise or a mango salsa. You can use any thick white fish fillets, such as hoki.

SERVES 10–12

15ml/1 tbsp sunflower oil, for greasing
350g/12oz oak-smoked salmon
900g/2lb haddock fillets, skinned
2 eggs, lightly beaten
105ml/7 tbsp crème fraîche
30ml/2 tbsp drained capers
30ml/2 tbsp drained soft green or pink peppercorns
salt and ground white pepper
crème fraîche, peppercorns, fresh dill and rocket (arugula), to garnish

1 Preheat the oven to 200°C/400°F/Gas 6. Grease a 1 litre/1¾ pint/4 cup loaf tin (pan) or terrine with the sunflower oil. Use some of the smoked salmon to line the loaf tin or terrine, allowing some of the ends to overhang the mould. Reserve the remaining smoked salmon until needed.

2 Cut two long slices of haddock the length of the tin or terrine and set aside. Cut the rest of the haddock into small pieces. Season all of the haddock with salt and ground white pepper.

3 Combine the eggs, crème fraîche, capers and green or pink peppercorns in a bowl. Add salt and pepper; stir in the haddock pieces. Spoon the mixture into the mould until it is one-third full. Smooth the surface with a spatula.

4 Wrap the long haddock fillets in the reserved salmon. Lay them on top of the layer of the fish mixture in the tin or terrine. Cover with the rest of the fish mixture, smooth the surface and fold the overhanging pieces of salmon over the top. Cover tightly with a double thickness of foil. Tap the terrine to settle the contents. Stand the terrine in a roasting tin and pour in boiling water to come halfway up the sides. Place in the oven and cook for 45 minutes–1 hour, until the filling is just set.

5 Take the terrine out of the roasting tin, but do not remove the foil cover. Place two or three large heavy tins on the foil to weight it and leave until cold. Chill in the fridge for 24 hours. About an hour before serving, remove the terrine from the fridge, lift off the weights and remove the foil. Carefully invert on to a serving plate and garnish with crème fraîche, peppercorns and sprigs of dill and rocket leaves.

Nutritional information per portion: Energy 154kcal/647kJ; Protein 22.5g; Carbohydrate 0.3g, of which sugars 0.3g; Fat 7.1g, of which saturates 3g; Cholesterol 78mg; Calcium 34mg; Fibre 0.2g; Sodium 571mg.

Chicken and **pork terrine**

This pale, elegant terrine is flecked with green peppercorns and parsley, which give it a wonderfully subtle flavour. For a sharper flavour, use fresh coriander instead of parsley.

SERVES 6–8

225g/8oz rindless, streaky (fatty) bacon
375g/13oz chicken breast fillets, skinned
15ml/1 tbsp lemon juice
225g/8oz lean minced (ground) pork
1/2 small onion, finely chopped
2 eggs, beaten
30ml/2 tbsp chopped fresh parsley
5ml/1 tsp salt
5ml/1 tsp green peppercorns, crushed
oil, for greasing
salad leaves, capers, sliced gherkins and beetroot (beets), to serve

1 Preheat the oven to 160°C/325°F/Gas 3. Put the bacon on a board and stretch it using the back of a knife before arranging it in overlapping slices over the base and sides of a 900g/2lb loaf tin (pan).

2 Cut 115g/4oz of the chicken into strips about 10cm/4in long. Sprinkle with lemon juice. Put the rest of the chicken in a food processor or blender with the minced pork and the onion. Process until fairly smooth.

3 Add the eggs, parsley, salt and peppercorns to the meat mixture and process again briefly. Spoon half the mixture into the loaf tin and then level the surface. Arrange the chicken strips on top, then spoon in the remaining meat mixture and smooth the top. Give the tin a couple of sharp taps to knock out any pockets of air.

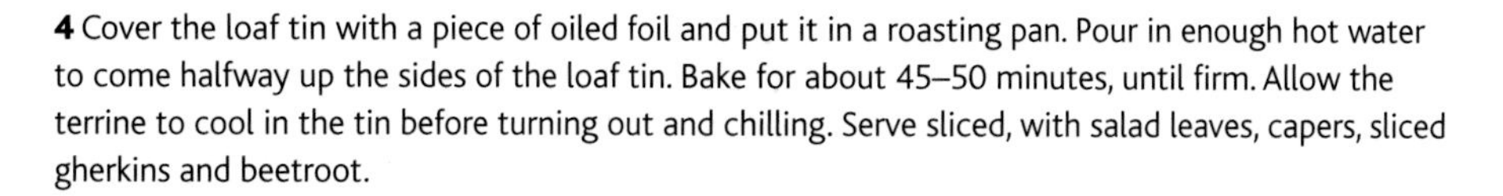

4 Cover the loaf tin with a piece of oiled foil and put it in a roasting pan. Pour in enough hot water to come halfway up the sides of the loaf tin. Bake for about 45–50 minutes, until firm. Allow the terrine to cool in the tin before turning out and chilling. Serve sliced, with salad leaves, capers, sliced gherkins and beetroot.

Nutritional information per portion: Energy 296kcal/1229kJ; Protein 3.5g; Carbohydrate 20.2g, of which sugars 19.7g; Fat 22.9g, of which saturates 3.4g; Cholesterol 0mg; Calcium 42mg; Fibre 3.8g; Sodium 169mg.

Vegetarian dishes

A wide variety of dishes from around the world are included in this chapter, with recipes from Europe to Asia. You can transport yourself to the Far East with Vegetable Tempura or enjoy a taste of the Mediterranean with Greek Aubergine and Spinach Pie.

Griddled tomatoes on soda bread

Nothing could be simpler than this delightful appetizer, yet a drizzle of olive oil and balsamic vinegar and shavings of Parmesan cheese transform it into something really rather special.

SERVES 4

olive oil, for brushing and drizzling
6 tomatoes, thickly sliced
4 thick slices soda bread
balsamic vinegar, for drizzling
salt and ground black pepper
shavings of Parmesan cheese, to serve

1 Brush a griddle pan with olive oil and heat. Add the tomato slices and cook for about 4 minutes, turning once, until softened and slightly blackened. Or, heat the grill (broiler) to high and line the rack with foil. Grill (broil) the slices for 4–6 minutes, turning once, until softened.

2 Meanwhile, lightly toast the soda bread. Place the tomatoes on top of the toast and then drizzle each portion with a little olive oil and balsamic vinegar. Season to taste with salt and black pepper and serve immediately with thin shavings of Parmesan cheese.

Nutritional information per portion: Energy 172kcal/724kJ; Protein 4g; Carbohydrate 25.1g, of which sugars 5.8g; Fat 6.9g, of which saturates 0.9g; Cholesterol 0mg; Calcium 63mg; Fibre 2.3g; Sodium 171mg.

Poached eggs Florentine

The term "à la Florentine" means "in the style of Florence" and refers to dishes cooked with spinach and topped with Mornay sauce. Here is a subtly spiced, elegant starter.

SERVES 4

675g/1½ lb spinach, washed and drained
25g/1oz/2 tbsp butter
60ml/4 tbsp double (heavy) cream
pinch of freshly grated nutmeg
salt and ground black pepper

FOR THE TOPPING
25g/1oz/2 tbsp butter
25g/1oz/¼ cup plain flour
300ml/½ pint/1¼ cups hot milk
pinch of ground mace
115g/4oz Gruyère cheese, grated
4 eggs
15ml/1 tbsp freshly grated Parmesan cheese, plus shavings to serve

1 Place the spinach in a large saucepan with very little water. Cook for 3–4 minutes or until tender, then drain and chop finely. Return the spinach to the pan, add the butter, cream, nutmeg and seasoning and heat through. Place in the base of one large or four small gratin dishes.

2 To make the topping, heat the butter in a small pan, add the flour and cook for 1 minute to a paste. Gradually blend in the hot milk, beating well as it thickens to break up any lumps.

3 Cook for 1–2 minutes, stirring. Remove from the heat and stir in the mace and three-quarters of the Gruyère cheese.

4 Preheat the oven to 200°C/400°F/Gas 6. Poach the eggs in lightly salted water for 3–4 minutes. Make hollows in the spinach with the back of a spoon, and place a poached egg in each one. Cover with the cheese sauce and sprinkle with the remaining Gruyère and Parmesan. Bake for 10 minutes or until golden. Serve at once with Parmesan shavings.

Nutritional information per portion: Energy 459kcal/1901kJ; Protein 21.7g; Carbohydrate 11.5g, of which sugars 6.5g; Fat 36g, of which saturates 20.3g; Cholesterol 270mg; Calcium 636mg; Fibre 3.8g; Sodium 626mg.

Dolmades

These stuffed vine leaves originated in Greece. If you can't find fresh vine leaves, use a packet or can of brined leaves. Soak in hot water for 20 minutes, then rinse and dry well on kitchen paper.

MAKES 20–24

24–28 fresh young vine leaves, soaked
30ml/2 tbsp olive oil
1 large onion, finely chopped
1 garlic clove, crushed
225g/8oz/2 cups cooked long grain rice
about 45ml/3 tbsp pine nuts
15ml/1 tbsp flaked (sliced) almonds
40g/1½ oz/¼ cup sultanas (golden raisins)
15ml/1 tbsp snipped fresh chives
15ml/1 tbsp finely chopped fresh mint
juice of ½ lemon
150ml/¼ pint/⅔ cup white wine
hot vegetable stock
salt and ground black pepper
mint sprig, to garnish
garlic yogurt and pitta bread, to serve

1 Cook the vine leaves in boiling water for 2–3 minutes. If using packet or canned leaves, place in a bowl, cover with boiling water and leave for 20 minutes until the leaves can be separated. Rinse and pat dry.

2 Heat the oil in a frying pan and fry the onion and garlic for 3–4 minutes. Spoon into a bowl, add the cooked rice and mix. Stir in 30ml/2 tbsp of the pine nuts, the almonds, sultanas, chives and mint. Add the lemon juice, salt and pepper and mix.

3 Reserve four vine leaves. Place the rest on a work surface with the veined side uppermost and put a spoonful of filling near each stem, fold the lower part of the leaf over it, roll up and fold in the sides.

4 Line the base of a deep frying pan with the reserved vine leaves. Place the dolmades close together in the pan, seam side down, in a single layer. Pour over the wine and enough stock to just cover. Place a plate on top of the dolmades, cover the pan and simmer for 30 minutes.

5 Cool and chill, then garnish with pine nuts and mint. Serve with the garlic yogurt and some pitta bread.

Nutritional information per portion: Energy 43kcal/181kJ; Protein 0.7g; Carbohydrate 6.7g, of which sugars 1.7g; Fat 1.1g, of which saturates 0.1g; Cholesterol 0mg; Calcium 12mg; Fibre 0.3g; Sodium 2mg.

Lemon, thyme and bean stuffed mushrooms

Portabello mushrooms have a rich flavour and a meaty texture that go well with this fragrant herb-and-lemon stuffing. The pine nut accompaniment is a traditional Middle Eastern dish.

SERVES 4–6

400g/14oz/2 cups canned aduki beans
45ml/3 tbsp olive oil, plus extra for brushing
1 onion, finely chopped
2 garlic cloves, crushed
30ml/2 tbsp fresh chopped thyme or 5ml/1 tsp dried
8 large field (portabello) mushrooms, stalks finely chopped
50g/2oz/1 cup fresh wholemeal (whole-wheat) breadcrumbs
juice of 1 lemon
185g/6½ oz/¾ cup goat's cheese, crumbled
salt and ground black pepper

FOR THE PINE NUT SAUCE
50g/2oz/½ cup pine nuts, toasted
50g/2oz/1 cup cubed white bread
2 garlic cloves, chopped
200ml/7fl oz/scant 1 cup milk
45ml/3 tbsp olive oil

1 Rinse the beans, drain, then set aside. Preheat the oven to 200°C/400°F/Gas 6. Heat the oil in a frying pan, add the onion and garlic and sauté for 5 minutes until softened. Add the thyme and the mushroom stalks and cook for 3 minutes, stirring occasionally, until tender.

2 Add the beans, breadcrumbs and lemon juice, season, then cook for 2 minutes. Mash two-thirds of the beans.

3 Brush an ovenproof dish and the base and sides of the mushrooms with oil, then top each one with a spoonful of the bean mixture. Place the mushrooms in the dish, cover with foil and bake for 20 minutes. Remove the foil. Top the mushrooms with the goat's cheese and bake for a further 15 minutes, until the mushrooms are tender.

4 To make the sauce, place all the ingredients in a food processor or blender and blend until smooth and creamy. Add more milk if the mixture appears too thick. Serve with the stuffed mushrooms.

Nutritional information per portion: Energy 403kcal/1680kJ; Protein 17g; Carbohydrate 25.8g, of which sugars 5.8g; Fat 26.5g, of which saturates 8g; Cholesterol 31mg; Calcium 158mg; Fibre 5.8g; Sodium 572mg.

Cannellini bean and rosemary bruschetta

This is a sophisticated variation on the theme of beans on toast, which, with the addition of the Mediterranean flavours of garlic and sun-dried tomatoes, makes an unusual starter.

SERVES 6

150g/5oz/$^2/_3$ cup dried cannellini beans
5 tomatoes
45ml/3 tbsp olive oil, plus extra for drizzling
2 sun-dried tomatoes in oil, drained and finely chopped
1 garlic clove, crushed
30ml/2 tbsp chopped fresh rosemary
12 slices Italian-style bread, such as ciabatta
1 large garlic clove
salt and ground black pepper
handful of fresh basil leaves, to garnish

1 Put the beans in a bowl, cover in water and soak overnight. Drain and rinse the beans, then place in a saucepan and cover with fresh water. Bring to the boil and boil rapidly for 10 minutes. Then simmer for 50–60 minutes or until tender. Drain, return to the pan and keep warm.

2 Meanwhile, place the tomatoes in a bowl, cover with boiling water; leave for 30 seconds, then peel, seed and chop the flesh. Heat the oil in a frying pan, add the fresh and sun-dried tomatoes, garlic and rosemary. Cook for 2 minutes until the tomatoes begin to break down and soften.

3 Add the tomato mixture to the cannellini beans and season to taste. Mix together well. Keep the bean mixture warm.

4 Rub the cut sides of the bread slices with the garlic clove, then toast them lightly. Spoon the cannellini bean mixture on top of the toast. Sprinkle with basil leaves and drizzle with a little extra olive oil before serving.

Nutritional information per portion: Energy 499kcal/2111kJ; Protein 20.2g; Carbohydrate 84.3g, of which sugars 8.5g; Fat 11.3g, of which saturates 1.7g; Cholesterol 0mg; Calcium 195mg; Fibre 8.1g; Sodium 749mg.

Glamorgan sausages

These tasty sausages, which are flavoured with herbs and mustard are ideal for vegetarians as they are made from cheese and leeks rather than meat.

MAKES 8

150g/5oz/2½ cups fresh breadcrumbs
150g/5oz generous cup grated Caerphilly cheese
1 small leek, very finely chopped
15ml/1 tbsp chopped fresh parsley
leaves from 1 thyme sprig, chopped
2 eggs
7.5ml/1½ tsp English (hot) mustard powder
about 45ml/3 tbsp milk
plain (all-purpose) flour, for coating
15ml/1 tbsp oil
15g/½ oz/1 tbsp butter, melted
salt and ground black pepper
salad leaves and tomato halves, to serve

1 Mix the breadcrumbs, cheese, leek, herbs and seasoning. Whisk the eggs with the mustard and reserve 30ml/2 tbsp. Stir the rest into the cheese mixture with enough milk to bind.

2 Divide the cheese mixture into eight portions and then form them into sausage shapes.

3 Dip the sausages in the reserved egg to coat. Season the flour, then roll the sausages in it to give a light, even coating. Chill for about 30 minutes until they are firm.

4 Preheat the grill (broiler) and oil the rack. Mix the oil and melted butter together and use to brush over the sausages. Cook the sausages for 5–10 minutes, turning them carefully every now and then, until golden brown all over. Serve hot or cold, with salad leaves and tomato halves.

Nutritional information per portion: Energy 193kcal/809kJ; Protein 8.8g; Carbohydrate 15.1g, of which sugars 0.9g; Fat 10.9g, of which saturates 5.7g; Cholesterol 70mg; Calcium 179mg; Fibre 0.8g; Sodium 309mg.

Potato skewers with mustard dip

Potatoes cooked on the barbecue have a great flavour and crisp skin. Try these delicious kebabs served with a thick, garlic-rich dip for an unusual start to a meal.

SERVES 6

FOR THE DIP

4 garlic cloves, crushed
2 egg yolks
30ml/2 tbsp lemon juice
300ml/½ pint/1¼ cups extra virgin olive oil
10ml/2 tsp wholegrain mustard
salt and ground black pepper

FOR THE SKEWERS

1kg/2¼ lb small new potatoes
200g/7oz shallots, halved
30ml/2 tbsp olive oil
15ml/1 tbsp sea salt

1 Prepare the barbecue, or preheat the grill (broiler). To make the dip place the garlic, egg yolks and lemon juice in a blender or a food processor fitted with a metal blade and process for just a few seconds until the mixture is smooth.

2 Keep the blender motor running and add the oil very gradually, pouring it in a thin stream, until the mixture forms a thick, glossy cream. Add the mustard and stir the ingredients together, then season with salt and pepper. Chill until ready to use.

3 Par-boil the potatoes in their skins in boiling water for 5 minutes. Drain well and then thread them on to metal skewers alternating with the shallots.

4 Brush the skewers with oil and sprinkle with salt. Barbecue or grill (broil) for about 10–12 minutes, turning occasionally. Serve with the mustard dip.

Nutritional information per portion: Energy 488kcal/2024kJ; Protein 4.3g; Carbohydrate 29.5g, of which sugars 4.1g; Fat 40g, of which saturates 6.1g; Cholesterol 65mg; Calcium 28mg; Fibre 2.2g; Sodium 49mg.

Deep-fried new potatoes with saffron aioli

Serve these crispy little golden potatoes dipped into a wickedly garlicky mayonnaise – then sit back and watch them disappear in a matter of minutes!

SERVES 4

1 egg yolk
2.5ml/½ tsp Dijon mustard
300ml/½ pint/1¼ cups extra virgin olive oil
15–30ml/1–2 tbsp lemon juice
1 garlic clove, crushed
2.5ml/½ tsp saffron threads
20 baby, new or salad potatoes
vegetable oil, for deep-frying
salt and ground black pepper

1 For the saffron aioli, put the egg yolk in a bowl with the Dijon mustard and a pinch of salt. Stir to mix together well. Beat in the olive oil very slowly, drop by drop at first and then in a very thin stream. Stir in the lemon juice.

2 Season the aioli with salt and pepper then add the crushed garlic and beat into the mixture thoroughly to combine.

3 Place the saffron in a small bowl and add 10ml/2 tsp hot water. Press the saffron threads with the back of a teaspoon, to extract the colour and flavour, and leave to infuse for 5 minutes. Beat the saffron and the liquid into the aioli.

4 Cook the potatoes in their skins in boiling salted water for 5 minutes, then turn off the heat. Cover the pan and leave for 15 minutes. Drain the potatoes, then dry them thoroughly in a dish towel.

5 Heat a 1cm/½in layer of vegetable oil in a deep pan. When the oil is very hot, add the potatoes and fry quickly, turning them constantly, until crisp and golden all over. Drain well on kitchen paper and then serve them hot with the saffron aioli.

Nutritional information per portion: Energy 788kcal/3266kJ; Protein 5g; Carbohydrate 40.3g, of which sugars 3.3g; Fat 68.6g, of which saturates 9.7g; Cholesterol 50mg; Calcium 21mg; Fibre 2.5g; Sodium 30mg.

Asparagus with raspberry dressing

The flavours of asparagus and raspberries complement each other wonderfully well. The tangy, fruity sauce gives this starter a real zing and the bright colours make it very attractive.

SERVES 4

675g/1½lb thin asparagus spears, trimmed
30ml/2 tbsp raspberry vinegar
2.5ml/½ tsp salt
5ml/1 tsp Dijon mustard
25ml/1½ tbsp sunflower oil
30ml/2 tbsp sour cream or natural (plain) yogurt
ground white pepper
175g/6oz/1 cup fresh raspberries, to garnish

1 Fill a large frying pan with water 10cm/4in deep and bring to the boil. Tie the asparagus spears into two bundles. Cook the bundles until just tender, for about 2 minutes.

2 Remove from the pan and immerse in cold water. Drain, untie and pat dry. Chill for 1 hour.

3 Mix the vinegar, salt and mustard in a bowl. Gradually stir in the oil until it is blended. Add the sour cream or yogurt and pepper to taste.

4 To serve, place the asparagus on individual plates and drizzle the dressing across the middle of the spears. Garnish with the raspberries.

Nutritional information per portion: Energy 104kcal/431kJ; Protein 5.8g; Carbohydrate 5.8g, of which sugars 5.6g; Fat 6.5g, of which saturates 1.6g; Cholesterol 5mg; Calcium 64mg; Fibre 4g; Sodium 43mg.

Greek aubergine and spinach pie

Aubergines layered with spinach, feta cheese and rice make a flavoursome and dramatic filling for a pie. It can be served warm or cold in elegant slices.

SERVES 12

375g/13oz shortcrust pastry, thawed if frozen
45–60ml/3–4 tbsp olive oil
1 large aubergine (eggplant), sliced
1 onion, chopped
1 garlic clove, crushed
175g/6oz spinach, washed
4 eggs
75g/3oz/½ cup crumbled feta cheese
40g/1½oz/½ cup freshly grated Parmesan cheese
60ml/4 tbsp natural (plain) yogurt
90ml/6 tbsp creamy milk
225g/8oz/2 cups cooked white or brown long grain rice
salt and ground black pepper

1 Preheat the oven to 180°C/350°F/Gas 4. Roll out the pastry thinly and use to line a 25cm/10in flan pan. Prick the base all over and bake in the oven for 10–12 minutes until the pastry is pale golden. (Alternatively, bake blind, using baking parchment as a lining, weighted with a handful of baking beans.)

2 Heat 30–45ml/2–3 tbsp of the oil in a frying pan and fry the aubergine slices for 6–8 minutes on each side until golden. You may need to add a little more oil at first, but this will be released as the flesh softens. Lift out and drain well on kitchen paper. Add the onion and garlic to the oil remaining in the pan then fry over a gentle heat for 4–5 minutes until soft, adding a little extra oil if necessary.

3 Chop the spinach finely, by hand or in a food processor. Beat the eggs in a large mixing bowl, then add the spinach, feta, Parmesan, yogurt, milk and the onion mixture. Season well with salt and ground black pepper and stir thoroughly to mix.

4 Spread the rice in an even layer over the base of the part-baked pastry case. Reserve a few aubergine slices for the top, and arrange the rest in an even layer over the rice.

5 Spoon the spinach and feta mixture over the aubergines and place the remaining slices on top. Bake for 30–40 minutes until lightly browned. Serve the pie while warm, or leave it to cool completely before transferring to a serving plate.

Nutritional information per portion: Energy 257kcal/1075kJ; Protein 6.5g; Carbohydrate 23.8g, of which sugars 2.1g; Fat 15.8g, of which saturates 4.7g; Cholesterol 73mg; Calcium 99mg; Fibre 1.5g; Sodium 267mg.

Son-in-law eggs

The name of this recipe comes from a story about a suitor who wanted to impress his future mother-in-law and devised a recipe from the only other dish he knew how to make – boiled eggs.

SERVES 4–6

75g/3oz/generous 1/3 cup palm sugar (jaggery)
60ml/4 tbsp light soy sauce
105ml/7 tbsp tamarind juice
oil, for frying
6 shallots, finely sliced
6 garlic cloves, finely sliced
6 red chillies, sliced
6 hard-boiled eggs, shelled
coriander (cilantro) sprigs, to garnish
lettuce, to serve

1 Combine the palm sugar, soy sauce and tamarind juice in a small saucepan. Bring to the boil, stirring until the sugar dissolves, then simmer the sauce for about 5 minutes.

2 Taste and add more palm sugar, soy sauce or tamarind juice, if necessary. It should be sweet, salty and slightly sour. Transfer the sauce to a bowl and set aside until needed.

3 Heat a couple of spoonfuls of the oil in a frying pan and fry the shallots, garlic and chillies until golden brown. Transfer to a bowl and set aside.

4 Deep-fry the eggs in hot oil for 3–5 minutes until golden brown. Drain the eggs on kitchen paper, quarter and arrange on a bed of lettuce. Scatter the shallot mixture over, drizzle with the sauce and garnish with coriander.

Nutritional information per portion: Energy 138kcal/578kJ; Protein 6.9g; Carbohydrate 16.3g, of which sugars 15.4g; Fat 5.6g, of which saturates 1.6g; Cholesterol 190mg; Calcium 45mg; Fibre 0.5g; Sodium 547mg.

Baked Mediterranean vegetables

Crisp and golden crunchy batter surrounds these vegetables, turning them into a substantial appetizer. Make sure the fat is really hot before adding the batter or it will not rise well.

SERVES 10–12

1 small aubergine (eggplant), trimmed, halved and thickly sliced
1 egg
115g/4oz/1 cup plain (all-purpose) flour
300ml/1/2 pint/1 1/4 cups milk
30ml/2 tbsp fresh thyme leaves, or 10ml/2 tsp dried
1 red onion, quartered
2 large courgettes (zucchini)
1 each red and yellow (bell) pepper, seeded and quartered
60–75ml/4–5 tbsp sunflower oil
salt and ground black pepper
30ml/2 tbsp freshly grated Parmesan cheese and fresh herbs, to garnish

1 Place the sliced aubergine in a colander or sieve (strainer), sprinkle generously with salt and leave for 10 minutes. Drain and pat dry on kitchen paper.

2 Meanwhile, to make the batter, beat the egg, then gradually beat in the flour and a little milk to make a smooth thick paste. Blend in the rest of the milk, add the thyme leaves and seasoning to taste and blend until smooth. Leave in a cool place until required.

3 Put the oil in a roasting pan and heat in the oven at 220°C/425°F/Gas 7. Add the vegetables, coat them well with the oil and return to the oven for 20 minutes until they start to cook.

4 Whisk the batter, pour over the vegetables and return to the oven for 30 minutes. If puffed up and golden, lower the heat to 190°C/375°F/Gas 5 for 10–15 minutes until crisp around the edges. Sprinkle with Parmesan and herbs and serve.

Nutritional information per portion: Energy 113kcal/473kJ; Protein 4.3g; Carbohydrate 11.9g, of which sugars 4.3g; Fat 5.7g, of which saturates 1.4g; Cholesterol 17mg; Calcium 89mg; Fibre 1.5g; Sodium 45mg.

Marinated feta cheese with capers

Marinating cubes of feta cheese with herbs and spices gives a marvellous flavour. This makes a delicious starter, served with hot crunchy toast.

SERVES 6

350g/12oz feta cheese
2 garlic cloves
2.5ml/1/2 tsp mixed peppercorns
8 coriander seeds
1 bay leaf
15–30ml/1–2 tbsp drained capers
oregano or thyme sprigs
olive oil, to cover
hot toast, kalamata olives, and chopped tomatoes, to serve

1 Cut the feta cheese into bitesize cubes. Thickly slice the garlic. Put the mixed peppercorns and coriander seeds in a mortar and crush lightly with a pestle.

2 Pack the feta cubes into a large preserving jar with the bay leaf, interspersing layers of cheese with garlic, crushed peppercorns and coriander, capers and the fresh oregano or thyme sprigs.

3 Pour in enough olive oil to cover the cheese. Close tightly and leave to marinate for two weeks in the fridge.

4 Lift out the feta cubes and serve on hot toast, with some chopped tomatoes, kalamata olives and a little of the flavoured oil from the jar drizzled over.

Nutritional information per portion: Energy 165kcal/683kJ; Protein 9.3g; Carbohydrate 1.3g, of which sugars 0.9g; Fat 13.6g, of which saturates 8.3g; Cholesterol 41mg; Calcium 211mg; Fibre 0.1g; Sodium 840mg.

Courgette fritters with **chilli jam**

Chilli jam is hot, sweet and sticky – rather like a thick chutney. It adds a delicious piquancy to these light courgette fritters, which are always a popular dish.

MAKES 12 FRITTERS

450g/1lb/3½ cups coarsely grated courgettes (zucchini)
50g/2oz/⅔ cup freshly grated Parmesan cheese
2 eggs, beaten
60ml/4 tbsp plain (all-purpose) flour
vegetable oil, for frying
salt and ground black pepper

FOR THE CHILLI JAM
75ml/5 tbsp olive oil
4 large onions, diced
4 garlic cloves, chopped
1–2 green chillies, seeded and sliced
30ml/2 tbsp soft dark brown sugar

1 First make the chilli jam. Heat the oil in a pan, then add the onions and the garlic. Reduce the heat to low, then cook for 20 minutes, stirring often, until the onions are soft. Cool.

2 Transfer to a food processor or blender. Add the chillies and sugar and blend until smooth, then return the mixture to the pan. Cook for 10 minutes, stirring often, until the mixture has the consistency of jam.

3 To make the fritters, squeeze the courgettes in a dish towel, then mix with the Parmesan, eggs, flour and salt and pepper.

4 Heat enough vegetable oil to cover the base of a frying pan. Add 30ml/2 tbsp of the mixture for each fritter. Cook for 2–3 minutes on each side. Cook the rest of the fritters. Drain on kitchen paper and serve with the chilli jam.

Nutritional information per portion: Energy 157kcal/652kJ; Protein 4.4g; Carbohydrate 11.1g, of which sugars 6.1g; Fat 10.8g, of which saturates 2.2g; Cholesterol 36mg; Calcium 85mg; Fibre 1.2g; Sodium 59mg.

Sesame seed-coated falafel with **tahini dip**

Sesame seeds are used to give a delightfully crunchy coating to these spicy chickpea patties. Serve with the tahini yogurt dip, and some warmed pitta bread too, if you like.

SERVES 6

250g/9oz/1⅓ cups dried chickpeas
2 garlic cloves, crushed
1 red chilli, seeded and finely sliced
5ml/1 tsp ground coriander
5ml/1 tsp ground cumin
15ml/1 tbsp chopped fresh mint
15ml/1 tbsp chopped fresh parsley
2 spring onions (scallions), finely chopped
1 large (US extra large) egg, beaten
sesame seeds, for coating
sunflower oil, for frying
salt and ground black pepper

FOR THE TAHINI YOGURT DIP

30ml/2 tbsp light tahini
200g/7oz/scant 1 cup natural (plain) live yogurt
5ml/1 tsp cayenne pepper, plus extra for sprinkling
15ml/1 tbsp chopped fresh mint
1 spring onion (scallion), finely sliced
fresh herbs, to garnish

1 In a bowl, cover the chickpeas with cold water and soak overnight. Drain and rinse, then place in a pan and cover with cold water. Bring to a rapid boil for 10 minutes, then simmer for 1½–2 hours.

2 Make the dip. Mix the tahini, yogurt, cayenne and mint. Sprinkle with the spring onion and extra cayenne and chill.

3 Mix the chickpeas with the garlic, chilli, spices, herbs, spring onions, seasoning and egg. Blend in a food processor until the mixture forms a coarse paste. If the paste seems too soft, chill in the fridge for 30 minutes.

4 Form the paste into 12 patties, then roll each in the sesame seeds. Fry, in batches, for 6 minutes. Serve with the dip and fresh herbs.

Nutritional information per portion: Energy 315kcal/1314kJ; Protein 14.3g; Carbohydrate 23.8g, of which sugars 3.8g; Fat 18.8g, of which saturates 2.6g; Cholesterol 32mg; Calcium 237mg; Fibre 5.8g; Sodium 63mg.

Charred artichokes with **lemon oil dip**

Here is a lip-smacking change from traditional fare. Artichokes are usually boiled, but dry-heat cooking also works very well. If you can get young artichokes, try roasting them over a barbecue.

SERVES 4

15ml/1 tbsp lemon juice or white wine vinegar
2 artichokes, trimmed
12 garlic cloves, unpeeled
90ml/6 tbsp olive oil
1 lemon
sea salt
flat leaf parsley sprigs, to garnish

1 Preheat the oven to 200°C/ 400°F/Gas 6. Add the lemon juice or vinegar to a bowl of cold water. Cut each artichoke into wedges. Pull the hairy choke out from the centre of each wedge and discard, then drop the wedges into the water.

2 Drain the wedges and place in a roasting pan with the garlic and 45ml/3 tbsp of the oil. Toss well to coat. Sprinkle with salt and roast for 40 minutes, until tender and a little charred.

3 Make the dip. Thinly pare rind from the lemon. Place the rind in a pan with water to cover. Bring to the boil, then simmer for 5 minutes. Drain, refresh in cold water, then chop.

4 Squeeze the flesh from the garlic cloves. Transfer to a bowl, mash to a paste, then add the lemon rind. Squeeze the juice from the lemon, then whisk the remaining olive oil and the lemon juice into the garlic paste. Garnish with parsley. Serve the artichokes with the lemon oil dip.

Nutritional information per portion: Energy 158kcal/651kJ; Protein 0.7g; Carbohydrate 1.3g, of which sugars 1.3g; Fat 16.7g, of which saturates 2.4g; Cholesterol 0mg; Calcium 52mg; Fibre 1.4g; Sodium 75mg.

Risotto frittata

Half omelette, half risotto, this makes a delightful appetizer. If possible, cook each frittata separately in a small, cast-iron pan, so that the eggs cook quickly but stay moist on top.

SERVES 4

30–45ml/2–3 tbsp olive oil
1 small onion, finely chopped
1 garlic clove, crushed
1 large red (bell) pepper, seeded and cut into thin strips
150g/5oz/¾ cup risotto rice
400–475ml/14–16fl oz/1⅔–2 cups simmering vegetable stock
25–40g/1–1½ oz/2–3 tbsp butter
175g/6oz/2½ cups button (white) mushrooms, finely sliced
60ml/4 tbsp freshly grated Parmesan cheese
6–8 eggs
salt and ground black pepper

1 Heat 15ml/1 tbsp oil in a frying pan and fry the onion and garlic over a gentle heat for 2–3 minutes. Add the pepper and cook, stirring, for 4–5 minutes, until soft.

2 Stir in the rice and cook gently for 2–3 minutes, stirring until the grains are evenly coated with oil.

3 Add a quarter of the vegetable stock and season. Stir over a low heat until the stock is absorbed. Add more stock, a little at a time. Let the rice absorb the liquid before adding more. Continue until the rice is al dente.

4 In a small pan, heat a little of the remaining oil and some of the butter and fry the mushrooms.

5 When the rice is tender, remove it from the heat. Stir in the mushrooms and the Parmesan.

6 Beat the eggs with 40ml/8 tsp cold water and season. Heat the remaining oil and butter in a pan and add the risotto. Spread the mixture in the pan, then add the beaten egg. Tilt the pan so that it cooks evenly. Fry over a moderate heat for 1–2 minutes, then transfer to a warmed plate and serve.

Nutritional information per portion: Energy 434kcal/1804kJ; Protein 19.5g; Carbohydrate 34.1g, of which sugars 3.6g; Fat 24.5g, of which saturates 9.5g; Cholesterol 314mg; Calcium 241mg; Fibre 1.4g; Sodium 311mg.

Wild mushroom and fontina tarts

Italian fontina cheese gives these tarts a creamy, nutty flavour. You can make the pastry cases in advance, then store in an airtight container for up to 2 days.

SERVES 4

25g/1oz/1/2 cup dried wild mushrooms
30ml/2 tbsp olive oil
1 red onion, chopped
2 garlic cloves, chopped
30ml/2 tbsp medium-dry sherry
1 egg
120ml/4fl oz/1/2 cup single (light) cream
25g/1oz fontina cheese, thinly sliced
salt and ground black pepper
rocket (arugula) leaves, to serve

FOR THE PASTRY

115g/4oz/1 cup wholemeal (whole-wheat) flour
50g/2oz/4 tbsp unsalted butter
25g/1oz/1/4 cup walnuts, roasted and ground
1 egg, lightly beaten

1 To make the pastry, rub the flour and butter together until the mixture resembles fine breadcrumbs. Add the nuts then the egg; mix to a soft dough. Wrap, then chill for 30 minutes.

2 Meanwhile, soak the dried wild mushrooms in 300ml/1/2 pint/1 1/4 cups boiling water for 30 minutes. Drain and reserve the liquid. Fry the onion in the oil for 5 minutes, then add the garlic and fry for about 2 minutes, stirring.

3 Add the soaked mushrooms and cook for 7 minutes over a high heat until the edges become crisp. Add the sherry and the reserved liquid. Cook over a high heat for about 10 minutes until the liquid evaporates. Season and set aside to cool.

4 Preheat the oven to 200°C/400°F/Gas 6. Lightly grease four 10cm/4in tart tins (muffin pans). Roll out the pastry on a lightly floured work surface and use to line the tart tins.

5 Prick the pastry, line with baking parchment and baking beans and bake blind for about 10 minutes. Remove the paper and the beans.

6 Whisk the egg and cream to mix, add to the mushroom mixture, then season. Spoon into the pastry cases, top with the cheese and bake for 18 minutes until the filling is set. Serve with rocket.

Nutritional information per portion: Energy 409kcal/1701kJ; Protein 10.2g; Carbohydrate 21.9g, of which sugars 2.3g; Fat 31g, of which saturates 13.4g; Cholesterol 143mg; Calcium 121mg; Fibre 2.3g; Sodium 199mg.

Chive scrambled eggs in brioches

This is an indulgent, truly delicious and slightly quirky start to a meal. Take care to cook the eggs at the right temperature and for the right time, otherwise they can become too dry or too sloppy.

SERVES 4

115g/4oz/1/2 cup unsalted butter
75g/3oz/generous 1 cup brown cap (cremini) mushrooms, finely sliced
4 individual brioches
8 eggs
15ml/1 tbsp chopped fresh chives, plus extra to garnish
salt and ground black pepper

1 Preheat the oven to 180°C/350°F/Gas 4. Place a quarter of the butter in a frying pan and heat until melted. Fry the mushrooms for about 3 minutes, then keep warm.

2 Slice the tops off the brioches, then scoop out the centres and discard. Put the brioches and lids on a baking sheet. Bake for 5 minutes until hot and slightly crisp.

3 Meanwhile, beat the eggs lightly and season to taste. Heat the remaining butter in a heavy pan over a gentle heat. When the butter has melted and is foaming slightly, add the eggs. Using a wooden spoon, stir constantly to ensure the egg does not stick.

4 Continue to stir gently until about three-quarters of the egg is semi-solid and creamy – this takes 2–3 minutes. Remove the pan from the heat – the egg will continue to cook – then stir in the chives.

5 To serve, spoon a little of the mushrooms into the base of each brioche and top with the scrambled eggs. Sprinkle with extra chives, balance the brioche lids on top and serve immediately.

Nutritional information per portion: Energy 533kcal/2218kJ; Protein 17.9g; Carbohydrate 31.9g, of which sugars 9.9g; Fat 38.2g, of which saturates 19.2g; Cholesterol 443mg; Calcium 137mg; Fibre 1.7g; Sodium 507mg.

Vegetable tempura

Tempura is a Japanese type of savoury fritter. Originally prawns were used, but a variety of vegetables can be cooked in the egg batter successfully too.

SERVES 4

2 courgettes (zucchini)
1/2 aubergine (eggplant)
1 large carrot
1/2 small Spanish (Bermuda) onion
1 egg
120ml/4fl oz/1/2 cup iced water
115g/4oz/1 cup plain (all-purpose) flour
salt and ground black pepper
vegetable oil, for deep-frying
sea salt flakes, lemon slices and Japanese soy sauce, to serve

1 Pare strips of peel from the courgettes and aubergine to give a striped effect. Using a chef's knife, cut the courgettes, aubergine and carrot into strips 7.5–10cm/3–4in long and 3mm/1/8in wide. Place in a colander and sprinkle with salt. Weigh down with a small plate, leave for 30 minutes, then rinse. Drain then dry with kitchen paper.

2 Thinly slice the onion from top to base, discarding the middle pieces. Separate the layers to make fine, long strips. Mix all the vegetables together and season well.

3 Make the batter just before frying. Mix the egg and iced water in a bowl, then sift in the flour. Mix briefly. Do not overmix: the batter should remain lumpy. Add the vegetables to the batter and mix.

4 Half-fill a wok with oil and heat to 180°C/350°F. Carefully lower a heaped tablespoonful of the mixture at a time into the oil. Cook batches for about 3 minutes, until golden and crisp. Drain on kitchen paper.

5 Serve with salt, lemon and Japanese soy sauce for dipping.

Nutritional information per portion: Energy 313kcal/1305kJ; Protein 7.1g; Carbohydrate 30.6g, of which sugars 7.3g; Fat 18.9g, of which saturates 2.5g; Cholesterol 48mg; Calcium 94mg; Fibre 3.6g; Sodium 28mg.

Leek and **onion tartlets**

Baking in individual tins makes for easier serving for a starter and it looks attractive, too. You could make tiny tartlets for parties.

SERVES 6

25g/1oz/2 tbsp butter
1 onion, thinly sliced
2.5ml/½ tsp dried thyme
450g/1lb leeks, thinly sliced
50g/2oz Gruyère or Emmenthal cheese, grated
3 eggs
300ml/½ pint/1¼ cups single (light) cream
pinch of freshly grated nutmeg
salt and ground black pepper
mixed salad leaves, to serve

FOR THE PASTRY

175g/6oz/1⅓ cups plain (all-purpose) flour
75g/3oz/6 tbsp cold butter
1 egg yolk
30–45ml/2–3 tbsp cold water
2.5ml/½ tsp salt

1 To make the pastry, sift the flour into a bowl and add the butter. Using your fingertips, rub the butter into the flour until it resembles fine breadcrumbs. Make a well in the centre of the mixture.

2 Beat together the egg yolk, water and salt, pour into the well and combine the flour and liquid until it begins to stick together. Form into a ball. Wrap and chill for 30 minutes.

3 Butter six 10cm/4in tartlet tins (muffin pans). On a lightly floured surface, roll out the dough until 3mm/⅛in thick, then using a 12.5cm/5in cutter, cut as many rounds as possible. Gently ease the rounds into the tins, pressing the pastry firmly into the base and sides. Re-roll the trimmings and line the remaining tins. Prick the bases all over and chill in the fridge for 30 minutes.

4 Preheat the oven to 190°C/375°F/Gas 5. Line the pastry cases with foil and fill with baking beans. Place on a baking sheet and bake for 6–8 minutes until golden at the edges. Remove the foil and beans and bake for a further 2 minutes until the bases appear dry. Transfer to a wire rack to cool. Reduce the oven temperature to 180°C/350°F/Gas 4.

5 In a large frying pan, melt the butter over a medium heat, then add the onion and thyme and cook for 3–5 minutes until the onion is just softened, stirring frequently. Add the thinly sliced leeks and cook for 10–12 minutes until they are soft and tender, stirring occasionally. Divide the leek mixture among the pastry cases and sprinkle each with cheese, dividing it evenly.

6 In a medium bowl, beat the eggs, cream, nutmeg and salt and pepper. Place the pastry cases on a baking sheet and pour in the egg mixture. Bake for 15–20 minutes until set and golden. Transfer the tartlets to a wire rack to cool slightly, then remove them from the tins and serve warm or at room temperature with salad leaves.

Nutritional information per portion: Energy 422kcal/1755kJ; Protein 11.5g; Carbohydrate 26.8g, of which sugars 3.9g; Fat 30.4g, of which saturates 17.7g; Cholesterol 200mg; Calcium 189mg; Fibre 2.7g; Sodium 215mg.

Tortilla wrap with tabbouleh and avocado

To be successful, tabbouleh needs spring onions, lemon juice, plenty of fresh herbs and lots of black pepper. Served at room temperature, it goes very well with the chilli and avocado mixture.

SERVES 6

175g/6oz/1 cup bulgur wheat
30ml/2 tbsp chopped fresh mint
30ml/2 tbsp chopped fresh flat leaf parsley, plus extra to garnish (optional)
1 bunch (about 6) spring onions (scallions), sliced
1/2 cucumber, diced
50ml/2fl oz/1/4 cup extra virgin olive oil
juice of 1 large lemon
salt and freshly ground black pepper
1 ripe avocado, stoned (pitted), peeled and diced
juice of 1/2 lemon
1/2 red chilli, seeded and sliced
1 garlic clove, crushed
1/2 red (bell) pepper, seeded and finely diced
4 wheat tortillas, to serve

1 To make the tabbouleh, place the bulgur wheat in a large heatproof bowl and pour over enough boiling water to cover. Leave for 30 minutes until the grains are tender but still retain a little resistance to the bite. Drain thoroughly in a sieve, then tip back into the bowl.

2 Add the mint, parsley, spring onions and cucumber to the bulgur wheat and mix thoroughly. Blend together the olive oil and lemon juice and pour over the tabbouleh, season to taste and toss well to mix. Chill for 30 minutes to allow the flavours to mingle.

3 To make the avocado mixture, place the avocado in a bowl and add the lemon juice, chilli and garlic. Season to taste and mash with a fork to form a smooth purée. Stir in the red pepper.

4 Warm the tortillas in a dry frying pan and serve either flat, folded or rolled up with the tabbouleh and avocado mixture. Garnish with parsley, if using.

Nutritional information per portion: Energy 336kcal/1408kJ; Protein 7.2g; Carbohydrate 53.9g, of which sugars 3.3g; Fat 11.4g, of which saturates 1.9g; Cholesterol 0mg; Calcium 88mg; Fibre 3.2g; Sodium 173mg.

Mini baked potatoes with blue cheese

These miniature potatoes can be eaten with the fingers. This dish is a great way of starting off an informal supper party, but it works just as well as a light snack, using ordinary baking potatoes.

MAKES 20

20 small new or salad potatoes
60ml/4 tbsp vegetable oil
coarse salt
120ml/4fl oz/1/2 cup sour cream
25g/1oz blue cheese, crumbled
30ml/2 tbsp chopped fresh chives, to garnish

1 Preheat the oven to 180°C/350°F/Gas 4. Wash and dry the potatoes. Toss with the oil in a bowl to coat.

2 Dip the potatoes in the coarse salt to coat lightly. Spread the potatoes out on a baking sheet. Bake for 45–50 minutes until the potatoes are tender.

3 In a small bowl, combine the sour cream and blue cheese, mixing together well.

4 Cut a cross in the top of each potato. Press gently with your fingers to open the potatoes.

5 Top each potato with a dollop of the blue cheese mixture. Place on a serving dish and garnish with the chives. Serve hot or at room temperature.

Nutritional information per portion: Energy 63kcal/262kJ; Protein 1.1g; Carbohydrate 6.3g, of which sugars 0.7g; Fat 3.9g, of which saturates 1.3g; Cholesterol 5mg; Calcium 14mg; Fibre 0.4g; Sodium 22mg.

Twice-baked Gruyère and potato soufflé

A great starter dish, this recipe can be prepared in advance if you are entertaining, to be given its second baking just before you serve it up.

SERVES 4

225g/8oz floury potatoes
2 eggs, separated
175g/6oz/1½ cups Gruyère cheese, grated
50g/2oz/½ cup self-raising (self-rising) flour
50g/2oz spinach leaves
butter, for greasing
salt and ground black pepper
salad leaves, to serve

1 Preheat the oven to 200°C/400°F/Gas 6. Peel the potatoes and cook in lightly salted boiling water for 20 minutes until very tender. Drain and mash with the egg yolks.

2 Stir in half of the Gruyère cheese and all of the flour. Season to taste with salt and ground black pepper. Finely chop the spinach and fold into the potato mixture.

3 Whip the egg whites until they form soft peaks. Fold a little of the egg white into the mixture to slacken it slightly. Using a large spoon, fold the remaining egg white into the mixture.

4 Grease 4 large ramekin dishes. Pour the mixture into the dishes; place on a baking sheet. Bake for 20 minutes. Remove from the oven and allow to cool.

5 Turn the soufflés out on to a baking sheet and scatter with the remaining cheese. Bake again for 5 minutes; serve with salad leaves.

Nutritional information per portion: Energy 304kcal/1270kJ; Protein 16.7g; Carbohydrate 19g, of which sugars 1.2g; Fat 17.5g, of which saturates 10.4g; Cholesterol 138mg; Calcium 380mg; Fibre 1.2g; Sodium 376mg.

Fried rice balls stuffed with mozzarella

These deep-fried balls of risotto go by the name of* suppli al telefono *in their native Italy. Stuffed with mozzarella cheese, they are very popular snacks and make a wonderful start to any meal.

SERVES 4

1 quantity Risotto alla Milanese, made without the saffron and with vegetable stock (see page 181)
3 eggs
breadcrumbs and plain (all-purpose) flour, to coat
115g/4oz/2/3 cup mozzarella cheese, cut into small cubes
oil, for deep-frying
dressed frisée lettuce and cherry tomatoes, to serve

1 Put the risotto in a bowl and allow it to cool completely. Beat two of the eggs, and stir them into the cooled risotto until well mixed.

2 Use your hands to form the rice mixture into balls the size of large eggs. If the mixture is too moist to hold its shape well, stir in a few spoonfuls of breadcrumbs. Poke a hole in the centre of each ball with your finger, then fill it with the mozzarella, and close the hole over again with the rice mixture.

3 Heat the oil for deep-frying until a small piece of bread sizzles as soon as it is dropped in.

4 Spread some flour on a plate. Beat the remaining egg in a shallow bowl. Sprinkle another plate with breadcrumbs. Roll the balls in the flour, then in the egg, and finally in the breadcrumbs. Fry the rice balls, a few at a time, in the hot oil until golden and crisp. Drain on kitchen paper while the remaining balls are being fried and keep warm. Serve at once, with a simple salad of frisée lettuce and cherry tomatoes.

Nutritional information per portion: Energy 813kcal/3389kJ; Protein 28.9g; Carbohydrate 89.6g, of which sugars 1.9g; Fat 37.9g, of which saturates 22.1g; Cholesterol 233mg; Calcium 464mg; Fibre 0.8g; Sodium 754mg.

Vegetable tarte tatin

This upside-down tart combines Mediterranean vegetables with rice, garlic, onions and olives. Courgettes and mushrooms could be used as well.

SERVES 4

30ml/2 tbsp sunflower oil
about 25ml/1½ tbsp olive oil
1 aubergine (eggplant), sliced lengthways
1 large red (bell) pepper, seeded and cut into long strips
5 tomatoes
2 red shallots, finely chopped
1–2 garlic cloves, crushed
150ml/¼ pint/⅔ cup white wine
10ml/2 tsp chopped fresh basil
225g/8oz/2 cups cooked white or brown long grain rice
40g/1½oz/⅔ cup stoned (pitted) black olives, chopped
350g/12oz puff pastry, thawed if frozen
ground black pepper
salad leaves, to serve

1 Preheat the oven to 190°C/375°F/Gas 5. Heat the sunflower oil with 15ml/1 tbsp of the olive oil and fry the aubergine slices for 4–5 minutes on each side. Drain on kitchen paper.

2 Add the pepper strips to the oil in the pan, turning them to coat. Cover the pan with a lid or foil and sweat the peppers over a moderately high heat for 5–6 minutes, stirring occasionally, until they are soft and flecked with brown.

3 Slice two of the tomatoes and set them aside. Plunge the remaining tomatoes briefly into boiling water, then peel them, cut them into quarters and remove the core and seeds. Chop the tomato flesh roughly.

4 Heat the remaining oil in the pan and fry the shallots and garlic for 3–4 minutes until softened. Add the chopped tomatoes and cook for a few minutes until softened. Stir in the wine and basil, with black pepper. Bring to the boil, then remove from the heat and stir in the rice and olives.

5 Arrange the tomato slices, aubergine slices and peppers in a single layer on the base of a heavy, 30cm/12in, shallow ovenproof dish. Spread the rice mixture on top.

6 Roll out the pastry to a circle slightly larger than the diameter of the dish and place on top of the rice, tucking the overlap down inside the dish. Bake for 25–30 minutes, until the pastry is golden. Cool slightly, then invert the tart on to a warmed serving plate. Serve in slices, with salad leaves.

Nutritional information per portion: Energy 535kcal/2240kJ; Protein 8.2g; Carbohydrate 59.1g, of which sugars 8.8g; Fat 29.5g, of which saturates 1.2g; Cholesterol 0mg; Calcium 89mg; Fibre 2.6g; Sodium 521mg.

Buckwheat blinis with mushroom caviar

These little Russian pancakes are traditionally served with fish roe caviar and sour cream. Here is a vegetarian alternative that uses a selection of delicious wild mushrooms in place of fish roe.

SERVES 4

115g/4oz/1 cup strong white bread flour
50g/2oz/1/2 cup buckwheat flour
2.5ml/1/2 tsp salt
300ml/1/2 pint/1 1/4 cups milk
5ml/1 tsp dried yeast
2 eggs, separated
200ml/7fl oz/scant 1 cup sour cream or crème fraîche

FOR THE CAVIAR

350g/12oz mixed wild mushrooms, such as chanterelle and porcini, trimmed and chopped
5ml/1 tsp celery salt
30ml/2 tbsp walnut oil
15ml/1 tbsp lemon juice
45ml/3 tbsp chopped fresh parsley
ground black pepper

1 To make the caviar, place the mushrooms in a glass bowl, toss with the salt and cover with a weighted plate. Leave for 2 hours until the juices have run out into the base of the bowl. Rinse to remove the salt, drain and press out as much liquid as you can with the back of a spoon. Return the mushrooms to the bowl and toss with walnut oil, lemon juice, parsley and pepper. Chill.

2 Sift the two flours together with the salt in a large mixing bowl. Gently warm the milk then add the yeast, stirring until dissolved. Pour into the flour, add the egg yolks and stir to make a smooth batter. Cover with a clean damp dish towel and leave in a warm place for 1 hour.

3 Whisk the egg whites in a clean grease-free bowl until stiff then fold into the risen batter. Heat an iron pan or griddle to a moderate temperature. Moisten with oil, then drop spoonfuls of the batter on to the surface. When bubbles rise to the top, turn them over and cook briefly on the other side. Spoon on the sour cream or crème fraîche, top with the caviar and serve.

Nutritional information per portion: Energy 380kcal/1586kJ; Protein 12.5g; Carbohydrate 38.8g, of which sugars 6.2g; Fat 20.6g, of which saturates 8.5g; Cholesterol 130mg; Calcium 205mg; Fibre 2.3g; Sodium 94mg.

Pears and **Stilton**

Stilton is the classic British blue cheese, but you could use other blue cheeses. Comice pears are a good choice for this dish, but for a dramatic colour contrast, select the excellent Red Williams.

SERVES 4

4 ripe pears, lightly chilled
75g/3oz blue Stilton
50g/2oz curd (farmer's) cheese
ground black pepper
watercress sprigs, to garnish

FOR THE DRESSING
45ml/3 tbsp light olive oil
15ml/1 tbsp lemon juice
10ml/2 tsp toasted poppy seeds
salt and ground black pepper

1 First make the dressing: place the olive oil and lemon juice, poppy seeds and seasoning in a screw-top jar and then shake together until emulsified.

2 Cut the pears in half lengthways, then scoop out the cores and cut away the calyx from the rounded end.

3 Beat together the Stilton, curd cheese and a little pepper. Divide this mixture among the cavities in the pears.

4 Shake the dressing to mix it again, then spoon it over the pears. Serve garnished with some watercress sprigs.

Nutritional information per portion: Energy 243kcal/1007kJ; Protein 7.2g; Carbohydrate 15.5g, of which sugars 15.5g; Fat 17.2g, of which saturates 6.4g; Cholesterol 21mg; Calcium 109mg; Fibre 3.5g; Sodium 208mg.

Fish and shellfish

Fish lends itself perfectly to appetizers because it is so versatile. In these recipes, fish is turned into sausages, kebabs, batons and delicious puff parcels. Easy-to-cook shellfish forms the basis for some of the great classic starters such as Marinated Mussels and Crab Cakes with Tartare Sauce.

Three-colour fish kebabs

Don't leave the fish to marinate for more than an hour. The lemon juice will start to break down the fibres of the fish after this time and it will then be difficult to avoid overcooking it.

SERVES 4

120ml/4fl oz/1/2 cup olive oil
grated rind and juice of 1 lemon
5ml/1 tsp crushed chilli flakes
350g/12oz monkfish fillet, cubed
350g/12oz swordfish fillet, cubed
350g/12oz thick salmon fillet, cubed
2 red, yellow or orange (bell) peppers, cored, seeded and cut into squares
30ml/2 tbsp chopped fresh parsley
salt and ground black pepper

FOR THE SWEET TOMATO AND CHILLI SALSA

225g/8oz ripe tomatoes, finely chopped
1 garlic clove, crushed
1 fresh red chilli, seeded and chopped
45ml/3 tbsp extra virgin olive oil
15ml/1 tbsp lemon juice
15ml/1 tbsp chopped fresh parsley
pinch of sugar

1 Put the oil in a shallow glass or china bowl and add the lemon rind and juice, the chilli flakes and pepper to taste. Whisk to combine, then add the fish chunks. Turn to coat evenly.

2 Add the pepper squares, stir, then cover and marinate in a cool place for 1 hour, turning occasionally with a slotted spoon.

3 Thread the fish and peppers on to eight oiled metal skewers, reserving the marinade. Barbecue or grill (broil) the skewered fish for 5–8 minutes, turning once.

4 Meanwhile, make the salsa by mixing all the ingredients in a bowl, and then add seasoning to taste. Heat the reserved marinade in a small pan, remove from the heat and stir in the parsley, with salt and pepper to taste. Serve the kebabs hot, with the marinade spooned over, accompanied by the salsa.

Nutritional information per portion: Energy 506kcal/2108kJ; Protein 37.4g; Carbohydrate 14.4g, of which sugars 0.6g; Fat 33.6g, of which saturates 13.7g; Cholesterol 130mg; Calcium 75mg; Fibre 0.6g; Sodium 1414mg.

Breaded sole batons

Goujons of lemon sole are coated in seasoned flour and then in breadcrumbs, and fried until deliciously crispy. They are served with piquant tartare sauce.

SERVES 4

275g/10oz lemon sole fillets, skinned
2 eggs
115g/4oz/1½ cups fine fresh breadcrumbs
75g/3oz/6 tbsp plain (all-purpose) flour
salt and ground black pepper
vegetable oil, for frying
tartare sauce and lemon wedges, to serve

1 Cut the fish fillets into long diagonal strips about 2cm/¾in wide, using a sharp knife.

2 Break the eggs into a shallow dish and beat well with a fork. Place the breadcrumbs in another shallow dish. Put the flour in a large plastic bag and season with salt and plenty of ground black pepper.

3 Dip the fish strips in the egg, turning to coat well. Place on a plate and then taking a few at a time, shake them in the bag of flour. Dip the strips in the egg again, then in the breadcrumbs, coating well. Place on a tray in a single layer. Let the coating set for 10 minutes.

4 Heat 1cm/½in oil in a large frying pan over a medium-high heat. When the oil is hot (a cube of bread will sizzle) fry the fish strips for about 2–2½ minutes in batches, turning once. Drain on kitchen paper and keep warm. Serve the fish with tartare sauce and lemon wedges.

Nutritional information per portion: Energy 363kcal/1522kJ; Protein 20.7g; Carbohydrate 36.9g, of which sugars 1g; Fat 15.8g, of which saturates 2.1g; Cholesterol 130mg; Calcium 98mg; Fibre 1.2g; Sodium 323mg.

Fish sausages

This unusual recipe originated in Hungary during the seventeenth century. It is still popular today as a satisfying and tasty way of using a variety of fish fillets.

SERVES 4

375g/13oz fish fillets, such as perch, pike, carp or cod, skinned
1 white bread roll
75ml/5 tbsp milk
25ml/1½ tbsp chopped fresh flat leaf parsley
2 eggs, well beaten
50g/2oz/½ cup plain (all-purpose) flour
50g/2oz/1 cup fine fresh white breadcrumbs
oil, for shallow frying
salt and ground black pepper
deep-fried parsley sprigs and lemon wedges dusted with paprika, to garnish

1 Mince or process the fish coarsely in a food processor or blender. Soak the roll in the milk for about 10 minutes, then squeeze it out. Mix the fish and bread together before adding the chopped parsley, one of the eggs and plenty of seasoning.

2 Using your fingers, shape the fish mixture into 10cm/4in long sausages, making them about 2.5cm/1in thick. Carefully roll the fish "sausages" in the flour, then in the remaining egg and finally in the breadcrumbs.

3 Heat the oil in a pan then slowly cook the sausages until golden brown all over. (You may need to work in batches.) Drain well on crumpled kitchen paper. Garnish with the deep-fried parsley sprigs and lemon wedges dusted with paprika.

Nutritional information per portion: Energy 238kcal/1007kJ; Protein 24.7g; Carbohydrate 25.8g, of which sugars 1.7g; Fat 4.8g, of which saturates 1.4g; Cholesterol 139mg; Calcium 82mg; Fibre 1.2g; Sodium 292mg.

Deep-fried whitebait

A spicy coating on these fish, which is a mixture of ground ginger, curry powder and cayenne pepper, gives this ever popular dish a crunchy bite.

SERVES 6

115g/4oz/1 cup plain (all-purpose) flour
2.5ml/1/2 tsp curry powder
2.5ml/1/2 tsp ground ginger
2.5ml/1/2 tsp cayenne pepper
pinch of salt
1.2kg/2 1/2 lb whitebait, thawed if frozen
vegetable oil, for deep-frying
lemon wedges, to garnish

1 Mix together the plain flour, curry powder, ground ginger, cayenne pepper and a little salt in a large bowl. Coat the fish in the seasoned flour, covering them evenly.

2 Heat the oil in a large, heavy pan until it reaches a temperature of 190°C/375°F. Fry the whitebait in batches for about 2–3 minutes until the fish is golden and crispy.

3 Drain the whitebait well on kitchen paper. Keep warm in a low oven until you have cooked all the fish. Serve at once, garnished with lemon wedges for squeezing over.

Nutritional information per portion: Energy 1050kcal/4348kJ; Protein 39g; Carbohydrate 10.6g, of which sugars 0.2g; Fat 95g, of which saturates 0g; Cholesterol 0mg; Calcium 1720mg; Fibre 0.4g; Sodium 460mg.

Herby plaice fritters

Serve these baby croquettes with a tartare sauce if you like, or use a good-quality mayonnaise and stir in some chopped capers and gherkins. Season to taste.

SERVES 4

450g/1lb plaice fillets
300ml/½ pint/1¼ cups milk
450g/1lb cooked potatoes
1 fennel bulb, finely chopped
45ml/ 3 tbsp chopped fresh parsley
2 eggs
15g/½ oz/1 tbsp unsalted butter
250g/9oz/2 cups white breadcrumbs
25g/1oz/2 tbsp sesame seeds
oil, for deep-frying
salt and ground black pepper

1 Gently poach the plaice fillets in the milk for about 15 minutes until the fish flakes. Drain and reserve the milk. Peel the skin off the fish and remove any bones. In a food processor fitted with a metal blade, process the fish, potatoes, fennel, parsley, eggs and butter.

2 Add 30ml/2 tbsp of the reserved cooking milk and season. Mix well. Chill for 30 minutes then shape into 20 even-size croquettes.

3 Mix together the breadcrumbs and sesame seeds, then roll the croquettes in this mixture to form a good coating.

4 Heat the oil in a large, heavy pan until it is hot enough to brown a cube of stale bread in 30 seconds. Deep-fry the croquettes in small batches for about 4 minutes until they are golden brown all over. Drain well on kitchen paper and serve the fritters hot.

Nutritional information per portion: Energy 596kcal/2510kJ; Protein 32.7g; Carbohydrate 67.5g, of which sugars 4g; Fat 23.7g, of which saturates 4.9g; Cholesterol 150mg; Calcium 208mg; Fibre 4.2g; Sodium 687mg.

Paella croquettes

Paella is probably Spain's most famous dish, and here it is used for a tasty fried tapas. In this recipe, the paella is cooked from scratch, but you could, of course, use left-over paella instead.

SERVES 4

pinch of saffron threads
150ml/¼ pint/⅔ cup white wine
30ml/2 tbsp olive oil
1 small onion, finely chopped
1 garlic clove, finely chopped
150g/5oz/⅔ cup risotto rice
300ml/½ pint/1¼ cups hot chicken stock
50g/2oz /½ cup cooked prawns (shrimp), peeled, deveined and coarsely chopped
50g/2oz cooked chicken, chopped
75g/3oz/⅔ cup petits pois, thawed if frozen
30ml/2 tbsp grated Parmesan cheese
1 egg, beaten
30ml/2 tbsp milk
75g/3oz/1½ cups fresh white breadcrumbs
vegetable or olive oil, for shallow-frying
salt and ground black pepper
flat leaf parsley, to garnish

1 Stir the saffron into the wine in a small bowl; set aside.

2 Heat the oil in a saucepan and gently fry the onion and garlic for 5 minutes until soft. Stir in the rice and cook, stirring, for 1 minute. Keeping the heat fairly high, add the wine and saffron mixture to the pan, stirring until it is all absorbed.

3 Gradually add the stock, stirring until the liquid is absorbed and the rice is cooked – about 20 minutes. Stir in the prawns, chicken, petits pois and Parmesan cheese. Season.

4 Cool the mixture slightly, then use spoons to shape the mixture into 16 lozenges.

5 Mix the egg and milk in a shallow bowl. Spread out the breadcrumbs on a sheet of foil. Dip the croquettes in the egg mixture, then coat them evenly in the breadcrumbs.

6 Heat the oil in a frying pan, then shallow fry the croquettes for 4–5 minutes until crisp and golden. Work in batches. Drain on kitchen paper and keep hot. Serve garnished with a sprig of flat leaf parsley.

Nutritional information per portion: Energy 524kcal/2183kJ; Protein 16.2g; Carbohydrate 48.4g, of which sugars 2.3g; Fat 27.3g, of which saturates 4.9g; Cholesterol 85mg; Calcium 160mg; Fibre 1.5g; Sodium 280mg.

Monkfish packages

With its meaty flesh and robust flavour, monkfish is perfect with garlic and chilli in this recipe. You could use a cheaper fish, like eel, but you'll lose that delicious taste.

SERVES 4

175g/6oz/1½ cups strong white bread flour
2 eggs
115g/4oz skinless monkfish fillet, diced
grated rind of 1 lemon
1 garlic clove, chopped
1 small red chilli, seeded and sliced
45ml/3 tbsp chopped fresh parsley
30ml/2 tbsp single (light) cream
salt and ground black pepper

FOR THE TOMATO OIL
2 tomatoes, peeled, seeded and finely diced
45ml/3 tbsp extra virgin olive oil
15ml/1 tbsp lemon juice

1 Place the bread flour, eggs and 2.5ml/½ tsp salt in a blender or food processor; pulse until it forms a soft dough. Knead for 2–3 minutes. Wrap in clear film and chill for 20 minutes. Clean the food processor.

2 Place the monkfish, lemon rind, garlic, chilli and parsley in the food processor; process until very finely chopped. Add the cream, with plenty of salt and ground black pepper, and process again until a very thick paste is formed. Make the tomato oil by stirring the diced tomatoes with the olive oil and lemon juice in a bowl. Add salt to taste. Cover and chill.

3 Roll out the dough thinly on a lightly floured surface and cut out 32 rounds, using a 4cm/1½in plain cutter. Divide the filling among half the rounds, then cover with the remaining rounds. Pinch the edges to seal.

4 Bring a pan of water to a simmer and poach the fish packages in batches, for 2–3 minutes. Drain and serve hot, drizzled with the tomato oil.

Nutritional information per portion: Energy 310kcal/1304kJ; Protein 12.9g; Carbohydrate 36.8g, of which sugars 3.4g; Fat 13.5g, of which saturates 3.1g; Cholesterol 103mg; Calcium 112mg; Fibre 2.7g; Sodium 54mg.

Salmon cakes with **butter sauce**

Salmon fish cakes make a real treat for the start of a dinner party. They are also economical, as you could use any small tail pieces that are on offer from your fishmonger or supermarket.

MAKES 6

225g/8oz salmon tail piece, cooked
30ml/2 tbsp chopped fresh parsley
2 spring onions (scallions), trimmed and chopped
grated rind and juice of ½ lemon
225g/8oz mashed potato (not too soft)
1 egg, beaten
50g/2oz/1 cup fresh white breadcrumbs
75g/3oz/6 tbsp butter, plus extra for frying (optional)
oil, for frying (optional)
salt and ground black pepper
courgette (zucchini) and carrot slices and sprig of coriander (cilantro), to garnish

1 Remove all the skin and bones from the fish and mash or flake it well. Add the parsley, spring onions and 5ml/1 tsp of the lemon rind, and season with salt and lots of black pepper. Gently work in the potato and then shape into six rounds, triangles or croquettes. Chill the salmon cakes for 20 minutes.

2 Preheat the grill (broiler). Coat the salmon cakes well in egg and then in the breadcrumbs. Grill (broil) gently for 5 minutes on each side, or until they are golden, or fry in butter and oil.

3 To make the butter sauce, melt the butter, whisk in the remaining lemon rind, the lemon juice, 15–30ml/1–2 tbsp water and seasoning to taste. Simmer for a few minutes and serve with the hot fish cakes and garnish with slices of courgette and carrot and a sprig of coriander.

Nutritional information per portion: Energy 188kcal/782kJ; Protein 9.5g; Carbohydrate 6.2g, of which sugars 0.7g; Fat 14.1g, of which saturates 6.8g; Cholesterol 68mg; Calcium 36mg; Fibre 0.9g; Sodium 101mg.

Thai fish cakes with cucumber relish

These wonderful small fish cakes are a very familiar and popular starter. They are usually accompanied with Thai beer – or choose a robust oaked Chardonnay instead.

MAKES ABOUT 12

300g/11oz white fish fillet, such as cod, cut into chunks
30ml/2 tbsp red curry paste
1 egg
30ml/2 tbsp fish sauce
5ml/1 tsp sugar
30ml/2 tbsp cornflour (cornstarch)
3 kaffir lime leaves, shredded
15ml/1 tbsp chopped fresh coriander (cilantro)
50g/2oz green beans, finely sliced
oil, for frying
Chinese mustard cress, to garnish

FOR THE CUCUMBER RELISH

60ml/4 tbsp Thai coconut or rice vinegar
60ml/4 tbsp water
50g/2oz sugar
1 whole bulb pickled garlic
1 cucumber, quartered and sliced
4 shallots, finely sliced
15ml/1 tbsp chopped fresh root ginger

1 To make the cucumber relish, bring the vinegar, water and sugar to the boil. Stir until the sugar dissolves, then remove from the heat and leave to cool.

2 Combine the rest of the relish ingredients together in a bowl and pour the vinegar mixture over.

3 Combine the fish, curry paste and egg in a food processor and process well. Transfer the mixture to a bowl then add the rest of the ingredients, except the oil and garnish. Stir to mix thoroughly.

4 Mould and shape the mixture into cakes about 5cm/2in in diameter and 5mm/¼in thick.

5 Heat the oil in a wok or deep-fryer. Fry the fish cakes, working in small batches, for about 4–5 minutes or until golden brown. Remove and drain on kitchen paper. Keep warm in a low oven. Garnish with Chinese mustard cress and serve with a little cucumber relish spooned on the side.

Nutritional information per portion: Energy 86kcal/361kJ; Protein 6.2g; Carbohydrate 8.1g, of which sugars 5.4g; Fat 3.4g, of which saturates 0.5g; Cholesterol 27mg; Calcium 16mg; Fibre 0.2g; Sodium 2040mg.

Marinated mussels

This is an ideal recipe to prepare and arrange up to 24 hours in advance. Remove from the fridge 15 minutes before serving to allow the flavours to develop fully.

MAKES ABOUT 48

1kg/2¼lb mussels, large if possible (about 48)
175ml/6fl oz/¾ cup dry white wine
1 garlic clove, finely crushed
120ml/4fl oz/½ cup olive oil
50ml/2fl oz/¼ cup lemon juice
5ml/1 tsp hot chilli flakes
2.5ml/½ tsp mixed (apple pie) spice
15ml/1 tbsp Dijon mustard
10ml/2 tsp sugar
5ml/1 tsp salt
15–30ml/1–2 tbsp chopped fresh dill or coriander (cilantro)
15ml/1 tbsp capers, drained and chopped if large
ground black pepper

1 With a stiff kitchen brush and under cold running water, scrub the mussels to remove any sand and barnacles; pull out and remove the "beards". Discard any open shells that will not shut when they are tapped.

2 In a large casserole or pan set over a high heat, bring the white wine to the boil with the garlic and freshly ground black pepper. Add the mussels and cover. Reduce the heat to medium and simmer for 2–4 minutes until the shells open, stirring occasionally.

3 In a large bowl combine the olive oil, lemon juice, chilli flakes, mixed spice, Dijon mustard, sugar, salt, the chopped dill or coriander and the capers. Stir well then set aside.

4 Discard any mussels with closed shells. With a small sharp knife, carefully remove the remaining mussels from their shells, reserving the half shells for serving. Add the mussels to the marinade. Toss the mussels to coat well, then cover and chill in the fridge for 6–8 hours or overnight, stirring gently from time to time.

5 With a teaspoon, place one mussel with a little marinade in each shell and arrange on a platter. To stop them wobbling, they can be placed on crushed ice, well washed seaweed or coarse salt.

Nutritional information per portion: Energy 21kcal/86kJ; Protein 1.1g; Carbohydrate 0.3g, of which sugars 0.3g; Fat 1.4g, of which saturates 0.2g; Cholesterol 3mg; Calcium 15mg; Fibre 0.1g; Sodium 23mg.

Thai-style seafood turnovers

These elegant appetizer-size turnovers are filled with fish, prawns and Thai fragrant rice, and are subtly flavoured with fresh coriander, garlic and ginger.

MAKES 18

plain (all-purpose) flour, for dusting
500g/1¼lb puff pastry, thawed if frozen
1 egg, beaten with 30ml/2 tbsp water
lime twists, to garnish

FOR THE FILLING

275g/10oz skinned white fish fillets, such as cod or haddock
seasoned plain (all-purpose) flour
8–10 large raw prawns (shrimp)
15ml/1 tbsp sunflower oil
about 75g/3oz/6 tbsp butter
6 spring onions (scallions), finely sliced
1 garlic clove, crushed
225g/8oz/2 cups cooked Thai fragrant rice
4cm/1½in piece fresh root ginger, grated
10ml/2 tsp finely chopped fresh coriander (cilantro)
5ml/1 tsp finely grated lime rind

1 Preheat the oven to 190°C/375°F/Gas 5. Make the filling. Cut the fish into 2cm/¾in cubes and dust with seasoned flour. Peel the prawns, remove the veins and cut each one into four pieces.

2 Heat half of the oil and 15g/½oz/1 tbsp of the butter in a frying pan. Fry the spring onions gently for 2 minutes.

3 Add the garlic and fry for a further 5 minutes, until the onions are very soft. Transfer to a large bowl.

4 Heat the remaining oil and a further 25g/1oz/2 tbsp of the butter in a clean pan. Fry the fish pieces briefly. As soon as they begin to turn opaque, use a slotted spoon to transfer them to the bowl with the spring onions. Cook the prawns in the fat remaining in the pan. When they begin to change colour, lift them out and add them to the bowl.

5 Add the cooked rice to the bowl, with the fresh root ginger, coriander and grated lime rind. Mix, taking care not to break up the fish.

6 Dust the work surface with a little flour. Roll out the pastry and cut into 10cm/4in rounds. Place spoonfuls of filling just off centre on the pastry rounds. Dot with a little of the remaining butter. Dampen the edges of the pastry with a little of the egg wash, fold one side of the pastry over the filling and press the edges together firmly.

7 Place the turnovers on two lightly greased baking sheets. Decorate them with the pastry trimmings, if you like, and brush them with egg wash. Bake in the oven for 12–15 minutes or until golden brown all over. Transfer to a plate and garnish with lime twists.

Nutritional information per portion: Energy 171kcal/715kJ; Protein 8.6g; Carbohydrate 18.7g, of which sugars 0.9g; Fat 7g, of which saturates 2.3g; Cholesterol 48mg; Calcium 34mg; Fibre 0.4g; Sodium 99mg.

Spinach empanadillas

These are little pastry turnovers, filled with ingredients that have a strong Moorish influence – pine nuts and raisins. Serve with pre-dinner drinks at an informal supper party.

MAKES 20

25g/1oz/2 tbsp raisins, soaked
25ml/1½ tbsp olive oil
450g/1lb fresh spinach, washed and chopped
6 drained canned anchovies, chopped
2 garlic cloves, finely chopped
25g/1oz/⅓ cup pine nuts, chopped
1 egg, beaten
350g/12oz puff pastry
salt and ground black pepper

1 Drain the raisins then chop roughly. Heat the oil in a pan, add the spinach, stir, cover and cook over a low heat for 2 minutes. Uncover and turn up the heat to evaporate any liquid. Add the anchovies, garlic and seasoning. Cook, stirring, for a further minute. Remove from the heat, add the raisins and pine nuts, and cool.

2 Preheat the oven to 180°C/350°F/Gas 4. Roll out the pastry to a 3mm/⅛in thickness. Using a 7.5cm/3in pastry cutter, cut out 20 rounds. Re-roll if necessary. Place two teaspoonfuls of the filling in the middle of each round, then brush the edges with water. Bring up the sides of the pastry and seal well.

3 Press the edges of the pastry together with a fork. Brush with egg. Place on a lightly greased baking sheet and bake for 15 minutes, until golden. Serve warm.

Nutritional information per portion: Energy 98kcal/409kJ; Protein 2.5g; Carbohydrate 8.6g, of which sugars 1.9g; Fat 6g, of which saturates 0.6g; Cholesterol 14mg; Calcium 29mg; Fibre 0.2g; Sodium 92mg.

Crab and ricotta tartlets

Use the meat from a freshly cooked crab, weighing about 450g/1lb, if you can. Otherwise, look out for frozen brown and white crab meat as an alternative.

SERVES 4

225g/8oz/2 cups plain (all-purpose) flour
pinch of salt
115g/4oz/½ cup butter, diced
225g/8oz/1 cup ricotta cheese
15ml/1 tbsp grated onion
30ml/2 tbsp grated Parmesan cheese
2.5ml/½ tsp mustard powder
2 eggs, plus 1 egg yolk
225g/8oz crab meat
30ml/2 tbsp chopped fresh parsley
2.5–5ml/½–1 tsp anchovy essence
5–10ml/1–2 tsp lemon juice
salt and cayenne pepper
salad leaves, to garnish

1 Preheat the oven to 200°C/400°F/Gas 6. Sift the flour and salt into a bowl, add the butter and rub it in until it resembles fine breadcrumbs. Stir in about 60ml/4 tbsp cold water.

2 Turn the dough on to a floured surface and knead lightly. Roll out and line four 10cm/4in tartlet tins (muffin pans). Prick the bases with a fork, then chill for 30 minutes.

3 Line with baking parchment and fill with baking beans. Bake for 10 minutes, remove the paper and beans and bake for 10 minutes.

4 Place the ricotta, onion, Parmesan and mustard powder in a bowl and beat until soft. Gradually beat in the eggs and egg yolk.

5 Stir in the crab meat and chopped fresh parsley, then add the anchovy essence and lemon juice. Season to taste with salt and cayenne pepper.

6 Remove the tartlet cases from the oven and reduce the temperature to 180°C/350°F/Gas 4. Spoon the filling into the cases and bake for 20 minutes, until set and golden. Serve hot, garnished with salad leaves.

Nutritional information per portion: Energy 644kcal/2685kJ; Protein 28.1g; Carbohydrate 46.3g, of which sugars 3.3g; Fat 39.8g, of which saturates 23g; Cholesterol 278mg; Calcium 288mg; Fibre 2.4g; Sodium 609mg.

Seafood pancakes

The combination of fresh and smoked haddock imparts a wonderful flavour to the filling. Using pancakes makes this a substantial starter for a dinner party.

SERVES 6

FOR THE PANCAKES

115g/4oz/1 cup plain (all-purpose) flour
pinch of salt
1 egg, plus 1 egg yolk
300ml/½ pint/1¼ cups milk
15ml/1 tbsp melted butter, plus extra for cooking
50–75g/2–3oz Gruyère cheese, grated
frisée lettuce, to serve

FOR THE FILLING

225g/8oz smoked haddock fillet
225g/8oz fresh haddock fillet
300ml/½ pint/1¼ cups milk
150ml/¼ pint/⅔ cup single (light) cream
40g/1½ oz/3 tbsp butter
40g/1½ oz/¼ cup plain (all-purpose) flour
freshly grated nutmeg
2 hard-boiled eggs, peeled and chopped

1 To make the pancakes, sift the flour and salt into a bowl. Make a well in the centre and add the egg and extra yolk. Whisk the egg, starting to incorporate some of the flour.

2 Gradually add the milk, whisking all the time until the batter is smooth and has the consistency of thin cream. Stir in the melted butter.

3 Heat a small crêpe pan or omelette pan until hot, then rub round the inside of the pan with a pad of kitchen paper dipped in melted butter.

4 Pour about 30ml/2 tbsp of the batter into the pan, then tip the pan to coat the base evenly. Cook for about 30 seconds until the underside of the pancake is brown.

5 Flip the pancake over and cook on the other side until it is lightly browned. Repeat to make 12 pancakes, rubbing the pan with melted butter between each pancake. Stack the pancakes as you make them, between sheets of baking parchment. Keep the pancakes warm on a plate that is set over a pan of simmering water.

6 Put the haddock fillets in a large pan. Add the milk and poach for 6–8 minutes, until just tender. Lift out the fish using a slotted spoon and, when cool enough to handle, remove the skin and any bones. Reserve the milk.

7 Measure the single cream into a jug then strain enough of the milk into the jug to make the quantity up to 450ml/¾ pint/scant 2 cups in total.

8 Melt the butter in a pan, stir in the flour and cook gently for 1 minute. Gradually mix in the milk mixture, stirring continuously to make a smooth sauce. Cook for 2–3 minutes, until thickened. Season with salt, black pepper and nutmeg. Roughly flake the haddock and fold into the sauce with the eggs. Leave to cool.

9 Preheat the oven to 180°C/350°F/Gas 4. Divide the filling among the pancakes. Fold the sides of each pancake into the centre, then roll them up to enclose the filling completely.

10 Butter six individual ovenproof dishes and then arrange two filled pancakes in each, or butter one large dish for all the pancakes. Brush with melted butter and cook for 15 minutes. Sprinkle over the Gruyère and cook for a further 5 minutes, until warmed through. Serve hot with lettuce leaves.

Nutritional information per portion: Energy 393kcal/1647kJ; Protein 26.7g; Carbohydrate 25.4g, of which sugars 5.7g; Fat 21.2g, of which saturates 11.9g; Cholesterol 203mg; Calcium 273mg; Fibre 0.8g; Sodium 514mg.

Aromatic tiger prawns

There is no elegant way to eat these aromatic prawns – just hold them by the tails, pull them off the sticks with your fingers and pop them into your mouth.

SERVES 4

16 raw tiger prawns (jumbo shrimp) or scampi (extra large shrimp) tails
2.5ml/½ tsp chilli powder
5ml/1 tsp fennel seeds
5 Sichuan or black peppercorns
1 star anise, broken into segments
1 cinnamon stick, broken into pieces
30ml/2 tbsp groundnut or sunflower oil
2 garlic cloves, chopped
2cm/¾in piece fresh root ginger, peeled and finely chopped
1 shallot, chopped
30ml/2 tbsp water
30ml/2 tbsp rice vinegar
30ml/2 tbsp soft brown or palm sugar (jaggery)
salt and ground black pepper
lime slices and spring onion (scallion), to garnish

1 If you are using whole prawns, remove the heads. Thread the prawns or scampi tails in pairs on 8 wooden cocktail sticks (toothpicks). Set aside. Heat a frying pan, put in all the chilli powder, fennel seeds, Sichuan or black peppercorns, star anise and cinnamon stick and dry-fry for 1–2 minutes to release the flavours. Leave to cool, then grind coarsely in a grinder or tip into a mortar and crush with a pestle.

2 Heat the groundnut or sunflower oil in a shallow pan, add the garlic, ginger and chopped shallot and then fry gently until very lightly coloured. Add the crushed spices and seasoning and cook the mixture gently for 2 minutes. Pour in the water and simmer, stirring, for 5 minutes.

3 Add the rice vinegar and soft brown or palm sugar, stir until dissolved, then add the prawns or scampi tails. Cook for about 3–5 minutes, until the seafood has turned pink, but is still very juicy. Serve hot, garnished with lime slices and spring onion.

Nutritional information per portion: Energy 142kcal/593kJ; Protein 13.4g; Carbohydrate 9g, of which sugars 8.7g; Fat 6g, of which saturates 0.7g; Cholesterol 146mg; Calcium 67mg; Fibre 0.2g; Sodium 144mg.

Italian prawn skewers

Parsley and lemon are all that is required to create a lovely tiger prawn dish. Grill them, or barbecue them for an informal al fresco summer appetizer.

SERVES 4

900g/2lb raw tiger prawns (jumbo shrimp), peeled
60ml/4 tbsp olive oil
45ml/3 tbsp vegetable oil
75g/3oz/1¼ cups very fine dry breadcrumbs
1 garlic clove, crushed
15ml/1 tbsp chopped fresh parsley
salt and ground black pepper
lemon wedges, to serve

1 Slit the prawns down their backs and remove the dark vein. Rinse in cold water and dry on kitchen paper.

2 Put the oils in a large bowl and add the prawns, coating them evenly. Add the breadcrumbs, garlic and parsley and season. Toss the prawns thoroughly, to give them an even coating of breadcrumbs. Cover and leave to marinate for 1 hour.

3 Carefully thread the tiger prawns on to four metal or wooden skewers, curling them up as you work, so that the tails are skewered neatly in the middle.

4 Preheat the grill (broiler) to a moderate heat. Place the skewers in the grill (broiling) pan and cook for 2 minutes on each side, until they are golden. Serve with the lemon.

Nutritional information per portion: Energy 415kcal/1734kJ; Protein 42.2g; Carbohydrate 14.9g, of which sugars 0.8g; Fat 21.1g, of which saturates 2.8g; Cholesterol 439mg; Calcium 227mg; Fibre 1.1g; Sodium 574mg.

Prawn cocktail

There is no nicer starter than a good, fresh prawn cocktail – but not with soggy prawns in a thin, vinegary sauce embedded in limp lettuce. This recipe shows how good a prawn cocktail can be.

SERVES 6

60ml/4 tbsp double (heavy) cream, lightly whipped
60ml/4 tbsp mayonnaise, preferably home-made
60ml/4 tbsp tomato ketchup
5–10ml/1–2 tsp Worcestershire sauce
juice of 1 lemon
1/2 cos or romaine lettuce
450g/1lb/4 cups cooked peeled prawns (shrimp)
salt, ground black pepper and paprika
6 large whole cooked unpeeled prawns (shrimp), to garnish (optional)
thinly sliced brown bread and lemon wedges, to serve

1 In a bowl, mix together the whipped cream, mayonnaise and ketchup. Add Worcestershire sauce to taste. Stir in enough lemon juice to make a really tangy sauce.

2 Finely shred the lettuce and fill six individual glasses one-third full. Stir the prawns into the sauce, then check the seasoning. Spoon the prawn mixture over the lettuce.

3 To prepare the garnish, if desired, peel the body shell from the whole cooked prawns and leave the tail "fan" for decoration. Drape one prawn over the edge of each glass. Sprinkle each of the cocktails with ground black pepper and some paprika. Serve immediately, with the thinly sliced brown bread and butter and lemon wedges for squeezing over.

Nutritional information per portion: Energy 194kcal/805kJ; Protein 13.9g; Carbohydrate 4.2g, of which sugars 4g; Fat 13.6g, of which saturates 4.6g; Cholesterol 167mg; Calcium 80mg; Fibre 0.4g; Sodium 384mg.

Hot crab soufflés

These delicious little soufflés must be served as soon as they are ready, so seat your guests at the table before taking the soufflés out of the oven.

SERVES 6

50g/2oz/1/4 cup butter
45ml/3 tbsp fine wholemeal (whole-wheat) breadcrumbs
4 spring onions (scallions), finely chopped
15ml/1 tbsp Malayan or mild Madras curry powder
25g/1oz/2 tbsp plain flour
105ml/7 tbsp coconut milk or milk
150ml/1/4 pint/2/3 cup whipping cream
4 egg yolks
225g/8oz white crab meat
mild green Tabasco sauce
6 egg whites
salt and ground black pepper

1 Use some of the butter to grease six ramekin dishes or a 1.75 litre/3 pint/7 1/2 cup soufflé dish. Sprinkle in the fine wholemeal breadcrumbs, roll the dishes or dish around to coat the base and sides completely, then tip out the excess breadcrumbs. Preheat the oven to 200°C/400°F/Gas 6.

2 Melt the remaining butter in a pan, add the spring onions and Malayan or mild Madras curry powder and cook over a low heat for about 1 minute, until softened. Stir in the flour and cook for a further 1 minute.

3 Gradually add the coconut milk or milk and the cream, stirring constantly. Cook until smooth and thick. Off the heat, stir in the egg yolks, then the crab. Season well with salt, black pepper and Tabasco sauce.

4 In a grease-free bowl, beat the egg whites stiffly with a pinch of salt. With a metal spoon stir one-third into the crab mixture then fold in the rest. Spoon into the dishes or dish.

5 Bake until well risen, golden brown and just firm to the touch. Individual soufflés will take 8 minutes; a large soufflé 15–20 minutes. Serve at once.

Nutritional information per portion: Energy 270kcal/1122kJ; Protein 14g; Carbohydrate 11.6g, of which sugars 2.2g; Fat 18.9g, of which saturates 12.1g; Cholesterol 181mg; Calcium 123mg; Fibre 1g; Sodium 426mg.

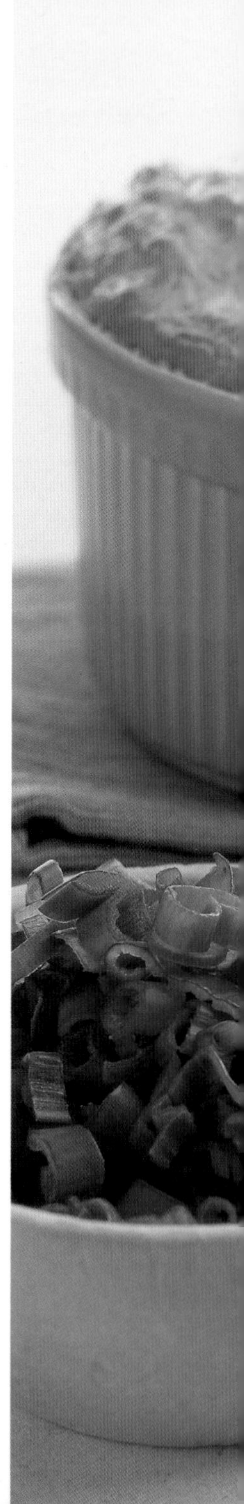

Crab cakes with tartare sauce

Sweet crab meat is offset by a piquant sauce. To make the crab go further, add 50g/2oz/1 cup fresh breadcrumbs and 1 more egg to the crab mixture. Divide into 12 cakes to serve 6.

SERVES 4

675g/1½ lb fresh crab meat
1 egg, beaten
30ml/2 tbsp mayonnaise
15ml/1 tbsp Worcestershire sauce
15ml/1 tbsp sherry
30ml/2 tbsp fresh parsley, finely chopped
15ml/1 tbsp fresh chives or dill, finely chopped
salt and ground black pepper
45ml/3 tbsp olive oil
salad leaves and lemon, to garnish

FOR THE SAUCE
1 egg yolk
15ml/1 tbsp white wine vinegar
30ml/2 tbsp Dijon-style mustard
250ml/8fl oz/1 cup vegetable or groundnut (peanut) oil
3ml/2 tbsp fresh lemon juice
60ml/4 tbsp spring onions (scallions), finely chopped
30ml/2 tbsp chopped drained capers
60ml/4 tbsp dill pickles, finely chopped
60ml/4 tbsp parsley, finely chopped

1 Pick over the crab meat, removing any pieces of shell or cartilage. In a mixing bowl, combine the beaten egg with the mayonnaise, Worcestershire sauce, sherry and herbs. Season with salt and lots of ground black pepper.

2 Gently fold in the crab meat. Divide the mixture into 8 portions and gently form each one into an oval cake. Place on a baking sheet between layers of baking parchment and chill for at least 1 hour.

3 Meanwhile, make the sauce. In a medium-size bowl, beat the egg yolk with a wire whisk until smooth. Add the vinegar, mustard, and salt and pepper to taste, and whisk for about 10 seconds to blend. Slowly whisk in the oil. Add the lemon juice, spring onions, capers, pickles and parsley, and mix well. Check the seasoning. Cover and chill.

4 Preheat the grill (broiler). Brush the crab cakes with the olive oil. Place on an oiled baking sheet, in one layer. Grill (broil) 15cm/6in from the heat until golden brown, for about 5 minutes on each side. Serve the crab cakes with the tartare sauce, garnished with salad leaves and lemon.

Nutritional information per portion: Energy 701kcal/2899kJ; Protein 33.4g; Carbohydrate 1.4g, of which sugars 1.3g; Fat 62g, of which saturates 8.1g; Cholesterol 225mg; Calcium 238mg; Fibre 0.4g; Sodium 1029mg.

Mussels and clams with lemon grass

Lemon grass has an incomparable flavour and is excellent used with seafood. If you cannot find clams, use extra mussels instead but buy a few more in case some need to be discarded.

SERVES 6

1.8–2kg/4–4$^1/_2$ lb mussels
120ml/4fl oz/$^1/_2$ cup dry white wine
1 bunch spring onions (scallions), chopped
2 lemon grass stalks, chopped
6 kaffir lime leaves, chopped
10ml/2 tsp Thai green curry paste
450g/1lb baby clams, washed
200ml/7fl oz/scant 1 cup coconut cream
30ml/2 tbsp chopped fresh coriander (cilantro)
salt and ground black pepper
whole garlic chives, to garnish

1 Clean the mussels. Pull off the "beards" and scrub the shells. Discard any that are broken or stay open when tapped.

2 Put the wine, spring onions, lemon grass, lime leaves and curry paste in a pan. Simmer the mixture until the wine almost evaporates.

3 Add the mussels and clams to the pan, cover tightly and steam the shellfish over a high heat for 5–6 minutes, until they open.

4 Using a slotted spoon, transfer the mussels and clams to a warmed serving bowl and keep hot. Discard any shellfish that remain closed. Strain the cooking liquid into a clean pan and then simmer to reduce the amount by half.

5 Stir in the coconut cream and coriander, with salt and pepper to taste. Heat through. Pour over the seafood and serve, garnished with garlic chives.

Nutritional information per portion: Energy 237kcal/993kJ; Protein 22.5g; Carbohydrate 2.8g, of which sugars 1.7g; Fat 13.8g, of which saturates 10.3g; Cholesterol 58mg; Calcium 238mg; Fibre 0.9g; Sodium 606mg.

Scallop-stuffed roast peppers with pesto

Serve these scallop-and-pesto-filled sweet red peppers with Italian bread, such as ciabatta or focaccia, to mop up the tasty juices.

SERVES 4

4 squat red (bell) peppers
2 large garlic cloves, cut into thin slivers
60ml/4 tbsp olive oil
4 shelled scallops
45ml/3 tbsp pesto sauce
salt and ground black pepper
freshly grated Parmesan cheese, to serve
salad leaves and basil sprigs, to garnish

1 Preheat the oven to 180°C/350°F/Gas 4. Cut the peppers in half lengthways, through their stalks. Scrape out and discard the cores and seeds. Wash the pepper shells and pat dry with kitchen paper.

2 Put the peppers, cut-side up, in an oiled roasting pan. Divide the slivers of garlic equally among them and sprinkle with salt and ground black pepper to taste. Then spoon the oil into the peppers and roast for 40 minutes.

3 Using a sharp knife, carefully cut each of the shelled scallops in half horizontally to make two flat discs each with a piece of coral. When cooked, remove the peppers from the oven and place a scallop half in each pepper half. Then top with the pesto sauce.

4 Return the pan to the oven and roast for 10 minutes more. Make sure you don't overcook the scallops otherwise they will become tough and rubbery. Transfer the peppers and scallops to individual serving plates, sprinkle with grated Parmesan and garnish each plate with a few salad leaves and basil sprigs. Serve warm.

Nutritional information per portion: Energy 285kcal/1186kJ; Protein 18.6g; Carbohydrate 16.7g, of which sugars 13.8g; Fat 16.3g, of which saturates 4.3g; Cholesterol 35mg; Calcium 168mg; Fibre 3.8g; Sodium 222mg.

Clams with chilli and yellow bean sauce

This delicious Thai-inspired dish is simple to prepare. It can be made in a matter of minutes so will not keep you away from your guests for very long.

SERVES 4–6

1kg/2¼ lb fresh clams
30ml/2 tbsp vegetable oil
4 garlic cloves, finely chopped
15ml/1 tbsp grated fresh root ginger
4 shallots, finely chopped
30ml/2 tbsp yellow bean sauce
6 red chillies, seeded and chopped
15ml/1 tbsp fish sauce
pinch of sugar
handful of basil leaves, plus extra to garnish

1 Wash and scrub the clams. Heat the oil in a wok or large frying pan. Add the garlic and ginger and fry for about 30 seconds, add the shallots and fry for a further minute.

2 Add the clams to the pan. Using a fish slice or spatula, turn them a few times to coat all over with the oil. Add the yellow bean sauce and half the chopped red chillies.

3 Continue to cook, stirring often, for 5–7 minutes, or until all the clams are open. You may need to add a splash of water. Adjust the seasoning with the fish sauce and a little sugar. Finally add the basil leaves and stir to mix.

4 Transfer the clams to a serving platter. Garnish with the remaining chopped red chillies and basil leaves and serve.

Nutritional information per portion: Energy 94kcal/393kJ; Protein 11.6g; Carbohydrate 2.4g, of which sugars 0.6g; Fat 4.3g, of which saturates 0.6g; Cholesterol 45mg; Calcium 75mg; Fibre 0.7g; Sodium 998mg.

Scallop and mussel kebabs

These delightfully crispy seafood skewers are served with hot toast spread with a lovely fresh herb butter.

SERVES 4

65g/2½oz/5 tbsp butter, at room temperature
30ml/2 tbsp fresh fennel or parsley, finely chopped
15ml/1 tbsp lemon juice
32 small scallops, removed from shells
24 large mussels, in the shell
8 bacon rashers
50g/2oz/1 cup fresh breadcrumbs
50ml/2fl oz/¼ cup olive oil
salt and ground black pepper
hot toast, to serve

1 Make the flavoured butter by combining the butter with the chopped herbs and lemon juice. Add salt and pepper to taste. Mix well and set aside.

2 In a small pan, cook the scallops in their own liquor until they begin to shrink. (If there is no scallop liquor – retained from the shells after shucking – use a little fish stock or white wine.) Drain the scallops well and then pat dry with kitchen paper.

3 Scrub the mussels well and remove their "beards", then rinse under cold running water. Place in a large pan with about 2.5cm/1in of water in the base. Cover and steam the mussels over a medium heat until they open. When cool enough to handle, remove them from their shells, and pat dry using kitchen paper. Discard any mussels that have not opened during cooking.

4 Take eight 15cm/6in wooden or metal skewers. Thread on each one, alternately, 4 scallops and 3 mussels. As you are doing this, weave a rasher of bacon between the scallops and mussels.

5 Preheat the grill (broiler). Spread the breadcrumbs on a plate. Brush the seafood with olive oil and roll in the crumbs to coat all over.

6 Place the skewers on the grill (broiling) rack. Cook until crisp and lightly browned, 4–5 minutes on each side. Serve immediately with hot toast and the flavoured butter.

Nutritional information per portion: Energy 506kcal/2108kJ; Protein 37.4g; Carbohydrate 14.4g, of which sugars 0.6g; Fat 33.6g, of which saturates 13.7g; Cholesterol 130mg; Calcium 75mg; Fibre 0.6g; Sodium 1414mg.

Salmon and scallop brochettes

With their delicate pastel colours and really superb flavour, these skewers make the perfect opener for a sophisticated dinner party.

SERVES 4

225g/8oz salmon fillet, skinned
8 shucked queen scallops, with their corals if possible
8 baby onions, peeled and blanched
1/2 yellow (bell) pepper, cut into 8 squares
8 lemon grass stalks
25g/1oz/2 tbsp butter
juice of 1/2 lemon
salt, ground white pepper and paprika

FOR THE SAUCE
30ml/2 tbsp dry vermouth
50g/2oz/1/4 cup butter
5ml/1 tsp chopped fresh tarragon

1 Preheat the grill (broiler) to medium-high. Cut the salmon into 12 2cm/3/4 in cubes. Thread the salmon, scallops, corals, onions and pepper squares on to the lemon grass stalks and place the brochettes in a grill (broiling) pan.

2 Melt the butter, add the lemon juice and a pinch of paprika and then brush over the brochettes. Grill (broil) the skewers for 2–3 minutes on each side, turning and basting the brochettes twice, until the fish and scallops are just cooked. Keep hot while you make the sauce.

3 Pour the dry vermouth and the leftover cooking juices from the brochettes into a small pan and boil fiercely to reduce by half. Add the butter and melt, then add the tarragon and salt and pepper. Serve the sauce with the brochettes.

Nutritional information per portion: Energy 321kcal/1336kJ; Protein 23.5g; Carbohydrate 4.8g, of which sugars 2.7g; Fat 22.4g, of which saturates 11.1g; Cholesterol 92mg; Calcium 36mg; Fibre 0.6g; Sodium 231mg.

Marinated asparagus and **langoustine**

For a really extravagant treat, you could make this attractive salad with medallions of lobster. For a cheaper version, use large prawns, allowing six per serving.

SERVES 4

16 langoustines
16 fresh asparagus spears, trimmed
2 carrots
30ml/2 tbsp olive oil
1 garlic clove, peeled
salt and ground black pepper
4 fresh tarragon sprigs and some chopped, to garnish

FOR THE DRESSING
30ml/2 tbsp tarragon vinegar
120ml/4fl oz/1/2 cup olive oil

1 Peel the langoustines and keep the discarded parts for stock.

2 Steam the asparagus over boiling salted water until just tender. Refresh under cold water, drain and place in a shallow dish.

3 Peel the carrots and cut into fine julienne shreds. Cook in a pan of lightly salted boiling water for about 3 minutes, until tender but still crunchy. Drain, refresh under cold water, drain again. Add the carrots to the asparagus.

4 For the dressing, whisk the vinegar with the oil. Season to taste. Pour over the asparagus and carrots and leave to marinate.

5 Heat the oil with the garlic in a frying pan until very hot. Add the langoustines and sauté until just heated through. Discard the garlic.

6 Divide the asparagus and carrots among four plates. Drizzle with the rest of the dressing and top each with four langoustine tails. Add the chopped tarragon and sprigs. Serve.

Nutritional information per portion: Energy 328kcal/1357kJ; Protein 20.7g; Carbohydrate 4g, of which sugars 3.8g; Fat 25.5g, of which saturates 3.7g; Cholesterol 195mg; Calcium 112mg; Fibre 2.3g; Sodium 197mg.

Garlic prawns in filo tartlets

Tartlets made with crisp golden layers of filo pastry and filled with spicy garlic and chilli prawns make a tempting starter, suitable for all occasions.

SERVES 4

FOR THE TARTLETS
50g/2oz/4 tbsp butter, melted
2–3 large sheets filo pastry

FOR THE FILLING
115g/4oz/$^1/_2$ cup butter
2–3 garlic cloves, crushed
1 red chilli, seeded and chopped
350g/12oz/3 cups cooked peeled prawns (shrimp)
30ml/2 tbsp chopped fresh parsley or chopped fresh chives
salt and ground black pepper

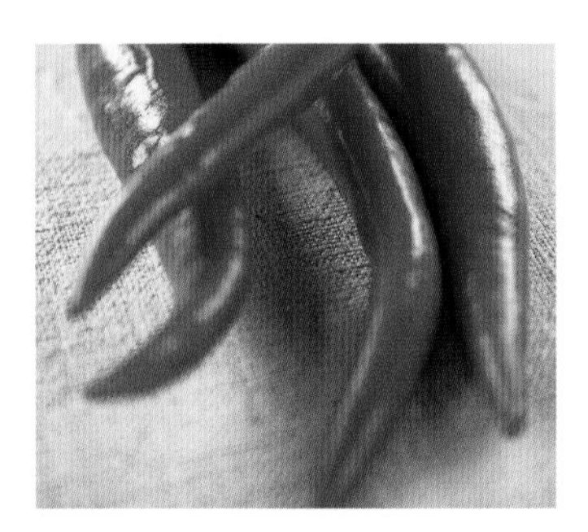

1 Preheat the oven to 200°C/400°F/Gas 6. Brush four individual 7.5cm/3in flan tins (pans) with the melted butter.

2 Cut the filo pastry into twelve 10cm/4in squares and brush with the melted butter. Place three squares of pastry inside each tin, overlapping them at slight angles and carefully frilling the edges and points while forming a good hollow in each centre.

3 Bake in the oven for 10–15 minutes, until crisp and golden. Leave to cool slightly then remove the pastry cases from the tins.

4 Meanwhile, make the filling. Melt the butter in a frying pan, then add the garlic, chilli and prawns and fry quickly for 1–2 minutes to warm through. Stir in the parsley or chives and season with salt and plenty of pepper. Spoon the prawn filling into the tartlets and serve at once.

Nutritional information per portion: Energy 440kcal/1825kJ; Protein 17.6g; Carbohydrate 15g, of which sugars 0.7g; Fat 34.8g, of which saturates 21.6g; Cholesterol 259mg; Calcium 118mg; Fibre 1g; Sodium 419mg.

Poultry and meat

Tasty and spicy bites of meat served as parcels, kebabs, meatballs or pies are popular in many different cultures around the world, including North Africa, Indonesia, Japan and India. Meat can also be included in more substantial appetizers such as a delicious creamy Italian risotto.

Golden Parmesan chicken

Served cold with the garlicky mayonnaise, these morsels of Parmesan-coated chicken make a great appetizer, especially if served informally as finger food.

SERVES 4

4 chicken breast fillets, skinned
75g/3oz/1½ cups fresh white breadcrumbs
40g/1½ oz Parmesan cheese, finely grated
30ml/2 tbsp chopped fresh parsley
2 eggs, beaten
120ml/4fl oz/½ cup mayonnaise
120ml/4fl oz/½ cup fromage frais (low-fat cream cheese)
1–2 garlic cloves, crushed
50g/2oz/4 tbsp butter, melted
salt and ground black pepper

1 Cut each fillet into four or five chunks. Mix together the breadcrumbs, Parmesan, parsley and seasoning in a shallow dish. Dip the chicken pieces in the egg, then into the breadcrumb mixture. Place in a single layer on a baking sheet; chill for 30 minutes.

2 To make the garlic mayonnaise, mix together the mayonnaise, fromage frais and garlic, and season to taste. Spoon into a small serving bowl. Chill.

3 Preheat the oven to 180°C/350°F/Gas 4. Drizzle the melted butter over the chicken pieces and cook them for about 20 minutes, until crisp and golden. Serve the chicken accompanied by the garlic mayonnaise for dipping.

Nutritional information per portion: Energy 591kcal/2460kJ; Protein 35.7g; Carbohydrate 16.7g, of which sugars 2.4g; Fat 43g, of which saturates 14.7g; Cholesterol 227mg; Calcium 216mg; Fibre 0.8g; Sodium 571mg.

Chicken with lemon and garlic

Extremely easy to cook and delicious to eat, this succulent tapas dish makes a great last-minute starter and tastes even better served with some home-made aioli.

SERVES 4

225g/8oz skinless chicken breast fillets
30ml/2 tbsp olive oil
1 shallot, finely chopped
4 garlic cloves, finely chopped
5ml/1 tsp paprika
juice of 1 lemon
30ml/2 tbsp chopped fresh parsley
salt and ground black pepper
flat leaf parsley, to garnish
lemon wedges, to serve

1 Sandwich the chicken breast fillets between two sheets of clear film (plastic wrap) or baking parchment. Bat out with a rolling pin or meat mallet until the fillets are about 5mm/¼in thick.

2 Cut the chicken into strips about 1cm/½ in wide. Heat the oil in a large frying pan. Stir-fry the chicken strips with the shallot, garlic and paprika over a high heat for about 3 minutes until lightly browned and cooked through. Add the lemon juice and parsley with salt and pepper to taste. Serve with lemon wedges, garnished with flat leaf parsley.

Nutritional information per portion: Energy 119kcal/496kJ; Protein 14.1g; Carbohydrate 1.5g, of which sugars 1.1g; Fat 6.3g, of which saturates 1g; Cholesterol 39mg; Calcium 32mg; Fibre 0.8g; Sodium 38mg.

Tandoori chicken sticks

This aromatic chicken dish is traditionally baked in a special clay oven called a tandoor. Here, the chicken is marinated and then grilled, with truly excellent results.

MAKES ABOUT 25

450g/1lb skinless chicken breast fillets

FOR THE CORIANDER YOGURT

250ml/8fl oz/1 cup natural (plain) yogurt
30ml/2 tbsp whipping cream
1/2 cucumber, peeled, seeded and finely chopped
15–30ml/1–2 tbsp fresh chopped mint or coriander (cilantro)
salt and ground black pepper

FOR THE MARINADE

175ml/6fl oz/3/4 cup natural (plain) yogurt
5ml/1 tsp garam masala or curry powder
1.5ml/1/4 tsp ground cumin
1.5ml/1/4 tsp ground coriander
1.5ml/1/4 tsp cayenne pepper (or to taste)
5ml/1 tsp tomato purée (paste)
1–2 garlic cloves, finely chopped
2.5cm/1in piece fresh root ginger, peeled and finely chopped
grated rind and juice of 1/2 lemon
15–30ml/1–2 tbsp chopped fresh mint

1 Prepare the coriander yogurt. Combine all the ingredients in a bowl and season with salt and ground black pepper. Cover with clear film (plastic wrap) and chill until you are ready to serve.

2 Prepare the marinade. Place all the ingredients in the bowl of a food processor, and process thoroughly until the mixture is smooth. Pour into a shallow dish.

3 Freeze the chicken breasts for 5 minutes to firm, then slice in half horizontally. Cut the slices into 2cm/3/4in strips and add to the marinade. Toss to coat well. Cover and chill in the fridge for 6–8 hours or overnight.

4 Preheat the grill (broiler) and line a baking sheet with foil. Using a slotted spoon, remove the chicken from the marinade and arrange the pieces in a single layer on the baking sheet. Scrunch up the chicken slightly so it makes wavy shapes. Grill for 4–5 minutes until brown and just cooked, turning once. When cool enough to handle, thread 1–2 pieces on to cocktail sticks (toothpicks) or short skewers and serve with the coriander yogurt dip.

Nutritional information per portion: Energy 32kcal/134kJ; Protein 5g; Carbohydrate 1.1g, of which sugars 0.8g; Fat 0.9g, of which saturates 0.4g; Cholesterol 14mg; Calcium 29mg; Fibre 0.2g; Sodium 23mg.

Barbecue-glazed chicken skewers

Known as yakitori *in Japan, these aromatic chicken and spring onion skewers are popular throughout the country and are often served as an appetizer with drinks.*

MAKES 12 SKEWERS AND 8 WING PIECES

8 chicken wings
4 chicken thighs, skinned
4 spring onions (scallions), blanched and cut into short lengths

FOR THE BASTING SAUCE
60ml/4 tbsp sake
75ml/5 tbsp/1/3 cup dark soy sauce
30ml/2 tbsp tamari sauce
15ml/1 tbsp mirin, or sweet sherry
15ml/1 tbsp sugar

1 Remove the wing tip of the chicken at the first joint. Chop through the second joint, revealing the two narrow bones. Take hold of the bones with a clean cloth and pull, turning the meat around the bones inside out. Remove the smaller bone and discard. Set the wings aside. Bone the chicken thighs and cut the meat into large dice. Thread the spring onions and thigh meat on to 12 skewers.

2 Measure the basting sauce ingredients into a stainless-steel or enamel pan and simmer until reduced by two-thirds. Cool.

3 Heat the grill (broiler) to a moderately high temperature. Grill (broil) the skewers without applying any oil. When juices begin to emerge from the chicken, baste liberally with the sauce. Allow a further 3 minutes for the chicken on skewers and not more than 5 minutes for the wings.

Nutritional information per portion: Energy 98kcal/415kJ; Protein 20.3g; Carbohydrate 1.9g, of which sugars 1.9g; Fat 0.9g, of which saturates 0.3g; Cholesterol 58mg; Calcium 7mg; Fibre 0.1g; Sodium 495mg.

Chicken parcels

These home-made chicken parcels look splendid piled high and golden brown. Flavoured with parsley and nutmeg, they will be an instant success with your guests.

MAKES 35

225g/8oz/2 cups strong white bread flour, plus extra for dusting
2.5ml/1/2 tsp salt
2.5ml/1/2 tsp caster (superfine) sugar
5ml/1 tsp easy-blend dried (rapid-rise) yeast
25g/1oz/2 tbsp butter, softened
1 egg, beaten, plus a little extra
90ml/6 tbsp warm milk
lemon wedges, to serve

FOR THE FILLING
1 small onion, finely chopped
175g/6oz/1 1/2 cups minced chicken
15ml/1 tbsp sunflower oil
75ml/5 tbsp chicken stock
30ml/2 tbsp chopped fresh parsley
pinch of grated nutmeg
salt and ground black pepper

1 Sift the flour, salt and sugar into a large bowl. Stir in the dried yeast, then make a well in the centre of the flour. Add the butter, egg and milk and mix to a soft dough. Turn on to a lightly floured surface and knead for 10 minutes, until the dough is smooth and elastic. Put the dough in a clean bowl, cover with clear film (plastic wrap) and then leave in a warm place to rise for 1 hour, or until the dough has doubled in size.

2 Meanwhile, fry the onion and chicken in the oil for about 10 minutes. Add the stock and simmer for 5 minutes. Stir in the parsley, grated nutmeg and salt and ground black pepper. Then leave to cool.

3 Preheat the oven to 220°C/425°F/Gas 7. Knead the dough, then roll it out until it is 3mm/1/8in thick. Stamp out rounds with a 7.5cm/3in cutter. Brush the edges with beaten egg. Put a little filling in the middle, then press the edges together. Leave to rise on oiled baking sheets, covered with oiled clear film (plastic wrap), for 15 minutes. Brush with more egg. Bake for 5 minutes, then for 10 minutes at 190°C/375°F/Gas 5, until well risen. Serve with lemon wedges.

Nutritional information per portion: Energy 554kcal/2310kJ; Protein 42.5g; Carbohydrate 14.8g, of which sugars 0.5g; Fat 36.6g, of which saturates 22g; Cholesterol 240mg; Calcium 138mg; Fibre 0.6g; Sodium 417mg.

Chicken bitki

This is a popular dish in its native country, Poland, and makes an attractive starter when offset by deep red beetroot and vibrant green salad leaves.

MAKES 12

15g/½oz/1 tbsp butter, melted
115g/4oz flat mushrooms, finely chopped
50g/2oz/1 cup fresh white breadcrumbs
350g/12oz chicken breast fillets, minced (ground) or finely chopped
2 eggs, separated
1.5ml/¼ tsp grated nutmeg
30ml/2 tbsp plain (all-purpose) flour
45ml/3 tbsp oil
salt and ground black pepper
salad leaves and grated pickled beetroot (beet), to serve

1 Melt the butter in a pan and fry the mushrooms for about 5 minutes until soft and the juices have evaporated. Allow to cool.

2 Mix the mushrooms and the breadcrumbs, the chicken, egg yolks, nutmeg, salt and pepper together.

3 Whisk the egg whites until they are stiff. Stir half of the egg whites into the chicken mixture to slacken it, then fold in the remainder. Shape into 12 even meatballs, about 7.5cm/3in long and about 2.5cm/1in wide. Roll in the flour to coat evenly.

4 Heat the oil in a frying pan and fry the bitki for about 10 minutes, turning until evenly golden brown and cooked through. Serve hot with some salad leaves and the grated pickled beetroot.

Nutritional information per portion: Energy 102kcal/426kJ; Protein 8.9g; Carbohydrate 5.2g, of which sugars 0.2g; Fat 5.2g, of which saturates 1.3g; Cholesterol 55mg; Calcium 16mg; Fibre 0.3g; Sodium 69mg.

Risotto alla Milanese

This classic risotto is often served with the hearty beef stew, osso buco, but it also makes a delicious first course in its own right.

SERVES 5–6

about 1.2 litres/2 pints/5 cups beef or chicken stock
good pinch of saffron threads
75g/3oz/6 tbsp butter
1 onion, finely chopped
275g/10oz/1½ cups risotto rice
75g/3oz/1 cup freshly grated Parmesan cheese
salt and ground black pepper

1 Bring the stock to the boil, then reduce to a low simmer. Ladle a little stock into a small bowl. Add the saffron and leave to infuse.

2 Melt 50g/2oz/4 tbsp of the butter in a large pan. Add the onion and cook gently for about 3 minutes until softened but not browned.

3 Add the rice. Stir until the grains start to swell and burst, then add a few ladlefuls of the stock, with the saffron liquid and seasoning. Stir over a low heat until the stock has been absorbed. Add the remaining stock, a few ladlefuls at a time, allowing the rice to absorb all the liquid before adding more, and stirring constantly. After about 20–25 minutes, the rice should be just tender and creamy.

4 Stir in about two-thirds of the grated Parmesan and the remaining butter. Heat through until the butter has melted. Transfer the risotto to a warmed serving bowl or platter and serve hot, with the remaining grated Parmesan served separately.

Nutritional information per portion: Energy 397kcal/1650kJ; Protein 10.6g; Carbohydrate 46.8g, of which sugars 0.8g; Fat 18.3g, of which saturates 11.3g; Cholesterol 49mg; Calcium 204mg; Fibre 0.2g; Sodium 265mg.

Lamb tikka

Creamy yogurt and ground nuts go wonderfully with the spices in these little Indian meatballs. If you intend to use wooden skewers, soak them in cold water for 30 minutes before cooking.

MAKES ABOUT 20

450g/1lb lamb fillet
2 spring onions (scallions), chopped

FOR THE MARINADE
350ml/12 fl oz/1½ cups natural (plain) yogurt
15ml/1 tbsp ground almonds, cashew nuts or peanuts
15ml/1 tbsp vegetable oil
2–3 garlic cloves, finely chopped
juice of 1 lemon
5ml/1 tsp garam masala or curry powder
2.5ml/½ tsp ground cardamom
1.5ml/¼ tsp cayenne pepper
15–30ml/1–2 tbsp chopped fresh mint

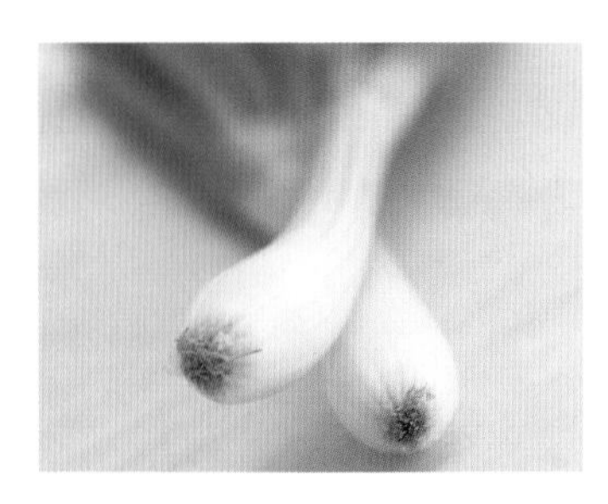

1 To prepare the marinade, stir together the marinade ingredients. In a separate small bowl, reserve about 120ml/4fl oz/½ cup of the mixture to use as a dipping sauce for the meatballs.

2 Cut the lamb into small pieces and put in the bowl of a food processor with the spring onions. Process until the meat is finely chopped. Add 30–45ml/2–3 tbsp of the marinade and process again. Test to see if the mixture holds together by pinching a little between your fingertips. Add a little more marinade if necessary, but do not make the mixture too wet and soft.

3 With moistened palms, form the meat mixture into slightly oval-shaped balls, measuring about 4cm/1½in long, and then arrange the meatballs in a shallow ovenproof dish.

4 Spoon over the remaining marinade. Chill the meatballs in the fridge for 8–10 hours or overnight.

5 Soak 20 wooden skewers for 30 minutes. Preheat the grill (broiler) and line a baking sheet with foil. Thread each meatball on to a skewer and arrange on the baking sheet.

6 Grill (broil) for 4–5 minutes, turning them occasionally, until crisp and golden on all sides. Serve with the marinade as a dipping sauce.

Nutritional information per portion: Energy 44kcal/182kJ; Protein 4.7g; Carbohydrate 0.4g, of which sugars 0.3g; Fat 2.6g, of which saturates 1.2g; Cholesterol 17mg; Calcium 12mg; Fibre 0.1g; Sodium 25mg.

Deep-fried lamb patties

These patties are a tasty North African speciality – called kibbeh – of minced meat and bulgur wheat. They are sometimes stuffed with additional meat and deep fried.

SERVES 6

450g/1lb lean lamb or lean minced (ground) lamb or beef
salt and ground black pepper
oil, for deep-frying
avocado slices and coriander (cilantro) sprigs, to serve

FOR THE PATTIES
225g/8oz/1 1/3 cups bulgur wheat
1 red chilli, seeded and roughly chopped
1 onion, roughly chopped

FOR THE STUFFING
1 onion, finely chopped
50g/2oz/2/3 cup pine nuts
30ml/2 tbsp olive oil
7.5ml/1 1/2 tsp ground allspice
60ml/4 tbsp chopped fresh coriander (cilantro)

1 Cut up the lamb and mince (grind) the pieces in a blender or food processor. Divide the minced meat into two equal portions.

2 For the patties, soak the bulgur wheat for 15 minutes in cold water. Drain then process in a blender or a food processor with the chilli, onion, half the meat and salt and pepper.

3 For the stuffing, fry the onion and pine nuts in the oil for 5 minutes. Add the allspice and remaining minced (ground) meat and fry gently, breaking up the meat with a wooden spoon, until browned. Stir in the coriander and seasoning. Shape the patty mixture into a cake. Cut into 12 wedges. Flatten one piece and spoon some stuffing into the centre. Bring the edges of the patty up over the stuffing, ensuring that the filling is completely encased.

4 Heat oil to a depth of 5cm/2in in a large pan until a few patty crumbs sizzle on the surface.

5 Lower half of the filled patties into the oil and fry for about 5 minutes until golden. Drain on kitchen paper and keep hot while cooking the remainder. Serve with avocado slices and coriander sprigs.

Nutritional information per portion: Energy 451kcal/1873kJ; Protein 19.2g; Carbohydrate 33.8g, of which sugars 1.6g; Fat 27.5g, of which saturates 5.9g; Cholesterol 57mg; Calcium 17mg; Fibre 1.2g; Sodium 66mg.

Spicy koftas

These koftas are cooked in batches and kept hot. Left-over koftas can be coarsely chopped and packed into pitta bread with chutney or relish for a delicious snack.

MAKES 20–25

450g/1lb lean minced (ground) beef or lamb
30ml/2 tbsp finely ground ginger
30ml/2 tbsp finely chopped garlic
4 green chillies, finely chopped
1 small onion, finely chopped
1 egg
2.5ml/½ tsp turmeric
5ml/1 tsp garam masala
50g/2oz coriander (cilantro) leaves, chopped
4–6 mint leaves, chopped, or 2.5ml/½ tsp mint sauce
175g/6oz raw potato
salt, to taste
vegetable oil, for deep-frying

1 Place the beef or lamb in a large bowl along with the ginger, garlic, chillies, onion, egg, spices and herbs. Grate the potato into the bowl, and season with salt. Knead together to blend well and form a soft dough.

2 Using your fingers, shape the kofta mixture into portions the size of golf balls. You should be able to make 20 to 25 koftas. Leave the balls to rest at room temperature for about 25 minutes.

3 In a wok or frying pan, heat the oil to medium-hot and fry the koftas in small batches until they are golden brown in colour. Drain well and serve hot.

Nutritional information per portion: Energy 96kcal/404kJ; Protein 5.2g; Carbohydrate 11.8g, of which sugars 1.2g; Fat 3.4g, of which saturates 1.4g; Cholesterol 18mg; Calcium 16mg; Fibre 1g; Sodium 28mg.

Pork satay

Originating in Indonesia, satay are skewers of meat marinated with spices and cooked quickly over charcoal. It's street food at its best, but it makes a great-tasting starter too.

MAKES ABOUT 20

450g/1lb lean pork
5ml/1 tsp grated fresh root ginger
1 lemon grass stalk, finely chopped
3 garlic cloves, finely chopped
15ml/1 tbsp medium curry paste
5ml/1 tsp ground cumin
5ml/1 tsp ground turmeric
60ml/4 tbsp coconut cream
30ml/2 tbsp fish sauce
5ml/1 tsp sugar
oil, for brushing
fresh herbs, to garnish

FOR THE SATAY SAUCE

250ml/8fl oz/1 cup coconut milk
30ml/2 tbsp red curry paste
75g/3oz crunchy peanut butter
120ml/4fl oz/½ cup chicken stock
45ml/3 tbsp soft light brown sugar
30ml/2 tbsp tamarind juice
15ml/1 tbsp fish sauce
2.5ml/½ tsp salt

1 Cut the pork thinly into 5cm/2in strips. Mix together the fresh root ginger, lemon grass, garlic, curry paste, cumin, turmeric, coconut cream, fish sauce and sugar. Pour over the pork and leave to marinate for about 2 hours.

2 Meanwhile, make the sauce. Heat the coconut milk over a medium heat, then add the red curry paste, peanut butter, chicken stock and sugar.

3 Cook and stir until the sauce is smooth, about 5–6 minutes. Add the tamarind juice, fish sauce and salt to taste.

4 Thread the meat on to skewers. Brush with oil and cook over charcoal or under a preheated grill (broiler) for 3–4 minutes on each side, turning occasionally, until cooked and golden brown.

5 Serve with the satay sauce garnished with fresh herbs.

Nutritional information per portion: Energy 83kcal/346kJ; Protein 6g; Carbohydrate 3.6g, of which sugars 3.1g; Fat 5g, of which saturates 2.6g; Cholesterol 14mg; Calcium 13mg; Fibre 0.4g; Sodium 243mg.

Savoury pork pies

These little pies come from Spain and are fun to eat. They look really appetizing served warm in a basket lined with a napkin.

MAKES 12 PASTRIES

350g/12oz shortcrust pastry, thawed if frozen

FOR THE FILLING

15ml/1 tbsp vegetable oil
1 onion, chopped
1 clove garlic, crushed
5ml/1 tsp thyme
115g/4oz/1 cup minced (ground) pork
5ml/1 tsp paprika
1 hard-boiled egg, chopped
1 gherkin, chopped
30ml/2 tbsp chopped fresh parsley
vegetable oil, for deep-frying
salt and ground black pepper

1 To make the filling, heat the vegetable oil in a saucepan or wok and soften the onion, garlic and thyme without browning, for about 3–4 minutes. Add the pork and paprika then brown evenly for 6–8 minutes. Season well, turn out into a bowl and cool. When the mixture is cool, add the hard-boiled egg, gherkin and parsley.

2 Turn the pastry out on to a floured work surface and roll out to a 38cm/15in square. Cut out 12 circles 13cm/5in in diameter. Place 15ml/1 tbsp of the filling on each circle, moisten the edges with a little water, fold over and seal.

3 Heat the vegetable oil in a deep-fryer fitted with a basket, to 196°C/385°F. Place three pies at a time in the basket and deep-fry until golden brown. Frying should take at least 1 minute or the inside filling will not be heated through. Serve warm.

Nutritional information per portion: Energy 209kcal/868kJ; Protein 4.2g; Carbohydrate 14.2g, of which sugars 0.7g; Fat 15.4g, of which saturates 3.8g; Cholesterol 26mg; Calcium 38mg; Fibre 0.9g; Sodium 131mg.

Mini sausage rolls

These miniature versions of old-fashioned sausage rolls are always popular – the Parmesan cheese gives them an extra special flavour.

MAKES ABOUT 48

15g/½ oz/1 tbsp butter
1 onion, finely chopped
350g/12oz good quality sausage meat (bulk sausage)
15ml/1 tbsp dried mixed herbs such as oregano, thyme, sage, tarragon or dill
25g/1oz finely chopped pistachio nuts (optional)
350g/12oz puff pastry, thawed if frozen
60–90ml/4–6 tbsp freshly grated Parmesan cheese
salt and ground black pepper
1 egg, lightly beaten, for glazing
poppy seeds, sesame seeds, fennel seeds and aniseeds, for sprinkling
mustard, to serve

1 In a small frying pan, over a medium heat, melt the butter. Add the onion and cook for about 5 minutes, until softened. Remove from the heat and cool. Put the onion, sausagemeat, herbs, salt and pepper and nuts (if using) in a mixing bowl and stir together until completely blended.

2 Divide the mixture into 4 equal portions and roll into thin sausages measuring about 25cm/10in long. Set aside. On a lightly floured surface, roll out the pastry to about 3mm/⅛in thick. Cut the pastry into 4 strips 25 x 7.5cm/10 x 3in long. Place a long sausage on each pastry strip and sprinkle each with a little Parmesan cheese.

3 Brush one long edge of each of the pastry strips with the egg glaze and roll up to enclose each sausage. Set them seam-side down and press gently to seal. Brush each with the egg glaze and sprinkle with one type of seed. Repeat with remaining pastry strips, using different seeds.

4 Preheat the oven to 220°C/425°F/Gas 7. Lightly grease a large baking sheet. Cut each of the pastry logs into 2.5cm/1in lengths and arrange on the baking sheet. Bake for about 15 minutes until the pastry is crisp and brown. Serve warm, with a pot of mustard to hand.

Nutritional information per portion: Energy 59kcal/245kJ; Protein 1.8g; Carbohydrate 3.7g, of which sugars 0.3g; Fat 4.3g, of which saturates 1.2g; Cholesterol 9mg; Calcium 24mg; Fibre 0.1g; Sodium 99mg.

Quail's eggs in aspic with prosciutto

These eggs, set attractively in aspic, are so easy to make, and are great for summer eating. Serve them with salad leaves and some home-made mayonnaise on the side.

MAKES 12

22g/3/4oz packet aspic powder
45ml/3 tbsp dry sherry
12 quail's eggs
12 fresh coriander (cilantro) or flat leaf parsley leaves
6 slices of prosciutto
salad leaves, to serve

1 Make up the aspic following the instructions but replacing 45ml/3 tbsp water with sherry. Leave in the fridge until it begins to thicken.

2 Put the quail's eggs in a pan of cold water and bring to the boil. Boil for 1½ minutes, pour off the hot water and add cold water. When cold, the yolks should be a little soft and the whites firm.

3 Rinse 12 dariole moulds and place them on a tray. Place a herb leaf in the base of each mould, then add an egg. As the aspic thickens add enough to almost cover each egg. Cut the prosciutto into 12 pieces. Fold to fit into the moulds. Put a slice of ham on each egg and pour in the rest of the aspic to fill the mould. Leave for 4 hours until set.

4 To serve, run a knife around the top rim of the aspic. Dip the moulds into warm water and tap gently until loosened. Invert on to small plates and serve with salad leaves.

Nutritional information per portion: Energy 31kcal/129kJ; Protein 3.9g; Carbohydrate 0.2g, of which sugars 0.2g; Fat 1.2g, of which saturates 0.3g; Cholesterol 36mg; Calcium 8mg; Fibre 0.1g; Sodium 97mg.

Eggs benedict

There is still debate over who created this recipe but the most likely story credits a Mr and Mrs LeGrand Benedict, who were regulars at New York's Delmonico's restaurant.

SERVES 4

5ml/1 tsp vinegar
4 eggs
2 English muffins or 4 rounds of bread
butter, for spreading
4 thick slices cooked ham, trimmed to fit the muffins
fresh chives, to garnish

FOR THE SAUCE

3 egg yolks
30ml/2 tbsp fresh lemon juice
1.5ml/¼ tsp salt
115g/4oz/½ cup butter
30ml/2 tbsp single (light) cream
ground black pepper

1 To make the sauce, blend the egg yolks, lemon juice and salt in a food processor or blender for 15 seconds.

2 Melt the butter in a saucepan until it bubbles. With the motor running, pour the butter into the food processor. Scrape the sauce into the top of a double boiler, over simmering water. Stir until thickened. (If it curdles, whisk in 15ml/1 tbsp boiling water.) Add the cream and pepper. Keep warm.

3 Bring a shallow pan of water to the boil. Stir in the vinegar. Break each egg into a cup, then slide it into the water. Gently turn the white around the yolk with a slotted spoon. Cook the eggs about 3–4 minutes. Remove from the pan and drain on kitchen paper. Gently trim any ragged edges with scissors.

4 While the eggs are poaching, split and toast the muffins or bread slices. Butter while still warm.

5 Place a piece of ham on each muffin half or slice of toast. Add an egg and spoon over the warm sauce. Garnish with chives and serve.

Nutritional information per portion: Energy 553kcal/2304kJ; Protein 19.8g; Carbohydrate 31.6g, of which sugars 2.2g; Fat 39.7g, of which saturates 18.9g; Cholesterol 427mg; Calcium 148mg; Fibre 1.3g; Sodium 635mg.

Salads

Making a salad is usually very simple and quick, as there is little cooking involved and the vibrant colours of the fresh ingredients add enormously to the pleasure of eating them. Try a simple classic such as Melon and Prosciutto Salad or a more substantial option such as Smoked Trout Pasta Salad.

Goat's cheese salad

Goat's cheese has a strong, tangy flavour, so choose robust salad leaves to accompany it. This dish looks lovely if you use a mixture of different colours and textures for the salad.

SERVES 4

30ml/2 tbsp olive oil
4 slices of French bread, 1cm/½in thick
8 cups mixed salad leaves, such as frisée lettuce, radicchio and red oak leaf, torn in small pieces
4 firm goat's cheese rounds, about 50g/2oz each, rind removed
1 yellow or red (bell) pepper, seeded and finely diced
1 small red onion, thinly sliced
45ml/3 tbsp chopped fresh parsley
30ml/2 tbsp chopped fresh chives

FOR THE DRESSING

30ml/2 tbsp white wine vinegar
1.5ml/¼ tsp salt
5ml/1 tsp wholegrain mustard
75ml/5 tbsp olive oil
ground black pepper

1 For the dressing, mix the vinegar and salt with a fork until dissolved. Stir in the mustard. Gradually stir in the olive oil until blended. Season with pepper and set aside until needed.

2 Preheat the grill (broiler). Heat the oil in a frying pan. When hot, add the bread slices and fry until golden, about 1 minute. Turn and cook on the other side, about 30 seconds more. Drain on kitchen paper and set aside.

3 Place the salad leaves in a bowl. Add 45ml/3 tbsp of the dressing and toss to coat well. Divide the dressed leaves among four salad plates.

4 Place the goat's cheeses, cut sides up, on a baking sheet and place on the grill (broiler). Grill (broil) until bubbling and golden, about 1–2 minutes.

5 Set a goat's cheese on each slice of bread and place in the centre of each plate. Scatter the diced pepper, red onion, parsley and chives over the salad. Drizzle with the remaining dressing and serve.

Nutritional information per portion: Energy 471kcal/1960kJ; Protein 15.8g; Carbohydrate 27.8g, of which sugars 6.3g; Fat 33.7g, of which saturates 12g; Cholesterol 47mg; Calcium 172mg; Fibre 3.2g; Sodium 556mg.

Panzanella salad

If sliced, juicy tomatoes layered with day-old bread sounds strange for a salad, don't be deceived – it's quite delicious. A popular Italian salad, this dish is ideal for serving as an appetizer.

SERVES 4–6

4 thick slices day-old bread, either white, brown or rye
1 small red onion, thinly sliced
450g/1lb ripe tomatoes, thinly sliced
115g/4oz mozzarella cheese, thinly sliced
5ml/1 tbsp fresh basil, shredded, or fresh marjoram
120ml/4fl oz/1/2 cup extra virgin olive oil
45ml/3 tbsp balsamic vinegar
juice of 1 small lemon
salt and ground black pepper
stoned (pitted) and sliced black olives or salted capers, to garnish

1 Dip the bread briefly in cold water, then carefully squeeze out the excess water. Arrange the bread in the base of a shallow salad bowl.

2 Soak the onion slices in cold water for about 10 minutes while you prepare the other ingredients. Drain and reserve.

3 Layer the tomatoes, cheese, onion, basil or marjoram, seasoning well in between each layer. Sprinkle with oil, vinegar and lemon juice.

4 Top with the olives or capers, cover with clear film (plastic wrap) and chill in the fridge for at least 2 hours or overnight, if possible.

Nutritional information per portion: Energy 237kcal/987kJ; Protein 6.3g; Carbohydrate 15.4g, of which sugars 3.5g; Fat 17.1g, of which saturates 4.5g; Cholesterol 11mg; Calcium 105mg; Fibre 1.3g; Sodium 213mg.

Caesar salad

This is a well-known and much-enjoyed salad, even though its origins are a mystery. Be sure to use cos lettuce and add the very soft eggs at the last minute.

SERVES 6

175ml/6fl oz/3/4 cup salad oil, preferably olive oil
115g/4oz French or Italian bread, cut in 2.5cm/1in cubes
1 large garlic clove, crushed with the flat side of a knife
1 cos or romaine lettuce
2 eggs, boiled for 1 minute
120ml/4fl oz/1/2 cup lemon juice
50g/2oz/2/3 cup freshly grated Parmesan cheese
6 anchovy fillets, drained and finely chopped (optional)
salt and ground black pepper

1 Heat 50ml/2fl oz/1/4 cup of the oil in a large frying pan. Add the bread cubes and garlic. Fry, stirring and turning constantly, until the cubes are golden brown all over. Drain on kitchen paper. Discard the garlic.

2 Tear large lettuce leaves into smaller pieces. Then put all the lettuce in a bowl. Add the remaining oil to the lettuce and season with salt and plenty of ground black pepper. Toss well to coat the leaves.

3 Break the eggs on top. Sprinkle with the lemon juice. Toss well again to combine. Add the Parmesan cheese and anchovies, if using. Toss gently to mix.

4 Scatter the fried bread cubes on top and serve immediately.

Nutritional information per portion: Energy 198kcal/824kJ; Protein 5.6g; Carbohydrate 13.8g, of which sugars 1.7g; Fat 13.8g, of which saturates 2.1g; Cholesterol 50mg; Calcium 64mg; Fibre 0.9g; Sodium 400mg.

Pear and Parmesan salad

This is a good starter when pears are at their seasonal best. Try Packhams or Comice when plentiful, drizzled with a poppy-seed dressing and topped with shavings of Parmesan.

SERVES 4

4 just-ripe dessert pears
50g/2oz piece Parmesan cheese
watercress, to garnish
water biscuits or rye bread, to serve (optional)

FOR THE DRESSING

30ml/2 tbsp extra virgin olive oil
15ml/1 tbsp sunflower oil
30ml/2 tbsp cider vinegar or white wine vinegar
2.5ml/½ tsp soft light brown sugar
good pinch of dried thyme
15ml/1 tbsp poppy seeds
salt and ground black pepper

1 Cut the pears in quarters and remove the cores. Cut each pear quarter in half lengthways and arrange them on four small serving plates. Peel the pears if you wish, though they look more attractive unpeeled.

2 Make the dressing. Mix the oils, vinegar, sugar, thyme and seasoning in a jug. Whisk well, then tip in the poppy seeds. Trickle the dressing over the pears. Garnish with watercress and shave Parmesan over the top. Serve with water biscuits or thinly sliced rye bread, if you like.

Nutritional information per portion: Energy 193kcal/804kJ; Protein 5.4g; Carbohydrate 15.7g, of which sugars 15.7g; Fat 12.5g, of which saturates 3.7g; Cholesterol 13mg; Calcium 167mg; Fibre 3.3g; Sodium 141mg.

Green bean and sweet red pepper salad

Serrano chillies are very fiery, so be cautious about their use. Wash your hands thoroughly after chopping them and make sure you don't touch your eyes.

SERVES 4

350g/12oz cooked green beans, quartered
2 red (bell) peppers, seeded and chopped
2 spring onions (scallions), chopped
1 or more drained pickled serrano chillies, rinsed, seeded and chopped
1 iceberg lettuce, coarsely shredded
olives, to garnish

FOR THE DRESSING
45ml/3 tbsp red wine vinegar
135ml/9 tbsp olive oil
salt and ground black pepper

1 Combine the cooked green beans, chopped peppers, chopped spring onions and chillies in a salad bowl.

2 Make the salad dressing. Pour the red wine vinegar into a bowl or jug. Add salt and ground black pepper to taste, then gradually whisk in the olive oil until well combined.

3 Pour the salad dressing over the prepared vegetables and toss lightly together to mix and coat thoroughly.

4 Line a large serving platter with the shredded iceberg lettuce leaves and arrange the salad vegetables attractively on top. Garnish with the olives and serve at once.

Nutritional information per portion: Energy 280kcal/1153kJ; Protein 3.1g; Carbohydrate 9.4g, of which sugars 8.4g; Fat 25.8g, of which saturates 3.8g; Cholesterol 0mg; Calcium 55mg; Fibre 3.9g; Sodium 5mg.

Egg and fennel tabbouleh with nuts

Tabbouleh is a Middle Eastern salad of steamed bulgur wheat, flavoured with parsley, mint and garlic as well as fennel. Small whole eggs, such as quail or guinea fowl, would be good in this dish.

SERVES 4

250g/9oz/1¼ cups bulgur wheat
4 small eggs
1 fennel bulb
1 bunch spring onions (scallions), chopped
25g/1oz/½ cup sun-dried tomatoes, sliced
45ml/3 tbsp chopped fresh parsley
30ml/2 tbsp chopped fresh mint
75g/3oz/½ cup black olives
60ml/4 tbsp olive oil, preferably Greek or Spanish
30ml/2 tbsp garlic oil
30ml/2 tbsp lemon juice
salt and ground black pepper

1 Cover the bulgur wheat with boiling water and leave to soak for 15 minutes. Transfer to a metal sieve (strainer), place over a pan of boiling water, cover and steam for 10 minutes. Spread out on a metal tray and leave to cool while you cook the eggs and fennel.

2 Hard-boil the small eggs for 8 minutes. Cool under running water, shell and quarter, or, if using an egg slicer, slice not quite all the way through.

3 Halve and then finely slice the fennel. Boil in salted water for 6 minutes, drain and cool under running water.

4 Combine the egg quarters, fennel, spring onions, sun-dried tomatoes, parsley, mint and olives with the bulgur wheat. If you have sliced the eggs, arrange them on top of the salad. Dress the tabbouleh with olive oil, garlic oil and lemon juice. Season well and serve.

Nutritional information per portion: Energy 624kcal/2587kJ; Protein 13.4g; Carbohydrate 49.3g, of which sugars 1.5g; Fat 42.2g, of which saturates 6.6g; Cholesterol 190mg; Calcium 97mg; Fibre 1.9g; Sodium 83mg.

Potato salad with **curry plant mayonnaise**

Potato salad can be made well in advance and is therefore a useful dish for serving as an appetizer at a party. Its popularity means that there are very rarely any leftovers to be cleared away.

SERVES 6

1kg/2¼lb new potatoes, in skins
300ml/½ pint/1¼ cups home-made or shop-bought mayonnaise
6 curry plant leaves, roughly chopped
salt and ground black pepper
mixed lettuce leaves or other salad leaves, to serve

1 Place the potatoes in a pan of salted water, bring to the boil and cook for 15 minutes or until tender. Drain and place in a large bowl to cool slightly.

2 Mix the mayonnaise with the curry plant leaves and black pepper, and stir into the potatoes while they are still warm. Leave to cool completely, then serve on a bed of mixed lettuce leaves or other assorted salad leaves.

Nutritional information per portion: Energy 474kcal/1967kJ; Protein 4.1g; Carbohydrate 29.1g, of which sugars 4.2g; Fat 38.7g, of which saturates 6g; Cholesterol 38mg; Calcium 37mg; Fibre 2.4g; Sodium 246mg.

Tricolour salad

A popular salad, this dish depends for success on the quality of its ingredients. Mozzarella is the best cheese to serve uncooked, and ripe plum tomatoes are essential.

SERVES 2–3

150g/5oz mozzarella, thinly sliced
4 large plum tomatoes, sliced
1 large avocado
about 12 basil leaves or a small handful of flat leaf parsley leaves
45–60ml/3–4 tbsp extra virgin olive oil
ground black pepper
ciabatta and sea salt flakes, to serve

1 Arrange the sliced mozzarella cheese and tomatoes randomly on two salad plates. Crush over a few good pinches of sea salt flakes. This will help to draw out some of the juices from the plum tomatoes. Set aside in a cool place and leave to marinate for about 30 minutes.

2 Just before serving, cut the avocado in half using a sharp knife and twist the halves to separate. Lift out the stone (pit) and remove the peel.

3 Carefully slice the avocado flesh crossways into half moons, or cut it into large chunks if that is easier.

4 Place the avocado on the salad, then sprinkle with the basil or parsley. Drizzle over the olive oil, add a little more salt if needed and some black pepper.

5 Serve at room temperature, with chunks of crusty Italian ciabatta for mopping up the dressing.

Nutritional information per portion: Energy 526kcal/2180kJ; Protein 17.5g; Carbohydrate 8.3g, of which sugars 7.2g; Fat 47.1g, of which saturates 16g; Cholesterol 44mg; Calcium 344mg; Fibre 5.8g; Sodium 327mg.

Pear and Roquefort salad

The flavours of pear and Roquefort complement each other beautifully in this classic dish. Choose ripe, firm Comice or Williams pears.

SERVES 4

3 ripe pears
lemon juice, for tossing
about 175g/6oz mixed salad leaves
175g/6oz Roquefort cheese
50g/2oz/1/2 cup hazelnut kernels, toasted and chopped

FOR THE DRESSING
30ml/2 tbsp hazelnut oil
45ml/3 tbsp olive oil
15ml/1 tbsp cider vinegar
5ml/1 tsp Dijon mustard
salt and ground black pepper

1 To make the dressing, mix together the oils, vinegar and mustard in a bowl or screw-top jar. Add salt and black pepper to taste. Stir or shake well.

2 Peel, core and slice the pears and toss them in lemon juice.

3 Arrange the salad leaves on serving plates, then place the pears on top. Crumble the cheese and scatter over the salad with the hazelnuts. Spoon over the dressing and serve at once.

Nutritional information per portion: Energy 409kcal/1694kJ; Protein 11.6g; Carbohydrate 12.9g, of which sugars 12.5g; Fat 35g, of which saturates 11g; Cholesterol 33mg; Calcium 258mg; Fibre 3.7g; Sodium 539mg.

Asparagus and **orange salad**

This is a really attractive salad with lots of bright colours. A simple dressing of olive oil and vinegar mingles with the orange and tomato flavours, with great results.

SERVES 4

225g/8oz asparagus, trimmed and cut into 5cm/2in pieces
2 large oranges
2 well-flavoured ripe tomatoes, each cut into eight pieces
50g/2oz romaine lettuce leaves, shredded
30ml/2 tbsp extra virgin olive oil
2.5ml/1/2 tsp sherry vinegar
salt and ground black pepper

1 Cook the asparagus in boiling, salted water for 3–4 minutes, until just tender. Drain and refresh under cold water. Set aside.

2 Grate the rind from half an orange and reserve. Peel all the oranges and cut into segments, removing the membrane. Squeeze out the juice from the membrane and reserve.

3 Put the asparagus, orange segments, tomatoes and lettuce into a salad bowl. Mix together the oil and vinegar and add 15ml/1 tbsp of the reserved orange juice and 5ml/1 tsp of the rind. Season with salt and plenty of ground black pepper. Just before serving, pour the dressing over the salad and mix gently to coat.

Nutritional information per portion: Energy 102kcal/424kJ; Protein 2.9g; Carbohydrate 9.3g, of which sugars 9.2g; Fat 6.1g, of which saturates 0.9g; Cholesterol 0mg; Calcium 58mg; Fibre 2.9g; Sodium 9mg.

Avocado and smoked fish salad

Avocado and smoked fish make a good combination and, flavoured with herbs and spices, create a delectable and elegant starter. Smoked haddock or cod can also be used in this salad.

SERVES 4

15g/½oz/1 tbsp butter or margarine
½ onion, finely sliced
5ml/1 tsp mustard seeds
225g/8oz smoked mackerel, flaked
30ml/2 tbsp fresh chopped coriander (cilantro)
2 firm tomatoes, peeled and chopped
15ml/1 tbsp lemon juice

FOR THE SALAD
2 avocados
½ cucumber
15ml/1 tbsp lemon juice
2 firm tomatoes
1 green chilli
salt and ground black pepper

1 Melt the butter or margarine in a frying pan, add the onion and mustard seeds and fry for about 5 minutes until the onion is soft but not browned. Add the fish, chopped coriander, tomatoes and lemon juice and cook over a low heat for about 2–3 minutes. Remove from the heat and leave to cool.

2 To make the salad, slice the avocados and cucumber thinly. Place together in a bowl and sprinkle with the lemon juice to prevent discoloration. Slice the tomatoes and seed and finely chop the chilli.

3 Place the fish mixture in the centre of a serving plate. Arrange the avocado slices, cucumber and tomatoes decoratively around the outside of the fish. Or, spoon a quarter of the fish mixture on to each of four serving plates and divide the avocados, cucumber and tomatoes equally among them. Then sprinkle with the chopped chilli and a little salt and black pepper, and serve.

Nutritional information per portion: Energy 386kcal/1596kJ; Protein 12.8g; Carbohydrate 4.6g, of which sugars 3.1g; Fat 35.2g, of which saturates 8.6g; Cholesterol 67mg; Calcium 32mg; Fibre 3.4g; Sodium 455mg.

Salade Niçoise

Made with the freshest ingredients, this classic Provençal salad makes a simple yet unbeatable summer dish. Serve with country-style bread and chilled white wine for a substantial appetizer.

SERVES 4–6

1 tuna steak, about 175g/6oz
olive oil, for brushing
115g/4oz French (green) beans
115g/4oz mixed salad leaves
1/2 small cucumber, thinly sliced
4 ripe tomatoes, quartered
50g/2oz canned anchovies, drained and halved lengthways
4 hard-boiled eggs, quartered
1/2 bunch radishes, trimmed
50g/2oz/1/2 cup small black olives
salt and ground black pepper
flat leaf parsley, to garnish (optional)

FOR THE DRESSING
90ml/6 tbsp virgin olive oil
2 garlic cloves, crushed
15ml/1 tbsp white wine vinegar
salt and ground black pepper

1 Whisk together the oil, garlic and vinegar, then season to taste.

2 Preheat the grill (broiler). Brush the tuna steak with olive oil and season with salt and black pepper. Cook for 3–4 minutes on each side until seared on the outside. Set aside and leave to cool.

3 Trim and halve the French beans. Cook them in a pan of boiling water for 2 minutes until only just tender, then drain, refresh and leave to cool.

4 Mix together the salad leaves, sliced cucumber, quartered tomatoes and French beans in a large, shallow bowl. Cut the tuna steak into two pieces or more, if you prefer.

5 Arrange the tuna over the salad, with the drained anchovies, hard-boiled eggs, radishes and small black olives. Pour over the dressing and then toss together lightly. Serve garnished with flat leaf parsley, if using.

Nutritional information per portion: Energy 218kcal/903kJ; Protein 12.3g; Carbohydrate 3.4g, of which sugars 3.2g; Fat 17.4g, of which saturates 3.2g; Cholesterol 135mg; Calcium 50mg; Fibre 1.7g; Sodium 256mg.

Smoked trout pasta salad

The fennel and dill really complement the flavour of the smoked trout in this delicious dish and the little pasta shells catch the trout, creating tasty mouthfuls.

SERVES 8

15g/½oz/1 tbsp butter
175g/6oz/1 cup chopped fennel bulb
6 spring onions (scallions), 2 finely chopped and the rest thinly sliced
225g/8oz skinless smoked trout fillets, flaked
45ml/3 tbsp chopped fresh dill
120ml/4fl oz/½ cup mayonnaise
10ml/2 tsp fresh lemon juice
30ml/2 tbsp whipping cream
450g/1lb/4 cups small pasta shapes, such as conchiglie
salt and ground black pepper
dill sprigs, to garnish

1 Melt the butter in a small pan. Cook the fennel and minced spring onions for 3–5 minutes. Transfer to a large bowl and cool slightly.

2 Add the sliced spring onions, trout, dill, mayonnaise, lemon juice and cream. Season and mix.

3 Bring a large pan of water to the boil. Salt to taste and add the pasta. Cook according to the instructions on the packet until just al dente. Drain thoroughly and leave to cool.

4 Add the pasta to the vegetable and trout mixture and toss to coat evenly. Check seasoning and add salt and ground black pepper, if necessary. Serve the salad lightly chilled or at room temperature, garnished with sprigs of dill.

Nutritional information per portion: Energy 369kcal/1548kJ; Protein 14.5g; Carbohydrate 42.7g, of which sugars 2.8g; Fat 16.8g, of which saturates 4g; Cholesterol 29mg; Calcium 31mg; Fibre 2.3g; Sodium 613mg.

Mixed seafood salad

If you cannot find all the seafood included in this dish in fresh form, then use a combination of fresh and frozen, but do use what is in season first.

SERVES 6–8

350g/12oz small squid
1 small onion, cut into quarters
1 bay leaf
200g/7oz raw unpeeled prawns (shrimp)
675g/1½lb fresh mussels, in the shell
450g/1lb small fresh clams
175ml/6fl oz/¾ cup white wine
1 fennel bulb

FOR THE DRESSING
75ml/5 tbsp extra virgin olive oil
45ml/3 tbsp lemon juice
1 garlic clove, finely chopped
salt and ground black pepper

1 Working near the sink, clean the squid by first peeling off the thin skin from the body section. Rinse well. Pull the head and tentacles away from the sac section. Some of the intestines will come away with the head. Remove and discard the translucent quill and any remaining insides from the sac. Sever the tentacles from the head. Discard the head and intestines. Remove the small hard beak from the base of the tentacles. Rinse the sac and tentacles of the squid well under cold running water. Drain in a colander.

2 Bring a large pan of water to the boil. Add the onion and bay leaf. Drop in the squid and cook for about 10 minutes, or until tender. Remove with a slotted spoon, and allow to cool before slicing into rings 1cm/½in wide. Cut each tentacle section into 2 pieces. Set aside.

3 Drop the prawns into the same boiling water, and cook until they turn pink, for about 2 minutes. Remove with a slotted spoon. Peel and remove the intestinal vein. (The cooking liquid may be strained and kept to make a soup. When cool, store in the freezer if not using immediately.)

4 Cut off the "beards" from the mussels. Scrub and rinse the mussels and clams well in several changes of cold water. Place in a large pan with the wine. Cover, and steam until all the shells have opened. (Discard any that do not open.) Lift the clams and mussels out.

5 Remove all the clams from their shells with a small spoon. Place in a large serving bowl. Remove all but 8 of the mussels from their shells, and add them to the clams in the bowl. Leave the remaining mussels in their half shells, and set aside. Cut the green, ferny part of the fennel away from the bulb. Chop finely and set aside. Chop the bulb into bite-size pieces, and add it to the serving bowl with the squid and prawns.

6 Make a dressing by combining the oil, lemon juice, garlic and chopped fennel green in a small bowl. Add salt and pepper to taste. Pour over the salad, and toss well. Decorate with the remaining mussels in the half shell. This salad may be served either at room temperature or lightly chilled.

Nutritional information per portion: Energy 166kcal/693kJ; Protein 19.3g; Carbohydrate 2.9g, of which sugars 1g; Fat 8.6g, of which saturates 1.3g; Cholesterol 177mg; Calcium 65mg; Fibre 0.9g; Sodium 480mg.

Wilted spinach and **bacon salad**

The spinach does not need to be cooked in this salad, as the hot dressing wilts it and provides a glorious taste sensation with the crispy bacon rashers.

SERVES 6

450g/1lb fresh young spinach leaves
225g/8oz streaky (fatty) bacon rashers
25ml/1½ tbsp vegetable oil
60ml/4 tbsp red wine vinegar
60ml/4 tbsp water
20ml/4 tsp caster (superfine) sugar
5ml/1 tsp mustard powder
8 spring onions (scallions), thinly sliced
6 radishes, thinly sliced
2 hard-boiled eggs, coarsely grated
salt and ground black pepper

1 Pull any coarse stalks from the spinach leaves and rinse well. Put the leaves in a large salad bowl.

2 Fry the bacon rashers in the oil until crisp and brown. Remove with tongs and drain on kitchen paper. Reserve the cooking fat in the pan. Chop the bacon and set aside until needed.

3 Combine the vinegar, water, sugar, mustard, and salt and ground black pepper in a bowl and stir until smoothly blended. Add to the fat in the frying pan and stir to mix. Bring the dressing to the boil, stirring.

4 Pour the hot dressing evenly over the spinach leaves. Scatter the bacon, spring onions, radishes and eggs over, and toss, then serve.

Nutritional information per portion: Energy 161kcal/667kJ; Protein 10.7g; Carbohydrate 5.3g, of which sugars 5.2g; Fat 10.9g, of which saturates 3.2g; Cholesterol 83mg; Calcium 148mg; Fibre 1.9g; Sodium 708mg.

Melon and prosciutto salad

Sections of cool fragrant melon wrapped with slices of air-dried ham make a delicious salad appetizer. If strawberries are in season, serve with a savoury-sweet strawberry salsa.

SERVES 4

1 large cantaloupe, Charentais or Galia melon
175g/6oz prosciutto or Serrano ham, thinly sliced

FOR THE SALSA
225g/8oz/2 cups strawberries
5ml/1 tsp caster (superfine) sugar
30ml/2 tbsp groundnut (peanut) or sunflower oil
15ml/1 tbsp orange juice
2.5ml/1/2 tsp finely grated orange rind
2.5ml/1/2 tsp finely grated fresh root ginger
salt and ground black pepper

1 Halve the melon and scoop the seeds out with a spoon. Cut the rind away with a paring knife, then slice the melon thickly. Chill until ready to serve.

2 To make the salsa, hull the strawberries and cut them into large dice. Place in a small mixing bowl with the sugar and crush lightly to release the juices. Add the oil, orange juice, rind and ginger. Season with salt and plenty of black pepper.

3 Arrange the melon on a serving plate, lay the ham over the top and serve with a bowl of salsa, handed round separately.

Nutritional information per portion: Energy 147kcal/614kJ; Protein 9.2g; Carbohydrate 12.2g, of which sugars 12.2g; Fat 7.1g, of which saturates 1.2g; Cholesterol 25mg; Calcium 29mg; Fibre 1.1g; Sodium 568mg.

Guide to techniques

This section looks at how garnishes can transform an appetizer into something really special by just adding a swirl of cream or a sprig of parsley. In addition, there are recipes for marinades to tenderize fish or meat, and oils and dressings that enhance the flavour of crisp salad vegetables.

Garnishes

Many garnishes are delicate works of art; others add a dash of texture or a hint of colour. Most garnishes are simple to do and that extra touch transforms a dish into something very special.

CREAM SWIRL

A swirl of cream or yogurt makes a bowl of soup look attractive.

1 Transfer cream to a jug (pitcher) with a good pouring lip. Pour a swirl on the surface of each bowl of soup.

2 Draw the tip of a fine skewer quickly through the cream to create a delicate feathered pattern. Serve the soup immediately.

CROÛTONS

Crispy croûtons use up stale bread and add crunch to any dish.

Cut the bread into small cubes, brush with oil and bake in the oven. Croûtons will keep in an airtight container for up to a week.

PARMESAN CURLS

Curls of Parmesan add a delicate touch to pasta or risotto.

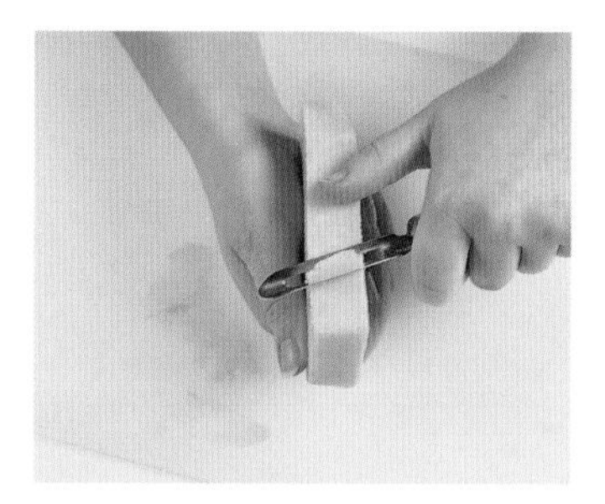

Holding a vegetable peeler at a 45 degree angle, draw it steadily across the block of Parmesan cheese to form a curl.

CHILLI FLOWERS

Make these chilli flowers several hours before they are needed. This will allow the "flowers" to open up.

1 Cut a chilli lengthways from the tip to within 1cm/½in of the stem end. Repeat at intervals around the chilli.

2 Rinse the chillies in cold running water and remove all the seeds. Place the chillies in a bowl of iced water and leave to chill for at least 4 hours.

3 For very curly flowers, leave the chillies in water in a cold place overnight. Wash your hands, knife and chopping board afterwards.

LEMON TWIST

This classic garnish is simple to make, but very effective.

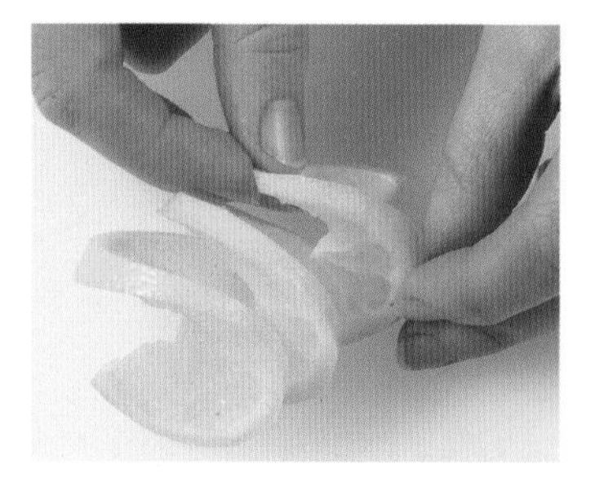

Cut a lemon into thin slices. Make a cut in each slice from the centre to the skin. Hold either side of the cut and twist to form an "S" shape.

CHIVE BRAIDS

Try floating a couple of edible braids of chives in a bowl of soup.

1 Hold three chives down with a bowl on one end. Plait the chives to within 2.5cm/1in of the end.

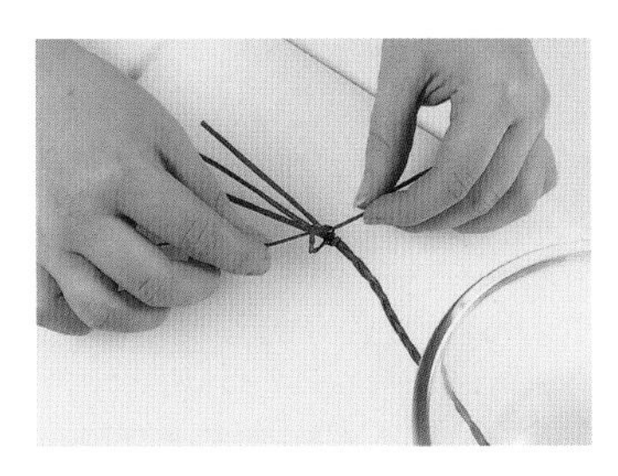

2 Tie a chive around each end of the plait. Trim both ends.

3 Pour boiling water over the braid in a bowl. Drain and refresh under cold running water. Drain again.

TOMATO SUNS

Colourful cherry tomato suns look good with most dishes, but especially with pâtés and terrines.

1 Place a tomato stem-side down. Cut lightly into the skin across the top, edging the knife down towards the base on either side. Repeat until the skin has been cut into eight separate segments, which are still joined at the base.

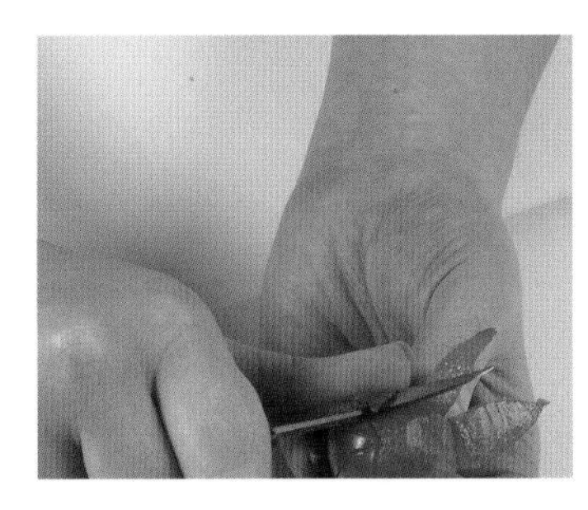

2 Carefully slide the top of the knife under the point of each segment and gradually ease the skin away towards the base. Gently fold the petals back to mimic the sun's rays.

AVOCADO FAN

Versatile avocados can serve as edible containers, be sliced or diced in a salad, or form the foundation of a soup or sauce. They also make very elegant garnishes.

1 Halve, stone (pit) and peel an avocado. Slice each half lengthways into quarters. Carefully and gently draw a cannelle knife (zester) across the quarters at 1cm/½in intervals, to create regular stripes.

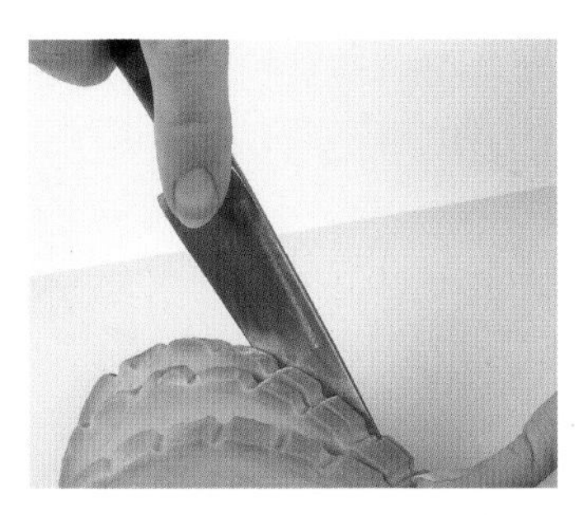

2 Make four cuts lengthways down each avocado quarter leaving 1cm/½in intact at the end. Carefully fan out the slices and arrange on a plate as a pretty garnish.

SPRING ONION TASSELS

This garnish is very popular in Chinese restaurants, where the appearance of a dish is as important as the taste. Spring onion (scallion) tassels will embellish most Chinese meals. Choose the freshest and crispest spring onions you can find with as much white part as possible.

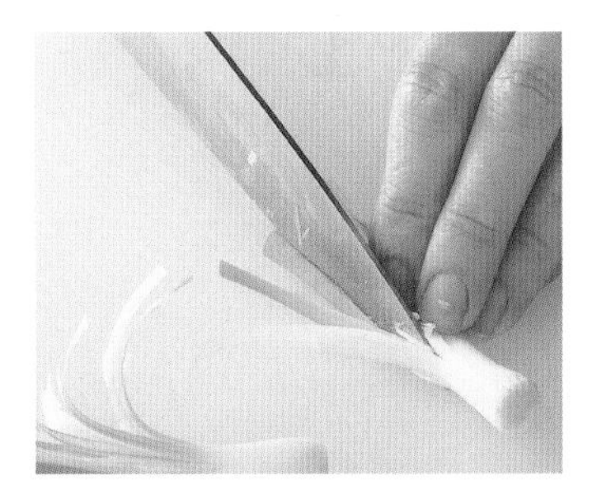

Using a sharp knife, cut the white part of a spring onion into a 6cm/2½in length. Shred one end, then place the spring onion in iced water for 30 minutes until the ends curl. Make several more tassels in the same way.

Marinades, oils and **dressings**

Marinades, flavoured oils and dressings can turn a piece of fish into a delectable appetizer or hors d'oeuvre. With a few ingredients, you can make a herb marinade to tenderize meat, a ginger and garlic oil for fried dishes, or a sour cream dressing to bring out the flavour of a crisp salad.

SUMMER HERB MARINADE

Make the best of summer herbs with this marinade. Any combination may be used, depending on what you have to hand, and it works well with veal, chicken, pork or lamb.

1 Discard any coarse and broken stalks, as well as any wilted and damaged leaves, from a wide selection of herb sprigs, such as chervil, thyme, parsley, sage, chives, rosemary and oregano, then, using a sharp knife, chop finely.

2 Mix the herbs with 90ml/6 tbsp olive oil, 45ml/3 tbsp tarragon vinegar, 1 garlic clove, crushed, 2 spring onions (scallions), chopped, and seasoning in a bowl. Add the meat or poultry, cover and chill for 2–3 hours.

GINGER AND LIME MARINADE

This refreshing marinade is particularly good with chicken.

1 Mix together the rind of one lime and the juice of three limes. Add 15ml/1 tbsp green cardamom seeds, crushed, 1 finely chopped onion, grated fresh root ginger (use a 2.5cm/1in piece and peel before grating), 1 large garlic clove, crushed and 45ml/3 tbsp olive oil.

2 Pour over the meat or fish. Stir gently to coat.

3 Cover the marinating meat and leave in a cool place for 2–3 hours.

CHILLI AND GARLIC MARINADE

Add extra chillies to this delicious marinade, but only if you like your food to be very spicy.

Combine 4 small chillies, seeded and finely diced, 10ml/2 tsp finely grated fresh root ginger, 1 large garlic clove, crushed, and 45ml/3 tbsp light soy sauce in a bowl. Add the meat or fish, cover and chill for 2– 4 hours.

CHINESE MARINADE

This marinade is traditionally used to flavour succulent duck breasts.

Mix 15ml/1 tbsp clear honey, 1.5ml/1¼ tsp five-spice powder, 1 garlic clove, finely chopped, 15ml/1 tbsp hoisin sauce and a pinch of salt and pepper in a large shallow bowl or dish. Add the duck breasts or other meat, turning them in the marinade. Cover with cling film (plastic wrap) and leave in a cool place to marinate for 2 hours.

ABOVE: *Flavourings for aromatic oils include cinnamon, coriander, fennel, garlic, chillies and ginger.*

AROMATIC SPICE OIL

As well as tasting delicious, oils make wonderful gifts. You can use many combinations of ingredients, such as chillies, coriander and lime leaves.
Peel and bruise a 6cm/2½in piece of fresh root ginger and place in a bottle. Fill with groundnut (peanut) oil, 2 garlic cloves and 3 small peeled shallots. Cover and leave in a cool dark place for 2 weeks before using.

SPICY TOMATO DRESSING

This tangy dressing goes extremely well with a robust salad, such as bean or potato salad. It can also be used as a delicious marinade for meat.
Mix together 5ml/1 tsp ground cumin, 15ml/1 tbsp tomato ketchup, 30ml/2 tbsp olive oil, 15ml/1 tbsp white wine vinegar and 1 garlic clove, crushed in a small bowl. Add a little salt and some hot pepper sauce to taste and stir again thoroughly.

SOUR CREAM AND DILL DRESSING

This unusual dressing can be made in only a couple of minutes.

Blend together 120ml/4fl oz/½ cup sour cream, 10ml/2 tsp creamed horseradish and 15ml/1 tbsp chopped fresh dill in a small bowl and season with a little salt and freshly ground black pepper. Use accordingly. If not using immediately, store the dressing in the refrigerator.

HERB GARDEN DRESSING

The dried mixture will keep throughout the winter until your herbs are growing again. It can also be used to sprinkle over vegetables, casseroles and stews.

1 Mix together 115g/4oz/1 cup dried oregano, 115g/4oz/1 cup dried basil, 50g/2oz/½ cup dried marjoram, 50g/2oz/½ cup dried dill, 50g/2oz/½ cup dried mint leaves, 50g/2oz/½ cup onion powder, 30ml/2 tbsp dry mustard, 10ml/2 tsp salt and 15ml/1 tbsp freshly ground black pepper and keep in a sealed jar to use as needed.

2 When making a batch of salad dressing, take 2 tbsp of the herb mixture and add it to 350ml/12fl oz/1½ cups of extra virgin olive oil and 120ml/4fl oz/½ cup cider vinegar in a bowl or jug (pitcher).

3 Mix the dressing thoroughly and allow to stand for 1 hour or so. Mix again before using.

Index

A

aromatic spice oil 221
artichokes
  charred artichokes with lemon oil dip 118
asparagus
  asparagus and egg terrine 90–1
  asparagus and orange salad 207
  asparagus with raspberry dressing 109
  chilled asparagus soup 64
  grilled asparagus with salt-cured ham 46
  marinated asparagus and langoustine 169
aubergines
  baba ganoush with Lebanese flatbread 20–1
  Greek aubergine and spinach pie 110–11
avocados
  avocado fan 219
  avocado and smoked fish salad 208
  avocado soup 60
  gazpacho with avocado salsa 52–3
  guacamole 16
  prawn, egg and avocado mousses 88
  tortilla wrap with tabbouleh and avocado 126

B

baba ganoush with Lebanese flatbread 20–1
baby carrot and fennel soup 62–3
bacon
  wilted spinach and bacon salad 204
baked Mediterranean vegetables 113
barbecue-glazed chicken skewers 178
basil and lemon dip 14–15
beans
  cannellini bean and rosemary bruschetta 104–5
  chilli bean dip 24–5
  clams with chilli and yellow bean sauce 164–5
  green bean and sweet red pepper salad 201
  lemon, thyme and bean stuffed mushrooms 103
beansprouts
  soya beansprout soup 58
beef
  beef satay with a hot mango dip 29
  spicy koftas 185
bread
  baba ganoush with Lebanese flatbread 20–1
  breaded sole batons 137
  broccoli soup with garlic toast 75
  cannellini bean and rosemary bruschetta 104–5
  chive scrambled eggs in brioches 122
  croûtons 218
  griddled tomatoes on soda bread 100
  prawn toasts 47
broccoli soup with garlic toast 75
brochettes *see* skewers
buckwheat blinis with mushroom caviar 132

C

caesar salad 199
cannellini bean and rosemary bruschetta 104–5
capers
  marinated feta cheese with capers 114–15
carrots
  baby carrot and fennel soup 62–3
celeriac fritters with mustard dip 13
charred artichokes with lemon oil dip 118
cheese
  cheese aigrettes 36
  crab and ricotta tartlets 151
  fried rice balls stuffed with mozzarella 129
  goat's cheese salad 196–7
  golden Parmesan chicken 174
  marinated feta cheese with capers 114–15
  mini baked potatoes with blue cheese 127
  Parmesan curls 218
  Parmesan fish goujons 27
  Parmesan thins 37
  pear and Parmesan salad 200
  pear and Roquefort salad 206
  pear and Stilton 133
  twice-baked Gruyère and potato soufflé 128
  wild mushroom and fontina tarts 120–1
chicken
  barbecue-glazed chicken skewers 178
  chicken bitki 180
  chicken with lemon and garlic 175
  chicken liver pâté 81
  chicken parcels 179
  chicken and pork terrine 96–7
  chicken satay with peanut sauce 32–3
  golden Parmesan chicken 174
  tandoori chicken sticks 176–7
chickpeas
  hummus bi tahina 10–11
  sesame seed-coated falafel with tahini dip 117
chilled soups *see* soups
chilli
  chilli bean dip 24–5
  chilli flowers 218
  chilli and garlic marinade 220
  clams with chilli and yellow bean sauce 164–5
  courgette fritters with chilli jam 116
Chinese marinade 220
chives
  chive braids 219
  chive scrambled eggs in brioches 122
chorizo pastry puffs 45
clams
  clams with chilli and yellow bean sauce 164–5
  mussels and clams with lemon grass 162
coconut
  lemon and coconut dhal dip 18–19
courgette fritters with chilli jam 116
crabs
  crab cakes with tartare sauce 160–1
  crab and ricotta tartlets 151
  hot crab soufflés 158–9
cream
  cream swirl 218
  soured cream and dill dressing 221
crispy spring rolls 40–1
croûtons 218
cucumber
  chilled prawn and cucumber soup 54
  cucumber flowers 218
  Thai fish cakes with cucumber relish 144–5
  tzatziki 22
curried parsnip soup 69

D

deep-fried dishes
  deep-fried lamb patties 184
  deep-fried new potatoes with saffron aioli 108
  deep-fried whitebait 139
dips
  baba ganoush with Lebanese flatbread 20–1
  basil and lemon dip 14–15
  beef satay with a hot mango dip 29
  celeriac fritters with mustard dip 13
  charred artichokes with lemon oil dip 118
  chilli bean dip 24–5
  guacamole 16
  hummus bi tahina 10–11
  king prawns in crispy batter 26
  king prawns with spicy dip 28
  lemon and coconut dhal dip 18–19
  potato skewers with mustard dip 107
  potato skins with Cajun dip 12
  quail's eggs with herbs and dips 23
  sesame seed-coated falafel with tahini dip 117
  Thai tempeh cakes with dipping sauce 17
  tzatziki 22
dolmades 102
dressings
  asparagus with raspberry dressing 109
  herb garden dressing 221
  soured cream and dill dressing 221
  spicy tomato dressing 221
duck wontons with spicy mango sauce 34–5

E

eggs
  asparagus and egg terrine 90–1
  chive scrambled eggs in brioches 122
  egg and fennel tabbouleh with nuts 202–203
  eggs benedict 193
  eggy Thai fish cakes 43
  hot crab soufflés 158–9
  pickled quail's eggs 39
  poached eggs Florentine 101
  prawn, egg and avocado mousses 88
  quail's eggs in aspic with prosciutto 192
  quail's eggs with herbs and dips 22–3

risotto frittata 119
son-in-law eggs 112
tapenade and quail's eggs 42
twice-baked Gruyère and potato soufflé 128

F
fennel
baby carrot and fennel soup 62–3
egg and fennel tabbouleh with nuts 202–3
fish
avocado and smoked fish salad 208
breaded sole batons 137
deep-fried whitebait 139
eggy Thai fish cakes 43
fish sausages 138
haddock and smoked salmon terrine 94–5
herby plaice fritters 140
mixed seafood salad 212–13
monkfish packages 142
Parmesan fish goujons 27
potted salmon with lemon and dill 86
salmon cakes with butter sauce 143
salmon rillettes 84–5
salmon and scallop brochettes 168
seafood pancakes 152–3
sea trout mousse 82–3
smoked haddock pâté 78
smoked salmon pâté 79
smoked trout pasta salad 210-11
Thai fish cakes with cucumber relish 144–5
Thai-style seafood turnovers 148–9
three-colour fish kebabs 136
five-spice rib-sticker 48
French onion and morel soup 71
fresh tomato soup 65
fried rice balls stuffed with mozzarella 129
fritters
celeriac fritters with mustard dip 13
courgette fritters with chilli jam 116
herby plaice fritters 140
vegetable tempura 123

G
garlic
broccoli soup with garlic toast 75
chicken with lemon and garlic 175
chilli and garlic marinade 220
deep-fried new potatoes with saffron aioli 108
garlic prawns in filo tartlets 170–1
Spanish garlic soup 56–7
garnishes 218–19
gazpacho with avocado salsa 52–3
ginger and lime marinade 220
Glamorgan sausages 106
goat's cheese salad 196–7
golden Parmesan chicken 174
Greek aubergine and spinach pie 110–11
green bean and sweet red pepper salad 201
griddled tomatoes on soda bread 100
grilled asparagus with salt-cured ham 46
grilled vegetable terrine 92–3
guacamole 16

H
haddock *see* fish
ham
grilled asparagus with salt-cured ham 46
melon and prosciutto salad 215
quail's eggs in aspic with Parma ham 192
herbs
basil and lemon dip 14–15
cannellini bean and rosemary bruschetta 104–5
chive braids 219
chive scrambled eggs in brioches 122
herb garden dressing 221
herbed liver pâté pie 80
herby plaice fritters 140
lemon, thyme and bean stuffed mushrooms 103
mussels and clams with lemon grass 162
pork balls with a minted peanut sauce 30
potted salmon with lemon and dill 86
quail's eggs with herbs and dips 22–3
scallop-stuffed roast peppers with pesto 163
soured cream and dill dressing 221
summer herb marinade 220
hot crab soufflés 158–9
hot-and-sour soup 55
hummus bi tahina 10–11

I
Italian prawn skewers 156

K
kebabs *see* skewers

L
lamb
deep-fried lamb patties 184
lamb tikka 182–3
skewered lamb with red onion salsa 49
spicy koftas 185
langoustine
marinated asparagus and langoustine 169
leek and onion tartlets 124–5
lemons 
basil and lemon dip 14–15
charred artichokes with lemon oil dip 118
chicken with lemon and garlic 175
lemon and coconut dhal 18–19
lemon, thyme and bean stuffed mushrooms 103
lemon twist 219
potted salmon with lemon and dill 86
liver
chicken liver pâté 81
herbed liver pâté pie 80

M
Malayan prawn laksa 66–7
mangos
beef satay with a hot mango dip 29
duck wontons with spicy mango sauce 34–5
marinades
beef satay with a hot mango dip 29
chicken satay with peanut sauce 32–33
chilli and garlic marinade 220
Chinese marinade 220
ginger and lime marinade 220
lamb tikka 182–3
marinated asparagus and langoustine 169
marinated feta cheese with capers 114–15
marinated mussels 146–7
summer herb marinade 220
tandoori chicken sticks 176–7
melon and prosciutto salad 215
mini baked potatoes with blue cheese 127
mixed seafood salad 212–13
monkfish packages 142
mousses
prawn, egg and avocado mousses 88
sea trout mousse 82–3
mushrooms
buckwheat blinis with mushroom caviar 132
French onion and morel soup 71
lemon, thyme and bean stuffed mushrooms 103
tortellini chanterelle broth 68
wild mushroom and fontina tarts 120–1
wild mushroom soup 72–3
mussels
marinated mussels 146–7
mussels and clams with lemon grass 162
scallop and mussel kebabs 166–7

N
nuts
chicken satay with peanut sauce 32–3
egg and fennel tabbouleh with nuts 202–3
pork balls with a minted peanut sauce 30
pork and peanut wontons with plum sauce 31
spicy peanut balls 38

O
onions
French onion and morel soup 71
leek and onion tartlets 124–5
skewered lamb with red onion salsa 49
spring onion tassels 219
oranges
asparagus and orange salad 207

P
paella croquettes 141
panzanella salad 198
Parmesan *see* cheese
parsnips
curried parsnip soup 69
pasta
smoked trout pasta salad 210–11
tortellini chanterelle broth 68
vermicelli soup 61
pâté
chicken liver pâté 81
herbed liver pâté pie 80
smoked haddock pâté 78
smoked salmon pâté 79
peanuts *see* nuts
pears
pear and Parmesan salad 200
pear and Roquefort salad 206
pear and Stilton 133
peas
split pea soup 70
peppers
chilled tomato and sweet pepper soup 76–7
green bean and sweet red pepper salad 201
roast pepper terrine 88–89
scallop-stuffed roast peppers with pesto 163
pies
Greek aubergine and spinach pie 110-11
herbed liver pâté pie 80

savoury pork pies 188–9
plaice *see* fish
poached eggs Florentine 101
pork
chicken and pork terrine 96–7
five-spice rib-sticker 48
pork balls with a minted peanut sauce 30
pork and peanut wontons with plum sauce 31
pork satay 186–7
savoury pork pies 188–9
potatoes
deep-fried new potatoes with saffron aioli 108
mini baked potatoes with blue cheese 127
potato salad with curry plant mayonnaise 204
potato skewers with mustard dip 107
potato skins with Cajun dip 12
twice-baked Gruyère and potato soufflé 128
potted prawns 87
potted salmon with lemon and dill 86
prawns
aromatic tiger prawns 154–5
chilled prawn and cucumber soup 54
garlic prawns in filo tartlets 170–1
Italian prawn skewers 156
king prawns in crispy batter 26
king prawns with spicy dip 28
Malayan prawn laksa 66-7
potted prawns 87
prawn cocktail 157
prawn, egg and avocado mousses 88
prawn toasts 47

Q

quail's eggs *see* eggs

R

raspberries
asparagus with raspberry dressing 109
rice
fried rice balls stuffed with mozzarella 129
paella croquettes 141
risotto alla Milanese 181 
risotto frittata 119
spinach and rice soup 74
roast pepper terrine 88–89

S

salads
asparagus and orange salad 207
avocado and smoked fish salad 208
caesar salad 199
goat's cheese salad 196–7
green bean and sweet red pepper salad 201
melon and prosciutto salad 215
mixed seafood salad 212–13
panzanella salad 198
pear and Parmesan salad 200
pear and Roquefort salad 206
potato salad with curry plant mayonnaise 204
salade Niçoise 209
smoked trout pasta salad 210–11
tricolour salad 205
wilted spinach and bacon salad 204
salmon *see* fish
salsa
gazpacho with avocado salsa 52–3
skewered lamb with red onion salsa 49
samosas 44
satay
beef satay with a hot mango dip 29
chicken satay with peanut sauce 32–3
pork satay 186–7
sausages
chorizo pastry puffs 45
fish sausages 138
Glamorgan sausages 106
mini sausage rolls 190–1
savoury pork pies 188–9
scallops
salmon and scallop brochettes 168
scallop and mussel kebabs 166–7
scallop-stuffed roast peppers with pesto 163
sea trout mousse 82–3
seafood *see* fish
sesame seed-coated falafel with tahini dip 117
skewers
barbecue-glazed chicken skewers 178
Italian prawn skewers 156
potato skewers with mustard dip 107
salmon and scallop brochettes 168
scallop and mussel kebabs 166–7
skewered lamb with red onion salsa 49
tandoori chicken sticks 176–7
three-colour fish kebabs 136
smoked trout pasta salad 210–11
sole *see* fish
son-in-law eggs 112
soups
avocado soup 60
baby carrot and fennel soup 62–3
broccoli soup with garlic toast 75
chilled asparagus soup 64
chilled prawn and cucumber soup 54
chilled tomato and sweet pepper soup 76–7
curried parsnip soup 69
French onion and morel soup 71
fresh tomato soup 65
gazpacho with avocado salsa 52–3
hot-and-sour soup 55
Malayan prawn laksa 66-7
soya beansprout soup 58
Spanish garlic soup 56–7
spinach and tofu soup 59
spinach and rice soup 74
split pea soup 70
tortellini chanterelle broth 68
vermicelli soup 61
wild mushroom soup 72–3
soured cream and dill dressing 221
Spanish garlic soup 56–7
spices
aromatic spice oil 221
curried parsnip soup 69
deep-fried new potatoes with saffron aioli 108
duck wontons with spicy mango sauce 34–5
five-spice rib-sticker 48
king prawns with spicy dip 30
mussels and clams with lemon grass 162
spicy koftas 185
spicy peanut balls 38
spicy tomato dressing 221
tandoori chicken sticks 176–7
turkey, juniper and peppercorn terrine 95
spinach
Greek aubergine and spinach pie 110–11
poached eggs Florentine 101
spinach and tofu soup 59
spinach empanadillas 150
spinach and rice soup 74
wilted spinach and bacon salad 214
split pea soup 70
spring onion tassels 219
spring rolls 44

T

tabbouleh
egg and fennel tabbouleh with nuts 202–3
tortilla wrap with tabbouleh and avocado 126
tahini
hummus bi tahina 10–11
sesame seed-coated falafel with tahini dip 117
tandoori chicken sticks 176–7
tapenade and quail's eggs 42
tarts
crab and ricotta tartlets 151
garlic prawns in filo tartlets 170–1
leek and onion tartlets 124–5
vegetable tarte tatin 130–1
wild mushroom and fontina tarts 120–1
terrines
asparagus and egg terrine 90–1
chicken and pork terrine 96–7
grilled vegetable terrine 92–3
haddock and smoked salmon terrine 94–5
roast pepper terrine 88–89
turkey, juniper and peppercorn terrine 95
Thai dishes
eggy Thai fish cakes 43
Thai fish cakes with cucumber relish 144–5
Thai tempeh cakes with dipping sauce 17
Thai-style seafood turnovers 148–9
three-colour fish kebabs 136
tofu
spinach and tofu soup 59
tomatoes
chilled tomato and sweet pepper soup 76–7
fresh tomato soup 65
griddled tomatoes on soda bread 100
spicy tomato dressing 221
tomato suns 219
tortellini chanterelle broth 68
tortilla wrap with tabbouleh and avocado 126
tricolour salad 205
trout *see* fish
turkey, juniper and peppercorn terrine 95
twice-baked Gruyère and potato soufflé 128
tzatziki 22

V

vegetables
baked Mediterranean vegetables 113
grilled vegetable terrine 92–3
vegetable tarte tatin 130–1
vegetable tempura 123
vermicelli soup 61

W

watercress
whitebait *see* fish
wilted spinach and bacon salad 214
wontons
duck wontons with spicy mango sauce 34–5